ARIS & PHILLIPS HIS

Road to Perfection

Camino de perfección

by

Pío Baroja

With Introduction, Translation and Notes by

Walter Borenstein

Aris & Phillips Hispanic Classics
are published by
Oxbow Books, Oxford, UK

© Walter Borenstein, 2008.
All rights reserved.
No part of this publication may be reproduced or stored in a retrieval system or transmitted in any form or by any means including photocopying without the prior permission of the publishers in writing.

Spanish text © estate of Pío Baroja.

ISBN 978-0-85668-796-9 (cloth)
ISBN 978-0-85668-791-4 (paper)

A CIP record for this book is available from the British Library

View of Toledo c. *1597–99*, El Greco,
© The Bridgeman Art Library, Getty Images

Printed and bound by
The University Press, Cambridge

CONTENTS

Acknowledgments	v
Introduction	1
Selected Bibliography	20
The Text and its Variants	29
Camino de Perfección / Road to Perfection	31
Notes	327

ACKNOWLEDGMENTS

I first came to know the work of Pío Baroja more than sixty years ago as an undergraduate student when I read his novel *Zalacain el aventurero* in a class offered by Professor Bernard Levy at C.C.N.Y. Some ten years later, I completed my doctoral dissertation, *Pío Baroja: His Contradictory Philosophy* under the direction of Professor Arthur Q. Hamilton at the University of Illinois. In that study of the author's work, I referred to *Camino de perfección* as "the most important of Baroja's works from a purely aesthetic point of view. The beauties in the interiors of the churches, the tender and sentimental descriptions of the *paisaje*, the sensitive and mystic spirit of the hero, as well as many other romantic elements all offer a degree of aesthetic feeling not found in many of the other novels." During the following years I wrote two often-cited articles on aspects of Baroja's work, one on his uncomplimentary stereotype of the Latin American, and the other on the impact of Baroja's Spain on the American novelist John Dos Passos.

I first began to seek a publisher for my translation of *Road to Perfection* almost fifty years ago. Several of the more than twenty presses with which I corresponded showed considerable interest and deliberated for some time before deciding that they could not publish it. But patience and persistence have their reward. Not long after I completed a third revision of the translation, I received a letter from Dr Jonathan Thacker of Merton College, Oxford, informing me that he had heard about my translation and would be interested in seeing it. He felt that the novel could be appropriate for the series of Hispanic Classics published by Aris and Phillips.

I would like to take this opportunity to thank Dr Thacker for his support in this endeavor to offer to the English-speaking public what is very probably one of Baroja's most important novels, one that is possibly the prototype of the novel of the Generation of 1898 in Spain, and is without question a work that has been a major influence on generations of Spanish writers since his time.

Most of the twelve translations of Baroja's work into English were published by Alfred Knopf between 1917 and 1928. The author had developed a personal relationship with the publisher, although he once wrote, partly in jest, that he and Knopf both considered Baroja one of the least read novelists

of his time. In 1959, Anthony Kerrigan published a translation of his novel *The Restlessness of Shanti Andia*. In 1997, a last translation of a Baroja novel was published, entitled *Zalacaín the Adventurer*, done by James P. Diendl.

I want to express my sincere thanks to the staff at Oxbow Books, especially Clare Litt and Tara Evans, who have displayed patience and understanding during the trying process involved in the publication of any book. Finally, I must thank my wife Audrey, who interrupted her own very busy schedule of literary work to help me with the formidable task of preparing and reading the manuscript. She has always served both as a steadfast support and an extraordinary model, who always gave me the needed encouragement to continue with an endeavor that I have always held in the very highest regard.

INTRODUCTION

I. Pío Baroja

"When I think," Pío Baroja wrote in 1917, "I am in favor of force, and I am inclined to believe that the world is a circus of athletes, in which one must only conquer, conquer by any means possible. And when I feel, I tend to believe in compassion, and then it seems to me that life is somewhat chaotic, absurd and sickly."[1] This dilemma of the struggle of the mind in opposition to the heart, of the rational versus the intuitive, perhaps the essence of the Spanish tragic sense of life from Don Quixote to Miguel de Unamuno, was to be a principal theme of much of Baroja's fiction and philosophy.[2] His *héroes fracasados*, the failed heroes who represent Unamuno's desire to "undertake a holy crusade to redeem the sepulcher of the Knight of Madness from the power of the Champions of Reason,"[3] were what the critic César Barja called "wanderers constantly on the move, explorers of adventure, eternal vagabonds on an unending *Road to Perfection.*"[4] In more than sixty novels, several collections of stories, hundreds of articles and a few plays and poems, Baroja was to travel through the cities, towns and roads of his Basque homeland, then the plains of Castile, the city of Madrid, the rest of Spain and many of the capitals and cities of Europe as a vigilant observer for his heroes on their endless journey, as he detailed the cruelty of the world around him, as he catalogued the countless persons encountered along the way, always restless, always moving, using the pages of his works vicariously as a vast arena into which to cast his characters into the struggle for existence, a struggle inevitably doomed to failure.

II. His Life

In Baroja's memoirs, in a brief introduction to a section on his childhood, he wrote the following portrayal of his character and his life:

> I am a man who has departed from his home, going along the road, with no destination in mind, his jacket slung over his shoulder, at the break of day, when the roosters throw their strident crowing into the air like a war cry, and the larks rise up in flight over the sown fields. By day and by night, under the sun of August and against the icy wind of December, I have made my way, haphazardly, sometimes frightened

over some chimerical dangers; other times, serene in the face of dangerous realities.
To keep me company in my solitude, I've walked along singing, whistling, humming happy and sad songs, according to my mood and the way in which my surroundings are reflected in my spirit.[5]

He concludes his conception of himself and his adaptation to the events of his life in this way:

Now I am not saddened by solitude, nor am I frightened by the mysterious murmurs of the countryside, nor the cawing of the crows. I now know the tree in which the nightingales sing and the star that casts its confidential glance in the night. I now find the inclemency of the weather soothing and I find the silent hours of dusk admirable, as a column of smoke rises up on the horizon. And so I go on my way, my jacket slung over my shoulder, along the road that I have not chosen, singing, whistling, humming. And when Destiny chooses to interrupt it, let it interrupt it; I, although I could protest, would not protest. . . .[6]

Baroja offers us a detailed autobiography in the second volume of his memoirs, *Familia, infancia y juventud*, taking us from a genealogical account of his ancestors, through his childhood and adolescence, his years as a medical student, the short period of his medical practice in Cestona, to the time he was involved in a family business in Madrid.

He was born in the Basque coastal city of San Sebastián, in the province of Guipúzcoa on December 28, 1872, at Number Six on the Calle de Orquendo. His father, Serafín Baroja y Zornosa, was an engineer with artistic and literary pretensions, who had contributed in both Spanish and Basque to the local newspapers and journals with poetry, prose and music. Roberta Johnson implies that the young Baroja's exposure to the many romantic books in his father's library had a great impact on his own romantic literary tendency and led to "his combination of the adventure story with the novel of contemporary social and philosophical concerns."[7] His father's work as a mining engineer made an orderly education and a stable family life difficult, as the demands of his profession took him to various parts of the peninsula.

The author was later to place great store in the importance of geographical determinism and one's racial heritage, and he attributed a considerable part of this aspect of his character to the constant movement, pointing out in his memoirs that

the trip had left a sad memory in me. The anticipation of a journey would take hold of me, and when we were in the house we were going to abandon, among the trunks, boxes and bundles, all tied up with rope made of esparto grass, I would dream that we were departing in search of some paradise filled with beautiful things, which would later turn out to be just another house, like any other..."[8]

From his father, he assumed that he had inherited his artistic temperament and his jovial, jesting character.

From his mother, Doña Carmen Nessi y Goñi, whose family was from Lombardy, he felt that he had inherited a spiritual, uneasy and turbulent foundation, a tendency toward skepticism, kindliness, hopelessness and despair. He attributed his disciplined habits as a writer to his mother's influence, and, unmarried, he lived with her in Madrid from 1902 until her death in 1935. After his father died in 1912, he purchased a summer home in Vera de Bidasoa in the Basque provinces and they spent their summers there.

Among the author's earliest recollections was the bombardment of San Sebastián by the Carlist forces during the last Carlist War. He admitted that all this was very vague and colored by things he had heard. Many of his early experiences were of a highly morbid and dramatic nature, like the execution of the prisoners he described in *Road to Perfection*, and they were to imbue in him a deeply romantic sensitivity and what Anthony Kerrigan called his sense of the ridiculous and the grandiose, his constant use of the word *farce* to designate a lack of honesty, the actions of "men defending causes they do not believe in, attacking beliefs they do not disbelieve, or even worse, men refusing to defend or practice what they do believe."[9]

The family moved to Madrid in 1879 and from there to Pamplona in 1881, returning to Madrid once again in 1884, where the young Baroja received his diploma in 1886. In his autobiographical collection of essays, *Youth and Egolatry*, he devotes several chapters to these early years. In one poignant and revealing piece, he speaks of some of the teachers whom he loathed, and of their firm conviction that "Baroja, you will never amount to anything."[10] His growing interest in the study of medicine led him to study in Valencia and in Madrid, where he received his doctorate in 1893, with a thesis not surprisingly entitled "Pain. A Psychophysical Study." In his novel *The Tree of Knowledge* and in the early sections of *Road to Perfection*, Baroja was to use his two protagonists, Andrés Hurtado and Fernando Ossorio, to relive

some of the painful memories as a young medical student. Baroja lost interest in the study of medicine quite early in his career and devoted himself to reading literature, his favorite writers being Dickens and Dostoevsky, and to strolling through the streets of the city, familiarizing himself with the places that would later fill his works.

It was also during his student years in Madrid that he took to reading philosophy. He read Kant, Fichte and Schopenhauer, searching for themes and inspiration that also characterized the Generation of 1898, of which he was to be an integral part. The emphasis on the will and the intellect was derived from Nietzsche and Schpenhauer. His reading of the works of Darwin and his followers had a profound impact on his concept of science. However, it was the influence of the Krausists who dominated the generation that preceded his that was to play a major role in the ideology of Baroja and the members of the Generation of 1898.[11]

After completing his doctoral thesis, he took up a medical practice in the Basque village of Cestona. After a short period as a rural doctor, he broke definitively with his chosen profession. He would later write that he was as much preoccupied with the ideas and feelings of the sick as he was by the symptoms of the illnesses themselves, indicating a preference for ideas over the practical aspect of medicine. It should be noted that he began to write a collection of stories while in Cestona with Basque settings, which would later be his *Vidas sombrías* (Somber Lives), in 1900.

He was called back to Madrid in 1896 to help his brother Ricardo, the artist, to operate a family business, a bakery on the Calle de la Misericordia. His experiences with the poorer classes of the city added to what he had previously observed while a medical student. It was at this time that he began to develop social theories bordering on intellectual anarchism. His trilogy of novels, *La lucha por la vida*, as well as numerous other novels, are filled with numberless characters, major and minor, observed during these years. Various characters present many social and political points of view that represent aspects of Baroja's thinking. John Dos Passos, in his all but forgotten work on Spain, *Rosinante to the Road Again*, tells of these "loafers and wanderers..., his artists and grotesque dreamers and fanatics..., descendants of the people in the *Quixote* and the *Novelas ejemplares*..., of the rogues and bandits of the *Lazarillo de Tormes*..."[12] He sees these characters, drawn from real life, as "men who have not had the willpower to continue in the fight for bread, they are men whose nerve has failed, who live furtively on the outskirts, snatching a little joy here and there, drugging their hunger

with gorgeous mirages."[13] The Spanish defeat in the war with the United States, a decisive and tragic moment in history that not only led to the loss of the last vestiges of Spain's once glorious empire, but also represented the focal point for the criticism and perspective of the Generation that took its very name from the date, contributed in part to the failure of the family enterprise and led Baroja to focus his efforts on a literary career.

Although he had occasionally contributed to a number of Basque journals, the publication of his story "Bondad oculta" in the periodical *Germinal* in 1897 can be said to mark his true initiation into literature. In 1899 he undertook the first of his numerous trips on the continent, this time to Paris; these solitary journeys were to represent a major influence as well as the themes in his development as a novelist. In the words of Juan Uribe Echeverría, he was "the universal Basque looking out over the world by a Spanish route; and, at the same time, an implacable observer of his native land from foreign watchtowers."[14] In the years that followed, Baroja was to collaborate on numerous journals, primarily short-lived periodicals of the newly born Generation of 1898. In 1900, he published his first major work, a collection of short stories entitled *Vidas sombrías*. He had now embarked on a literary career.

Since 1902, Baroja had been living in a house on the Calle de Mendizábal, Number 34, with his parents, and eventually, his entire family would occupy three floors of the building. His sister Carmen and his brother Ricardo formed an artistic circle that was to become a cultural center for the author's acquaintances. He continued to travel abroad, to London in 1906, to Florence in 1907, to Rome in 1908 and to Switzerland shortly thereafter, and these journeys gave him many of the characters and landscapes for his novels and essays. His sister's husband, whom she married in 1913, Rafael Caro Raggio, was to publish many of his works.

The years preceding the Spanish Civil War (1936–39) were relatively undisturbed for Baroja. After 1912, he would spend part of the year in Madrid and the summers in Vera de Bidasoa. A brief period of political activism ended in failure and he moved into a more intellectualized and sedentary level of involvement. The protagonists of his novels confronted the social and political problems that would have confronted him. He was totally dedicated to writing and produced an astonishing number of novels and essays during these years. In 1911, he embarked on a major historical endeavor, a work that was to culminate in twenty-two novels in a series entitled *Memorias de un hombre de acción*, a fictional journey in nineteenth

century Spain built around his protagonist, Eugenio de Aviraneta, a distant relative. Half of the novels he wrote between 1912 and 1935 were in this series. As in the realist novels by Benito Pérez Galdós, Baroja undertook to portray Spanish history during this turbulent century. There is a difference between his works and the forty-seven novels of Galdós's *Episodios nacionales*. Roberta Johnson says of Baroja's that they give a sense "of ordinary people's lives during these turbulent times of struggle to change Spain from a medieval to a modern bourgeois society."[15] She says, "Rather than a history of great political events, it is a history seen from below, from the perspective of common people and of the small-time conspirator working in a small corner of the huge map of the Spanish nineteenth century."[16]

While in Madrid, the author moved generally in a narrow and ritualized milieu, between the Banco de España and the Puerta del Sol, along the Calle de Alcalá and the Carrera de San Jerónimo, meeting with the same circle of friends and associates, maintaining a routine that was to become quite characteristic of much of his own literary work. The dictatorial rule of General Miguel Primo de Rivera (1923–30) during the reign of Alfonso XIII forced his Basque compatriot Miguel de Unamuno into exile, but did little to change Baroja's life. Always the critic of society, prepared to see all the defects in all social systems, Baroja was considered a negativist, a pessimist and a cynic. He was tolerated by a power structure that had learned to accept his caustic vision of all aspects of Spanish life.

The fall of the monarchy in 1931 brought a new republic to Spain. The shift in power brought both political factions down on Baroja. He had never truly found a direction he could admire or follow; Anthony Kerrigan says of him, "Baroja, far from being a socialist, was not even a believer in democracy... He had concerned himself...with rebels and been the associate of socialist romantics and anarchist conspirators."[17] Baroja had referred to himself as a radical liberal, an individualist and an anarchist. He saw himself first of all as "an enemy of the Church; then of the State; while these two great powers are in conflict," he wrote, "I am a partisan of the State against the Church; the day the State prevails, I'm an enemy of the State."[18]

In 1934, Baroja was elected to the Royal Spanish Academy, much to the dismay of his enemies on the right and the left. Not long after his mother's death in 1935, fighting erupted and would last for three bloody years. Since his summer home was close to the French frontier, he was advised to flee immediately. He was taken prisoner by Carlist forces and might easily have been shot as an enemy of tradition, but was released after the intervention

of an officer who was a family friend. He made his way over the mountains into France and established residence in Paris. His fellow member of the Generation, Azorín, suffered the same fate. Except for a brief and secret visit to Madrid in 1937, he remained here until 1940, when, fearing the anger of invading German forces, he returned to a war-ravaged Spain in Madrid. He rented an apartment on the Calle de Ruiz de Alarcón, Number 12, near the Prado Museum. He continued to write at a furious pace, now under the watchful eye of the censors. His sister Carmen died in 1953 and his brother Ricardo shortly thereafter. He lived with his nephew, the anthropologist Julio Caro Baroja, for his remaining years.

His major literary efforts were dedicated to the eight volumes of his memoirs, *Desde la última vuelta del camino*, a book of poems and a series of novels. His health was rapidly deteriorating and he suffered from severe arteriosclerosis. He fractured his femur in May 1956 and was bedridden for a time. He received frequent visits from the younger generation and was looked upon as a "living legend," a member of a generation that had revitalized Spanish literature. He was visited by one of his most stalwart admirers, Ernest Hemingway, who had earlier questioned the failure to grant Baroja the Nobel Prize. But, after all, neither Pérez Galdós nor Unamuno had received it. Don Pío died on October 30, 1956 at the age of eighty-three.

Anthony Kerrigan tells us that Pío Baroja is buried in the Cementerio Civil del Este in Madrid, in close proximity to the graves of Nicolás Salmerón, a president of the First Spanish Republic, and Pablo Iglesias, a socialist leader in the First and Second Internationals. Kerrigan wrote, "Death, if less facetious than life, again proved equally as ironic, circumstantial and just; its justice, hurried and rather sarcastic, was a poetic justice."[19] He concluded, "If the three men had nothing else in common they were astoundingly alike in their virtue, in perhaps the most sacred of virtues: they had been incorruptible in life."[20]

III. His Works

"Probably," Baroja wrote in the prologue to his novel *La dama errante* in 1914, "A book like ... does not have the conditions to live for a long time; it is not a painting intended for a museum, but rather an impressionist canvas; it is, perhaps, as a work, too rough, too harsh, not serene enough..."[21] He concludes, somewhat pessimistically

this ephemeral character of my work does not upset me. We are men of the immediate present, people enamored of the moment that is passing, of that which is fleeting, of what is transitory, and the lasting quality or the absence of it in our work preoccupies us very little, so little, that it almost doesn't trouble us at all."[22]

Many years later, in 1953, not long before he died, he wrote a brief testimony to solitude and his life as a writer: "sometimes, you make up a novel to your taste, about loves and intrigues, with the supposition that what was initiated so energetically and then passed on like a cloud carried off by the wind, without leaving any trace whatsoever, had its development, its denouement, its outcome in time."[23] And he goes on:

After all, what difference does it make? Thousands of projects, empty and inferior, about intrigues and machinations, that have no purpose, nor even the appearance of development, dissolve in the air and leave nothing more behind than a flimsy cloud of melancholy, like the seed that falls to the dusty ground or like the fish that remains imprisoned in the dried up hole in the sand on the beach."[24]

Few writers have been so bitterly criticized in Spain and abroad and he took the time to respond to much of this hostile and negative view of his work. He entitled the first volume of his memoirs *El escritor según él y según los críticos*.[25] He was especially castigated for his indifference to grammar, style and structure. Yet he has his staunch defenders. Federico de Onís said of his style that

it is therefore idle to seek in his novels a harmonious structure, orderly, rounded and complete. For the spirit of Baroja is as errant as that of his characters; he loves digressing; he delights in details. And in this very fact lies his originality and charm. Some have called these qualities defects, as they have his careless, natural, but vigorous and spontaneous style, when it is precisely these apparent defects that constitute his never-to-be-forgotten enchantment.[26]

Baroja had said himself that he saw his novels as "a sack capable of containing everything."[27] The English critic C. J. Brown argued that Baroja believed that "art is vastly inferior to life, and should therefore be based on observation of life."[28] He felt that Baroja saw that "style is ideally a matter of expressing oneself briefly, directly, and exactly; and the novel is a shapeless,

informal genre which should be judged on the strength of its capacity to entertain the reader."[29] Some critics accused Baroja of a disregard for the traditional art of the novel, implying also that his philosophy was shallow and naïve. Others felt that his Basque origins had had a deleterious impact on his writing of Castilian. In spite of much of this, Brown points out that his influence on the Spanish novel following him was far greater than all of his contemporaries put together. Salvador Madariaga, the eminent Spanish critic, pointed out that Baroja

> came to write his novels in a disconnected succession of short episodes, having no particular rhythm or shape, beginning just anywhere and ending just any way, having no other relations than those between the characters which run through them, and no other unity than a vague continuity in time and the mood of the whole novel which they build up ultimately by their cumulative effect.[30]

William A. Drake argues that Baroja's style "is acrid, economical to rigidity, almost brusquely direct, and innocent of the rhetorical subtleties and the finished periods hallowed by his forbears and assiduously cultivated by most of his contemporaries."[31] For this reason, Drake thinks that more cultivated and orthodox Castilian ears felt that his style was crude and ungrammatical in structure. The novelist and critic Ramón Sender wrote, "In his vast work there is not a single rhetorical phrase. He wrote in an oral, careless and direct manner and said lively, original and deep things with frequent errors in syntax."[32] Anthony Kerrigan pointed out "there is no 'style' in Baroja, his style being an attempt to bypass rhetoric in a driving attempt to get at the things described."[33] He concluded that "his dramatic end he achieves by understatement. What he chooses to say is a resumé of the unsaid, and his characters are sketched with the rapidity of a sharp-eyed draftsman. His visual approach is that of an artist filling his sketchbook."[34] Baroja himself often seemed to be amused by much of the criticism and may have even encouraged it. Gregorio Marañón defended Baroja's influence saying that he played a major role in the development of an awareness of the tragedy of Spanish life among the bourgeois youth of his time.

Baroja cultivated the novelistic form for more than half a century, presenting a vast panorama of Spanish society, just as his predecessor Benito Pérez Galdós had offered a somewhat earlier view of life in the late nineteenth century. He wrote thirty-one novels as parts of trilogies, in which a general theme might include works seemingly unrelated. The first,

Tierra vasca, was written between 1900 and 1909. The second, *La vida fantástica,* which includes *Road to Perfection,* was written between 1901 and 1906. *La lucha por la vida,* perhaps the most cohesive, has been most widely discussed, and Isaac Goldberg translated all of its novels into English between 1922 and 1924. The novels of *El pasado* were written between 1905 and 1907. *La raza* was written between 1908 and 1911. The first two novels of *Las ciudades* were written in 1910 and 1912, but the final work was not written until 1920. *El mar,* which includes his most well known work in English, *The Uneasiness of Shanti Andia,* written in 1911, contained four novels and was not completed until 1930. The novels of *Agonías de nuestro tiempo* were written in 1926 and 1927. All three novels of *La selva oscura* were written in 1932, and the novels of *La juventud perdida* were written between 1934 and 1938. He began a final series, *Saturnales,* in 1950, but only completed a second novel in 1952. If we include the twenty-two novels of his lengthy historical work, *Memorias de un hombre de acción,* written between 1913 and 1935, almost all of his novelistic output is contained in the trilogies and the historical series.

His *Vidas sombrías,* written in 1900, was a collection of short stories. He wrote many other stories afterwards and many were collected in single volumes. He published several collections of essays and many of his other articles are collected in Volumes V and VIII of his *Obras Completas.* The seven volumes of his memoirs, *Desde la última vuelta del camino,* were begun in 1944 and completed in 1949. In addition, he is the author of a small number of dramatic works, a biography and a book of poetry.

Most of the writers who have discussed Baroja's work have drawn from his novels written between 1900 and 1927, and those written up to 1912 have been the basis for much of the critical writing about him. Ernest Boyd said of his work, "His power resides in the lines of an etcher bitten with acid—the acid of an ironical and pessimistic humor. The logical end of the lawless world surveyed by Baroja is anarchy."[35] Salvador de Madariaga wrote of his work, "In renouncing most of the attractive methods of literary art, he has gained a freer scope for the intensity and power of his vision. The result is a writing which for directness and simplicity has no rival in Spain."[36] John Dos Passos said, "Baroja is a great novelist, not only in his time, on railway bookstalls and in editorial offices, but in that vigorous emanation of life and events that...people...call literature."[37] Dwight Bolinger compared the author's career to the three stages in the lives of his heroes, "At the first, enthusiasm for action, and heroes who sweep all opposition before them;

then doubt, and semi-heroes who start well but end in failure; and at the last disillusionment, and men who are endowed like heroes but see the futility of heroics, and do not even make a beginning in action."[38] V.S. Pritchett wrote of Baroja's works

> He set down his 'brief lives' of people and families, recording their hopes, errors, pretences and fates, with sardonic precision... No idea forces daily life into some pattern of value or moral struggle, unless it is pity for illusion. Disbeliever, pessimist, anthropologist, collecting data in which gossip has its place... He is an anarchist. Society is disagreeable. He looks for the inexplicable outbreak in human character... For Baroja, the core of difference in us is the very source of life. He is interested in what is unanswerably ourselves.[39]

Sherman E. Eoff characterized Baroja as a spokesman of his age, who, as a very subjective writer, "reveals his intense loneliness." A reader who followed him on his "restless journey," would recognize his "dissatisfaction with human society." But, he should better reflect on man's place in the cosmos. "The novelist's outlook, in fact, appears to be an all-inclusive pessimism impregnated with a paralyzing doubt growing out of the scientific and philosophical literature of the nineteenth century."[40] Baroja's negativism may have arisen, not so much from his sense of social injustice, of which he was well aware, as from his low esteem of mankind. His philosophy flowed from a dark vision, almost Darwinian, of the human race, in a struggle one of his characters saw as "somewhat painful, empty and absurd." More than anything else, he was torn by inevitable contradictions, in which momentary bursts of faith were dashed by fits of weakness or compassion. His heroes turned out to be *héroes fracasados* (failed heroes), oppressed by an inevitable "abulia," in which, in the words of Fernando Ossorio in *Road to Perfection*, "some spring is broken in my life," and all their efforts ended on a note of failure. His confidence in the "man of action" seemed to flounder in the midst of the "struggle for life," in which all action becomes futile when men are affected with feeling and sensitivity and shackled by their sense of pity and humanitarianism, at the very time when cruelty and indifference are required in the crises of action. Some of his heroes often become *abúlicos* and refuse to enter the fray from the beginning, others enter the battle and fall by the wayside for one reason or another, while yet others watch the struggle for existence from their armchairs, urging others to carry on toward inevitable failure.

Baroja remarked that he often was awakened to the thought of doing something truly extraordinary, only to realize soon after that there was nothing to do. In his novels, he created the protagonists who would concern themselves with such issues in the "struggle for life." He once said that he would have never felt the need to write novels if he had undertaken the struggle himself. His novels, filled with autobiographical elements, are not so much the consequence of the life he lived, as the life created for his heroes to live. Baroja, the great admirer of Nietzsche, once commented that the German philosopher might have thought himself as cruel and terrible as Attila the Hun; yet he was "incapable of killing a fly." One could just as well say this of Baroja.

He was a true loner, and yet he loved to stroll about aimlessly with friends, untidily dressed, stopping occasionally in old, dirty cafés, always observing. In his torn jacket, his black hat or a beret, his hands in his pockets, he always gave an appearance of being ill humored and frustrated. A rabid individualist, his sense of impotence in the face of an impossible world drove him to put words in an anarchist character's mouth, said in a blind fury, seeking the utter annihilation of all humanity. Unlike his hero, who rushes out into the streets to join the mob, and encounters death in the streets of Madrid, Baroja is content to write novel after novel delineating the inevitable end of such efforts. Doomed to contradiction, he is at once a sentimental and intellectual anarchist and an elitist reactionary, an aristocratic nihilist and a man in love with a suffering people.

Many critics in many languages have tried to define the man, the meaning of his novels and the philosophy in which he may have believed. The critic Ernesto Giménez Caballero may have come close to the truth when he wrote, "There is really no way to dissect Baroja. He is elusive and squirms about like a fish. He is in constant movement, going voluptuously back and forth ... and one sets out suggestively after him, without ever knowing where he may stop, as he passes through the magic depths that are always new."[41]

IV. Road to Perfection

Many critics have called Baroja's novel *Camino de perfección* the most representative novel of the Generation of 1898, the one that typifies the complex, contradictory and tragic vision of the past, present and future in the heart of Spain. Beatrice P. Patt wrote, "With its harsh social criticism and its portrayal of a fundamentally flawed protagonist, *The Road to Perfection*

takes its place next to Azorín's *La voluntad* as one of the earliest authentic literary manifestations of the temper of the Generation of 1898..."[42] The novel first appeared in serial form in a supplement to the newspaper *La Opinión* in 1901. It was first published in book form in 1902. In an event characteristic of the Generation of 1898, a banquet was organized by Azorín and the publisher to celebrate the publication of the novel.

The protagonist of the novel, Fernando Ossorio, had already appeared in an earlier novel by Baroja published in 1901, *Aventuras, inventos y mixtificaciones de Silvestre Paradox*. In Chapter XVII of this earlier work, it is clearly implied that a considerable part of the later novel had already been conceived. An earlier unpublished work, written in 1889 or 1890, contained some of the material used for this novel. Laura, the youngest of Fernando's three aunts, in whose house he had been living, appears in the novel and tells Silvestre of her nephew, whom she calls a *golfo*. María Flora, Fernando's cousin, also speaks to Fernando in this chapter about her relationship to him, in fact.

In the first two chapters of *Road to Perfection*, the author appears and serves as a narrator, guide and confidant of the hero. Once he has established this relationship and offered his vision of Ossorio as a "decadent being, a visionary and *abúlico* with upset nerves," he leaves him to his own resources through the remainder of the work. Before he decides to leave Madrid in Chapter IX, he abandons a medical career, moves into his great-uncle's house after the old man's death, and becomes involved in a degenerate incestuous love affair with one of his aunts. Roberta Johnson suggests that he is not seeking mystical perfection, "but for a way to integrate the several aspects of his being—the artistic, the sensual, and the spiritual—into a way of life that can be sustained in the modern, secular, bourgeois world."[43] Turning from science and art, medicine and painting, he goes on a philosophical and spiritual search of a new life, believing he has been damaged by a tainted genetic inheritance and a hostile environment that is insensitive to his needs.

From Chapter IX through Chapter XIX, Ossorio embarks on a spiritual and physical journey through parts of central Spain. He heads north from Madrid, primarily on foot, offering Baroja ample opportunity to paint many word descriptions of the Castilian landscapes, often reminiscent of Titian, Watteau and El Greco. In the tradition of the heroes of the endless journeys in Spanish literature undertaken from the time of the *Cantar de Mio Cid*, through the *Lazarillo de Tormes* and the many picaresque antiheroes who

followed him, and the spiritual journey of Santa Teresa in her *Camino de perfección*, Fernando Ossorio follows their footsteps on his lonely venture along the back roads of Castile. He passes through the towns of Rascafría, Colmenar and Fuencarral and many others, encountering people along the way, just as his close friend Azorín would travel only a few years later in his autobiographical work *The Route of Don Quixote*. Among his many encounters is one with a German traveler, Max Schulze, a fanatic disciple of Nietzsche, who undoubtedly is Paul Schmitz, a Swiss writer, known to Baroja and many of his friends, who had made this journey with the novelist some years earlier. Ossorio moves on to Segovia, where his experiences are described in four chapters. Finally, he departs from Segovia in the company of a philosophical old wagon driver, Nicolás Polentinos, whom Ossorio refers to as a "King Lear of La Mancha" because one of his daughters had betrayed his trust.

Ossorio arrives in Toledo in Chapter XX and will remain there through Chapter XXXI. This is the city associated with the painter El Greco. The reader may wish to look upon the famous painting *View of Toledo* as he reads Baroja's descriptions of the city and its surroundings. The stark, mystical tone of the painter is a dominant factor in understanding the spiritual search of Ossorio, who has still not abandoned all his sensibility as a painter. The conflict between art and life may be the primary force in the protagonist's struggle to find his bearings. Some critics have suggested that Baroja was influenced by Max Nordau in writing this novel; Nordau was a German writer who held artists responsible for much of European degeneration in his *Degeneration* (1892–93). Ossorio struggles with these contradictions of the spirit when he visits a church one night with some friends to admire the painting by El Greco, *The Burial of the Count of Orgaz*. They stand before it late that night, gazing at it by the light of candles, as the shadows play on the gaunt figures. All this is a part of the protagonist's search for spiritual purification.

Ossorio eventually departs from Toledo in Chapter XXXII and goes to the city of Yécora, where he will remain through Chapter XLIV. This city, which in reality is Yecla, about 110 miles southwest of Valencia, is the city where Ossorio had gone to a Piarist school as a boarding student years earlier. It is interesting to note that Azorín had actually gone to this boarding school in Yecla and wrote of his experiences there in his *Confessions of a Little Philosopher*. Roberta Johnson believes, "Changes of geographical location are very important to nearly all of Baroja's protagonists, as they

are often accompanied by hope that leaving one environment and replacing it with another will alleviate their misfortunes."[44] This part of the novel contains most of the material damning the Catholic Church and the impact of its education upon the mind of a young boy. His reaction to the bitter and oppressive memories of childhood when he visits the school with some friends and sees the young boys undergoing the same corrupting and debilitating indoctrination offers Baroja an irresistible opportunity to castigate the Church and its extraordinary power over the minds of the young. Here, also, Ossorio finds himself compelled to engage in distasteful and painful arguments with a young Piarist; he decides to abandon Yécora and move on to someplace else.

From Chapter XLVI to the end of the novel, Baroja allows the protagonist to speak for himself. The strange and personal style of the first person is very similar to the technique of Azorín, a style in which the action moves closer to the present by using the present perfect tense in place of the preterit. Ossorio visits an uncle's house in a small town near Valencia and is invited to stay for a while. He is in constant conflict with his uncle, a doctor, who does not share any of his views and resists his nephew's growing involvement with his older daughter. Ossorio eventually marries her, in spite of the differences in their character and intellectual levels. When a boy is born, after their first child, a girl, dies at birth, he tries to convince himself that his new vigor and style of life has freed him from his earlier mystical preoccupations. In the final chapter, he stands by his son, dreaming of the way in which he will bring him up, free of all superstition and religion. Baroja rejects a positive conclusion at the very end when he allows us to observe the child's devout grandmother, quietly sewing a page of Scripture into an amulet to be worn by the baby. Ossorio's son will in all likelihood have to face the same struggle as did his father. José Corrales Egea, in his introduction to the French translation of the novel by Robert Marrast, sees the conclusion as pessimistic, believing that all of Ossorio's earlier illusions have disappeared. He feels that the hero has become a man like all others, blended into his society.

Juan Uribe Echeverría sees in this novel "all the fundamental attitudes, rejections and tastes, the ideological ingredients of the famous literary generation."[45] Azorín characterized it simply as a "collection of landscapes," a panoramic vision of Castilian life and a somber explication of its decay. César Barja held that the novel, with its subtitle *Pasión mística*, is a truly tortured work, dealing with

a young man..., in whom the influences of family, education and environment have destroyed all natural and healthy instincts of life, filling his soul with superstition and mystic preoccupation. He is not a believer, but rather simply, a victim of religious tradition and self-analysis; an hysteric, a degenerate, one of so many examples of an impoverished will, as are found in Baroja's novels.[46]

Many critics have analyzed the novel in the same way, seeing the work as related to the turbulent and sickly spirit of Spanish youth at the time. Pedro Laín Entralgo, in his outstanding study of the Generation of 1898, sees Ossorio as a "disoriented, timid, indecisive escapist and impressionist...," who does not know what to do with his life, and "lets it flow freely, like an uneasy stream of blood, along all the length of the Spanish byways." He calls him a "wanderer without repose..., a restless spirit, moving through landscape after landscape; an insatiable drinker, threading together impressions and landscapes in search of impossible peace of mind."[47]

V. *Camino de Perfección* and the Censors

When Pío Baroja fled Spain in July of 1936, it was apparent to him that not only his life, but the books that he had written for so many years, were in serious danger. In *Ayer y hoy*, written in Paris while he was living in exile, he described the circumstances of his escape and his close brush with death. He observed books being burned, among them some he contributed to a library. He recalls that a Spanish officer accused him of being "that miserable old man who had insulted religion and traditionalism in his books." By 1938, the Loyalist *News of Spain* announced that the rebel paper *Diario de Burgos* had listed some of his books as banned.

In an interview in 1952, Baroja was reported to have said that several of his novels had been expurgated in the newly published *Obras completas* that had come out in a deluxe edition in eight volumes. As early as 1942, Stanley J. Kunitz and Howard Haycraft had intimated that Baroja's works had been banned in Spain. "In any event, they wrote, "it is not likely that his books are now permitted circulation in Spain, since his unsparing picture of the wretchedness of the workers and peasants is an implicit condemnation of their exploitation, whatever personal views he may express in articles."[48] His nephew Pío Caro Baroja wrote of his uncle's interest in writing a novel on the war, *Miserias de la Guerra*, but that the censors would not permit

it.[49] Camilo José Cela, awarded the Nobel Prize in 1989, had asked Baroja to write a prologue for his first novel, *The family of Pascual Duarte*. Baroja had refused, fearing that he could go to jail for so reckless an act.[50]

It was announced in 1946 that the first volume of the *Obras completas* of Baroja would soon appear, published in Madrid by Biblioteca Nueva in a deluxe edition. This brought relief to many scholars and students who had long been working with individual works in varying conditions. The second volume appeared in 1947, four more in 1949 and the eighth in 1951. The pattern, declared earlier by the publishers, of printing the novels in the order of their trilogies, was broken from the start. The first trilogy, *Tierra vasca*, is in the first volume, followed by three other trilogies. The trilogy, *La vida fantástica*, opens the second volume, but the second novel in it, *Camino de perfección*, is omitted and does not appear until the sixth volume. The publishers had never made mention of any changes or expurgations. However, in 1952, the same editors mentioned the edition of the *Obras completas* on the cover of another book and in journals, saying it had been revised by the author. The three years between the publication of the first volume and the sixth were required to determine what the censors were willing to accept in the publication of this one novel. *Camino de perfección* may thus be the work that is most indicative of the attitudes of the censors of that time. It is apparent that there were some who felt it should not be published at all.

In a conversation with Carmen Iglesias, she said she knew of the expurgation of Baroja's work, and regretted having to use the edition for her study because of its convenience.[51] Other commentators on his work, including Luis S. Granjel, in his *Retrato de Pío Baroja*, also refer to this edition in their notes. The editors at Las Américas Publishing Company in New York reported, in their edition of *Camino de perfección* in 1952, that there were four previous editions, the first by Rodríguez Serra in 1902, the second by Editorial Renacimiento in 1913, the third by Rafael Caro Raggio in 1920, and the fourth in Volume VI of the *Obras Completas* in 1948. They commented that several passages had been suppressed in the edition of 1948.[52] Donald Shaw, in his book on the Generation of 1898, pointed out that some works had been censored in the same edition.[53] Ricardo Landeira, in a study of the modern Spanish novel, said that the new edition of Baroja's works had been savagely cut by the censors.[54] Luis Granjel, in his extensive analysis of Baroja and his works, does not mention the expurgations, and Sebastián Juan Arbó, though he does not mention the censorship, does say

that Baroja was not permitted to have his book on the civil war published.[55]

There are nineteen examples of expurgation in Baroja's novel *Road to Perfection*, varying in length from three words to twenty lines. They deal with a variety of subjects, but primarily focus on religion and sex. I have placed footnotes in the text where sections have been suppressed. In addition to material portraying the Catholic Church, its priests, its educational system and its influence, the censors seem to have been troubled by immoral acts and thoughts and an incestuous relationship between Ossorio and his aunt. The portrayal of Spain, its culture and people in a degrading manner is also suspect. I was astonished at the many contradictions in what was a superficial examination of the text, where biting attacks on priests are cut and unwarranted indictment of nuns permitted. This novel was the one that brought out the greatest antipathy toward the author's views. My collation of the texts in the other novels revealed far fewer passages suppressed.

In the early years after the end of the civil war in 1939, it was far simpler to ban the works of certain Spanish writers. Fernando Entrerios, in a brief article on Spanish censorship in 1962, pointed out that the works of Unamuno, Baroja, Valle-Inclán and others had been banned for some time.[56] As the government of Francisco Franco sought to gain a degree of respectability in Europe and America, it was apparent that some softening of policy was required. Entrerios implied that the censors, eager to display their social, political and religious orthodoxy, vied with one another to suppress all damaging references. At times, nothing more than hostility toward a certain writer would explain the expurgation. He concludes that there was no fixed policy, that few priests participated and that most of the censors were low-level bureaucrats, often lacking in cultural background, anxious to please the regime. E. Inman Fox has pointed out the expurgation in the novel *La voluntad* by Azorín,[57] in the fourth edition of the novel, published in 1940 by Biblioteca Nueva, the same publisher that did Baroja's works. Stanislaw Baranczak, commenting on censorship in Poland in 1977, wrote that "the more 'responsibility' the censor feels toward a higher authority, the more passionate his zeal and greater his impunity vis-à-vis the injured person (the author). In this way the criteria for excision become more and more fanciful."[58]

The censors in Spain, hard pressed to recognize Baroja's international reputation and seeking to avoid becoming the pariah of Europe, produced a deluxe edition, calf-bound, that sold for 250 pesetas per volume in 1952. The tragedy in all of this is the lost opportunity to create an excellent and

accurate edition of the author's work. Instead, they chose to spend their time in a naïve, vindictive and careless enterprise, out of fear for the work of a tired old man of seventy-seven who had long ceased to represent a threat to their regime, and then conspire to conceal their expurgation and delude the scholarly world into believing that all was well in the literary world of Spain and that they were honoring a venerable man of letters. Baroja, in a moment of utter cynicism, commented on the lack of revolutionary ideas in works of Azorín and Valle-Inclán and Benavente, and added, "If there is something revolutionary in some of the works of these authors, one can say that they have had no real influence on the public because it hasn't read them."[59]

VI: Conclusion

Many critics from a number of nations have recognized the importance of Pío Baroja and his work, not only for Spain, but for the entire world. His novels have been translated into many languages, and *Road to Perfection* into Italian and French. Readers of English know him best for his trilogy of novels, *The Struggle for Life*. Although Baroja scorned honors for most of his life and wrote a disparaging article on the Nobel Prize in Literature, he was often mentioned as an obvious candidate for that honor, including by Ernest Hemingway. His influence on later writers of the novel cannot be measured. Roberta Johnson wrote that these writers,

> whose first vivid memories are of a Spain in conflict and who began their writing careers in the dreary, repressive, reactionary ambience of the Franco regime, found in Baroja's terse, unrhetorical style a frank treatment of Spanish social problems and an effective incorporation of ideological issues into the narrative fabric. Thus Baroja provided a model for their own attempts to re-create in fiction their frustrations and disillusionment with the unencouraging atmosphere of their historical moment. Although the perspective of the twenty-first century may ultimately determine otherwise, at present Baroja remains Spain's foremost novelist of the twentieth century. His is the largest and most sustained body of fiction to deal in a significant way with the complexities of modern life.[60]

SELECTED BIBLIOGRAPHY

Works of Baroja in English Translation
Novels

El árbol de la ciencia/The Tree of Knowledge. Tr. by Aubrey F. G. Bell. New York: Knopf, 1928. Excerpt in Seymour Resnick and Jeanne Pasmantier, eds, *An Anthology of Spanish Literature in English Translation.* New York: Ungar, 1958. London: Calder, 1958. Excerpt in Seymour Resnick and Jeanne Pasmantier, eds, *Highlights of Spanish Literature.* New York: Ungar, 1963.

Aurora roja/Red Dawn. Tr. by Isaac Goldberg. New York: Knopf, 1924.

La busca/The Quest. Tr. by Isaac Goldberg. New York: Knopf, 1922. Excerpt in H. Haydn and J. Cournos, eds, *A World of Great Stories.* New York: Crown, 1947. Called "Blasa's Tavern."

César o nada/Caesar or Nothing. Tr. by Louis How. New York: Knopf, 1919.

La feria de los discretos The City of the Discreet. Tr. by Jacob S. Fasset, Jr. New York: Knopf, 1917.

Las inquietudes de Shanti Andía/In The Restlessness of Shanti Andía, and Other Writings. Tr. by Anthony Kerrigan. Ann Arbor, Mich.: University of Michigan Press, 1959. 30–261. In *The Restlessness of Shanti Andía and Selected Stories.* Tr. by Anthony and Elaine Kerrigan. New York and Toronto: New American Library, 1962. 41–301. A selection in *Introduction to Modern Spanish Literature,* ed. By Kessel Schwartz. New York: Twayne Publishers, 1968. 89–102.

Mala hierba/Weeds. Tr. by Isaac Goldberg. New York: Knopf, 1923.

El Mayorazgo de Labraz/Lord of Labraz. Tr. by A.F.G. Bell. New York and London: Knopf, 1926.

Paradox, rey/Paradox, King. Tr. by Nevill Barbour. London: Wishart, 1931. Selections in Introduction to Modern Spanish Literature: an Anthology of Fiction, Poetry and Essay, ed. By Kessel Schwartz. New York: Twayne Publishers, 1968. 75–89.

La sensualidad pervertida (excerpt) *"Amorous Experiments of a Simpleminded Man in a Degenerate Age."* Tr. by Samuel Putnam. In *The European Caravan: An Anthology of the New Spirit in European Literature. Part I, France, Spain, England and Ireland.* New York: Brewer, Warren and Putnam, 1931.

Zalacaín, el aventurero/Zalacain, the Adventurer: the History of the Good Fortune and the Wanderings of Martin Zalacain of Urbia. Tr. by James P. Dendl. Fort Bragg, Cal., 1997.

Plays

La leyenda de Jaun de Alzate/The Legend of Jaun de Alzate. Tr. by Anthony Kerrigan. In *The Restlessness of Shanti Andía and Other Writings.* Ann Arbor, Mich., 1962. 303–415.

Essays and Other Writings

"The Basque Character," Tr. by Emilia Doyaga. In *Chelsea,* 29 (1971) 110–11.

"Gálvez the Absurd" Tr. by Anthony Kerrigan from Baroja's Memoirs. In *The Restlessness of Shanti Andía and Other Writings.* Ann Arbor, Mich., 1962. 293–98. In *The Restlessness of Shanti Andía and Selected Stories.* New York and Toronto: New American Library, 1962. 318–24.

Juventud, egolatría/Youth and Egolatry. Tr. by Jacob S. Fassett, Jr. and Francis L. Phillips. New York: Knopf, 1920. Excerpts in *The World's Best: Stories, Humor, Drama, History, Essays, Poetry,* ed. by Whit Burnett. New York: Dial, 1950.

"Mistakes of the Spanish Republic," Tr. anon. In *Living Age,* 351 (1937), 422–27.

"The Renegade Friar." Tr. by Anthony Kerrigan. Taken from Baroja's Memoirs. In *The Restlessness of Shanti Andía and Other Writings.* Ann Arbor, Mich.: University of Michigan Press, 1962, 286–92.

"The Tale of a Wig." Tr. by Anthony Kerrigan. Taken from Baroja's Memoirs. In *The Restlessness of Shanti Andía and Other Writings.* Ann Arbor, Mich.: University of Michigan Press, 1962, 299–300.

"The Way I Write." Tr. by Isaac Goldberg. Introduction to *The Quest.* New York: Knopf, 1922. Also in Anthony Kerrigan, *The Restlessness of Shanti Andía and Other Writings.* Ann Arbor, Mich.: University of Michigan Press, 1962, 279–85.

Short Stories

"Angelus." Tr. by Pedro and Claire Villa Fernández. In *Twentieth Century Short Stories,* Sylvia C. Bates, Ed. Boston and New York: Houghton, Mifflin, 1933. In *Best of Modern European Literature,* K. Mann and H. Kesten, eds Philadelphia: Blakeston, 1945.

"Blas the Knifegrinder." Tr. by V.S. Pritchett. In *Fortnightly Review,* 147 (New Series 141), 1937, 586–95.

"El carbonero." "The Charcoal Maker." Tr. by Anthony Kerrigan and Elaine Kerrigan. In *The Restlessness of Shanti Andía and Selected Stories.* New York and Toronto: New American Library, 1962. 325–27.

"Las coles del cementerio." "The Cabbages of the Cemetery." Tr. by Harriet de Onís. In *Spanish Stories and Tales,* Harriet de Onís, ed. New York: Knopf,

1956. In *Spanish Stories and Tales*, Harriet de Onís, ed. New York: Pocket Library, 1956. 182–87. In *The Restlessness of Shanti Andía and Other Writings*, by Anthony Kerrigan, Ann Arbor, Mich.: University of Michigan Press, 1959. 265–69. In *The Restlessness of Shanti Andía And Selected Stories*. By Anthony and Elaine Kerrigan, New York And Toronto: New American Library, 1962. 302–07. In *Honey and Wax*, Richard Stern, ed. Chicago: University of Chicago Press, 1966.

"Lo desconocido." "The Unknown." Tr. by Pedro and Claire Villa Fernández. In *Twentieth Century Short Stories*, Sylvia C. Bates, ed. Boston and New York: Houghton Mifflin, 1933.

"Elizabide, el vagabundo." "The Love Story of a Vagabond." Tr. by H. C. Schweikert. In *World Fiction*, 1 (1923) 50–55. "Elizabide, the Rover." Tr. by W.E. Colford. In *Classic Tales from Modern Spain*, William E. Colford, ed. Great Neck, N.Y.: Barron's, 1964.

"La sima." "The Abyss." Tr. by Warre B. Wells. In *Great Spanish Short Stories Representing the work of the Leading Spanish Writers of the Day*, Warre B. Wells, ed., Boston: Houghton Mifflin, 1932. In *The Spanish Omnibus*. London: Eyre and Spottiswode, 1932. In *Stories of Many Nations*, Irwin H. Braun and David E. Safarjian, eds, Boston: D. C. Heath, 1942. In *The Restlessness of Shanti Andía and Other Writings,* by Anthony Kerrigan, Ann Arbor, Mich.: University of Michigan Press, 1959. 270–75. In *The Restlessness of Shanti Andía and Selected stories,* by Anthony and Elaine Kerrigan, New York and Toronto: New American Library, 1962. 308–14.

"La trapera." "The Madrid Ragpicker." Tr. by Elaine Kerrigan. *New Mexico Quarterly*, 30 (1960). 3–5. In *The Restlessness of Shanti Andía and Selected Stories*, by Anthony and Elaine Kerrigan. New York and Toronto: New American Library, 1962. 328–30.

"El vago." "The Bum." In *The Restlessness of Shanti Andía and Selected Stories*, by Anthony and Elaine Kerrigan. New York and Toronto: New American Library, 1962. 315–17.

Other stories by Baroja may possibly be found in English translation in journals and anthologies. They are not listed in Robert S. Rudder's *The Literature of Spain in English Translation*, New York: Frederick Ungar Publishing Co., 1975, 366–68. Baroja was not a prolific writer of short stories and wrote hundreds of articles. Outside of the 33 very short stories he wrote for his *Vidas sombrías* in 1900, only 12 stories appear in the edition of his *Obras completas* published in 1948.

Books and Articles in English on Baroja

In the course of my gathering of bibliographical material in English dealing with Baroja, I was astonished at the number of books and articles written in Spanish about this important figure of the Spanish Generation of 1898. I also realized that there were probably three or four times as many as the hundreds I was able to find listed. In addition, I came across more than 125 doctoral dissertations written in English about Baroja. There are probably many more written in Spanish here and in Spain and Latin America. I am listing only selected books and articles written in English for the purpose of this translation.

Barrow, Leo L. *Negation in Baroja: A Key to His Novelistic Creativity*. Tucson: University of Arizona Press, 1971.

Bell, Aubrey F.G. *The Novel."* In his *Contemporary Spanish Literature*. New York: Alfred A. Knopf, 1925: 107–21.

Bolinger, Dwight. "Heroes and Hamlets: The Protagonists of Baroja's Novels." *Hispania*, XXIV, No. 1 (February 1941): 91–94.

Borenstein, Walter. "Baroja's Uncomplimentary Stereotype of the Latin American." *Symposium: A Journal Devoted to Modern Languages and Literatures*, XI, No. 1 (Spring 1957): 46–60.

Borenstein, Walter. "The Failure of Nerve: The Impact of Pío Baroja's Spain On John Dos Passos." In *Nine Essays in Modern Literature*, Donald E. Stanford, ed. Baton Rouge: Louisiana State University Press, 1965: 63–87.

Boyd, Ernest. "Pío Baroja." In his *Studies from Ten Literatures*. Port Washington: Kennikat Press, 1968: 72–86.

Brenan, Gerald. *The Literature of the Spanish People*. Boston: Cambridge University Press, 1951: 449–53.

Brown, C.G. *A Literary History of Spain: the 20th Century*. London: Ernest Benn, Ltd., 1972: 31–37.

Bruyne. Jacques de. "Aspects of Pío Baroja's Anticlericalism." *Neophilologus* {Amsterdam, Neth.} LX (January 1976): 56–74.

Buseth, Cedric. "The Role of Landscape in Baroja's *Camino de perfección*. In *Ensayos de literature europea e hispanoamericana*, Felix Menchacatorre, ed. San Sebastián: Universidad del País Vasco, 1990: 47–52.

Cappuccio, Brenda L. "Baroja's Andrés Hurtado and the Search for Self." *Crítica Hispánica*, 14, nos. 1–2 (1992): 59–68.

Chandler, Richard and Kessel Schwartz, *A New History of Spanish Literature*. Baton Rouge: Lousiana State University Press, 1961: 238– 43; 569–71.

Ciplijauskaite, Birute. "Anti-Heroic Vision in *Memorias de un hombre de Acción.*" *Pacific Coast Philology* {Los Angeles, CA} VII (1972): 29–35.
Ciplijauskaite, Birute. "Pío Baroja on Two Worlds." *Americas* {Washington}, XXV (January 1973): 19–24.
Crispin, John. "The Relationship between Theme and Structure in Pío Baroja's *El mundo es ansí*. In *Los hallazgos de la lectura: Estudio Dedicado a Miguel Enguidanos*, Luis Lorenzo-Rivero, ed. Madrid: Porrúa Turanzas, 1989.
Deaver, William O., Jr. "A Deconstruction of Patriarchal Law in *Camino de perfección.*" *Romance Language Annual* VI (1994): 439–43.
Dictionary of the Literature of the Iberian Peninsula, A-K, Germán Bleiberg, Maureen Ihrie and Janet Pérez, eds Westport, CN and London: Greenwood Press, 1993: 168–70.
Dos Passos, John. "Baroja Muzzled." *The Dial* {N. Y.}, LXXIV (1923): 199–200.
Dos Passos, John. "A Novelist of Disintegration." *Freeman* (October 20, 1920).
Dos Passos, John. "A Novelist of Revolution." In his *Rosinante to the Road Again*. New York: George H. Doran Co., 1922: 88–100.
Drake, William A. "Pío Baroja." In his *Contemporary European Writers*. New York: The John Day Co., 1928: 114–23.
Eller, Kenneth C. "The Autobiographical Sources of Baroja's *El árbol de La ciencia.*" *Revista de Estudios Hispánicos* {University, AL} XII (1978): 323–35.
Eller, Kenneth C. "Favorable Portrayals of Women in Pío Baroja's Novels." *The Language Quarterly*, XXIII, Nos. 1–2 (Fall-Winter, 1984): 17–21.
Eller, Kenneth C. "Form and Content of Baroja's Novels: Harmony or Chaos?" *Neophilologus* LXXI, No.1 (January 1987): 72–80.
Eoff, Sherman H. "The Persuasion to Passivity." In his *The Modern Spanish Novel: Comparative Essays Examining the Philosophical Impact of Science on Fiction*. New York: New York University Press, 1961: 164–85.
Fitzmaurice-Kelly, James, *A New History of Spanish Literature*. London: Humphrey Milford, 1926: 484–85.
Flint, Weston and Norma N. Flint. *Camino de perfección (Pasión mística)*. London, Grant and Cutler, Ltd., 1980.
Fox, E. Inman. "Baroja and Schopenhauer: *El árbol de la ciencia. Revue de Littérature Comparée*. {Tours, France} XXXVII, No. 3 (July–September 1963): 350–59.
Fox, E. Inman. "Pío Baroja." In *Encyclopedia of World Literature in the 20th Century* (Steven R. Serafin, ed.), 3rd ed. Vol. I, Farmington Hills, MI: St. James Press, 1999: 204–05.
Franz, Thomas R. "Cela's *La familia del héroe* as homage to Baroja. *Revista de Estudios Hispánicos* {St. Louis, MO} XXVI, No. 3 (October 1992): 437–51.

Franz, Thomas R. "*El árbol de la ciencia* and the Demythologizing of Faust." *Letras Peninsulares* (Fall 200–Winter 2001): 739–50.
Franz, Thomas R. "Explorers, Travelers and Tourists in Baroja." *Letras Peninsulares*, VIII, N*o. 2 (Fall 1995): 311–28.*
Galerstein, Carolyn. "The Crisis of Reason in Baroja's *The Tree of Knowledge*." *LFAR* II, No.1 (January 1982): 34–41.
Ginsburg, Judith. "In Search of a Voice: Baroja's Early Writings and Political Career." *Revista de Estudios Hispánicos* {St. Louis, MO} XV, No. 2 (May 1981): 221–32.
Gleaves, Edwin S. "Hemingway and Baroja: Studies in Spiritual Anarchism." *Revista de Estudios Hispánicos* {University, AL} V (1971): 363–75.
Goldberg, Isaac. Introduction to *Red Dawn*. New York: Alfred Knopf, 1924.
Henn, David. "History, Philosophy and Fiction: Pío Baroja's *César o nada.*" *Neophilologus* LXXXVII, No. 2 April 2003): 233–46.
Johnson, Roberta "Pío Baroja" in *European Writers:* Vol. IX: *The Twentieth Century: Pío Baroja to Franz Kafka* (George Stade, ed.). New York: Charles Scribners and Sons, 1989: 589–616.
Joly, Susan J. "*The Tree of Knowledge* as the Fall into Pessimism: The Affinity of Baroja with Schopenhauer." In *Selected Proceedings of the Pennsylvania Foreign Language Conference*, Gregorio C. Martín, ed. Pittsburgh: Department of Modern Languages, Duquesne University, 1993: 173–77.
Jurkevich, Gaijana. "Double Voices and Forking Paths: Baroja's *Camino de Perfección*. *Symposium: A Quarterly Journal in Modern Literatures*, XLVI, No. 3 (Fall 1992): 209–24.
Kerrigan, Anthony, "The World of Pío Baroja." In *The Restlessness of Shanti Andía and Other Writings*, by Pío Baroja. Ann Arbor {MI}: The University of Michigan Press, 1959: 3–27. Also in *The Restlessness Of Shanti Andía and Selected Stories*. New York and Toronto: New American Library, 1962: ix–xxxix.
King-Arjona, Doris. "*La* 'voluntad' and 'abulia' in Contemporary Spanish Ideology." *Revue Hispanique* LXXIV (1928): 573–667.
Kunitz, Stanley J. and Howard Haycraft. *Twentieth Century Authors*. New York: H. W. Wilson Co., 1942: 75–77.
LaRubia-Prado, Francisco. "*Camino de perfección:* Pío Baroja's Re-Vision Of Bildungsgeschichte." *Siglo XX/20th Century* XI, Nos. 1–2 (1993): 49–70.*A Library of Literary Criticism: Modern Romance Literatures*, Dorothy N Curley and Arthur Curley, eds New York: Frederick Unger Publishing Co., 1967: 36–41.
Longhurst, C.A. *El mundo es ansí.* London: Grant and Cutler, Ltd., 1977.
Longhurst, C.A "*Camino de perfección* and the Modernist Aesthetic." In *Hispanic*

Studies in Honour of Geoffrey Ribbans, Ann L. Mackenzie and Dorothy S. Severin, eds Liverpool: Liverpool University Press, 1992.

López-Aranguren, Nancy. "Bums, Scoundrels and the Ideal Society in *Vidas Sombrías (Somber Lives),* by Pío Baroja. In *Imagination, Emblems and Expressions: Essays on Latin America, Caribbean and Continental Culture and Identity,* Helen Ryan-Ranso, ed. *Popular.* Bowling Green {OH}, 1993.

Macklin, J.J. "The Modernist Mind: Identity and Integration in Pio Baroja's *Camino de perfección." Neophilologus* LXVII, No. 4 (October 1983): 540–55.

Macklin, J.J. "Religion and Modernity in Spain: *Camino de perfección* and *La voluntad." Anales de la Literatura Española Contemporánea* XXIII, Nos. 1–2 (1998): 10–11; 217–33.

Madariaga, Salvador de. *The Genius of Spain.* London: Oxford University Press, 1930: 111–27.

Madland, Helga S. "Baroja's *Camino de perfección* and Schnitzler's *Leutenant Gusti*: Fin de siècle Madrid and Vienna." *Comparative Literature Studies* XXI, No. 3 (Fall 1984): 306–22.

Mencken, H.L. Introduction to *Youth and Egolatry,* by Pío Baroja. New York: Alfred A. Knopf, 1920: 11–20.

Murphy, Katharine. "Intertexts in the City: Edwardian London in Pío Baroja's *La ciudad de la niebla* and Six English Novels." *Modern Language Review* XCVII, No. 1 (January 2002): 149–63.

Nicholson, Helen S. "The Novel of Protest and the Spanish Republic." *The University of Arizona Bulletin,* Humanities Bulletin No. 3, vol. X, No. 3. Tucson: University of Arizona, 1939.

Northup, George T.. *An Introduction to Spanish Literature.* Chicago: The University of Chicago Press, 1936: 433–35.

Olstad, Charles. "Symbolic Structure in Baroja's *Camino de perfección." Kentucky Romance Quarterly* XXIII, No. 4 (1976): 451–65.

Onís, Federico de. Introduction to *Zalacaín el aventurero,* Arthur L. Owen, Ed. New York: D.C. Heath, 1926: v-xix.

Onís, Federico de. "Pío Baroja and the Contemporary Spanish Novel." *New York Times Book Review* (May 4, 1919): VII, 257: 1.

Ouimette, Victor. "The Liberalism of Baroja and the Second Republic." *Hispania: A Journal Devoted to the Interests of Spanish and Portuguese* LX (1947): 21–34.

Owen, Arthur L. "Concerning the Ideology of Pío Baroja." *Hispania* XV (February 1, 1932): 15–24.

Patt, Beatrice P. *Pío Baroja.* New York: Twayne Publishers, 1971.

Patt, Beatrice P. and Martin Nozick. *The Generation of 1898 and After.* New York: Dodd, Mead and Co., 1960: 84–86.

"People." *Time* LXVIII, No. 18 (October 29, 1956): 47.
Pritchett, V.S. "A Chat with Don Pío Baroja." *The Dearborn Independent* (January 22, 1927)
Pritchett, V.S. *The Spanish Temper.* New York" Alfred A. Knopf, 1955: 33–35.
Pritchett, V.S. *Pío Baroja:* La busca *1903 to* La busca *1904.* Durham Modern Language Series. Durham: University of Durham, 1982.
Ramsden, Herbert. *La busca.* London: Grant and Cutler, 1982.
Redding, Catherine. *The Generation of 1898 in Spain as Seen Through Its Fictional Hero.* Northampton, MA: Smith College, Vol. XVII (1936) nos. 3, 4.
Reid, John T. *Modern Spain and Liberalism: A Study in Literary Contrasts.* Stanford, CA and London: Stanford University Press, 1937: 222–25.
Rivkin, Laura. "Pain and Physiological Form in Baroja's *Camino de Perfección.*" *Symposium: A Quarterly Journal in Modern Literature* XXXIX, No. 3 (Fall 1985): 207–16.
Rodríguez, Alfred, "Baroja's Faustian Parody." *Discurso Literario: Revista De Temas Hispánicos* VI, No. 2 (Spring 1989): 477–85.
Rodríguez-Luis, Julio. "Andrés Hurtado's Failure: Grafting Modernismo into *The Tree of Knowledge.*" *Romance Quarterly* XXXV, No. 2 (May 1988): 193–204.
Rosenberg, Solomon L. and Laurence D. Bailiff. Introduction to *Zalacaín el Aventurero: historia de las buenas andanzas y fortunas de Martín Zalacaín de Urbia,* by Pío Baroja. New York: Appleton Century Crofts, 1926.
Rosenberg, Solomon L Introduction to *Páginas escogidas (selecciones y notas del autor,* by Pío Baroja. New York F. S. Crofts, 1928.
Sanders, Jeremy L. "A Missing Link to the Work of Pío Baroja." *Bulletin of Hispanic Studies* {Glasgow, Scotland} LXI, No. 1 (1984): 14–30.
Seeleman, Rosa. "The Treatment of Landscape in the Novelists of the Generation of 1898." *Hispanic Review,* IV, No. 3 (1936): 226–38.
Sender, Ramón. "Posthumous Baroja." *New Mexico Quarterly* XXX, No. 1 (Spring 1960): 6–10.
Seris, Homero. *The Second Golden Age of Spanish Literature* (Translation of Spanish edition published in Paris). Coral Gables, Fla.: University of Miami. Hispanic Studies, no. 1 (November 1939): 108–20.
Servodidio, Mirella. "Speculations on Intertextualities: Baroja and Valle- Inclán." *Hispania: A Journal Devoted to the Teaching of Spanish and Portuguese* LXVI, No. 1 (March 1983): 11–16.
Shaw, Donald L. "Classifying *Camino de perfección. Romance Quarterly* XXXVI, No. 3 (August 1989): 353–59.
Shaw, Donald L. "Baroja: Anguish and Action and Ataraxia." *The Generation of 1898.* London: E. Benn; New York: Barnes and Noble, 1975.

Shaw, Donald L. *A Literary History of Spain: The Nineteenth Century.* London: Benn; New York: Barnes and Noble, 1972: 166–71.
Shaw, Donald L. "A Reply to 'Deshumanización': Baroja on the Art of the Novel." *Hispanic Review* XXV, No. 2 (April 1957): 105–11.
Shaw, Donald L. "Two Novels of Baroja: An Illustration of His Technique." *Bulletin of Hispanic Studies* {Liverpool, Eng.} XL (1963): 151–59.
Smith, Gilbert. "Feminism and Decadence in Baroja's *El mundo es ansí.*" *Romance Quarterly* XXXVI, No. 3 (August 1989): 361–68.
Smith, Horatio (ed.). *Columbia Dictionary of Modern European Literature.* New York: Columbia University Press, 1942: 51–53.
Starkie, Walter. "Some Novelists of Modern Spain." *The Nineteenth Century and After 48*, No. 583 (September 1925): 452–61.
Talbot, Lynn K. "Did Baroja Influence Lawrence? A Reading of *César o nada* And *The Plumed Serpent.*" *The D.H. Lawrence Review* XXII, No. 1 (Spring 1990): 39–51.
Templin, Ernest H. "Pío Baroja and Science." *Hispanic Review* XV, No. 1 (January 1947): 165–92.
Templin, Ernest H. "Pío Baroja: Three Pivotal Concepts." *Hispanic Review* XII, No. 4 (October 1944): 306–29.
"Thoughts on Pío Baroja." *Critical Inquiry: A Voice for Reasoned Inquiry into Significant Creations of the Human Spirit* {Chicago, IL} 1 (1974) 415–46.
Trend, John B. *The Civilization of Spain.* 2nd ed. London, New York: Oxford University Press, 1967.

THE TEXT AND ITS VARIANTS

There is no definitive edition of *Camino de perfección*. For the Spanish text and the English translation, I relied primarily on the edition published in Madrid in 1913 by Renacimiento. In addition, I collated all six editions of the novel published between 1902 and 1956. I am especially grateful to the library of the University of Toronto for providing me with a microfilm of the extremely rare first edition of 1902. A number of newer editions and reprints have appeared since 1956.

The text of this novel offers us an extraordinary example of the liberties taken by editors and even printers in Spain since the beginning of the century. In the course of collating, I found hundreds of variations from one edition to another. They were either minor changes, like punctuation, or more serious changes, like adverbs. Baroja recognized the extent to which his work, more than that of many others, was being constantly changed. Some of this may be attributed to the fact that he was considered a Basque who did not write in a form acceptable to many more *castizo* readers.

Although I did eliminate the accents on some words of one syllable, as used in most earlier editions, I did preserve accent marks for words like "*fué*" and "*dió*."

CAMINO DE PERFECCIÓN

ROAD TO PERFECTION

(PASIÓN MÍSTICA)

NOVELA

I

Entre los compañeros que estudiaron medicina conmigo, ninguno tan extraño y digno de observación como Fernando Ossorio. Era un muchacho alto, moreno, silencioso, de ojos intranquilos y expresión melancólica. Entre los condiscípulos, algunos aseguraban que Ossorio tenía talento; otros, en cambio, decían que era uno de esos estudiantes pobretones que, a fuerza de fuerzas, pueden ir aprobando cursos.

Fernando hablaba muy poco, sabía con frecuencia las lecciones, faltaba en ciertos períodos del curso a las clases y parecía no darle mucha importancia a la carrera.

Un día vi a Ossorio en la sala de disección, que quitaba cuidadosamente un escapulario al cadáver de una vieja, que después envolvía el trapo en un papel y lo guardaba en la caja de los bisturís.

Le pregunté para qué hacía aquello y me dijo que coleccionaba todos los escapularios, medallas, cintas o amuletos que traían los cadáveres al Depósito.

Desde entonces intimamos algo y hablábamos de pintura, arte que él cultivaba como aficionado. Me decía que a Velázquez le consideraba como demasiado perfecto para entusiasmarle. Murillo le parecía antipático; los pintores que le encantaban eran los españoles anteriores a Velázquez, como Pantoja de la Cruz, Sánchez Coello y, sobre todo, el Greco.

A pesar de sus opiniones, que a mí me parecían excelentes, no podía comprender que un muchacho que andaba a todas horas con Santana, el condiscípulo más torpe y más negado de la clase, pudiera tener algún talento. Después, cuando en el curso de Patología general comenzamos a ir a la clínica, veía siempre a Ossorio, sin hacer caso de las explicaciones del profesor, mirando con curiosidad a los enfermos, haciendo dibujos y croquis en su álbum. Dibujaba figuras locas, estiradas unas, achaparradas las otras; tan pronto grotescas y risibles como llenas de espíritu y de vida.

– Están muy bien – le decía yo contemplando las figuras de su álbum –, pero no se parecen a los originales.

– Eso ¿qué importa? – replicaba él –. Lo natural es sencillamente estúpido. El arte no debe ser nunca natural.

– El arte debe de ser la representación de la naturaleza, matizada al reflejarse en un temperamento – decía yo que estaba entonces entusiasmado con las ideas de Zola.

– No. El arte es la misma naturaleza. Dios murmura en la cascada y canta en el poeta. Los sentimientos refinados son tan reales como los toscos, pero aquéllos son menos torpes. Por eso hay que buscar algo agudo, algo finamente torturado.

– Con estas ideas – le dije una vez –, ¿cómo puede usted resistir a ese idiota de Santana, que es tan estúpidamente natural?

I

Among the classmates who studied medicine with me, none was so strange and deserving of observation as Fernando Ossorio. He was a tall, dark, silent boy, with restless eyes and a melancholy expression. Among our fellow students, some were certain that Ossorio was quite gifted; on the other hand, others said that he was nothing more than one of those mediocre students who are able to keep passing courses by sheer effort.

Fernando spoke very little, was frequently prepared for his lessons, would miss classes during certain times in the academic year, and seemed to attach little importance to his program of studies.

One day I saw Ossorio in the dissection room carefully removing a scapular from an old woman's cadaver. He then wrapped the tattered cloth in a piece of paper and put it away in his surgical knife case.

I asked him why he was doing that and he told me he collected all the scapulars, medals, ribbons or amulets on the cadavers when they were brought to the Morgue.

From that time on, we became quite friendly and would talk about painting, an art that he cultivated as an amateur. He told me he considered Velázquez too perfect to arouse his enthusiasm; Murillo seemed distasteful to him; the painters who most delighted him were the Spaniards who came before Velázquez: Pantoja de la Cruz[1], Sánchez Coello[2], and above all, El Greco.

In spite of his opinions, which seemed quite excellent to me, I couldn't understand how a fellow with his talent could run around all the time with Santana, the stupidest and most incompetent of our fellow students. Later on, when we started going to the clinic for our course in General Pathology, I would always see Ossorio, paying no attention whatsoever to the professor's explications, gazing curiously at the sick patients and making drawings and sketches in his notebook. He would draw freakish figures, some elongated, others stunted; grotesque and ridiculous, yet filled with spirit and life at the same time.

"They're very good," I said to him as I contemplated the figures in his notebook, "but they don't resemble the originals."

"So what difference does that make?" he replied. "What is natural is simply stupid. Art ought never to be natural."

"Art should be the representation of Nature, tinged by the temperament in which it is reflected," I said, impressed at that time by Zola's ideas.

"No. Art is Nature itself. God murmurs in the waterfall and sings in the poet. Refined feelings are every bit as real as unpolished ones, but the former aren't as clumsy. That's why you have to look for something subtle, something delicately tortured."

"With ideas like these," I once told him, "how are you able to put up with that idiot of a Santana, who is so stupidly natural?"

"Oh! He's a very interesting fellow," he replied with a smile. "To tell the truth,

—¡Oh! Es un tipo muy interesante —contestó, sonriendo —. A mí, la verdad, la gente que me conoce me estima, él no: siente un desprecio tan profundo por mí, que me obliga a respetarle.

Un día, en una de esas conversaciones largas en que se vuelca el fondo de los pensamientos una conciencia, le hablé de lo poco clara que resultaba su persona; de cómo en algunos días me parecía un necio, un completo badulaque, y otros, en cambio, me asombraba y le creía un hombre de grandísimo talento.

— Sí —murmuró Ossorio, vagamente —. Hay algo de eso: es que soy un histérico, un degenerado.

—¡Bah!

— Como lo oye usted. De niño fuí de esas criaturas que asombran a todo el mundo por su precocidad. A los ocho años dibujaba y tocaba el piano; la gente celebraba mis disposiciones; había quien aseguraba que sería yo una eminencia; todos se hacían lenguas de mi talento, menos mis padres, que no me querían. No es cosa de recordar historias tristes, ¿verdad? Mi nodriza, la pobre, a quien quería más que a mi madre, se asustaba cuando yo hablaba. Por una de esas cuestiones tristes, que decía, dejé a los diez años la casa de mis padres y me llevaron a la de mi abuelo, un buen señor, baldado, que vivía gracias a la solicitud de una vieja criada; sus hijos, mi madre y sus dos hermanas no se ocupaban del pobre viejo absolutamente para nada. Mi abuelo era un volteriano convencido, de esos que creen que la religión es una mala farsa; mi nodriza, fanática como nadie; yo me encontraba combatido por la incredulidad de uno y la superstición de la otra. A los doce años mi nodriza me llevó a confesar. Sentía yo por dentro una verdadera repugnancia por aquel acto, pero fuí y, en vez de parecerme desagradable, se me antojó dulce, grato, como una brisa fresca de verano. Durante algunos meses tuve una exaltación religiosa grande; luego, poco a poco, las palabras de mi abuelo fueron haciendo mella en mí, tanto que, cuando a los catorce o quince años me llevaron a comulgar, protesté varias veces. Primero, yo no quería llevar lazo en la manga; después dije que todo aquello de comulgarse era una majadería y una farsa, y que en una cosa que va al estómago y se disuelve allí no puede estar Dios, ni nadie. Mi abuelo sonreía al oirme hablar; mi madre, que aquel día estaba en casa de su padre, no se enteró de nada; mi nodriza, en cambio, se indignó tanto que casi reprendió a mi abuelo porque me imbuía ideas antirreligiosas. Él la contestó riéndose. Poco tiempo después. al ir a concluir yo el bachillerato, mi abuelo murió, y la presencia de la muerte y algo

people who know me think highly of me, but he doesn't: he is filled with such a profound scorn for me that I feel obliged to respect him."

One day, during one of those long conversations, when you turn the very depths of your thoughts inside out, and you spiritually drain your consciousness, I spoke to him of how vague his entire being seemed to me; how on some days he appeared to me to be a fool, a complete nincompoop, and how, on other days, on the other hand, he would astonish me and make me consider him a man of considerable intelligence.

"Yes," Ossorio murmured vaguely. "There is something to that: the fact is that I am an hysteric, a degenerate."

"Come now!"

"It's just as I say. When I was a little boy, I was one of those children who astonish everyone with their precocity. At the age of eight, I was already drawing pictures and playing the piano; people celebrated my natural talents; there were even some who were certain that I would eventually be quite famous; everyone raved about my intelligence, except my parents, who didn't love me. It isn't that I want to recall sad stories, is it? My nursemaid, the poor thing, whom I loved more than I did my mother, would get frightened when I spoke. Because of one of those sad issues I spoke of, I left my parents' home when I was ten years old and they took me to live with my grandfather, a kindly gentleman, a cripple, who was able to get along thanks to the diligent care of an old maidservant; his children, my mother and her two sisters, took absolutely no interest in the pitiful old man. My grandfather was a confirmed Voltairian, one of those who believe that religion is an evil farce; my nursemaid was as fanatic as one can be; I found myself torn between the skepticism of the one and the superstition of the other. When I was twelve years old, my nursemaid took me to Confession. Deep down, I was filled with real repugnance for that act, but I went anyway, and instead of turning out to be distasteful, it left me with a feeling that was sweet and pleasant, like a cool summer breeze. For several months thereafter, I was possessed by great religious exaltation; later, little by little, my grandfather's words began making a greater impression on me, so much so, that at the age of fourteen or fifteen, when they took me to take communion, I protested a number of times. First of all, I didn't want to wear an armband on my sleeve; in addition, I said that all that business of taking communion was a lot of nonsense and a farce, and that neither God nor anyone else could be within anything that goes into the stomach and is dissolved there.[3] My grandfather smiled when he heard me talk like that; my mother, who happened to be in her father's house that day, didn't find out anything at all about this; my nursemaid, on the other hand, got so angry that she all but rebuked my grandfather for instilling such anti-religious ideas in me. He answered her by laughing. A short time afterward, just as I was going to complete my secondary school studies, my grandfather died, and the presence of death, as well as some distressing facts that I discovered about my family, disturbed my spirit

doloroso que averigué en mi familia me turbaron el alma de tal modo que me hice torpe, huraño, y mis brillantes facultades desaparecieron, sobre todo mi portentosa memoria. Yo, por dentro, comprendía que empezaba a ver las cosas claras, que hasta entonces no había sido más que un badulaque; pero los amigos de casa decían: "Este chico se ha entontecido." Mi madre, a quien indudablemente estorbaba en su casa y que no quería tenerme a su lado, me envió a que concluyese el grado de bachiller a Yécora, un lugarón de la Mancha, clerical, triste y antipático. Pasé en aquella ciudad levítica tres años, dos en un colegio de escolapios y uno en casa del administrador de unas fincas nuestras, y allí me hice vicioso, canalla, mal intencionado; adquirí todas estas gracias que adornan a la gente de sotana y a la que se trata íntimamente con ella. Volví a Madrid cuando murió mi padre; a los diez y ocho años me puse a estudiar, y yo, que antes había sido un prodigio, no he llegado a ser después ni siquiera un mediano estudiante. Total: que gracias a mi educación han hecho de mí un degenerado.

–¿Y piensa usted ejercer la carrera cuando la concluya? – le pregunté yo.

– No, no. Al principio me gustaba; ahora me repugna extraordinariamente. Además, me considero a mí mismo como un menor de edad, ¿sabe usted?; algún resorte se ha roto en mi vida.

Ossorio me dió una profunda lástima.

Al año siguiente no estudió ya con nosotros, no le volví a ver y supuse que habría ido a estudiar a otra universidad; pero un día le encontré y me dijo que había abandonado la carrera, que se dedicaba a la pintura definitivamente. Aquel día nos hablamos de tú, no sé por qué.

II

En la Exposición de Bellas Artes, años después, vi un cuadro de Ossorio colocado en las salas del piso de arriba, donde estaba reunido lo peor de todo, lo peor en concepto del Jurado.

El cuadro representaba una habitación pobre con un sofá verde, y encima un retrato al óleo. En el sofá, sentados, dos muchachos altos, pálidos, elegantemente vestidos de negro, y una joven de quince o diez y seis años; de pie, sobre el hombro del hermano mayor, apoyaba el brazo una niña de falda corta, también vestida de negro. Por la ventana, abierta, se veían los tejados de un pueblo industrial, el cielo cruzado por alambres y cables gruesos y el humo de las chimeneas de cien fábricas que iba subiendo lentamente en el aire. El cuadro se llamaba *Horas de silencio*.

to such an extent that I became stupid and unsociable, and all my brilliant faculties disappeared, above all, my prodigious memory. Deep down, I now understood that I was beginning to see things clearly, that I had been nothing but a simpleton until that time; but friends of the family kept saying, "This boy has really become foolish." Since my mother undoubtedly felt that I was getting in her way in the house and she didn't want me near her, she sent me to finish my secondary school studies in Yécora, a graceless, sad, unpleasant town in La Mancha, dominated by the clergy. I spent three years in that priestly city, two in a school run by Piarist priests, and one in the home of the administrator for some farm property we owned, and it was there that I turned vicious, mean and ill-intentioned; I acquired all of these charming qualities that embellish those who wear a cassock and those who deal intimately with them. I returned to Madrid when my father died; at eighteen years of age, I started my studies, and I, who had once been a prodigy, haven't even been able to attain the level of an average student since then. In a word: thanks to the way I was brought up and educated, they've made a degenerate out of me."

"And you intend to practice your profession when you finish?" I asked him.

"No, no. I liked it at first; now I find it extremely repugnant. Besides, I consider myself a minor, do you understand?; some spring has broken in the fabric of my life."

Ossorio filled me with profound pity.

The following year, he no longer studied with us; I didn't see him again, and I supposed that he'd probably gone to study at another university, but I ran into him one day and he told me that he had abandoned his professional studies and was devoting himself to painting once and for all. That day we spoke to one another in the familiar tú form, I don't really know why.

II

Some years later, at the Fine Arts Exhibition, I saw one of Ossorio's paintings that had been placed in the exhibit rooms on the upper floor, where all the worst pieces had been gathered together, that is, the worst in the opinion of the Jury.

The painting represented a humble room with a green sofa and a portrait in oil above it. Seated on the sofa were two boys, tall, pale and elegantly dressed in black, and a young girl, fifteen or sixteen years old; a little girl in a short skirt, also dressed in black, was standing, leaning her arm on the shoulder of her older brother. Through the open window, you could see the tile roofs of an industrial town, the sky crisscrossed with wires and heavy cables, and the smoke from the smokestacks of a hundred factories that kept rising slowly into the air. The painting was entitled *Hours of Silence*. It was painted inconsistently; but there was an atmosphere of

Estaba pintado con desigualdad, pero había en todo él una atmósfera de sufrimiento contenido, una angustia, algo tan vagamente doloroso, que afligía el alma.

Aquellos jóvenes enlutados, en el cuarto abandonado y triste, frente a la vida y al trabajo de una gran capital, daban miedo. En las caras alargadas, pálidas y aristocráticas de los cuatro se adivinaba una existencia de refinamiento, se comprendía que en el cuarto había pasado algo muy doloroso; quizás el epílogo triste de una vida. Se adivinaba en lontananza una terrible catástrofe; aquella gran capital, con sus chimeneas, era el monstruo que había de tragar a los hermanos abandonados.

Contemplaba yo absorto el cuadro, cuando se presentó Ossorio delante de mí. Tenía aspecto de viejo; se había dejado la barba; en su rostro se notaban huellas de cansancio y demacración.

– Oye, tú; esto es muy hermoso – le dije.

– Eso creo yo también; pero aquí me han metido en este rincón y nadie se ocupa de mi cuadro. Esta gente no entiende nada de nada. No han comprendido a Rusiñol, ni a Zuloaga, ni a Regoyos; a mí, que no sé pintar como ellos, pero que tengo un ideal de arte más grande, me tienen que comprender menos.

–¡Bah! ¿Crees tú que no comprenden? Lo que hacen es no sentir, no simpatizar.

– Es lo mismo.

–¿Y qué ideal es ese tuyo tan grande?

–¡Qué sé yo! Se habla siempre con énfasis y exagera uno sin querer. No me creas; yo no tengo ideal ninguno, ¿sabes? Lo que sí creo es que el arte, eso que nosotros llamamos así con cierta veneración, no es un conjunto de reglas, ni nada; sino que es la vida: el espíritu de las cosas reflejado en el espíritu del hombre. Lo demás, eso de la técnica y el estudio, todo eso es m...

– Ya se ve, ya. Has pintado el cuadro de memoria, ¿eh?, sin modelos.

–¡Claro! Así se debe pintar. ¿Que no se recuerda, lo que me pasa a mí, los colores? Pues no se pinta.

– En fin, que todas tus teorías han traído tu cuadro a este rincón.

–¡Pchs! No me importa. Yo quería que alguno de esos críticos imbéciles de los periódicos, porque mira que son brutos, se hubieran ocupado de mi cuadro, con la idea romántica de que una mujer que me gusta supiera que yo soy hombre capaz de pintar cuadros. ¡Una necedad! Ya ves tú, a las mujeres qué les importará que un hombre tenga talento o no.

– Habrá algunas...

–¡Ca! Todas son imbéciles. ¿Vámonos? A mí esta Exposición me pone enfermo.

restrained suffering in its total effect, a sense of anguish, something so vaguely grievous that it afflicted your very soul.

Those young people, dressed in mourning, in that abandoned and sad room, confronting the life and toil of a great capital city, filled you with fear. In the elongated, pale, aristocratic faces of the four children, you could surmise an existence filled with refinement, you could understand that something very distressing had taken place in the room; perhaps the sad epilogue of a life. You could foresee a terrible catastrophe in the distant future; that great capital with its smokestacks was the monster that was going to swallow up the abandoned children.

I was absorbed in the contemplation of the painting when Ossorio suddenly appeared before me. He had the appearance of an old man; he had let his beard grow; traces of weariness and emaciation were evident on his face.

"I must tell you, this is very beautiful," I said to him.

"I think so too; but they've stuck it here in this corner and nobody pays any attention to my painting. These people don't understand anything at all. They didn't understand Rusiñol[4], nor Zuloaga[5], nor Regoyos[6]; they must understand me even less, since I don't know how to paint as well as they did, though I do have a greater artistic ideal."

"Nonsense! Do you really think they don't understand? What they are doing is showing no feeling, no affinity."

"It's the same thing."

"And what's this great ideal of yours?"

"How would I know! One always speaks emphatically and exaggerates without intending to. You don't have to believe me; I have no ideal at all, don't you see? What I do believe is that art, as we seem to call it with a certain veneration, is not a collection of rules, nor anything like that; it is rather life itself: the spirit of things reflected in the spirit of man. Everything else, the business of technique, study, all that is sh..."

"That's very apparent, very. You painted the picture from memory, right?, with no models."

"Of course! That's how one ought to paint. And if, as often happens with me, you can't remember the colors? Then you don't paint it."

"In the end, all your theories have brought your painting to this corner."

"Pshaw! It makes no difference to me. I used to wish that one of those imbecilic critics at the newspapers, and believe me, they really are brutes, would have taken an interest in my painting, with the romantic notion that a woman whom I like would realize that I'm a man who is truly capable of painting pictures. That's stupid nonsense! As you can plainly see, women don't really care whether a man has any talent or not."

"There are probably some..."

"Come now! They're all imbeciles. Shall we leave? This Exhibition is making me sick."

– Vamos.

Salimos del Palacio de Bellas Artes. Nos detuvimos a contemplar la puesta del sol, desde uno de los desmontes cercanos.

El cielo estaba puro, limpio, azul, transparente. A lo lejos, por detrás de una fila de altos chopos del Hipódromo, se ocultaba el sol, echando sus últimos resplandores anaranjados sobre las copas verdes de los árboles, sobre los cerros próximos, desnudos, arenosos, a los que daba un color cobrizo de oro pálido.

La sierra se destacaba como una mancha azul violácea, suave en la faja del horizonte cercana al suelo, que era de una amarillez de ópalo; y sobre aquella ancha lista opalina, en aquel fondo de místico retablo, se perfilaban claramente, como en los cuadros de los viejos y concienzudos maestros, la silueta recortada de una torre, de una chimenea, de un árbol. Hacia la ciudad, el humo de unas fábricas manchaba el cielo azul, infinito, inmaculado...

Al ocultarse el sol se hizo más violácea la muralla de la sierra; aún iluminaban los últimos rayos un pico lejano del poniente, y las demás montañas quedaban envueltas en una bruma rosada y espléndida, de carmín y de oro, que parecía arrancada de alguna apoteosis del Ticiano.

Sopló un ligero vientecillo; el pueblo, los cerros, quedaron de un color gris y de un tono frío; el cielo se obscurió.

Oíase desde arriba, desde donde estábamos, la cadencia rítmica del ruido de los coches que pasaban por la Castellana, el zumbido de los tranvías eléctricos al deslizarse por los railes. Un rebaño de cabras cruzó por delante del Hipódromo; resonaban las esquilas dulcemente.

–¡Condenada Naturaleza! – murmuró Ossorio –. ¡Es siempre hermosa!

Bajamos a la Castellana, comenzamos a caminar hacia Madrid. Fernando tomó el tema de antes y siguió:

– Esto no creas que me ha molestado; lo que me molesta es que me encuentro hueco, ¿sabes? Siento la vida completamente vacía: me acuesto tarde, me levanto tarde, y al levantarme ya estoy cansado; como que me tiendo en un sillón y espero la hora de cenar y de acostarme.

–¿Por qué no te casas?

–¿Para qué?

–¡Toma! ¿Qué sé yo? Para tener una mujer a tu lado.

– He tenido una muchacha hasta hace unos días en mi casa.

– Y ¿ya no la tienes?

– No; se fué con un amigo que la ha alquilado una casa elegante y la lleva por las noches a Apolo. Los dos me saludan y me hablan; ninguno de ellos cree que ha obrado mal conmigo. Es raro, ¿verdad? Si vieras; está mi casa tan triste...

– Trabaja más.

– Chico, no puedo. Estoy tan cansado, tan cansado...

"Let's go then."

We left the Palace of Fine Arts. We stopped to contemplate the sunset from one of the nearby clearings.

The sky was pure, limpid, blue, transparent. In the distance, behind a row of tall black poplar trees near the Hippodrome, the sun was hiding, casting its dying orange-hued brilliance upon the green treetops, upon the nearby barren and sandy hills, coloring them with copper and pale gold.

The mountain range stood out like a patch of soft violaceous blue, against the band of the horizon, so very close to the ground, that was the color of yellow opal; and over that wide opaline strip, against that background resembling a mystic retable, you could see clearly profiled, as in the paintings of the old and scrupulous masters, the outlined silhouette of a tower, of a smokestack, of a tree. Toward the city, the smoke from the factories was staining the infinite, immaculate blue sky...

When the sun was completely obscured, the face of the mountain turned even more violaceous; its dying rays still illuminated a far off peak in the west, and the other mountains remained wrapped in a splendid rose-colored mist, of carmine and gold, which seemed to have been torn from some apotheosis of Titian.

A gentle breeze was blowing; the town, the hills remained gray-colored, with a cold tint; the sky grew dark.

From where we were standing up above, you could hear the rhythmic cadence of the sound of the carriages as they passed along the Paseo de la Castellana, and the hum of the electric trolleys as they glided along the rails. A flock of goats crossed in front of the Hippodrome; their bells resounded melodiously.

"Confounded Nature!" Ossorio muttered. "It is always beautiful."

We descended to the Castellana and began to walk toward Madrid. Fernando picked up his earlier theme and continued:

"Don't think that all this has bothered me; what really does disturb me is that I find myself hollow, you understand? I feel that life is totally empty: I go to bed late, I get up late, and when I do get up, I'm already tired; so I stretch out in an armchair and wait till it's time to eat dinner and go to bed."

"Then why don't you get married?"

"For what purpose?"

"Come on! How should I know? Just to have a woman by your side."

"I had a girl in my house until just a few days ago."

"And you don't have her any more?"

"No; she ran off with a friend of mine, who rented an elegant house for her and takes her out at night to the Apolo. They both greet me and even speak to me; neither one of them thinks I've been treated very badly. That's strange, isn't it? If you could only see; my house is so very sad..."

"You ought to work harder."

"My dear fellow, I just can't do it. I'm so tired, so tired..."

– Haz voluntad, hombre. Reacciona.
– Imposible. Tengo la inercia en los tuétanos.
–¿Pero es que te ha pasado alguna cosa nueva; has tenido desengaños o penas últimamente?
– No; sí fuera de mis inquietudes de chico, mi vida se ha deslizado con relativa placidez. Pero tengo el pensamiento amargo. ¿De qué proviene esto? No lo sé. Yo creo que es cuestión de herencia.
–¡Bah! Te escuchas demasiado.
Mi amigo no contestó.

Volvíamos andando por la Castellana hacia Madrid. El centro del paseo estaba repleto de coches; los veíamos cruzar por entre los troncos negros de los árboles; era una procesión interminable de caballos blancos, negros, rojizos, que piafaban impacientes; de coches charolados con ruedas rojas y amarillas, apretados en cuatro o cinco hileras, que no se interrumpían; de cocheros y lacayos sentados en los pescantes con una tiesura de muñecos de madera. Dentro de los carruajes, señoras con trajes blancos en posturas perezosas de sultanas indolentes, niñas llenas de lazos con vestidos llamativos, jóvenes *sportsmen* vestidos a la inglesa y caballeros ancianos, mostrando la pechera resaltante de blancura.

Por los lados, a pie, paseaba gente atildada, esa gente de una elegancia enfermiza que constituye la burguesía madrileña pobre. Todo aquel conjunto de personas y de coches parecía moverse, dirigido por una batuta invisible.

Avanzamos Fernando Ossorio y yo hasta el Obelisco de Colón, volvimos sobre nuestros pasos, llegamos al Obelisco, y desde allá, definitivamente, nos dirigimos hacia el centro de Madrid.

El cielo estaba azul, de un azul líquido: parecía un inmenso lago sereno, en cuyas aguas se reflejaran tímidamente algunas estrellas.

La vuelta de los coches de la Castellana tenía algo del afeminamiento espiritual de un paisaje de Watteau.

Sobre la tierra, entre las dos cortinas de follaje formadas por los árboles macizos de hojas, nadaba la niebla tenue, nacida del vaho caluroso de la tarde.

– Sí; la influencia histérica – dijo Ossorio al cabo de unos minutos, cuando yo creí que había olvidado ya el tema desagradable de su conversación–; la influencia histérica se marca con facilidad en mi familia. La hermana de mi padre, loca; un primo, suicida; un hermano de mi madre, imbécil, en un manicomio; un tío, alcoholizado. Es tremendo, tremendo. – Luego, cambiando de conversación, añadió:– El otro día estuve en un baile en casa de unos amigos, y me sentí molesto porque nadie se ocupaba de mí, y me marché en seguida. Estas mujeres – y señaló unas muchachas que pasaron riendo y hablando alto a nuestro lado – no nos quieren.

"Make an effort, old chap. Snap out of it."

"Impossible. I'm overwhelmed to the very marrow by inertia."

"But did something new happen to you; have you had any disappointments or afflictions lately?"

"No; in fact, outside of my childhood anxieties, my life has slipped by with relative serenity. Yet my thoughts are filled with bitterness. Where does all this come from? I just don't know. I think it's a question of heredity."

"Nonsense! You think too much about yourself."

My friend didn't answer.

We were on our way back, walking along the Castellana toward Madrid. The center of the boulevard was filled with carriages; we could see them crossing by through the black trunks of the trees; it was an interminable procession of white, black and reddish-colored horses, stamping their feet impatiently; of shiny carriages with red and yellow wheels, squeezed together in four or five lines, without interruption; the coachmen and footmen seated on the coachboxes with a stiffness not unlike that of wooden dolls. Inside the carriages, ladies in white dresses, in the languid postures of indolent sultanas, young girls covered with bows, attired in provocative dresses, young *sportsmen* dressed in the English fashion, and old gentlemen, making a show of the whiteness of their protruding shirt fronts.

On either side, well-dressed people were strolling along on foot, the kind of people marked by a sickly elegance that characterizes the poorer bourgeoisie of Madrid. All that mass of people and carriages seemed to be moving, directed by an invisible baton.

Fernando Ossorio and I advanced toward the Obelisco de Colón, we then retraced our steps, and from the Obelisk, we definitively made our way toward the center of Madrid.

The sky was blue, a kind of liquid blue; it looked like an immense, serene lake and a number of stars were timorously reflected in its waters.

The movement of the carriages on the Castellana possessed something of the spiritual effeminacy of a landscape by Watteau.

The tenuous mist, rising from the warm vapors of the afternoon, seemed to swim above the ground, between the two curtains of foliage formed by the trees that were now thick with leaves.

"Yes, the influence of hysteria," Ossorio said after a few moments, when I thought that he had already forgotten the unpleasant subject of his conversation; "the influence of hysteria in my family can easily be observed. My father's sister, insane; a cousin, a suicide; my mother's brother, an imbecile in an asylum; an uncle, an alcoholic. It's dreadful, just dreadful." Then, changing the subject of his conversation, he added, "The other day, I was at a dance at the home of some friends of mine, and I was upset because nobody seemed to be paying any attention to me, and so I hurriedly walked out. These women," and he pointed at some girls who were passing alongside us, laughing and speaking in loud voices, "they don't like

Somos tristes, ya somos viejos también...; si no lo somos, lo parecemos.

—¡Qué le vamos a hacer! – le dije yo –. Unos nacen para buhos, otros para canarios. Nosotros somos buhos o cornejas. No debemos intentar cantar. Quizá tengamos también nuestro fin.

—¡Ah! ¡Si yo supiera para qué sirvo! Porque yo quisiera hacer algo, ¿sabes?; pero no sé qué.

— La literatura quizá te gustaría.

— No; es poco plástico eso.

— Y la medicina, ¿por qué no la sigues?

— Me repugna ese elemento de humanidad sucio con el que hay que luchar: la vieja que tiene la matriz podrida, el señor gordo que pesca indigestiones..., eso es asqueroso. Yo quisiera tener un trabajo espiritual y manual al mismo tiempo; así como ser escultor y tratar con esas cosas tan limpias como la madera y la piedra, y tener que decorar una gran iglesia y pasarme la vida haciendo estatuas, animales fantásticos, canecillos monstruosos y bichos raros; pero haciéndolo todo a puñetazos, ¿eh?... Sí, un trabajo manual me convendría.

— Si no te cansabas.

— Es muy probable. Perdóname, me marcho. Voy detrás de aquella mujer vestida de negro... ¿Sabes? Ese entusiasmo es mi única esperanza.

Habíamos llegado a la plaza de la Cibeles; Ossorio se deslizó por entre la gente y se perdió.

La conversación me dejó pensativo. Veía la calle de Alcalá iluminada con sus focos eléctricos, que nadaban en una penumbra luminosa. En el cielo, enfrente, muy lejos, sobre una claridad cobriza del horizonte, se destacaba la silueta aguda de un campanario. Veíanse por la ancha calle en cuesta correr y deslizarse los tranvías eléctricos con sus brillantes reflectores y sus farolillos de color; trazaban ziszás las luces de los coches, que parecían los ojos llenos de guiños de pequeños y maliciosos monstruos; el cielo, de un azul negro, iba estrellándose. Volvía la gente a pie por las dos aceras, como un rebaño obscuro, apelotonándose, subiendo hacia el centro de la ciudad. Del jardín del Ministerio de la Guerra y de los árboles de Recoletos llegaba un perfume penetrante de las acacias en flor; un aroma de languideces y deseos.

Daba aquel anochecer la impresión de la fatiga, del aniquilamiento de un pueblo que se preparaba para los placeres de la noche, después de las perezas del día.

us. We are sad and we are also old before our time..., and if we aren't, we seem to be that way."

"What can we do about it!" I said to him. "Some of us are born to be owls and others to be canaries. We are owls or crows. We shouldn't try to sing. Perhaps we too have our purpose in life."

"Ah! If only I knew what I'm good for! Because I would like to do something, you understand?; but I don't know what."

"Perhaps you would like literature?"

"No, that isn't plastic enough."

"And how about medicine, why don't you go on with that?"

"I find that filthy element of humanity with which you have to struggle quite repugnant: the old lady who has a rotten womb, the fat gentleman who suffers from attacks of indigestion..., all that is loathsome. I would like to have some kind of work that is spiritual and manual at the same time; like being a sculptor and dealing with those things that are as clean as wood and stone, and having a great church to adorn, and spending my life carving statues, fantastic animals, monstrous modillions and strange creatures, but doing it all with my fists, eh?... Yes, manual work would suit me well."

"If you didn't get tired of it."

"That's very likely. Excuse me, but I have to go. I'm going to walk after that woman dressed in black... Do you want to know something? That kind of excitement is my only hope."

We had reached the Plaza de la Cibeles; Ossorio slipped away and was lost in the crowd.

The conversation left me rapt in thought. I could see the Calle de Alcalá illuminated by electric lights, swimming in a luminous penumbra. In the sky, before me, far in the distance, you could see the pointed silhouette of a bell tower profiled against the coppery brightness of the horizon. Along the wide, sloping street, you could see the electric trolleys with their brilliant reflector lights and colored little lanterns as they raced and glided by; the lights of the carriages seemed like the ever winking eyes of small, wicked monsters as they traced their zigzag movements; the blue-black sky was filling with stars. The people were returning on foot along the two sidewalks like a shadowy herd, crowding one another, moving up toward the heart of the city. The penetrating perfume of the blooming acacias emanated from the garden of the Ministry of War and the trees of the Paseo de Recoletos; an aroma of languor and desire.

That hour of dusk left you with an impression of the fatigue, of the annihilation of a people, preparing for the pleasures of the night after the indolence of the day.

III

Días más tarde, al llegar Fernando a su casa, se encontró con una invitación para ir a una kermesse que se celebraba en el Jardín del Buen Retiro.

Se dirigió hacia allí pensando si la invitación sería de aquella mujer que tanto le preocupaba. Daban las doce cuando llegó.

Era verano, hacía un calor sofocante. El jardín estaba espléndido: mujeres hermosas vestidas de blanco, ojos brillantes, gasas, cintas, joyas llenas de reflejos, pecheras impecables de los caballeros, uniformes negros, azules y rojos, roces de faldas de seda, risas, murmullos de conversaciones.

En la obscuridad, entre el negruzco follaje verde lustroso, brillaban focos eléctricos y farolillos de papel. Los puestos, adornados de percalinas de colores nacionales y banderolas también amarillas y encarnadas, estaban llenos de cachivaches colocados en los estantes. Una fila de señoritas en pie, sofocadas, rojas, sacaban papeletas de unas urnas y se las daban a los elegantes caballeros, que iban dejando al mismo tiempo monedas y billetes en una bandeja.

Otras señoronas elegantes iban con *carnets* vendiendo números para una rifa. A seguida de los puestos había una rifa, un diorama y una horchatería, servida por jóvenes de la alta crema madrileña.

Y en el paseo, mientras la música tocaba en el quiosco central, se agrupaba la gente y se oía más fuerte el crujir de las faldas de seda, carcajadas y risas contenidas; voces agudas de las muchachas elegantes que hablaban con una rapidez vertiginosa, risas claras y argentinas de las señoras, voces gangosas y veladas de las viejas. Brillaban los ojos de las mujeres alumbrados con un fulgor de misterio; en los corros había conversaciones a media voz, que no tenían más atractivo e incitante que el ser vehículo de deseos no expresados; una atmósfera de sensualidad y de perfumes voluptuosos llenaba el aire.

Y en la noche, templada, parecía que aquellos deseos estallaban como los capullos de una flor al abrirse; los cohetes subían en el aire, detonaban y caían deshechos en chispas azules y rojas, que a veces quedaban inmóviles en el aire brillando como estrellas...

Estaba también la mujer de luto hablando con un húsar. Ossorio la contempló desde lejos.

Era para él aquella mujer, delgada, enfermiza, ojerosa, una fantasía cerebral e imaginativa, que le ocasionaba dolores ficticios y placeres sin realidad. No la deseaba, No sentía por ella el instinto natural del macho por la hembra; la consideraba demasiado metafísica, demasiado espiritual; y ella, la pobre muchacha, enferma y triste, ansiosa de vida, de juventud, de calor, quería que él la desease, que él la amara con furor de sexo, y coqueteaba con uno y otro para arrancar a Fernando

III

Several days later, when Fernando came home, he found an invitation to go to a kermess that was taking place in the Garden of the Parque del Buen Retiro.

He made his way there, wondering if the invitation might have come from that woman who was so much on his mind. It was striking midnight when he arrived.

It was summer and the heat was stifling. The garden was splendid: lovely women dressed in white, radiant eyes, chiffons, ribbons, jewels sparkling with reflected brilliance, gentleman in impeccably white shirt fronts, black, blue and red uniforms, the rustling of silk skirts, laughter, the murmur of conversations...

Electric light bulbs and Chinese lanterns were shining in the darkness, amid the lustrous blackish-green foliage. The booths, decorated with percaline in the national colors, and banderoles, also yellow and red, were filled with all manner of knickknacks set up on the shelves. A row of young ladies were standing, sweltering and flushed, drawing paper tickets from urns and giving them to the elegant gentlemen who kept leaving coins and bills on a tray at the same time.

Other elegantly dressed and distinguished looking ladies were walking around with *carnets*, selling numbers for a raffle. Beyond the stalls, there were a raffle, a diorama exhibit and a stand with orgeat drinks served by young ladies of the very cream of Madrilenian society.

And on the promenade, while the music was being played in the central bandstand, people gathered about and you could hear even more plainly the rustle of silk skirts, peals of laughter and restrained titters; the high-pitched voices of elegant girls speaking with vertiginous rapidity, the clear and silvery laughter of the matrons and the nasal, muffled voices of the older ladies. The eyes of the ladies, illuminated by a mysterious brilliance, were shining; there were subdued conversations among the circles of guests, which were seductive and exciting only because they served as vehicles for unexpressed desires; an atmosphere of sensuality and voluptuous perfumes filled the air.

And it seemed as if those desires, in that mild night, were erupting like the buds of a flower as it opened; the rockets rose up into the air, exploded and fell to earth, bursting into blue and red sparks, and at times remaining motionless in the air, shining like stars...

The woman in mourning black was also there, speaking with a hussar. Ossorio contemplated her from a distance.

That woman, slender, sickly, with dark circles under her eyes, was a cerebral and imaginative fantasy for him, occasioning imaginary afflictions and unreal pleasures within him. He didn't desire her, nor did he feel for her the natural instinct of the male for the female; he considered her much too metaphysical, too spiritual; and she, the poor girl, sickly and sad, anxious for living, for youth and warmth, wanted him to desire her with a sexual frenzy, and so she played the coquette with one man or another, in

de su apatía; y al ver lo inútil de sus infantiles maquinaciones, tenía una mirada de tristeza desoladora, una mirada de entregarse a la ruina de su cuerpo, de sus ilusiones, de su alma, de todo...

Aquella noche la muchacha de luto hallábase transformada. Hablaba con calor, estaba con las mejillas rojas y la mirada brillante; a veces dirigía la vista hacia donde estaba Fernando.

Ossorio experimentó una gran tristeza, mezcla de celos y de dolor.

Se dispuso a salir, y pasó sin fijarse al lado de su prima.

– No, pues ahora no te vas, golfo –le dijo ella.

–¡Sabes que estás hoy la mar de guapa!

–¿Sí?

–¡Vaya! Como no se ve bien, ¿comprendes?...

– Hombre, ¡qué fino! A ver. ¿Te sientas? ¿Vas a tomar algunas papeltas?

– Espera. No me puedo decidir así como así. Hay que saber las ventajas que tiene una cosa y otra.

–¡Viene la Reina! –dijo una de las que estaban con la prima de Ossorio.

Con la noticia se conmovió el grupo de horchateras, y Fernando, aprovechándose de la conmoción, se escabulló.

Venía la Reina con sus hijos por entre dos filas de gente que la saludaban al pasar con grandes reverencias.

Las mujeres encontraban gallardo a Caserta, al príncipe consorte, a quien miraban con curiosidad.

Fernando, al separarse de María Flora, se dispuso a salir.

Iba a hacerlo, cuando la señorita de luto, que iba paseando con sus amigas, se le acercó y le dijo con voz suave y algo opaca:

–¿Quiere usted papeletas para la rifa de la Reina?

– No, señora –contestó él brutalmente.

Salió de los Jardines. En la puerta esperaban grupos de lacayos y un gran semicírculo de coches con los faroles encendidos.

– Es extraño – murmuró Ossorio –. Yo no estaba antes enamorado de esta mujer; hoy he sentido más que amor, ira, al verla con otro. Mis entusiasmos son como mis constipados: empiezan por la cabeza, siguen en el pecho y después...se marchan. Esta muchacha era para mí algo musical y hoy ha tomado carne. Y por dentro veo que no la quiero, que no he querido nunca a nadie; quizás si estuve enamorado alguna vez fué cuando era chico. Sí; cuando tenía diez o doce años.

Recordaba en la vecindad de casa de su abuelo una muchacha de pelo rojizo y ojos ribeteados, a la cual no se atrevía a mirar, y que a veces soñaba con ella. Luego, ya de estudiante, esperaba a que pasara una modista por el mismo camino

order to draw Fernando out of his apathy; when she saw the uselessness of her childish machinations, she was overcome by a look of disconsolate sadness, a look that implied the surrender of her body, her illusions, her soul, her very being, to utter ruin...

The girl dressed in mourning black seemed to be transformed that night. She spoke animatedly, her cheeks were flushed, her eyes were shining; every so often she would turn her glance to where Fernando was standing.

Ossorio experienced an extraordinary sadness, a mixture of jealousy and sorrow.

He prepared to leave and passed alongside his cousin without realizing it.

"No, you're not leaving now, you *rascal*," she said to him.

"You know, you're extremely lovely tonight!"

"Really?"

"Of course! As if one couldn't see that, you understand?"

"Well, how very nice of you! Let's see now. Would you like to sit down? Are you going to get any raffle tickets?"

"Wait a moment. I can't make up my mind just like that. I'd have to know the advantages one way or the other."

"Here comes the Queen!"[7] said one of the girls with Ossorio's cousin.

The group of girls who were selling orgeat drinks were excited at the news and Fernando took advantage of the commotion and slipped away.

The Queen came in with her children between two rows of people who bowed deeply to greet her as she passed.

The women found Caserta,[8] the prince consort, quite handsome and they looked at him with curiosity.

After getting away from María Flora, Fernando made ready to leave. He was just about to do so when the young lady in black mourning, who was strolling with her friends, came over to him and said in a soft, somewhat pathetic voice:

"Would you like some tickets for the Queen's raffle?"

"No, señora," he answered abruptly.

He left the Gardens. Groups of footmen and a great semicircle of carriages with lighted lanterns were waiting at the gate.

"It's strange," Ossorio murmured, "I wasn't in love with this woman before; today, when I saw her with someone else, I felt something more than just love, real anger. My infatuations are like my colds: they begin in my head, they go down to the chest and then...they go away. This girl used to be something almost musical for me, and today she has become flesh and blood. And deep down, I see that I don't really love her and that I've never loved anyone; perhaps, if I was ever in love at all, it was when I was a child. Yes; when I was ten or twelve years old."

He recalled that there had been a girl in the neighborhood of his grandfather's house, who had reddish-colored hair and red-ringed eyes, and that he never dared look at her and that sometimes he would dream of her. Later on, as a student, he

que llevaba él para ir al Instituto, y al cruzarse con ella le temblaban las piernas.

Mientras traía a la imaginación estos recuerdos lejanos, caminaba por Recoletos, obscuro, lleno de sombras misteriosas. Al verle pasar tan elegante, con la pechera blanca que resaltaba en la obscuridad, las busconas le detenían; él las rechazaba y seguía andando velozmente, movido por el ritmo de su pensamiento, que marchaba con rapidez y sin cadencia.

Al llegar a la calle de Génova tomó por ella; siguió por el paseo de Santa Engracia, y a la izquierda entró por una callejuela, se detuvo frente a una casa alta, abrió la puerta y fué subiendo la escalera sin hacer ruido. Entró en el estudio, encendió una vela, se desnudó y se sentó en la cama.

Se sentía allí un aire de amarga desolación: los bocetos, antes clavados en las paredes pintadas de azul, estaban tirados en el suelo, arrollados; la mesa llena de trastos y de polvo, los libros deshechos amontonados en un armario.

–¡Cómo está esto! – murmuró – ¡Qué sucio! ¡Qué triste! Apagaré la luz, aunque sé que no voy a dormir.

Puso un libro encima de la vela, la apagó, y se tendió en la cama.

IV

No conocía Fernando al hermano de su abuelo. No le había visto más que de niño alguna vez, y si no le hubiese escrito su tía Laura diciéndole que el tío había muerto y que se presentara en la casa, Fernando no se hubiera ocupado para nada de un pariente a quien no conocía. Aunque murmurando y de mala gana, Ossorio fué por la tarde a casa del hermano de su abuelo, a un caserón de la calle del Sacramento. Llegó a la casa y le hicieron pasar inmediatamente a un gabinete. Se habían reunido allí los notables de la familia. Acababa el juez de abrir y leer el testamento del anciano señor y todos los parientes bufaban de rabia; una de las partes más saneadas de la fortuna se les marchaba de entre las manos e iba a parar a la hija de una querida del viejo. El marqués, cuñado de Luisa Fernanda, se había sentado en el sofá, y su abultado abdomen, en forma puntiaguda, le bajaba entre las dos piernecillas de enano; vestía chaleco blanco y corbata también blanca; llevaba a sus labios húmedos con sus dedos gordos y amorcillados un cigarro puro y escuchaba los distintos pareceres, aprobándolos o desaprobándolos. Su hermano dormitaba en una butaca y un primo de ambos, que parecía un pez por su cara, se paseaba de un lado a otro, apoyándose en el respaldo de las sillas.

would wait for a dressmaker to pass by him along the same route he took on his way to the Institute, and when they passed one another, his legs would tremble.

While these distant memories kept returning to his imagination, he continued walking along the Paseo de Recoletos, which was now dark and filled with mysterious shadows. When the streetwalkers saw him go by, so elegantly dressed, his white shirtfront gleaming in the darkness, they tried to stop him; he brushed them aside and kept walking ahead swiftly, moved by the rhythm of the thoughts that swept over him rapidly, without cadence.

He followed the Calle de Génova when he reached it; he then continued along the Paseo de Santa Engracia, turned into a small side street on the left, stopped in front of a tall house, opened the door and made his way up the stairs without making a sound. He went into the studio, lit a candle, undressed and sat down on the bed.

You could feel an air of bitter desolation in the room; the sketches, which had been fastened to the blue-painted walls before, were rolled up and thrown all over the floor; the table was covered with artist's supplies and dust, the books were lying open and piled up in a cabinet.

"How dreadful all this is!" he muttered. "How filthy! How sad! I'll put out the light, even though I'm quite sure I won't be able to fall asleep."

He put a book on top of the candle, extinguishing it, and stretched out on the bed.

IV

Fernando did not know his grandfather's brother. He had only seen him one time as a child, and if his Aunt Laura hadn't written to him, telling him his uncle had died and that he should appear at the house, he would have paid no attention whatsoever to a relative whom he hardly knew. That afternoon, though he grumbled and was reluctant to go, Ossorio went to his grandfather's brother's home, a large rambling old house on the Calle del Sacramento. When he arrived at the house, they immediately had him go into a sitting room. The most important members of the family had all gathered there. The magistrate had just opened and read the old gentleman's will and all the relatives were snorting with anger; one of the most unencumbered parts of his fortune was slipping right out of their hands and was going to end up with the daughter of the old man's mistress. Luisa Fernanda's brother-in-law, the marquis, had taken a seat on the sofa and his protruding, sharp-pointed abdomen hung down between his two scrawny, dwarf-like legs; he was wearing a white vest and a tie, also white; he kept raising a cigar to his humid lips with his plump, sausage-like fingers as he listened to the various opinions, approving or disapproving of them. His brother was dozing in an armchair and a cousin of the two, who had a face that looked like a fish, kept pacing back and forth, leaning on the backs of the chairs.

– Hay que solucionar el conflicto – decía a cada momento. Parecía que le había tomado gusto a la palabra solucionar.

Estaban, además de éstos, un militar, también pariente de Fernando, y dos chicos altos, jóvenes, vestidos de negro, hijos del marqués: uno, el menor, serio y grave; el otro, movedizo y alegre. En medio de todos ellos se hallaba el administrador del tío abuelo, hombre triste, de barba negra y hablar meloso, por el cual en aquel momento sentían todos los parientes extraordinario cariño. Después de ver que gran parte de la fortuna se llevaba la niña de la *pelandusca*, se trataba de salvar de la ruina un almacén de aceites que había puesto el tío para dar salida al de sus olivares andaluces, y una casa de préstamos, Pero aparecía que el almacén, que estaba a nombre del administrador, tenía deudas. ¡Pero si no se comprendían aquellas deudas!

El administrador dijo que se había vendido mucho más aceite de lo que daban los olivares del señor y se había recurrido a otros cosecheros.

–¿De manera que eso podría ser un buen negocio? – preguntó el marqués.

– Sí; llevándolo bien es un gran negocio.

El marqués miró al administrador fijamente.

–¿Pero qué hacía el tío con ese dinero? – murmuró el hombre-pez.

El administrador sonrió discretamente y torció la cabeza con resignación.

El odio se acentuó en contra de Nini, de la grandísima pelandusca que arruinaba a la familia.

El marqués dijo que aquellas manifestaciones eran extemporáneas. La cuestión estaba en poner a flote el aceite y quedarse libre de las deudas.

Se trataba de esto, aunque parecía que se hablaba de otra cosa.

– Un procedimiento sencillo – dijo el primo de la cara de pez, con su voz afeminada – es vender el género, figurar falsos acreedores y declararse en quiebra. Luego se ponía la casa a nombre de otro y ya estaba hecho todo.

El marqués no aprobó por lo pronto la idea de su pariente y estudió la cara del administrador, el cual manifestó que él no podía prestar su nombre a una combinación de aquella clase. El pez comentó la desaprobación. Otra opinión era ir a los principales acreedores, prometerles a ellos sólo el pago y declararse en quiebra.

Fernando, al que no le interesaba aquello, salió del despacho y tras de él salieron los hijos del marqués.

–¿Dónde está el muerto? – preguntó Ossorio.

– Ahí, en ese gabinete – le dijo el primo. – Pero no vayas a verle. Está completamente en descomposición.

"We have to resolve this conflict," he kept saying over and over. It seemed that he had become partial to the word resolve.

In addition to these people, there was an army officer, also one of Fernando's relatives, and two tall, young fellows, dressed in black, sons of the marquis: one of them, the younger, was serious and solemn; the other was fidgety and cheerful. In the very midst of them all was his great uncle's administrator, a sad-looking man, with a black beard and a saccharine voice, for whom all the relatives seemed to have an extraordinary affection at that particular moment. After they saw how great a portion of the fortune the *strumpet*'s little girl had taken away, it turned into a question of saving from ruin a business selling olive oil their uncle had set up in order to create an outlet for the produce from his Andalusian olive groves, as well as a money-lending establishment. But it turned out that the business was in the name of the administrator and encumbered with debts. And nobody could understand those debts!

The administrator said that much more oil had been sold than the total production of the old man's groves and that they had been compelled to turn to other growers.

"So you think this could turn out to be a good business?" the marquis asked.

"Yes; if it were well run, it could be a great business."

The marquis looked fixedly at the administrator.

"But what did uncle do with all that money?" muttered the man with the fish-face.

The administrator smiled discreetly and turned his head aside in resignation.

All their hatred was now focused against Nini, that awful strumpet who was ruining the family.

The marquis said that those outbursts were irrelevant. The question at hand was how to get the oil business on its feet and how to be free of all debt.

This was what they were dealing with, although it seemed they were talking about something else.

"A simple procedure," said the fish-faced cousin in his effeminate voice, "would be to sell all the merchandise, make up some false creditors and declare bankruptcy. You could then put the firm in someone else's name and it would all be taken care of."

For the time being, the marquis couldn't approve of his relative's idea and he studied the face of the administrator, who let him know that he couldn't lend his name to any scheme like that. The fish-face expounded on their disapproval. Another opinion consisted of going to the principal creditors and promising payment to them alone and then declaring bankruptcy.

Fernando, who wasn't much interested in all that, went out of the study and the marquis's sons followed him.

"Where is the dead man?" Ossorio asked.

"In there, in that parlor," his cousin told him. "But don't go in to see him. He's completely decomposed."

—¿Sí, eh?
— Uf.
Fernando apenas conocía a sus primos, pero le parecieron alegres y desenvueltos.
— Y vosotros, ¿le conocéis a ella? — les preguntó.
—¿A quién, a Nini? Sí, hombre.
—¿Y qué tal es?
— Más bonita que el mundo — contestó el más joven.— Y no creas, que le quería al tío. La última vez que les vi juntos fué en Romea. Estaban los dos en un palco; yo estaba en otro con una amiga... Bailaba la bella Martínez, y cuando terminó de bailar, Nini, que es amiga de la Martínez, la echó al escenario un ramillete de flores.
—¿Y sabe ella que ha muerto el tío?
— Sí ¡ah! ¿Pero no te han dicho lo que ha ocurrido?
— No.
— Pues que ha mandado una corona de flores naturales, y estaba puesta en el cuarto, cuando se enteran que es de ella, y se indignan todas las señoras, y va papá y dice que aquel atrevimiento no se puede soportar, y coge la corona y la echa a un cuarto obscuro. Ya le he dicho yo a papá cuatro cosas, para que no vuelva a hacer tonterías.
— Vamos a dar una vuelta — preguntó uno de ellos —. El coche de mamá debe estar abajo. Volveremos al anochecer.
— Vamos. ¿Se lo decimos a mamá?
— Para qué? Está ahí muy entretenida.
Efectivamente, en el salón en donde estaban las señoras se oía una conversación muy animada y un murmullo de voces que subía y bajaba de intensidad.
Fueron los tres a la calle, entraron en el coche y se dirigieron a la Castellana. Los dos jóvenes comentaban riéndose la avaricia de su papá.
Pasaron en un coche una señorita y una señora. Los dos primos de Fernando las saludaron.
—¿Quiénes son? — preguntó Fernando.
— Lulú Cortenay y su madre.
— Es bonita.
— Preciosa.
— Esta chica no se casará — dijo el más serio de los hermanos.
—¿Porque no tiene capital?
— No...si lo debe tener...pero mordido.
—¿Mordido? — preguntó Fernando extrañado.

"Is that so?"

"Ugh!"

Fernando hardly knew his cousins, but they seemed cheerful and easygoing to him.

"Do you two know her?"

"Whom, Nini? We sure do."

"What's she like?"

"She's as pretty as a picture," the younger one replied. "And don't believe what you hear, she really loved our uncle. The last time I saw them together was at the Romea Theatre. The two of them were together in a theater box and I was in another with a girl friend of mine... The beautiful Martínez[9] was dancing, and when she finished dancing, Nini, who is a friend of La Martínez, threw a bouquet of flowers onto the stage for her."

"And does she know that uncle died?"

"Yes. Oh, I see! So they didn't tell you what happened?"

"No."

"Well, she sent a wreath of fresh flowers and it was placed in the room, and when they find out it's from her, all the ladies get indignant and papa goes and says we don't have to put up with such audacity and so he grabs the wreath and throws it into some dark room.

"I really told papa a thing or two so he won't do a stupid thing like that again."

"Are we going for a ride?" one of them asked. "Mama's carriage is probably downstairs. We can be back by nightfall."

"Let's go then. But shouldn't we tell mama?"

"What for? She seems to be well entertained."

As a matter of fact, you could hear a very animated conversation and the murmur of voices rising and falling in intensity in the parlor where all of the ladies were gathered.

The three of us went out into the street, got into the carriage and headed for the Castellana. The two young men kept making comments and laughing at their father's greed.

A young lady and an older woman passed by in a carriage. Fernando's two cousins greeted them.

"Who are they?" Fernando asked.

"Lulú Cortunay and her mother."

"She's pretty."

"Exquisite."

"This girl isn't going to get married," said the more serious brother.

"Why? Because she doesn't have any money?"

"No..., she ought to have some..., but it's all been nibbled away."

"Nibbled away?" Fernando asked in astonishment.

– Sí; mordido por un condesito, amigo suyo.

El otro hermano comenzó a reírse al oír aquello.

–¡Admirable, chico, admirable!

Pasaron las hijas de un general y su madre, en un landó grande y destartalado. Hubo nuevos saludos y nuevas sonrisas.

– Son feas.

– Y cursis.

– Ahora viene la condesa y sus hijas.

Pasaron; se descubrieron los dos primos de Fernando y éste hizo lo mismo; una de las muchachas saludó con risa irónica, levantando el brazo por encima de la cabeza con la mano abierta.

–¿A éstas las conocerás – preguntó el menos serio de los primos de Fernando.

– Sí; creo que las conozco de vista.

–¡Pero si son populares! A esta muchacha la conoce ya todo Madrid. En el teatro habla alto, se suena fuerte, se ríe a carcajadas, lleva el compás con el abanico y se hace señas con los amigos.

–¡Demonio! Pues es una mujer extraña.

–¡Vaya, y de talento! ¡Suele dar unas tabarras a los jovencitos que la hacen la rosca.!

Y el primo contó algunas anécdotas.

Una vez estaban reunidos en su casa la madre, que debe ser una mujer de éstas que tienen furor sexual, y algunos amigos. La madre tenía un amigo íntimo, joven. Se oye sonar el timbre del teléfono. Se acerca la muchacha. Pregunta que quién llama, y al oír que es el amigo de su madre, le dice: – "¡Mamá!" – "¿Que quién es?" – responde la vieja. – "¡Tu héroe!"

Otra vez le salió mal la broma, porque se encontró en los pasillos del Real a la de Ortiz de Estúñiga, y le dijo:

– Oye, ¿Has visto a mi marido? Se ha marchado del palco y no sé dónde anda.

– Pues, Échale los *mansos* – le replicó ésta.

– Hija, ¿Está tu padre ahí?

Y las anécdotas llovían.

Tenía ya la chica fama y todas las historias desvergonzadas se las atribuían a ella, como antes las anécdotas grotescas a un señor riquísimo.

– Lo que es ésa, cuando se case, va a eclipsar a su madre – terminó diciendo como conclusión el pollo.

– Bah. Según –murmuró el más serio –. Yo no creo que esta chica tenga la lubricidad de su madre. Indudablemente en ella hay un instinto de perversidad moral. Es más; es posible que esta manera de ser nazca de un romanticismo fracasado al

"Yes; all nibbled away by a young count, a boyfriend among her friends."
The other brother began to laugh when he heard all that.
"Wonderful, old chap, wonderful!"
A general's wife and daughters passed by in a large and dilapidated landau. There were renewed greetings and smiles.
"They're ugly."
"And quite pretentious."
"Here comes the countess with her daughters."
They passed by; Fernando's two cousins tipped their hats and he did the same; one of the girls greeted them with ironic laughter, raising her arm over her head with her hand open.
"You probably know those girls?" the less serious of Fernando's cousins asked.
"Yes, I think I may know them by sight."
"Well, they really are popular. Everyone in Madrid knows this girl by now. At the theater she speaks loudly, she blows her nose noisily, she's always bursting into laughter, she keeps time with her fan and makes all manner of signs to her male friends."
"The devil you say! Then she's really an unusual woman."
"You can say that again, and she's quite clever! She's really gives a lot of trouble to all the young fellows who try to play up to her!"
His cousin recounted a number of anecdotes.
One time, the mother, who must be one of those women filled with a sexual frenzy, was at home with a number of friends. The mother had an intimate, young male friend. They hear the telephone ring. The girl goes over. She asks who's calling, and when she hears that it's her mother's male friend, she calls out, "Mama!" "Who is it?" the old lady replies. "Your hero!"
Another time the joke didn't turn out well because she met that Ortiz de Estúñiga woman in the corridors of the Real Theatre and said to her:
"Tell me, have you seen my husband? He seems to have gone off from the box and I have no idea where he may be gadding about."
"Well, why don't you try sending out the tame oxen to get him,"[10] she replied to her.
"Child, is your father there?"
And the anecdotes poured on and on.
The girl already had quite a reputation and the most shameless stories were told with reference to her, just as many grotesque anecdotes had been told before about a very rich gentleman.
"The way that girl carries on, when she gets married, she's going to eclipse her mother," the young dandy ended up saying in conclusion.
"Nonsense! It all depends," muttered the more serious one. "I don't think this girl has her mother's lascivious nature. There is undoubtedly an instinct for perversity in her, but for a more moral type of perversity. I'll go further; it is altogether possible

vivir en un ambiente imposible para la satisfacción de sus deseos. Yo no sé, pero no creo en la maldad ni en el vicio de los que sonríen con ironía.

– Te advierto, Fernando, que éste es un filósofo.

– No; veo nada más y observo. Fijaos. Vuelven otra vez. Mirad la madre. Es seria, tranquila; de soltera sería soñadora. La hija sigue riendo, riendo, con su risa irónica y sus ojos brillantes. Hay algo de romanticismo en esa risa burlona, que niega, que parece que ridiculiza.

– Habrá todo lo que quieras, pero yo no me casaría con ella.

– Eso no quiere decir nada. ¿Vamos a casa?

Volvieron. El primo, más alegre y jovial, inclinándose al oído de Fernando, iba mostrándole y nombrándole al mismo tiempo la gente que pasaba en coche. Aristócratas viejos con aspecto humilde y encogido, nobles de nuevo cuño estirados y petulantes, senadores, diputados, bolsistas. Todos, en sus coches que se apretaban en las filas del paseo, sintiendo el placer de verse, de saludarse, de espiarse, casi todos aguijoneados por las tristezas de la envidia y las sordideces de una vida superficialmente fastuoso e íntimamente miserable y pobre.

Y seguían las historias, que no terminaban nunca, y los apodos que trascendían a romanticismo trasnochado: La Bestia Hermosa, La Judía Verde, la Preciosa Ridícula, el Lirio del Valle, y seguían las murmuraciones. A una muchacha no le gustaban los chicos; tres jovencitos que iban en un coche, eran los *liones* que cambiaban las queridas, las mujeres más elegantes y hermosas de Madrid.

– Esta sociedad aristocrática –dijo sentenciosamente el primo filósofo – está muy bien organizada. Es la única que tiene buen sentido y buen gusto, Los maridos andan *golfeando* con una y otra, de acá para allá, de casa de Lucía a casa de Mercedes, y de ésta a casa de Marta. Las pobrecitas de las mujeres se quedan abandonadas y se las ve vacilar durante mucho tiempo y pasear con los ojos tristes. Hasta que un día se deciden, y hacen bien, toman un queridito y a vivir alegremente.

Al entrar en la calle Mayor, los dos primos saludaban a dos muchachas y a una señora que pasaron en un coche.

– El padre de éstas –dijo el primo filósofo – es un católico furibundo. Es de los que van a los jubileos con cirio; en cambio, las chicas andan de teatrucho en teatrucho, escotadas, riéndose y charlando con sus amigos. Es una sociedad muy amable esta madrileña.

– Ya te habrás fijado en el aspecto místico que tiene la mayor de las hermanas

that a way of life like that may be born of a frustrated romanticism, living in a milieu which is impossible for the fulfillment of her desires. I just don't know, but I can't believe in the evil or vice of those who smile ironically."

"I'm warning you, Fernando, this fellow is a philosopher."

"No; all I do is look and observe. Take a good look. They're coming back again. Look at the mother. She is serious and calm; when she was single, she was probably a dreamer. The daughter keeps on laughing, with that ironic laughter and those shining eyes. There is something romantic in that mocking laugh, a sort of denial, that seems to be ridiculing."

"She may be everything you say, but I still wouldn't marry her."

"That doesn't mean anything. Shall we go back to the house?"

They started back. The more carefree and jovial cousin leaned over Fernando's ear, and kept pointing out and naming, at the same time, all the people passing in their carriages. Old aristocrats, humble and reserved in appearance, snobbish and arrogant nobles with newly acquired titles, senators, deputies, stockbrokers. All of them, in their carriages, which were crowded together in the lanes of that boulevard, all experiencing the pleasure of seeing one another, greeting one another, and spying on one another, almost all of them goaded on by the wretchedness of envy and the sordid quality of a life that was ostentatious on the surface and inwardly miserable and impoverished.

And the stories kept running on and on and never seemed to end, and all manner of sobriquets that went back to a trite romanticism: The Beautiful Beast, the Green Jewess, the Ridiculous Précieuse, the Lily of the Valley, and the gossip kept flowing. One girl didn't like young men; three young fellows riding in a carriage were the *lions*, who exchanged their mistresses with one another, counted among the most elegant and beautiful women in Madrid.

"This aristocratic society," said the philosophical cousin sententiously, "is very well organized. It's the only kind that has good sense and good taste. The husbands go *chasing around* after one woman or another, from here to there, from Lucía's house to Mercedes's house and from there to Marta's house. Their pitiful wives are left abandoned and you can see them hesitate for a long time as they stroll about with sad eyes. Until one day they make up their minds and do the right thing, and take a young lover and start living more lightheartedly."

As they came into the Calle Mayor, the two cousins greeted two girls and an older woman as they passed by in a carriage.

"These girls' father," said the philosophical cousin, "is a fanatic Catholic. He's one of those people who goes to jubilees with a candle; the young girls, on the other hand, run around from one squalid theater to another, wearing low-cut dresses, laughing and chattering with their male friends. This Madrilenian society is really very pleasant."

"You must have noticed that mystical expression on the older sister," said the

– dijo el primo jovial –. Dicen que tiene ese aspecto tan espiritual desde que se acostaba con un obispo.

Llegaron a la calle del Sacramento y subieron a casa.

En el despacho se seguía hablando de la cuestión del aceite; en la sala se comentaban en voz baja los escándalos de Nini; los criados andaban alborotados por si les despedían o no de la casa, y mientras tanto, el tío abuelo, solo, bien solo, sin que nadie le molestara con gritos, ni lamentos, ni otras tonterías por el estilo, se pudría tranquilamente en su ataúd, y de su cara gruesa, carnosa, abultada, no se veía a través del cristal más que una mezcla de sangre rojiza y negra, y en las narices y en la boca algunos puntos blancos de pus.

V

Cuando Fernando Ossorio se encontró instalado en la nueva casa de la calle del Sacramento, comprendió que debía haber llegado a un extremo de debilidad muy grande. Precisamente entonce la herencia de su tío abuelo le daba medios para vivir con cierta independencia; pero como no tenía deseos, ni voluntad, ni fuerza para nada, se dejó llevar por la corriente. No entraba en la decisión de sus tías de llevarle a vivir con ellas ningún móvil interesado. Luisa Fernanda le tenía cariño a su sobrino y al mismo tiempo pensaba que cuatro mujeres solas en una casa no tenían la autoridad que podría tener un hombre. Antes Fernando tuvo una conferencia con su tía Laura, y desde entonces ya no se volvió a hablar del matrimonio de María Flora con Fernando.

Las tías, que fueron a ocupar el segundo piso de la casa del señor difunto, destinaron para su sobrino dos cuartos grandes, una sala con dos balcones que daban a la calle del Sacramento y una alcoba con ventanas a un jardín de la vecindad. La sala, que había estado cerrada durante mucho tiempo, tenía un aspecto marchito que agradaba a Fernando. Era grande y de techo bajo, lo que le hacía parecer de más tamaño; estaba tapizada con papel amarillo claro con dibujos geométricos en las paredes y cubierta en el techo con papel blanco.

Un zócalo de madera de limoncillo corría alrededor del cuarto.

Los balcones, altos y anchos, rasgados en la gruesa pared, no abrían en toda su altura, sino sólo en la parte de abajo; los cristales eran pequeños y sujetos por gruesos listones pintados de blanco.

Una sillería vieja de terciopelo amarillo formada por sillas curvas, un sofá y dos sillones ajados, adornaban la sala. En las paredes y en el suelo había un amontonamiento de muebles, cuadros y cachivaches; un piano viejo con las teclas

jovial cousin. "They say she's had that spiritual look ever since she started sleeping with a bishop."[11]

They reached the Calle del Sacramento and went up into the house. They were still talking about the problem of the olive oil in the study; they were commenting on the scandalous behavior of that Nini in hushed voices in the drawing room; the servants were going around all upset, wondering whether or not they would be dismissed from that house, and all the while, great-uncle, all alone, truly alone, without anyone to trouble him with shouts or lamentations, nor any other nonsense of that kind, was tranquilly decaying in his casket, and through the glass, all you could see of his heavy, fleshy, bulky face, was a mixture of reddish-black blood and several white bits of pus in his nostrils and his mouth.

V

When Fernando found himself settled down in his new home on the Calle del Sacramento, he realized that he must have reached the very depths of extreme weakness. Precisely at that time, the inheritance from his great-uncle gave him the means to live with a certain degree of independence, but since he had neither the desire, nor the will power nor the energy to accomplish anything, he allowed himself to carried along by the current. There was no self-serving motive in his aunts' decision to have him come live with them. Luisa Fernanda had considerable affection for her nephew and, at the same time, she thought that four women alone in a house didn't have the authority that one man could have. Before anything else, Fernando had a chat with his Aunt Laura, and from that time on, they never again spoke of a possible marriage of María Flora with Fernando.

His aunts, who moved upstairs to occupy the second floor of the deceased old man's house, set apart two large rooms for their nephew, a sitting room with two balcony windows facing the Calle del Sacramento and a bedroom facing a neighborhood garden. The sitting room, which had been kept closed up for a long time, had a faded appearance that appealed to Fernando. It was spacious and had a low ceiling that made it seem even greater in size; the walls were done in bright yellow paper with geometrical designs and the ceiling was papered in white.

A baseboard made of yellow limoncillo wood ran around the entire room.

The balcony windows, tall and broad, carved out of the thick wall, did not open all the way up, just the lower part; the panes of glass were small and held in place by thick strips of white-painted wood.

An old living room suite of yellow velvet that decorated the sitting room consisted of curved chairs, a sofa and two shabby armchairs. The walls and the floor were piled up with pieces of furniture, paintings and all manner of knickknacks; an

amarillentas, dos o tres cornucopias, una consola de mármol que sostenía dos relojes ennegrecidos de metal dorado, un pupitre de porcelana y una poltrona vieja cubierta de tela dorada con dibujos negros.

En esta poltrona pasaba Ossorio las horas muertas, contemplando las rajaduras del techo, que parecían las líneas que representan los ríos en los mapas, y las manchas redondeadas, rojizas, que dejaban las moscas.

En las paredes no había sitio libre donde poner la punta de un alfiler: estaban llenas de cuadros, de apuntes, de fotografías de iglesias, de grabados y de medallas. Había reunido allí los mejores cuadros de la casa, antes colocados en los sitios más obscuros.

Desde los balcones se veía un montón de tejados parduscos, grises. Por encima de ellos, enfrente, la iglesia de San Andrés, la única quizá agradable de Madrid; más lejos, a la derecha, se destacaba la parte superior de la cúpula gris de San Francisco el Grande; y cerca, a un lado, la torre de Santa María de la Almudena.

Reinaba en la sala un gran silencio. De cuando en cuando se oía el timbre de los tranvías de la calle Mayor y las campanas de la iglesia próxima.

La alcoba, cuyas ventanas daban a un jardín de la vecindad, tenía una cama de madera, grande, baja, con cortinas verdes, un armario y un gran sillón.

Abajo, desde las ventanas, se veía un jardín con un estanque redondo en medio, adornado con macetas.

El cambio de medio moral influyó en Ossorio grandemente; dejó sus amistades de bohemio y se reunió con una caterva de señoritos de buena sociedad, viciosos, pero correctos siempre; comenzó a presentarse en la Castellana y en Recoletos en coche, y en los palcos de los teatros, elegantemente vestido, acompañando señoras.

Era una vida desconocida para Fernando, que tenía atractivos.

Toda la gente distinguida se ve por la mañana, por la tarde, por la noche. El gran entretenimiento de ellos no es presenciar óperas, dramas, pasear, andar en coche o bailar; la satisfacción es verse todos los días, saber lo que hacen, descubrir por el aspecto de una familia su encumbramiento o su ruina, estudiarse, espiarse, observarse unos a otros. Por esto, que mientras lo fué conociendo pareció interesantísimo a Fernando, ya conocido no lo encontró nada digno de observación.

La prima de Osssorio tenía relaciones co un chico artillero, de buena familia, pero pobre, con el que se pasaba la vida hablando desde el balcón y mirándose en los teatros; Octavio, el primo, estaba en un colegio de Francia; la familia parecía encontrarse en un buen período de calma y de tranquilidad.

Una noche, Fernando, que solía quedarse con mucha frecuencia en casa y empezaba a abandonar su vida elegante, oyó a través del tabique vagos murmullos

old piano with yellowed keys, two or three sconces with mirrors, a marble console table supporting two blackened clocks of gilded metal, a porcelain-topped writing desk and an old easy chair covered with gold-colored fabric with black designs.

Ossorio would spend the lifeless hours in this easy chair contemplating the cracks in the ceiling that resembled lines representing the rivers on a map, and also the rounded, reddish specks left by the flies.

There wasn't enough empty space on the walls to accommodate the head of a pin: they were covered with pictures, sketches, photographs of churches, engravings and plaques. He had brought together there the best paintings in the house, which had been placed in the darkest corners before.

From the balcony windows, you could see a mass of brownish and gray tile roofs. Rising above them, facing his room, stood the Church of San Andrés, perhaps the only pleasant-looking one in Madrid; farther away, to the right, you could see the upper part of the cupola of San Francisco el Grande outlined, and nearby, to one side, the tower of Santa María de Almudena.

A heavy silence reigned in the sitting room. From time to time, you could hear the clang of the streetcar bells on the Calle Mayor and the bells from the nearby church.

The bedroom, with its two windows facing a neighborhood garden, contained a large, low, wooden bed with green curtains, a wardrobe and a spacious armchair.

From the windows, you could see a garden down below with a round pool in the center, decorated with potted plants.

The change in his moral environment had a tremendous influence on Ossorio; he abandoned his bohemian friendships and started meeting with a crowd made up of young gentlemen from high society, given to vice, but always correct; he began to appear on the Castellana and on the Paseo de Recoletos in a carriage, and in boxes at the theater, elegantly dressed, in the company of gracious ladies.

It was an unfamiliar life for Fernando, but it had its attractions.

All distinguished people see one another in the morning, in the afternoon and in the evening. Their major form of amusement isn't going to see operas, plays, taking a stroll, riding around in a carriage or going to a dance; their satisfaction lies in seeing one another every day, knowing what others are doing, determining the rise to eminence or ruin of a family by their appearance, studying one another, spying on one another, observing one another. But all this, which had seemed quite interesting to Fernando during the time he was learning about it, didn't seem worthy of observation at all once he was aware of it.

Ossorio's cousin was being courted by a young fellow in the Artillery Corps, from a good family, but poor, and she spent most of her time talking to him from her balcony, and exchanging glances with him at the theatres; his cousin Octavio was away at a school in France; the family seemed to find itself in an agreeable period of calm and tranquility.

One night, Fernando, who was now staying home quite frequently and was just beginning to abandon his elegant life, heard indistinct, barely perceptible murmurs

apenas perceptibles. Separaba su cuarto del de Laura otro cuarto intermedio. Encendió la luz y vió que oculta por las cortinas de su cama, había una ventana condenada. De día abrió la ventana condenada que daba a un cuarto lleno de armarios y de cajas, que casi siempre estaba cerrado.

A la noche siguiente abrió de par en par el montante y escuchó: oyó la voz de la tía Laura y la de su doncella, y luego gritos, risas, estallido de besos; después, lamentos, súplicas, gritos voluptuosos...

Laura tenía de treinta a treinta y cinco años. Era morena, de ojos algo claros, el pelo muy negro, la nariz gruesa, los labios abultados; la voz fuerte, hombruna, que a veces se hacía opaca, como en sus hermanas; gangueaba algo, por haberse educado en un colegio de monjas de París, una sucursal de Lesbos, en donde se rendía culto a la *joie imparfaite*. Los andares de Laura eran decididos, de marimacho; vestía con mucha frecuencia trajes que las mujeres llaman de sastre, y sus enaguas se ceñían estrechamente a la carne.

Cuando se ponía a reñir, su voz era molesta de tal modo, que se sentía odio por ella, sin más razón que la voz. Tenía en su aspecto algo indefinido, neutro, parecía una mujer muy poco femenina y, sin embargo, había en ella una atracción sexual grande. A veces su palabra sonaba a algo afrodisíaco, y su movimiento de caderas, hombruno por lo violento, era ásperamente sexual, excitante como la cantárida.

Algunas noches se quedaba Fernando en casa. Luisa Fernanda y Laura se sentaban en el comedor al lado del fuego.

Luisa Fernanda, hundida en la poltrona, miraba las llamas. Ella y su hermana no hablaban más que del tiempo y de lo que sucedía en casa.

Flora se aburría, leía o dormía de rabia.

Sonaba lentamente el reloj de caja del pasillo.

Cuando se acercaba la hora de irse a acostar, las dos hermanas mayores llamaban primero a la cocinera y se discutía la comida del día siguiente.

Luisa Fernanda preguntaba a todos lo que querían para comer.

Luego venían una serie de recomendaciones largas.

Muchas veces María Flora y Fernando se quedaban en el comedor charlando a los lados de la chimenea.

from the other side of the thin wall. His room was separated from his Aunt Laura's by another room in between; he put on a light and saw that there was a blocked-up window hidden by the curtains of his bed. When day came, he opened the blocked window that opened into a room filled with wardrobes and boxes and which was almost always kept closed.

The following night, he opened the transom wide and listened: he heard his Aunt Laura's voice and that of her maid, and then cries, laughter, the explosive sound of kisses; then, moaning, pleading, voluptuous cries...[12]

Laura was about thirty or thirty-five years old. She was dark, with pale blue-gray eyes, very black hair, a broad nose and thick lips; she had a strong, mannish voice which sometimes took on a muffled quality, as was the case with her sisters; she spoke with a nasal quality, due to the fact that she had been educated in an academy for girls in Paris, run by nuns, a subsidiary of Lesbos, where they rendered homage to the *joie imparfaite*. Laura's walk was quite resolute, like that of a mannish woman; she frequently wore suits which women call tailored and her underskirts were fitted tightly to confine her flesh.

Whenever she would start a quarrel, her voice would become annoying, to such an extent that you would feel true hatred for her, and for no other reason than her voice. There was something undefined, neuter, in her appearance; she seemed to be a woman of very little femininity, and nevertheless, she exuded a considerable sexual attraction. Her words would sometimes assume an aphrodisiacal quality and the movement of her hips, quite mannish in its violence, was abrasively sexual, as stimulating as cantharides.

Fernando would stay at home some nights.

Luisa Fernanda and Laura would sit in the dining room beside the fire.

Luisa Fernanda, buried in her easy chair, would look at the flames. She and her sister would speak of nothing more than the weather or what was going on about the house.

Flora would act quite bored and would read or fall asleep out of sheer desperation.

The grandfather clock in the hallway would slowly chime the hours. When it was almost time to go to bed, the two older sisters would first call the cook and discuss the meal for the coming day.

Luisa Fernanda would ask everyone what they would like to eat.

That would be followed by a series of long recommendations.

Many times María Flora and Fernando would remain in the dining room chatting as they sat on either side of the fireplace.

VI

Por entonces ya Fernando comenzaba a tener ciertas ideas ascéticas,
Sentía desprecio por la gimnasia y el atletismo.
La limpieza le parecía bien con tal de que no ocasionase cuidados.
Tenía la idea del cristiano, de que el cuerpo es una porquería, en la que no hay que pensar.
Todas esas fricciones y flagelaciones de origen pagano le parecían repugnantes.
Ver un atleta en un circo le producía una repulsión invencible.
El ideal de su vida era un paisaje intelectual, frío, limpio, puro, siempre cristalino, con una claridad blanca, sin un sol bestial; la mujer soñada era una mujer algo rígida, de nervios de acero; energía de domadora y con la menor cantidad de carne, de pecho, de grasa, de estúpida brutalidad y atontamiento sexuales.
Una noche de Carnaval en que Fernando llegó a casa a la madrugada, se encontró con su tía Laura, que estaba haciendo té para Luisa Fernanda, que se hallaba enferma.
Fernando se sentía aquella noche brutal; tenía el cerebro turbado por los vapores del vino.
Laura era una mujer incitante, y en aquella hora aun más.
Estaba despechugada; por entre la abertura de su bata se veía su pecho blanco, pequeño y poco abultado, con una vena azul que lo cruzaba; en el cuello tenía una cinta roja con un lazo.
Fernando se sentó junto a ella sin decir una palabra; vió como hacía todos los preparativos; calentaba el agua, apartaba después la lamparilla del alcohol, vertía el líquido en una taza e iba después hacia el cuarto de su hermana con el plato en una mano mientras que con la otra movía la cucharilla, que repiqueteaba con un tintineo alegre en la taza.
Fernando esperó a que volviera, entontecido, con la cara inyectada por el deseo. Tardó Laura en volver.
–¿Todavía estás aquí? – le preguntó a su sobrino.
– Sí.
– Pero ¿qué quieres?
–¿Qué quiero? – murmuró Fernando sordamente, y acercándose a ella tiró de la bata de una manera convulsiva y besó a Laura en el pecho con labios que ardían.
Laura palideció profundamente y rechazó a Ossorio con un ademán de desprecio. Luego pareció consentir; Fernando la agarró del talle y la hizo pasar a su cuarto.

VI

At about that time Fernando began to have certain ascetic ideas.

He felt contemptuous toward gymnastics and athletics.

Cleanliness seemed acceptable to him as long as it didn't entail any special efforts.

He embraced the Christian attitude that the body is something nasty and that one ought not even think about it.

All that abrasive scraping and flagellation of pagan origin seemed repugnant to him. The mere sight of an athlete in a circus produced an overpowering repulsion in him.

His life's ideal was an intellectual landscape, cold, limpid, pure, always crystalline, with a white brilliance, away from the brutal sun. The woman of his dreams was a somewhat rigid woman, with nerves of steel, the energy of an animal tamer and the least amount of flesh, bosom, fat, one with stupid sexual brutishness and dullness.

One night during Shrovetide, when Fernando came home in the early hours of the morning, he met his Aunt Laura making tea for Luisa Fernanda who happened to be ill.

Fernando was feeling quite brutal that night; his brain was clouded by the vapors of wine.

Laura was a provocative woman and more than ever at that moment.

Her bosom was partially bared; through the opening of her dressing gown, he could see a white breast, small, not very full, with a blue vein crossing over it; she was wearing a red ribbon with a bow around her neck.

Fernando sat down beside her without saying a word; he saw how she went through all the preparations; she heated the water, then pushed aside the small spirit lamp, poured the liquid into a cup, and then went toward her sister's room with the saucer in one hand, while, with the other, she kept stirring the teaspoon, which tinkled with a merry, jingling sound in the cup.

Fernando waited for her to return, feeling dazed, his faced suffused with desire. Laura took some time to return.

"So you're still here?" she asked her nephew.

"Yes."

"Well, what do you want?"

"What do I want?" Fernando muttered in a muffled voice and, walking over to her, he pulled her dressing gown aside with a convulsive move and kissed Laura on the breast with burning lips.

Laura turned deeply pale and pushed Ossorio away with a scornful gesture. Then she seemed to acquiesce; Fernando grabbed her by the waist and made her go to his room with him.

La luz eléctrica estaba allí encendida; había fuego en la chimenea. Al llegar allí él se sentó en un sofá y miró estúpidamente a Laura; ella, de pie, le contempló; de pronto, abalanzándose sobre él, le echó los brazos al cuello y le besó en la boca; fué un beso largo, agudo, doloroso. Al retroceder ella, Fernando trató de sujetarla, primero del talle, después agarrándola de las manos. Laura se desasió, y tranquilamente, despacio, rechazándole con un gesto violento cuando él quería acercarse, fué dejando la ropa en el suelo y apareció sobre el montón de telas blancas su cuerpo desnudo, alto, esbelto, moreno, iluminado por la luz del techo y por las llamaradas rojas de la chimenea.

La cinta que rodeaba su cuello parecía una línea de sangre que separaba su cabeza del tronco. Fernando la cogió en sus brazos y la estrechó convulsivamente, y sintió en la cara, en los párpados, en el cuello los labios de Laura, y oyó su voz áspera y opaca por el deseo.

A medianoche, Ossorio se despertó; vió que Laura se levantaba y salía del cuarto como una sombra blanca. Al poco rato volvió.

—¿A dónde has ido? Te vas a enfriar – le dijo.

– A ver a Luisa. Hace frío – y apelotonándose se enlazó a Fernando estrechamente.

Y así en los demás días. Como las fieras que huyen a la obscuridad de los bosques a satisfacer su deseo, así volvieron a encontrarse mudos, temblorosos, poseídos de un erotismo bestial nunca satisfecho, quizá sintiendo el uno por el otro más odio que amor. A veces, en el cuerpo de uno de los dos quedaban huellas de golpes, de arañazos, de mordiscos. Fernando fué el primero que se cansó. Sentía que su cerebro se deshacía, se liquidaba. Laura no se saciaba nunca: aquella mujer tenía el furor de la lujuria en todo su cuerpo.

Su piel estaba siempre ardiente, los labios secos, en sus ojos se notaba algo como requemado. A Fernando le parecía una serpiente de fuego que le había envuelto entre sus anillos y que cada vez le estrujaba más y más, y él iba ahogándose y sentía que le faltaba el aire para respirar. Laura le excitaba con sus conversaciones sensuales. De ella se desprendía una voluptuosidad tal, que era imposible permanecer tranquilo a su lado.

Cuando con sus palabras no llegaba a enloquecer a Fernando, ponía sobre su hombro un gato de Angora blanco muy manso que tenían y allí lo acariciaba como si fuera un niño: ¡Pobrecito, ¡pobrecito!, y sus palabras tenían entonaciones tan brutalmente lujuriosas, que a Fernando le hacían perder la cabeza y lloraba de rabia y de furor. Laura quería gozar de todas estas locuras y salían y se daban cita en una casa de la calle de San Marcos, Era una casa estrecha, con dos balcones en cada piso; en uno del principal había una muestra que ponía: "Sastre y modista", y sostenidos en los hierros de los balcones, abrazados por un anillo, tiestos con plantas. En el piso bajo había un obrador de plancha. Fernando solía esperar a Laura

The electric light was lit there; there was a fire in the fireplace. As soon as he came in, he sat down on a sofa and stared vacantly at Laura; she stood there contemplating him; suddenly she threw herself upon him, wrapped her arms around his neck and kissed him on the mouth; it was a long, piercing, painful kiss. When she drew back, Fernando tried to hold on to her, first by the waist, then by seizing hold of her hands. Laura freed herself, pushing him away with a violent gesture when he tried to approach her, and calmly and slowly, she began to let her clothes drop to the floor, and her naked, tall, lithe, dark body, illuminated by the light from the ceiling and by the red flashes of flame from the fireplace, appeared over the heap of white garments.

The ribbon that encircled her neck seemed like a line of blood that separated her head from her torso. Fernando seized her in his arms and pressed her close convulsively, and he felt Laura's lips on his face, his eyelids and his neck, and heard her voice, harsh and muffled by desire.

Ossorio awoke at midnight; he saw that Laura was getting up and leaving the room like a white shadow. In a short while she returned.

"Where did you go? You're going to catch a chill," he said to her.

"To see Luisa. It's cold," and cuddling up close to him, she wrapped herself tightly around Fernando.

And so it went on the days that followed.[13] Like beasts that flee into the darkness of the forests to gratify their desire, so did they come together again, silent, trembling, possessed by a savage eroticism that was never sated, feeling perhaps more hatred than love for one another. Sometimes one or the other would bear the traces of blows, deep scratches and bites. Fernando was first to grow tired of it all. He felt that his brain was coming undone, that it was dissolving. Laura never seemed to be satisfied; that woman seemed to be possessed of a frenzied lust over her entire body.

Her skin was always feverish, her lips dry; a trace of something scorched could be seen in her eyes. To Fernando she resembled a serpent of fire that had wrapped him in its coils and kept crushing him more and more each moment, and he kept choking and felt that he didn't have enough air to breathe. Laura excited him with her sensual conversations. So great a voluptuousness emanated from her that it was impossible to remain calm by her side.

When her words didn't succeed in driving Fernando wild, she would place a white Angora cat, a very tame cat they kept there, on his shoulder, and there she would caress it as if it were a child, saying, "Poor little thing!, poor little thing!" and her words would have intonations so brutally lustful that they made Fernando lose his head and weep from anger and fury. Laura wanted the full enjoyment of all this madness, and so they would go out and arrange to meet at a house on the Calle de San Marcos. It was a narrow house with two balconies on each floor; on one of those on the second floor, there was a sign that read: "Tailor and dressmaker," and some potted plants, surrounded by metal bands and hanging from the iron bars of the balconies. On the ground floor there was an ironing business. Fernando used to

en la calle. Ella llegaba en coche, llamaba en el piso principal; una mujer *barbiana*, gorda, que venía sin corsé, con un peinador blanco y en chanclas, le abría la puerta y le hacía pasar a un gabinete amueblado con un diván, una mesa, varias sillas y un espejo grande, frente al diván.

Todo aquello le entretenía admirablemente a Laura; leía los letreros que se habían escrito en la pared y en el espejo.

Algunas veces, buscando la sensación más intensa, iban a alguna casa de la calle de Embajadores o de Mesón de Paredes. Al salir de allá, cuando los faroles brillaban en el ambiente limpio de las noches de invierno, se detenían en los grupos de gente que oía a algún ciego tocar la guitarra. Laura se escurría entre los aprendices de taller embozados hasta las orejas en sus tapabocas, entre los golfos, asistentes y criadas. Escuchaba en silencio los arpegios, punteados y acordes, indispensable introducción del *cante jondo*.

Carraspeaba el cantor, lanzaba doloridos ayes y *jipíos*, y comenzaba la copla, alzando los turbios ojos, que brillaban apagados a la luz de los faroles.

Con los ojos cerrados, la boca abierta y torcida, apenas articulaba el ciego las palabras del lamento gitano y sus frases sonaban subrayadas con golpes de pulgar sobre la caja sonora de la guitarra.

Aquellas canciones nostálgicas y tristes, cuyos principales temas eran el amor y la muerte, la sangrecita y el presidio, el corazón y las cadenas y los camposantos y el ataúd de la madre, hacían estremecer a Laura, y sólo cuando Fernando le advertía que era tarde se separaba del grupo con pena y cogía el brazo de su amigo e iban los dos por las calles obscuras.

Muchas veces Fernando, al lado de aquella mujer, soñaba que iba andando por una llanura castellana seca, quemada y que el cielo era muy bajo, que cada vez bajaba más, y él sentía sobre su corazón una opresión terrible, y trataba de respirar y no podía.

De vez en cuando, un detalle sin importancia reavivaba sus deseos: un vestido nuevo, un escote más pronunciado. Entonces andaba detrás de ella por la casa como un lobo, buscando las ocasiones para encontrarla a solas, con los ojos ardientes y la boca seca; y cuando la cogía, sus manos nerviosas se agarraban como tenazas a los brazos o el pecho de Laura, y con la voz rabiosa murmurada entre dientes: "Te mataría," y a veces tenía que hacer un esfuerzo para no coger entre sus dedos la garganta de Laura y estrangularla.

Laura le excitaba con sus caricias y sus perversidades, y cuando veía a Fernando gemir dolorosamente con espasmos, le decía con una sonrisa entre lúbrica y canalla:

– Yo quiero que sufras, pero que sufras mucho.

Muchas noches Fernando se escapaba de casa y se reunía con sus antiguos amigos bohemios; pero en vez de hablar de arte bebía frenéticamente.

wait for Laura in the street. She would arrive in a carriage, knock at the door on the second floor; a fat, *brazen-looking woman*, in a white peignoir and slippers, without a corset, would open the door for her and have her go to a sitting room furnished with a divan, a table, several chairs and a large mirror facing the divan.

All that was a source of extraordinary amusement to Laura; she loved to read the graffiti that had been scribbled on the wall and on the mirror. A number of times, in their search for the most intense sensations, they would go to some house on the Calle de Embajadores or de Mesón de Paredes. As they left there, when the streetlamps were shining in the limpid atmosphere of the winter nights, they would stop among the groups of people listening to some blind man playing his guitar. Laura would slip through and stand among the shop apprentices, huddled up to their ears in their heavy scarves, among the street urchins, the army orderlies and the servant girls. They would listen in silence to the arpeggios, the plucking of the guitar strings and the chords, the indispensable introduction to the *cante jondo*.[14]

The singer would break into his hoarse chant, crying out heartbreaking ayes and *jipíos*, and then he would begin the ballad, raising his turbid eyes, shining sightless by the light of the streetlamps.

With his eyes closed, his mouth open and twisted, the blind man barely articulated the words of the gypsy lament and his phrases resounded, underscored by the striking of his thumb against the wooden body of the guitar.

Those nostalgic and sad songs, the principal themes of which were love and death, the spilling of precious blood and imprisonment, the heart and the chains, the cemeteries and the mother's coffin, made Laura tremble, and only when Fernando warned her that it was getting late, would she withdraw sorrowfully from the group, and grasp her lover's arm, and the two of them would go on their way along the dark streets.

Many times, when Fernando was beside that woman, he would dream that he was walking along a dry and scorched Castilian plain, and that the sky was very low and kept lowering more and more, and he felt a terrifying pressure over his heart, and that he was trying to breathe and wasn't able to do so.

Every so often, some unimportant detail would revive his desire: some new dress, a more pronounced and lower neckline. Then he would follow her around the house like a wolf, searching for any opportunities to find her alone, his eyes blazing, his mouth dry; and when he would catch hold of her, his nervous hands would seize Laura's arms or breasts like pincers and he would mutter in an enraged voice, with teeth clenched, "I could kill you," and sometimes he would have to make a special effort in order not to grab Laura by the throat with his fingers and strangle her.

Laura would excite him with her caresses and her perversities, and when she would see Fernando moan with distress in the midst of a spasm, she would say with a smile, lubricious and vicious at the same time:

"I want you to suffer, but really suffer a great deal."

Many nights, Fernando would escape from the house and join his former bohemian friends; but instead of speaking about art, he would drink frenziedly.

Por la mañana, cuando iba a casa, cuando por el frío del amanecer se disipaba su embriaguez, sentía un remordimiento terrible, no un dolor de alma, sino un dolor orgánico en el epigastrio y una angustia brutal que le daban deseos de echar a correr dando vueltas y saltos mortales por el aire como los payasos, lejos, muy lejos, lo más lejos posible.

Solía recordar en aquellos amaneceres una impresión matinal de Madrid, de cuando era estudiante; aquellas mañanas frescas de otoño cuando iba a San Carlos se le representaban con energía como si fueran los pocos momentos alegres de su vida.

Laura parecía rejuvenecerse por momentos; en cambio, Fernando se avejentaba por momentos, e iba perdiendo el apetito y el sueño. Una neuralgia de la cara le mortificaba horriblemente; de noche le despertaba el dolor, tenía que vestirse y salir a la calle a pasear.

Quizá por contraste, Fernando, que estaba hastiado de aquellos amores turbulentos, se puso a hacer el amor a la muchacha de luto que era amiga de su prima, y se llamaba Blanca.

Laura lo supo y no se incomodó.

–¡Si debías de casarte con ella! – le dijo a Fernando –. Te conviene. Tiene una fortuna regular.

A Ossorio le pareció repugnante la observación, pero no dijo nada.

Una noche Fernando fué a los Jardines y vió a Blanca paseándose, mirando a un nuevo galán. A Fernando empezaba a parecerle otra vez bonita y agradable. Devoró su rabia, y al salir siguió tras ella, que no sólo no disimulaba, sino que exageraba la afabilidad con el joven. Iba la muchacha en un grupo de varias personas que volvían a casa.

La siguió por Recoletos, y la oyó una risa tan irónica, tan burlona, que se acercó sin saber para qué. Fernando se adelantó a ella, y se detuvo a encender un cigarro. Pasaron Blanca y su amiga, y detrás dos señoras y un caballero, las dos muchachas del brazo, balanceándose, moviendo las caderas, y al llegar cerca de Fernando, éste se retiró tan torpemente que casi tropezó con ellas. Blanca se llevó la mano a la boca fingiendo que contenía la risa y murmuró:

–¡Está chiflado!

En todas las amigas de Blanca, Fernando notaba la misma mezcla de ironía y de compasión que le exasperaba.

Por la amistad de María Flora llegó a acompañar a Blanca algunos días; pero en vez de enamorarse con el trato, le sucedió lo contrario.

Cada detalle le molestaba más y más. ¡Hacían unos desprecios a la institutriz!, pobre muchacha que había cometido el delito de tener unos ojos muy grandes y muy hermosos y una cara tranquila, de expresión dulce. La hacían ir siempre detrás; si

In the morning, when he would come home, just as his intoxication was beginning to wear off with the early morning cold, he would feel a terrible remorse, not an affliction of the soul, but rather an organic pain in the epigastrium, and a savage anguish that filled him with a desire to start running, to whirl round and round, to do somersaults in the air, like clowns, far, very far, as far away as possible.

Those hours at daybreak would bring to mind an impression of Madrid at early morning, at a time when he was a student; those cool, autumn mornings when he used to go to San Carlos, would reappear vividly before him as if they were the few happy moments of his life.

Laura seemed to be rejuvenated through their relationship; Fernando, on the other hand, was looking older all the time, was losing his appetite and his ability to sleep. A facial neuralgia was tormenting him terribly; at night, the pain would awaken him and he had to get dressed and go out to take a walk in the street.

Perhaps for contrast, because he was getting thoroughly disgusted with that turbulent love affair, Fernando started paying court to the girl in mourning black, who was his cousin's friend and was named Blanca.

Laura found out about it and it didn't seem to upset her at all.

"You ought to get married to her!" she said to Fernando. "She's just right for you. She has a sizeable fortune."

This observation seemed utterly loathsome to Ossorio, but he didn't say anything.

One night Fernando went to the Gardens and saw Blanca taking a stroll, looking at a new admirer. She was beginning to appear quite pretty and pleasant to Fernando again. He overcame his rage, and he followed her when she left, noting that she not only didn't conceal her friendliness toward the young man, but she even exaggerated it. The girl was walking along with a group of people who were on their way home.

He followed her along the Paseo de Recoletos and heard her laughter, so ironic and mocking that he moved closer to her without knowing why. Fernando got ahead of her and stopped to light a cigar. Blanca and her girl friend passed by and two women and a gentleman came behind them, the two girls walking arm in arm, swaying back and forth, moving their hips; and as they came closer to Fernando, he drew back so awkwardly that he almost bumped into them. Blanca raised her hand to her mouth pretending to suppress her laughter and murmured:

"He's touched!"

Fernando noted the same mixture of irony and pity that exasperated him among all of Blanca's friends.

Because of her friendship with María Flora, he was able to accompany Blanca on several occasions; but instead of falling in love through their continuing familiarity, just the opposite occurred.

Every detail disturbed him more and more. They would act with contempt toward the governess!, a poor girl whose only crime was that she had big, beautiful eyes and a tranquil face with a sweet expression. They would always make her walk

formaban un corro para hablar, la dejaban fuera. Quizá había en la muchacha una gran serenidad, y todos los desdenes resbalaban en ella.

Blanca era de una desigualdad de carácter perturbadora, y Fernando tuvo que desistir de sus intentos.

Laura trató de consolarle; ella, que no quería perder a Fernando, ansiaba comprender aquel temperamento opuesto al suyo, aquel carácter irregular, tan pronto lleno de ilusiones como aplanado por un desaliento sin causa. Había un verdadero abismo entre la manera de ser de los dos; no se entendían en nada, y Fernando, con la indignación de su debilidad, pegaba a su querida. A veces a ella le entraba un terror pánico al ver a su sobrino hablando solo por las habitaciones obscuras.

Ella quería experimentar el placer a todo pasto, sentir vibrando las entrañas con las voluptuosidades más enervadoras, llegar al límite en que el placer, de intenso, se hace doloroso; pero turbar su espíritu, no.

Nunca se habían dicho Fernando y Laura una palabra tierna propia de enamorados; cuando sus ojos no manifestaban odio, más bien huían que buscaban encontrarse.

Y cada día Fernando estaba más intranquilo, más irritado y desigual en su manera de ser. De afirmaciones categóricas pasaba a negaciones de la misma clase, y si alguno le contrariaba, balbuciaba por la indignación palabras incoherentes. Una de sus frases era decir:

– Estoy azorado.

–¿Por qué – se le preguntaba.

– Que sé yo – contestaba irritado.

VII

Fueron tres meses terribles para Fernando.

Una noche, después de salir de la casa en donde se reunían los dos, en vez de callejear, entraron en la iglesia de San Andrés, que estaba abierta. Se rezaba un rosario o una novena; la iglesia estaba a obscuras; había cuatro o cinco viejas arrodilladas en el suelo. Laura y Fernando entraron hasta el altar mayor, y como la verja que comunica la iglesia con la Capilla del Obispo estaba abierta, pasaron adentro y se sentaron en un banco. Después, Laura se arrodilló. El lugar, la irreverencia que allí se cometía, impulsaron a Fernando a interrumpir los rezos de Laura, inclinándose para hablarla al oído. Ella, escandalizada, se volvió a reprenderle; él la tomó del talle, Laura se levantó, y entonces Fernando, bruscamente, la sentó sobre sus rodillas.

behind them; if they formed a group to chat, they would always leave her out. It may have been that there was a quiet serenity about that girl and all their disdainful slights simply slid past her.

Blanca had a disturbing unevenness of character and Fernando had to abandon his intentions.

Laura tried to console him; since she didn't want to lose Fernando, she was anxious to understand that temperament, so opposite to her own, his irregular character, so filled with illusions one moment, and overcome by some inexplicable discouragement the next. There was a veritable abyss between each of their ways of life; they didn't understand one another in any way at all, and Fernando, out of indignation brought on by his weakness, would hit his mistress. At times, when she would see her nephew talking to himself in dark rooms, a panicky terror would seize hold of her.

She wanted to experience pleasure without limitations, to feel her innermost being vibrate with a most enervating voluptuousness, to reach that limit at which pleasure, because of its intensity, becomes painful; but as for disturbing her inner spirit, not that.

Never had Fernando and Laura exchanged a single tender word with one another, as lovers often do; if their eyes didn't actually show signs of hatred, they would avoid one another rather than seek one another out.

And with each passing day, Fernando grew more and more uneasy, more irritable and erratic in his conduct. From categorical affirmations, he moved to negations of the same kind, and if someone contradicted him, he would stammer incoherent words in indignation. One of his favorite expressions was:

"I'm all upset."

"Why?" someone would ask.

"How should I know," he would answer with irritation.

VII

They were three dreadful months for Fernando.

One night, after they left the house where the two of them would meet, instead of strolling through the streets, they entered the Church of San Andrés, which was open. They were saying a rosary or a novena; the church was in darkness; there were four or five old ladies kneeling on the floor. Laura and Fernando entered and went right up to the high altar and, since the grille that leads from the church into the Bishop's Chapel was open, they went inside and sat down on a bench. After a while, Laura knelt down. The place, the irreverence being committed there, induced Fernando to interrupt Laura's prayers and he leaned over and whispered in her ear. She was scandalized and turned around to reproach him; he seized her by the waist, Laura stood up and then Fernando quite brusquely sat her down on his knees.

– Te he de besar aquí – murmuró riéndose.

– No – dijo ella temblorosamente –, aquí no. – Después, mostrándole un Cristo en un altar, apenas iluminado por dos lamparillas de aceite, murmuró:– Nos está mirando. – Ossorio se echó a reír, y besó a Laura dos o tres veces en la nuca. Ella se pudo desasir y salió de la iglesia; él hizo lo mismo.

De noche, al entrar en la cama, sin saber por qué, se le apareció claramente sobre el papel de su cuarto un Cristo grande que le contemplaba. No era un Cristo vivo de carne, ni una imagen del Cristo; era un Cristo momia. Fernando veía que el cabello era de alguna mujer, la piel de pergamino; los ojos debían de ser de otra persona. Era un Cristo momia, que parecía haber resucitado de entre los muertos, con carne y huesos y cabellos prestados.

–¡Farsante! – murmuró con ironía Ossorio –. ¡Imaginación, no me engañes! – Y no había acabado de decir esto, cuando sintió un escalofrío que le recorría la espalda.

Se levantó de su asiento, apagó la luz, se acercó a su alcoba y se tendió en la cama. Mil luces le bailaban en los ojos; ráfagas brillantes, espadas de oro. Sentía como avisos de convulsiones que le espantaban.

– Voy a tener convulsiones – se decía a sí mismo, y esta idea le producía un terror pánico.

Tuvo que levantarse de la cama; encendió una luz, se puso las botas y salió a la calle. Llegó a la Plaza de Oriente a toda prisa. Se revolvían en su cerebro un *maremagnum* de ideas que no llegaban a ser ideas.

A veces sentía como un aura epiléptica, y pensaba: me voy a caer ahora mismo; y se le turbaban los ojos y se le debilitaban las piernas, tanto, que tenía que apoyarse con las manos en la pared de alguna casa.

Por la calle del Arenal fué hasta la Puerta del Sol. Eran las doce y media.

Llegó a Fornos y entró, En una mesa vió a un antiguo condiscípulo de San Carlos quen estaba cenando con una mujerona gruesa, y que le invitó a cenar con ellos.

Fernando contestó haciendo un signo negativo con la cabeza, y ya iba a marcharse, cuando oyó que le llamaban. Se volvió y se encontró a Paco Sánchez de Ulloa, que estaba tomando café.

Paco Sánchez era hijo de una familia ilustre. Se había gastado toda su fortuna en locuras, y debía una cantidad crecida. Eso sí, cuando se sentía vanidoso y se emborrachaba, decía que era el señor del estado de Ulloa y de Monterroto, y de otros muchos más.

Fernando contó, espantado, lo que le había sucedido.

"I have to kiss you here," he murmured with a laugh.

"No," she said trembling, "not here." Then, pointing to a figure of Christ on an altar, barely illuminated by two small oil lamps, she murmured, "He's watching us." Ossorio burst into laughter and kissed Laura on the back of the neck two or three times. She succeeded in pulling free and walked out of the church; he did the same.

That night, when he got into bed, a large figure of Christ appeared to him clearly on the wallpaper of his room and contemplated him, without his knowing why. It was not a living Christ, of flesh and bone, nor an image of Christ: it was a mummified Christ. Fernando could see that the hair was that of some woman, the skin was like parchment; the eyes must have been those of another person. It was a mummified Christ, which seemed to have been resurrected from among the dead, with its flesh and bones and hair borrowed from others.

"You fraud!" Ossorio muttered ironically. "Imagination, do not deceive me." And he had no sooner said this than he felt a chill run down his back.[15]

He got up from his chair, put out the light, went into his bedroom and lay down on the bed. A thousand lights were dancing in his eyes; brilliant flashes, swords of gold. He felt something very much like a premonition of convulsions that filled him with fear.

"I'm going to have convulsions," he kept saying to himself and the very idea of this filled him with panic and terror.

He felt compelled to rise up from his bed; he turned on a light, put on his boots and went down into the street. He reached the Plaza de Oriente as quickly as possible. A confused multitude of ideas were churning round and round in his brain, but they never developed.

At times he felt something like an epileptic aura and he would think: I am going to fall down right now; and his eyes blurred and his legs grew so weak that he had to lean against the wall of a nearby house with his hands.

He continued along the Calle del Arenal till he reached the Puerta del Sol. It was twelve-thirty.

He came to the Café de Fornos and went inside. He saw an old schoolmate from San Carlos seated at a table, who was dining with a coarse, heavyset woman, and he was invited to dine with them.

Fernando replied by making a negative sign with his head and was just about to walk away when he heard someone calling him. He turned around and found that it was Paco Sánchez de Ulloa, who was having a cup of coffee.

Paco Sánchez was the son of an illustrious family. He had squandered his entire fortune in frivolous ways and was now heavily in debt. One thing though, when he was feeling vain and when he was drunk, he would say that he was the lord of the manor of Ulloa and Monterroto and many other places.

Fernando was still frightened and recounted all that had happened.

– Bah – murmuró Sánchez de Ulloa –. Si estuvieras en mi caso, no tendrías esos terrores.
–¿Pues qué te pasa?
– Nada. Que ha entrado un imbécil en el ministerio, uno de esos ministros honrados que se dedican a robar el papel, las plumas, y me dejará cesante. Este otro que se ha marchado era una buena persona.
– Pues, chico, no tenía una gran fama.
– No. Es un ladrón; pero siquiera roba en grande. El dice: ¿Cuánto se puede sacar al año del ministerio? ¿Veinte mil pesetas? Pues las desprecia; las abandona a nosotros. Que luego divida a España en diez pedazos y los vaya vendiendo uno a Francia, otro a Inglaterra, etc., etc. Hace bien. Cuanto antes concluyan con este cochino país, mejor.

En aquel momento se sentó una muchacha pintada en la mesa en que estaban los dos.
– Vete, joven prostituta – le dijo Ulloa –; tengo que hablar con este amigo.
–¡Desaborío! –murmuró ella al levantarse.
– Será lo único que sabrá decir esa imbécil – masculló Fernando con rabia.
–¿Tú crees que las señoras saben decir más cosas? Ya ves María la *Gallega*, la *Regardé*, la *Churretes* y todas esas otras si son bestias; pues nuestras damas son más bestias todavía y mucho más golfas.
–¿Qué, salimos? – preguntó Fernando.
– Sí. Vamos. – dijo Ulloa.

Salieron de Fornos y echaron a andar nuevamente hacia la Puerta del Sol.
Ulloa maldecía de la vida, del dinero, de las mujeres, de los hombres, de todo.
Estaba decidido a suicidarse si la última combinación que se traía no le resultaba.
– A mí todo me ha salido mal en esta perra vida – decía Ulloa –, todo. Verdad que en este país el que tiene un poco de vergüenza y de dignidad está perdido. ¡Oh! Si yo pudiera tomar la revancha. De este indecente pueblo no quedaba ni una mosca. Que me decía uno: Yo soy un ciudadano pacífico, –No importa. ¿Ha vivido usted en Madrid? – Sí, señor. – Que le peguen cuatro tiros. Te digo que no dejaría ni una mosca, ni una piedra sobre otra.

Fernando le oía hablar sin entenderle. ¿Qué querrá decir? – se preguntaba.
Se traslucían en Ulloa todos los malos instintos del aristócrata arruinado.
Al desembocar en la Puerta del Sol, vieron a dos mujeres que se insultaban rabiosamente.

"Nonsense!" Sánchez de Ulloa murmured. "If you were in my circumstances, you wouldn't be terrified like that."

"So what's happening to you?"

"Nothing much. Just that some imbecile has taken over the Ministry. one of those overly honest ministers who spend their time stealing paper and pens and who will end up dismissing me. This other one, who left the post, he was a fine person."

"But really, old boy, he didn't have a very good reputation."

"No, he's a thief. But at least he steals on a large scale. He says: How much can one squeeze out of the Ministry in one year? Twenty thousand *pesetas*? Well, that much is beneath him; he leaves it all for us. As far as I'm concerned, let him go ahead and divide Spain into ten pieces and go around selling one to France, another to England, etc., etc. He's doing the right thing. The sooner they finish with this filthy country, the better."

At that moment, a heavily painted young girl sat down at the table where they were both seated.

"Get out of here, my young prostitute," Ulloa said to her; "I have to talk to this friend of mine."

"*You ninny, you!*" she muttered as she stood up.

"That's probably the only thing that imbecile knows how to say," Fernando mumbled angrily.

"Do you really think our fine ladies know how to say anything better? We can all see that María the *Gallega*, La *Regardé* and La *Churretes* and all those others are really bestial; but our fine ladies are even more bestial and worse tramps than that."

"How about it, shall we go?" asked Fernando.

They walked out of Fornos and started to make their way toward the Puerta del Sol again.

Ulloa kept cursing life, money, women, men, everything. He made up his mind to kill himself if the latest round of political appointments being considered didn't work out for him.

"Everything in this rotten life has turned out badly for me," said Ulloa, "everything. It's quite true that in this country any man with just a little sense of shame and dignity is doomed. Oh! If only I could take revenge. Not even one fly would be left in this indecent town. Suppose a person were to say to me, 'I'm a peaceable citizen.' It makes no difference. Have you lived in Madrid? 'Yes, indeed.' Have him shot. I tell you I wouldn't leave even one fly, not one stone on top of another."

Fernando heard what he was saying without understanding him. "What can he possibly mean?" he wondered.

All the harmful instincts of a ruined aristocrat were apparent in Ulloa.

When they came out at the Puerta del Sol, they saw two women savagely insulting one another.

Cuatro o cinco desocupados habían formado corro para oírlas. Fernando y Ulloa se acercaron. De pronto una de las mujeres, la más vieja, se abalanzó sobre la otra. La joven se terció el mantón y esperó con la mano derecha levantada, los dedos extendidos en el aire. En un momento, las dos se agarraron del moño y empezaron a golpearse brutalmente. Los del grupo reían. Fernando trató de separarlas, pero estaban agarradas con verdadera furia.

– Déjalas que se maten – dijo Ulloa, y tiró del brazo a Fernando.

Las dos mujeres seguían arañandose y golpeándose en medio de la gente, que las miraba con indiferencia.

De pronto se acercó un chulo, cogió a la muchacha más joven del brazo y le dió un tirón que la separó de la otra; tenía la cara llena de arañazos y de sangre.

–¡Vaya un sainete! – gritó Ulloa –. ¡Y la policía sin aparecer por ninguna parte! ¡Para qué servirá la policía en Madrid!

Las palabras de su amigo, la riña de las dos mujeres, Laura, la aparición de la noche, todo se confundía y se mezclaba en el cerebro de Fernando.

Nunca había estado su alma tan turbada. Ulloa seguía hablando, haciendo fantasías sobre el motivo del país. En este país... ¡Si estuviéramos en otro país!

Dieron una vuelta por la Plaza de Oriente y se dirigieron hacia el Viaducto. Desde allá se veía hacia abajo la calle de Segovia, apenas iluminada por las luces de los faroles, las cuales se prolongaban después en dos líneas de puntos luminosos que corrían en ziszás por el campo negro, como si fueran de algún malecón que entrara en el mar.

– Me gusta sentir el vértigo, suponer que aquí no hay una verja a la que uno puede agarrarse – dijo Ulloa.

Por una callejuela próxima a San Francisco el Grande salieron cerca de la Plaza de la Cebada, y bajando por la calle de Toledo, pasaron por la puerta del mismo nombre. Antes de llegar al puente oyeron gritos y sonido de cencerros. Traían las reses al Matadero. Fernando y Ulloa se acercaron al centro de la carretera.

–¡Eh! ¡Fuera de ahí! – les gritó un hombre con gorra de pelo que corría enarbolando un garrote.

–¿Y si no nos da la gana? – preguntó Ulloa.

– Maldita sea la... –exclamó el hombre de la gorra.

–¡A que le pego un palo a este tío! – murmuró Ulloa.

–¡Eh! ¡eh! ¡fuera! ¡fuera! – gritaron desde lejos.

Fernando hizo retroceder a su amigo; el hombre de la gorra echó a correr con el garrote al hombro y comenzaron a pasar las reses saltando, galopando, como una ola negra.

Four or five idlers had formed a circle to listen to them. Fernando and Ulloa moved closer. Suddenly, one of the women, the older one, pounced on the other. The younger one threw her shawl obliquely across her breast and waited, her right hand raised, her fingers extended in the air. A moment later, the two women seized one another by the chignon in their hair and began to beat on one another viciously. The people gathered round were laughing. Fernando tried to separate them but they were clutching one another with real frenzy.

"Let them kill one another," said Ulloa, and he tugged Fernando by the arm.

The two women kept scratching and beating one another in the midst of all those people who were looking on indifferently.

Suddenly a tough came over, seized the younger girl by the arm and tugged at her till he separated her from the other; her face was covered with deep scratches and blood.

"What a farce!" Ulloa shouted. "And the Police nowhere to be found! What use can the Police possibly be in Madrid!"

His friend's words, the fight between the two women, Laura, the nocturnal apparition, all of this was confused and interwoven in Fernando's brain.

Never had his spirit been so distressed. Ulloa continued speaking, creating fantasies concerning the motif of the country. In this country... If only we were in some other country!

They strolled around the Plaza de Oriente and then headed toward the Viaduct. From there they could see the Calle de Segovia down below, barely illuminated by the light of the streetlamps, which stretched out from there in two lines of luminous dots that ran zigzagging through the dark countryside, as if they were part of a dike reaching out into the sea.

"I like to feel this vertigo and make believe there is no railing here for me to grab hold of," said Ulloa.

Walking along a side street next to San Francisco el Grande, they came out near the Plaza de la Cebada, and after descending along the Calle de Toledo, they passed through the Gate of the same name. Before reaching the bridge, they heard shouts and the sound of cowbells. They were taking the cattle to the slaughterhouse. Fernando and Ulloa approached the center of the road.

"Hey! Get away from there!" shouted a man wearing a bearskin cap as he ran along brandishing a cudgel in the air.

"And what if we don't feel like it?" asked Ulloa.

"You god damned...," exclaimed the man with the cap.

"I bet I could really give this fellow a sound thrashing!" Ulloa muttered.

"Hey! Hey! Get out of the way!" some shouts came from a distance.

Fernando convinced his friend to move back; the man wearing the cap began to run with the cudgel over his shoulder and the cattle started to pass by, jumping and galloping like a black wave.

Detrás del ganado venían tres garrochistas a caballo. Ya cerca del Matadero, los jinetes gritaron, se encabritaron los caballos y todo el tropel de reses desapareció en un momento.

La noche estaba sombría, el cielo con grandes nubarrones, por entre los cuales se filtraba de vez en cuando un rayo blanco y plateado de luna.

Ossorio y Ulloa siguieron andando por el campo llano y negro, camino de Carabanchel Bajo. Llegaron a este pueblo, bebieron agua en una fuente y anduvieron un rato por campos desiertos llenos de surcos. Era una negrura y un silencio terribles. Sólo se oían a lo lejos ladridos desesperados de los perros. Enfrente un edificio con las ventanas iluminadas.

— Eso es un manicomio — dijo Ulloa.

A la media hora llegaron a Carabanchel Alto por un camino a cuya derecha se veía un jardín que terminaba en una plaza iluminada con luz eléctrica.

— La verdad es que no sé para qué hemos venido tan lejos — murmuró Ulloa.

— Ni yo.

— Sentémonos.

Estuvieron sentados un rato sin hablar, y cuando se cansaron salieron del pueblo. Se veía Madrid a lo lejos, extendido, lleno de puntos luminosos, envuelto en una tenue neblina.

Llegaron al cruce de la carretera de Extremadura y pasaron por delante de algunos ventorros.

—¿Tú tienes dinero? — preguntó Ulloa.

— Un duro.

— Llamemos en una venta de éstas.

Hiciéronlo así; se les abrieron en un parador y pasaron a la cocina, iluminada por un candil que colgaba de la campana de una chimenea.

— Se encuentra aquí uno en plena novela de Fernández y González, ¿verdad? — dijo Ulloa —. Le voy a hablar de vos al posadero.

—¡Eh, *seor* hostelero: ¿qué tenéis para comer?

— Pues hay huevos, sardinas, queso...

— Está bien. Traed las tres cosas y poned la mesa junto al fuego. Pronto. ¡Voto a bríos! Que no estoy acostumbrado a esperar.

Fernando no tenía ganas de comer; pero en cambio su amigo tragaba todo lo que le ponían por delante. Los dos bebían con exageración; no hablaban. Vieron que unos arrieros con sus mulas salían del parador. Debía de estar amaneciendo.

— Vámonos — dijo Fernando.

Pero Ulloa estaba allí muy bien y no quería marcharse.

Three herdsmen on horseback armed with goads came riding behind the cattle. Once they were near the Slaughterhouse, the horsemen started to shout, the horses reared up and the entire herd of cattle disappeared in an instant.

The night was gloomy, the sky, filled with big, black clouds, and a silvery-white moonbeam kept filtering through every so often.

Ossorio and Ulloa continued walking through the flat, dark countryside on the road to Carabanchel Bajo. They reached this town, drank some water at a fountain and then kept walking for a while through deserted fields filled with furrows. The darkness and the silence were terrifying.

The only sound you could hear in the distance was the desperate barking of dogs. A building with lighted windows stood opposite them.

"That is an insane asylum," said Ulloa.

They arrived in Carabanchel Alto within half an hour, along a road to the right of which you could see a garden that ended in a square illuminated by electric lights.

"The truth of the matter is that I don't know to what purpose we came so far," Ulloa murmured.

"Neither do I."

"Let's sit down."

They remained seated for a while without speaking and when they grew tired of this, they left the town. Madrid could be seen in the distance, spread out, filled with luminous dots, wrapped in a tenuous mist.

They reached the intersection with the road to Extremadura and passed in front of some shabby roadside inns.

"Do you have any money?" asked Ulloa.

"One *duro*."

"Why don't we knock at the door of one of those inns?"

They did this; they were admitted into an inn and made their way into the kitchen, which was illuminated by an oil lamp hanging from the funnel over a fireplace.

"You find yourself in the very midst of a Fernández y González novel[16] when you're here, don't you think so?" said Ulloa. "I do believe that I'm going to speak to the innkeeper using the antiquated vos form."

"Hey there, *seor* innkeeper! What do you have to eat?"

"Well, we have eggs, sardines, cheese..."

"That's fine. Kindly bring us all three and set the table near the fire. Quickly now. Confound it! I'm not accustomed to waiting."

Fernando didn't feel much like eating, but his friend, on the contrary, devoured everything put in front of him. They both kept drinking to excess, without speaking a word. They saw that several mule drivers were leaving the inn with their mules. Dawn was probably breaking.

"Let's go," said Fernando.

But Ulloa felt quite at ease there and didn't want to depart.

—Entonces me marcho solo.
—Bueno; pero dame el duro.
Ossorio se lo dio. Salió de la venta.
Empezaba a apuntar el alba; enfrente se veía Madrid envuelto en una neblina de color de acero. Los faroles de la ciudad ya no resplandecian con brillo; sólo algunos focos eléctricos, agrupados en la plaza de la Armería desafiaban con su luz blanca y cruda la suave claridad del amanecer.

Sobre la tierra violácea de obscuro tinte, con alguna que otra mancha verde, simétrica de los campos de sembradura, nadaban ligeras neblinas; allá aparecía un grupo de casuchas de basurero, tan humildes que parecían no atreverse a salir de la tierra; aquí un tejar; más lejos una corraliza con algún grupo de arbolillos enclenques y tristes y alguna huerta por cuyas tapias asomaban masas de follaje verde.

Por la carretera pasaban los lecheros montados en sus caballejos peludos de largas colas; mujeres de los pueblos inmediatos arreando boriquillos cargados de hortalizas; pesadas y misteriosas galeras, que nadie guiaba, arrastradas por larga reata de mulas medio dormidas; carros de los basureros destartalados, con las bandas hechas de esparto, que iban dando barquinazos, tirados por algún esquálido caballo precedido de un valiente boriquillo; traperos con sacos al hombro, mujeres viejas, haraposas con cestas al brazo. A medida que se acercaba Ossorio a Madrid iba viendo los paradores abiertos y hombres y mujeres negruzcos que entraban y salían en ellos. Se destacaba la ciudad claramente: el Viaducto, la torre de Santa Cruz, roja y blanca; otras puntiagudas, piramidales, de color pizarroso, San Francisco el Grande...

Y en el aéreo mar celeste se perfilaban sobre desmontes amarillentos, tejados, torres, esquinazos y paredones del pueblo.

Sobre el bloque blanco del Palacio Real, herido por los rayos del sol naciente, aparecía una nubecilla larga y estrecha, rosado dedo de la aurora; el cielo comenzaba a sonreír con dulce melancolía y la mañana se adornaba con sus más hermosas galas azules y rojas.

Subió Ossorio por la cuesta de la Vega, silenciosa, con sus jardines abandonados; pasó por delante de la Almudena, salió a la calle Mayor; Madrid estaba desierto, iluminado por una luz blanca, fría, que hacía resaltar los detalles todos. En el barrio en donde vivía Fernando, las campanas llamaban a los fieles a la primera misa; alguna que otra vieja encogida, cubierta con una mantilla verdosa se encaminaba hacia la iglesia como deslizándose cerca de las paredes.

"Then I'll leave myself."
"Fine; but give me the *duro*."
Ossorio gave it to him. He left the inn.

Dawn was just beginning to show; he could see Madrid before him, wrapped in a mist the color of steel. The streetlamps in the city were no longer shining so brightly; only a few electric lights, grouped together on the Plaza de la Armería, challenged the gentle brightness of early morning with their white, harsh light.

Delicate mists were floating over the darkly tinted violet ground, with a green, symmetrical patch of sown fields scattered here and there; over there, a group of garbage collectors' shacks appeared, so humble that they seemed reluctant to rise up from the ground; here, a tile works; further away, an enclosed area for animals, with a group of sad, languishing little trees and a garden with masses of green foliage peering over its earthen walls.

Dairymen were passing along the road, riding on their shaggy, long-tailed nags; women from nearby towns driving little donkeys loaded down with garden vegetables; heavy, mysterious, four-wheeled covered wagons, with nobody guiding them, dragged along by a long line of half-sleeping mules; dilapidated garbage collectors' carts, the sides of their bodies made with esparto grass, were moving along, bumping and jolting, drawn by some squalid horse, preceded by a valiant little donkey out in front; rag pickers, with sacks slung over their shoulders, old women in tatters with baskets on their arms. As Ossorio kept approaching Madrid, he kept seeing that the roadside inns were now open and blackish-looking men and women were going in and out. The city now stood out clearly: the Viaduct, the tower of Santa Cruz, red and white; others, sharp-pointed, like pyramids, the color of slate, San Francisco el Grande...

And in the celestial sea of air, over the yellowish heights, you could see the profiles of the roofs, towers, street corners and thick walls of the town.

A long, narrow, little cloud, the rose-colored finger of dawn, appeared over the white stone mass of the Royal Palace as it was struck by the rays of the rising sun; the sky was beginning to smile with a sweet melancholy, and the morning bedecked itself with its loveliest blue and red finery.

Ossorio made his way up the Cuesta de la Vega, now silent, its gardens abandoned. He passed in front of the Cathedral of Nuestra Señora de La Almudena and came out on the Calle Mayor. Madrid was deserted, illuminated by a cold, white light that made all the details stand out. In the quarter where Fernando lived, the church bells were calling the faithful to the first Mass; an occasional old woman, hunched over, covered with a greenish mantilla, would make her way toward the church, as if she were gliding along close to the walls.

VIII

Al día siguiente, Ossorio se levantó de la cama tarde, cansado, con la espalda y los riñones doloridos. Seguía pensando en el fenómeno de la noche anterior, e interpretándolo de una porción de maneras; unas veces se inclinaba a creer en lo inconsciente; otras suponía la existencia de fuerzas supranaturales, o por lo menos suprasensibles. Había momentos en que se creía en una farsa inventada por él mismo sin darse consciencia clara del hecho; pero fuese cualquiera la explicación que admitiera, el fenómeno le producía un miedo horrible.

Siempre había sido inclinado a la creencia en lo sobrenatural, pero nunca de una manera tan rotunda como entonces. La época de la pubertad de Fernando, además de ser dolorosa por sus descubrimientos desagradables y penosos, lo fué también por el miedo. De noche, en su cuarto, oía siempre la respiración de un hombre que estaba detrás de la puerta. Además era sonámbulo; se levantaba de la cama muchas veces, salía al comedor y se escondía debajo de la mesa; cuando el frío de las baldosas le despertaba, volvía a la cama sin asombrarse.

Tenía dolores de distinto carácter; de distinto color le parecía a él.

Cuando todavía era muchacho fué a ver cómo agarrotaban a los tres reos de la Guindalera, llevado por una curiosidad malsana, y por la noche al meterse en la cama, se pasó hasta el amanecer temblando; durante mucho tiempo, al abrir la puerta de un cuarto obscuro veía en el fondo la silueta de los tres ajusticiados: la mujer en medio, con la cabeza para abajo; uno de los hombres, aplastado sobre el banquillo; el otro, en una postura jacarandosa con el brazo apoyado en una pierna.

Pero aunque el miedo hubiera sido un huésped continuo de su alma, nunca había llegado a una tan grande intranquilidad, de todos los momentos. Desde aquella noche la vida de Fernando fué imposible.

Parecía que la fuerza de su cerebro se disolvía, y con una fe extraña en un hombre incrédulo, intentaba levantar por la voluntad las mesas y las sillas y los objetos más pesados.

Fué una época terrible de inquietudes y dolores.

Unas veces veía sombras, resplandores de luz, ruidos, lamentos; se creía transportado en los aires o que le marchaba del cuerpo un brazo o una mano.

Otra vez se le ocurrió que los fenómenos medianímicos que a él le ocurrían tenían como causa principal el demonio.

En su cerebro débil, todas las ideas locas mordían y se agarraban, pero aquélla no; por más que quiso aferrarse y creer en Satanás, la idea se le escapaba.

VIII

On the following day, Ossorio got up late, very tired, with a pain in his back and in his sides. He kept thinking about the phenomenon of the previous night and he interpreted it in a number of ways: at times he was inclined to believe in the unconscious; at other times he would assume the existence of supernatural forces, or at least, supersensory ones. There were moments when he tended to believe that he was involved in a farce invented by himself without his even being clearly conscious of the fact; but whatever explanation he might be willing to accept, the phenomenon still produced a terrifying fear in him.

He had always been inclined to believe in the supernatural, but never in such a categorical way as then. Fernando's period of puberty, in addition to being painful because of its unpleasant and distressing discoveries, was also so because of his fear. At night, in his room, he would always hear a man's breathing behind the door. In addition to this, he was a somnambulist; he would get out of bed many times, go out into the dining room and hide under the table; when the coldness of the floor tiles would awaken him, he would return to his bed without being astonished.

He suffered from pains of different kinds; they would seem to him to be of different colors.

When he was still a boy, drawn by a morbid curiosity, he went to see how they garroted the three condemned men from La Guindalera,[17] and that night, when he got into bed, he lay there trembling until dawn; for a long time afterward, whenever he would open the door of a dark room, he would see the silhouette of the three executed prisoners in the background: the woman in the middle with her head lowered; one of the men looking crushed on the stool; the other in a sprightly posture with his arm leaning on one of his legs.

But even though fear had long been a constant guest in his spirit, he had never reached so total a state of uneasiness at every possible moment. Ever since that night, Fernando's life became impossible.

It seemed that the vigor of his brain was dissolving and, with a faith that was uncommon in nonbelievers, he kept trying to levitate tables and chairs and the heaviest of objects by the sheer power of his will.

It was a terrifying period of uneasiness and suffering.

At times he would see shadows, flashes of light, and hear noises and moans; he felt that he was being transported through the air or that one of his arms or legs was departing from his body.

Another time it occurred to him that it was the Devil who was the principal cause of the somewhat psychic phenomena that he was experiencing.

All these wild ideas kept gnawing at his weakened brain and were taking a firm hold, except that one; no matter how much as he wanted to attach himself to this notion and believe in Satan, the idea would elude him.

Intimamente su miedo era creer que los fenómenos que experimentaba eran única y exclusivamente síntomas de locura o de anemia cerebral.

Al mismo tiempo sentía una gran opresión en la comumna vertebral, y vértigos y zumbidos, y la tierra le parecía como si estuviera algodonada.

Un día que encontró a un antiguo condiscípulo suyo, le explicó lo que tenía y le preguntó después:

–¿Qué haría yo?

– Sal de Madrid.

–¿Adónde?

– A cualquier parte. Por los caminos, a pie, por donde tengas que sufrir incomodidades, molestias, dolores...

Fernando pensó durante dos o tres días en el consejo de su amigo, y viendo que la intranquilidad y el dolor crecían por momentos, se decidió. Pidió dinero a su administrador, cosió unos cuantos billetes en el forro de su americana, se vistió con su peor traje, compró un revólver y una boina y, una noche, sin despedirse de nadie, salió de casa con intención de marcharse de Madrid.

IX

Llegó al final de la Castellana, subió por los desmontes del Hipódromo, y fue siguiendo maquinalmente las vueltas y revueltas del Canalillo.

La noche estaba negra, calurosa, pesada; ni una estrella brillaba en el cielo opaco, ni una luz en las tinieblas. De algunas casas cercanas salían perros al camino, que se ponían a ladrar con furia.

A Fernando le recordaba la noche y el lugar, noches y lugares de los cuentos en donde salen trasgos y ladrones.

Se sentó al borde del Canalillo. Era así como la noche su porvenir: obscuro, opaco, negro. No quería emperezarse. Se levantó, y en una de las revueltas del camino se encontró con dos hombres garrote en mano. Eran consumeros.

–¿Adónde salgo por aquí? – les preguntó Fernando.

– Si sigue usted por esta senda, a la Castellana; por esta otra, a los Cuatro Caminos.

Se veían aquí y allá filas de faroles que brillaban, se interrumpían, volvían a formar otra hilera y a brillar a lo lejos.

Ossorio siguió hacia los Cuatro Caminos. Cuando llegó a los merenderos

In his innermost thoughts, his fear consisted of the conviction that the phenomena he was experiencing were solely and exclusively symptoms of madness or cerebral anemia.

At the same time, he felt severe pressure on his spinal column, and a feeling of vertigo, a constant buzzing, and the ground would seem to him to be made of cotton.

One day he met one of his former schoolmates and explained what it was that was troubling him. Then he asked him:

"What should I do?"

"Leave Madrid."

"To go where?"

"Anywhere. Take to the roads, on foot, any place where you may have to put up with inconveniences, hardships, suffering..."

Fernando thought about his friend's advice for two or three days, and when he saw that his restlessness and pain were increasing with every passing moment, he made up his mind. He asked the estate administrator for some money, he sewed several banknotes into the lining of his jacket, he put on his worst suit, bought a revolver and a beret and, one night, without saying goodbye to anyone, he left his house with the intention of departing from Madrid.

IX

He reached the end of the Castellana, walked up through the clearings around the Hippodrome[18] and automatically kept following the winding and turning of the Canalillo.

The night was dark, warm and oppressive; not a single star was shining in the murky sky, not a single light in all that darkness. Dogs would occasionally come out onto the road from some nearby house and begin to bark frenziedly.

The night and the place reminded Fernando of nights and places in stories where goblins and thieves come out.

He sat down at the edge of the Canalillo. His future was very much like the night: dark, murky, black. He didn't want to waste any time. He stood up and ran into two men with cudgels in their hands at one of the turns in the road. They were guards assigned to looking for smugglers.

"Where do I get to if I go this way?" Fernando asked them.

"If you follow this road, to the Castellana; if you go the other way, to Cuatro Caminos."[19]

Here and there, you could see rows of lamps shining, suddenly coming to an end, and then forming another line, glowing in the distance.

Fernando continued toward Cuatro Caminos. When he reached the roadside

empezaba a amanecer. En una taberna preguntó cuál era aquella carretera; le dijeron que la de Fuencarral, y comenzó a marchar por ella.

A ambos lados de la carretera se veían casuchas roñosas, de piso bajo sólo, con su corraliza cercada de tapia de adobe; la mayoría sin ventanas, sin más luz ni más aire que el que entraba por la puerta.

Blancas nubes cruzaban el cielo pálido; en la sierra aún resaltaban grandes manchas de nieve. A lo lejos se veía un pueblo envuelto en una nube cenicienta. De los tejares próximos llegaba un olor irrespirable a estiércol quemado.

Salió el sol que, aun dando de soslayo, comenzó a fatigarle. Al poco rato sudaba a mares. No había sombra allí para tenderse, ni ventorro cercano; después de vacilar Ossorio muchas veces, entró en un cobertizo rodeado por una cerca hecha con latas de petróleo.

Allí dentro, un viejo estaba amontonando botes de pimiento en un rincón.

– Oiga usted, buen hombre, ¿quiere usted darme algo de comer, pagando por supuesto? – preguntó Ossorio.

– Pase usted, señorito.

Entró Fernando en el cobertizo, y el viejo le hizo pasar de aquí a su casa, hecha de adobe, con un coralillo para las gallinas, cercado por latas extendidas y clavadas en estacas.

El viejo era encorvado, con el pelo de color gris sucio, las manos temblorosas y los ojos rojizos; ejercía su profesión de basurero desde la infancia. Antes que Sabatini tuviera sus carros y su contrata con el Ayuntamiento, le dijo a Fernando, conocía él todo lo conocible en cuestión de basuras.

Después de exponer sus grandes conocimientos en este asunto, preguntó a Ossorio:

–¿Y adónde va usted, si se puede saber?

– Difícil es, porque yo no lo sé.

El viejo movió la cabeza con un ademán compasivo y de duda al mismo tiempo, y no dijo nada.

–¿Adónde va la carretera? – preguntó Fernando.

– La de la izquierda, a Colmenar; la otra es la carretera de Francia.

– Pues iré a Colmenar. ¿Me dejará usted dormir un rato aquí?

– Sí, señor. Duerma usted. ¡Pues no faltaba más!

Fernando se tendió en un montón de paja y quedó amodorrado.

Soñó que se acercaba a él por los aires, amenazadora, una nube negra, muy negra, y de repente se abría en su centro una especie de cráter rojo.

Se despertó de repente y se levantó.

–¿Qué le debo a usted? – le preguntó al viejo.

– A mí, nada.

inns, dawn was just beginning to break. He asked at a tavern which road he was on; they told him it was the one to Fuencarral[20] and he started to walk along it. On both sides of the road, you could see grimy, squalid shacks, with only a lower floor, with an enclosed area for animals, surrounded by an earthen wall; the majority without any windows, with no more light or air than that which came in through the door.

White clouds were crossing the pale sky; large patches of snow still stood out on the mountain range. In the distance, you could make out a town, wrapped in an ash-colored cloud. From the nearby tile works, there came a suffocating odor of burnt manure.

The sun came out and, although its rays were coming down obliquely, he began to feel exhausted. In a short while he was sweating profusely. There wasn't any shade around where you might stretch out, or even some wretched roadhouse nearby; after hesitating a number of times, Ossorio went into a covered shed surrounded by a fence made of petroleum drums.

Inside there, an old man was piling up pepper cans in a corner.

"Listen here, my good man, would you be able to let me have something to eat, if I pay you, of course?" Ossorio asked him.

"Come on in, my dear young man."

Fernando went into the shed and the old man had him go from here into his house, which was made of adobe, with a small yard for the hens, surrounded by tin cans that had been flattened and nailed onto stakes.

The old man was stooped over, with hair that was a dirty gray, with hands that trembled and eyes that were bloodshot; he had carried on his trade as a garbage collector since his childhood. He told Fernando that even before Sabatini[21] had his carts and his contract with the Municipal Government, he knew everything there was to know regarding garbage.

After expounding on his great knowledge on this matter, he asked Ossorio:

"And where are you headed for, if I may ask?"

"It's difficult to say, because I really don't know."

The old man moved his head with a gesture that was both compassionate and incredulous at the same time, but he didn't say anything.

"Where does the road go?" Fernando asked.

"The one on the left, to Colmenar;[22] the other one is the road to France."

"Well, I'll be going to Colmenar. Will you let me sleep here for a little while?"

"Yes, indeed. Just go to sleep. Just go ahead!"

Fernando stretched out on a pile of straw and fell fast asleep.

He dreamed that a black cloud, very black and threatening, was coming toward him through the air, and that a sort of red crater was suddenly opening up in the center.

He woke up suddenly and got to his feet.

"What do I owe you?" he asked the old man.

"Owe me? Why nothing."

—¡Pero, hombre!
— Nada, nada.
— Pues, muchas gracias.

Se despidió del viejo dándole un apretón de manos, y siguió andando por la carretera llena de polvo. Pasaban carromatos y mujeres montadas en borriquillos. La tierra era estéril; en la carretera, sólo a largo trecho había algún arbolillo raquítico y torcido, y en algunas partes cuadros de viñas polvorientas.

A las nueve estaba Ossorio en Fuencarral. En la entrada del pueblo, a la derecha, hay una ermita blanca, acabada de blanquear, con la puerta de azul rabioso, cúpula de pizarra y un tinglado de hierro para las campanas.

El pueblo estaba solitario y triste, como si estuviera abandonado; se olía, al entrar en él, un olor fuerte a paja quemada.

En Fuencarral se divide la carretera; Ossorio tomó la que pasa próxima a la tapia de El Pardo.

Nubarrones grises y pálidos celajes llenaban el cielo; algunos rebaños pacían en la llanura. La carretera se extendía llena de polvo y de carriles hechos por los carros entre los arbolillos enclenques. El paisaje tenía la enorme desolación de las llanuras manchegas. A media tarde vió entre las colinas áridas y yermas, las copas de unos cuantos cipreses que se destacaban negruzcos en el cielo.

Era algún jardín o cementerio de un convento abandonado y ruinoso que se veía a pocos pasos.

Fernando se echó allá, a la sombra, y descansó un par de horas. Sentía un terrible cansancio que no le dejaba discurrir con gran satisfacción suya, y al mismo tiempo una vaguedad y laxitud grandes.

Al ver que pasaba la tarde, tuvo que hacer un gran esfuerzo para levantarse; bordeando la cerca de El Pardo, sentándose aquí, echándose allá, fue acercándose a Colmenar.

Se veía el pueblo desde lejos sobre una loma. Por encima de él, nubes espesas y plomizas formaban en el horizonte una alta muralla, encima de la cual parecían adivinarse las torres y campanarios de alguna ciudad misteriosa, de sueño.

Aquella masa de color de plomo, estaba surcada por largas hendeduras rojas que al reunirse y ensancharse parecían inmensos pájaros de fuego con las alas extendidas.

La masa azulada de la sierra se destacó al anochecer y perfiló su contorno, línea valiente y atrevida, detallada en la superficie más clara del cielo.

Obscureció; lo plomizo fue tomando un tono frío y gris; comenzó a oírse a lo lejos el tañido de una campana; pasó una cigüeña volando...

"But, my dear man!"
"Nothing, nothing at all."
"Well, thank you very much."
He bade the old man goodbye, clasping his hand tight, and again started walking along the dust-covered road. Covered two-wheeled carts and women riding on small donkeys kept passing. The earth was sterile; along the road, there was only an occasional scrawny, twisted little tree, and patches of dusty vineyards in some places.

By nine o'clock Ossorio was in Fuencarral. At the entrance to the town, on the right, there is a white hermitage, recently whitewashed, with a door painted in a garish blue, a dome of slate and an iron roof covering for the bells.

The town was lonely and sad, as if it were abandoned; as you entered, you could smell a very pronounced odor of burnt straw.

The road divides in Fuencarral; Ossorio took the one that passes close to the wall of El Pardo.

Large gray clouds and pale colored cloud effects filled the sky; several flocks were grazing on the plain. The road was covered with dust and full of ruts made by the carts, and extended between the sickly little trees. The landscape possessed the stark desolation of the Manchegan plains. By mid-afternoon, he was able to see the tops of several cypresses profiled blackish against the sky among the arid, barren hills.

It was some garden or cemetery of an abandoned and ruined monastery that could be seen only a short distance away.

Fernando stretched out there in the shade, and he rested for a couple of hours. He was overcome by a terrible weariness that, to his great satisfaction, made it impossible to think rationally, and at the same time he was filled with a great sense of vagueness and laxity.

When he saw that the afternoon was passing by, he was forced to make a great effort to stand up; skirting the wall of El Pardo, sitting down in one place, lying down in another, he kept drawing closer to Colmenar.

From a distance, you could see the town on a low hill. Above it, on the horizon, thick, leaden clouds formed a high wall, on top of which you seemed to make out above them the towers and bell gables of some mysterious city of dreams.

That mass of leaden color was streaked with long red clefts, that seemed to be immense firebirds with wings extended as they first joined together and then expanded.

As it grew dark, the bluish mass of the mountain range stood out, and its outline, strong and bold, was profiled against the extremely bright surface of the sky.

It got even darker; the lead color started taking on a cold, gray tone; you began hearing the tolling of a bell in the distance; a stork came flying by...

X

Cuando se despertó al día siguiente en una posada de Colmenar, eran ya las dos de la tarde. No había pododo conciliar el sueño hasta el amanecer. Se levantó encorvado, con los pies doloridos, comió y salió de casa. El día era caluroso, asfixiante; el cielo azul, blanquecino; la tierra quemaba.

Fernando se tendió a esperar a que el sol se ocultase para seguir su marcha y se durmió. Era el anochecer cuando salió del pueblo; la carretera estaba obscura, sombría después; a medida que la obscuridad se hacía mayor, quedando imponente.

La noche, estrellada, había refrescado; a un lado y a otro se oía el tintineo de los cencerros de las vacas y toros que pastaban en las deshesas.

Pasaron por el camino carros de bueyes en fila cargados de leña dirigidos por boyerizos con sombreros anchos; cruzaron por delante de Fernando algunos jinetes como negros fantasmas; después la carretera quedó completamente desierta y silenciosa; no se oyó nada más que el tañido de las esquilas de las vacas, tan pronto cerca, tan pronto lejos, rápido y vocinglero unas veces, triste y pausado otras.

Fernando se puso a cantar para ahuyentar el miedo, cuando oyó junto a él los ladridos broncos de un perro. Debía de ser un perrazo enorme, de esos de ganado; en la obscuridad no se le veía; pero se notaba que se acercaba de pronto y retrocedía después. Ossorio sacó el revolver y lo amartilló.

El perro parecía entender la advertencia y se fué alejando, quedándose atrás hasta que dejaron de oírse sus ladridos.

Como sucede siempre, después de experimentar una impresión de miedo, Fernando se quedó turbado, y con predisposición ya para sentirlo y experimentarlo fuertemente por cualquier motivo, grande o pequeño. De pronto vió en la carretera una cosa blanca y negra que se movía. Se figuró que debía ser un toro o una vaca.

Fernando se sintió lleno de terror, y como para aquel caso de nada le servía el revólver, lo guardó en el bolsillo del pantalón después de ponerlo en el seguro; y hecho esto, salió de la carretera, saltando la cerca de un lado, se internó en una dehesa, sin pensar que el peligro era allí mayor por estar pastando multitud de reses bravas. Dentro de la dehesa trató de hacer una curva, dejando en medio a la vaca, toro o lo que fuese y seguir la carretera adelante.

Por desdicha, el terreno en el soto era muy desigual, y Ossorio se cayó de bruces desde lo alto de un ribazo, sin más daño que una rozadura en las rodillas.

La viajata empezaba a parecerle odiosa a Fernando, sobre todo larguísima. No pasaba nadie a quien preguntarle si se había equivocado o no de camino. Seguía oyéndose monótono y triste el son de las esquilas; alguna que otra hoguera de llamas rojas brillaba entre los árboles.

X

When he awoke on the following day in an inn in Colmenar, it was already two in the afternoon. He hadn't been able to fall asleep until daybreak. He got up, his back stooped over, his feet aching; he ate and walked outside. It was a warm, stifling day; the sky, blue, with a touch of white; the earth, scorched.

Fernando stretched out to wait for the sun to hide so that he could continue his journey, and he fell asleep. It was nightfall when he left town; the road was dark, and then even somber; as it grew ever darker, it ended up being virtually pitch-black.

The starry night had turned cool; on either side of the road, you could hear the tinkling of the bells on the cows and the bulls grazing in the meadows.

Carts passed by along the road, drawn by oxen in a single file, loaded with wood and led by cowherds wearing wide-brimmed hats; several horsemen crossed in front of Fernando like black phantoms; then the road remained totally deserted and silent; nothing could be heard but the sound of the cowbells, now nearby, now far off, sometimes rapid and uproarious, at other times sad and deliberate.

Fernando started to sing in order to drive away his fear, when suddenly he heard the raucous barking of a dog nearby. It must have been a fierce, enormous dog, of the kind used with cattle; you couldn't see it in the darkness; but you could tell that it was suddenly getting closer and then moving away. Ossorio took out his revolver and cocked it.

The dog seemed to understand the warning and kept moving away, remaining even further behind, till its barking could no longer be heard at all.

As always seems to happen after experiencing a sensation of fear, Fernando was left very distraught and predisposed to feel and experience fear even more strongly now, for any reason whatsoever, large or small. Suddenly he saw something white and black moving along the road. He imagined it must be a bull or a cow.

Fernando felt overcome by terror, and, since his revolver would be of no use whatsoever to him in this situation, he put it away in his pants pocket, after setting the safety catch; and having done this, he left the main road, jumping over a fence that ran along one side, and made his way deep into a meadow, without realizing that the danger was even greater there because a herd of fierce bulls was probably grazing there. Once inside the meadow, he tried to circle around, leaving the cow or the bull or whatever it might be in the middle, and follow the main road once more after that.

Unfortunately, the terrain in the thicket was very uneven and Ossorio fell headlong from the top of an embankment, with no more injury to himself than some abrasions on his knees.

The whole journey was beginning to seem odious to Fernando and entirely too long. He hadn't passed anyone of whom he could inquire whether or not he had taken the wrong road. He kept hearing the monotonous, sad sound of the cowbells; the red flames of a bonfire could be seen shining here and there between the trees.

Se mezcló después al tañer de los cencerros el graznido de las ranas, alborotador, escandaloso.

Al poco rato de esto, Fernando vió a un hombre, que debía ser molinero o panadero, porque estaba blanco de harina y que venía jinete en un borriquillo tan pequeño, que iba rozando el suelo con los pies.

–¿Este es el camino de Manzanares? – le preguntó Ossorio de sopetón.

El hombre, en vez de contestar, dió con los talones al borriquillo, que echo a correr; luego desde lejos, gritó:

– Sí.

– Ha creído que soy algún bandido – pensó Fernando, mirando al hombre que se alejaba; y acompañándole con sus maldiciones, siguió Ossorio camino adelante, cada vez más turbado y medroso, cuando a la revuelta de la carretera se encontró con un castillo que se levantaba sobre una loma.

– Debe ser un efecto de óptica – pensó Ossorio –, y se fué acercando con susto, como quien se aproxima a un fantasma que sabe que se va a desaparecer.

Era real el castillo, y parecía enorme. La luna pasaba por una galleria destrozada que tenía en lo alto, y producía un efecto fantástico.

No lejos se comenzaba a ver el pueblo, envuelto en una neblina plateada. Era un pueblo de sierra, de pobres casas desparramadas en una loma.

Fernando se acercó a él y entró por una calle ancha y obscura, que era continuación de la carretera. Las casas todas estaban cerradas; ladraban los perros. En la plaza, de piso desigual, salía luz por la rendija de una puerta.

Ossorio llamó.

–¿Es posada ésta? – dijo.

– Sí, posada es.

Abrióse la puerta y entró en el zaguán, grande, blanqueado, con vigas en el techo.

A un lado, debajo de una tosca escalera, había un cajón de madera sin pintar, con un mostrador recubierto de cinc, y en el mostrador un hombre ceñudo, de boina, que asomaba el cuerpo tras de una balanza de platillos de hierro.

Era el posadero; hablaban con él dos tipos de aspecto brutal: el uno, con la chaqueta al hombro, faja y boina; el otro, con sombrero ancho, de tela.

El de la boina pedía al del mostrador aguardiente y tabaco al fiado, y el posadero se lo negaba y miraba al suelo amargamente, mientras daba vuelta entre los labios a una colilla apagada.

Viendo que la conversación seguía sin que el posadero se fijara en él, Fernando preguntó:

–¿Se puede cenar?

– Pagando...

Then the obstreperous and scandalous croaking of the frogs started mixing with the tinkle of the cowbells.

In a little while, Fernando saw a man who must have been a miller or a baker, because he was coated white with flour, and was riding along on a little donkey, so small that the man kept scraping the ground with his feet.

"Is this the road to Manzanares?"[23] Ossorio asked him unexpectedly.

Instead of answering, the man pressed his heels to the little donkey's flanks and it started to run; then he shouted from a distance:

"Yes."

"He must have thought I am some bandit," Ossorio mused as he watched the man draw further away,; and accompanying him with his curses, Ossorio kept following the road, ever more distraught and fearful, when, at a turn in the road, he came upon a castle rising up on a small hill.

"It must be an optical illusion," thought Ossorio, and he kept moving toward it fearfully, like someone approaching a phantom that he knows is going to disappear.

The castle was real and seemed enormous. The moon was shining through a ruined gallery located in the upper part, and it produced a fantastic effect.

Not far from there, you could begin to see the town, wrapped in a silvery mist. It was a mountain village consisting of impoverished-looking houses scattered along a hillside.

Fernando drew nearer and entered along a wide, dark street, which was a continuation of the main road. The houses were all closed up; the dogs were barking. In the square, which had an uneven surface, a light was showing through a crack in one of the doors.

Ossorio knocked.

"Is this an inn?" he asked.

"Yes, it's an inn."

The door opened and he walked into the vestibule, large, whitewashed, with beams along the ceiling.

On one side, under a rough staircase, there was a stall made of unpainted wood, with a counter covered over with zinc, and at the counter, a scowling man wearing a beret, was poking his body out from behind a set of scales with iron pans.

It was the innkeeper; two brutish-looking fellows were talking to him: one had his jacket thrown over his shoulder and was wearing a sash and a beret; the other was wearing a wide-brimmed felt hat.

The one with the beret was asking the man behind the counter for *aguardiente* and tobacco on credit and the innkeeper kept refusing and looking at the floor bitterly, while he kept shifting the extinguished stub of cigar between his lips.

When Fernando saw that the conversation was continuing without the innkeeper taking any notice of him, he asked:

"Would one be able to eat dinner here?"

"If you pay..."

– Se pagará. ¿Qué hay para cenar?
– Usted dirá.
–¿Hay huevos?
– No, señor; no hay.
–¿Habrá carne?
– A estas horas carne, tú... – dijo con ironía el del mostrador a uno de sus amigos.
–¿Pues qué demonios hay entonces?
– Usted dirá.
–¿Quiere usted hacer unas sopas? Y no hablemos más.
– Bueno. ¡Vaya por las sopas! Dentro de un momento están aquí.

Vinieron las sopas en una gran cazuela, con una capa espesísmima de pimentón. No estaban agradables, ni mucho menos; pero con un esfuerzo de voluntad eran casi comestibles.

–¿Hay algún pajar? – preguntó después Ossorio al posadero.
– No hay pajar.
– Entonces, ¿dónde se puede dormir>
– Aquí se duerme en la cama.
– Y en todas partes; pero como en este pueblo parece que no hay nada, creía que no habría cama tampoco.
– Pues hay dos. Ahí enfrente está el cuarto.

Fernando entró en él. Era un cuarto ancho, negro, con una cama de tablas y un colchón muy delgado.

Ossorio se tendió vestido, y no pudo dormir un momento: veía caminos que se alargaban hasta el infinito, y él los seguía y los seguía, y siempre estaba en el mismo sitio. De vez en cuando se despertaban sus sentidos; escuchaba avizorado por un temor sin causa, y oía afuera, en el silencio de la noche, el canto de los ruiseñores.

XI

Después de un rato corto de amodorramiento, Ossorio se despertó de madrugada con sobresalto; saltó de la dura cama, abrió una ventanuca y se asomó a ella. Era un amanecer espléndido y alegre: despertaba la naturaleza con una sonrisa tímida; cantaban los gallos, chillaban las golondrinas; el aire estaba limpio, saturado de olor a tierra húmeda.

Cuando Ossorio iba a salir se encontró con la puerta cerrada por fuera. Llamó varias veces, hasta que oyó la voz del dueño.

"You'll be paid. What is there to eat?"
"Just ask."
"Are there any eggs?"
"No, sir, there aren't any."
"You wouldn't have any meat?"
"Meat, at this hour, you..." the man at the counter said ironically to one of his friends.
"Then what the devil do you have?"
"You only have to ask."
"Would you mind making me some soup with bread sops? And let's not discuss it any more."
"All right. Here's to the soup and bread sops! It'll be here in just a minute."
The bread sops and soup arrived in a large earthen casserole, coated with a thick layer of pepper. It wasn't very tasty, to say the least; but with considerable effort and will power, it was almost edible.
"Is there a straw loft around here?" Ossorio then asked the innkeeper.
"There's no straw loft."
"Then where can one sleep?"
"Around here, people sleep in beds."
"So do they everywhere, but since it seems they don't have anything else in this town, I thought there wouldn't be a bed either."
"Well, there are two. The room is over there, facing us."
Fernando went inside. It was a wide, dark room, with a bed made of boards and a very thin mattress.
Ossorio stretched out fully dressed, and he wasn't able to sleep for even a moment: he kept seeing roads that stretched out into infinity, and he kept following them and following them, and yet he was always in the same place. From time to time, his senses would awaken; he would listen, as if he were being spied upon by an inexplicable fear, and he would hear the song of the nightingales outside in the silence of the night.

XI

After a short space of heavy sleep, Ossorio awoke with a start at the break of day; he jumped out of the hard bed, opened the roughly made window and peered out. It was a splendid, cheerful morning: Nature was awakening with a timid smile; the cocks were crowing, the swallows were chirping; the air was clean, saturated with the fragrance of the humid earth.

When Ossorio was about to leave, he found that the door was locked from the outside. He called out several times until he heard the voice of the landlord.

¡Voy, voy!

—¿Es que tenía usted miedo de que me marchara sin pagar? – le dijo Fernando.

— No; pero todo podia ser.

Ossorio no quiso reñir; pagó la cuenta, que subía a una peseta, y salió del pueblo.

El castillo, con la luz de la mañana, no era, ni mucho menos, lo que de noche había parecido a Fernando; lo que tenía era una buena posición: estaba colocado admirablemente, dominado el valle.

Sería en otros tiempos más bien lugar de recreo que otra cosa; los señores de la corte irían allí a lancear los toros, y en los bancos de piedra de las torres, próximos a las ventanas, contemplarían las señoras las hazañas de los castellanos.

Pronto Ossorio perdió de vista el castillejo y comenzó a bordear dehesas, en las cuales pastaban toros blancos y negros que le miraban atentamente. Algunos pastores famélicos, sucios, desgreñados, le contemplaban con la misma indiferencia que los toros. Un zagal tocaba en el caramillo una canción primitiva, que rompía el aire silencioso de la mañana.

El cielo iba poniéndose negruzco, plomizo, violado por algunos sitios; una gran nube obscura avanzaba. Empezó a llover, y Ossorio apresuró su marcha. Iba acercándose a un bosquecillo frondoso de álamos, de un verde brillante. Ocultábase entre aquel bosquecillo una aldehuela de pocas casas, con su iglesia de torre piramidal terminada por un enorme nido de cigüeñas. Tocaban las campanas a misa. Era domingo.

Fernando entró en la iglesia, que se hallaba ruinosa, con las paredes recubiertas de cal, llenas de roñas y desconchaduras.

Al entrar no se percibía más que unas cuantas luces en el suelo, colocadas sobre cuadros de tela blanca; después se iban viendo el altar mayor, el cura con su casulla bordada con flores rojas y verdes; luego se percibían contornos de mujeres arrodilladas, con mantillas negras echadas sobre la frente, caras duras, denegridas, tostadas por el sol, rezando con un ademán de ferviente misticismo; y en la parte de atrás de la iglesia, debajo del coro, por una ventana con cristales empolvados, entraba una claridad plateada que iluminaba las cabezas de los hombres sentados en fila en un banco largo.

El cura, desde el altar, cantaba la misa con una voz cascada que parecía un balido; el órgano sonaba en el coro con una voz también de viejo. La misa estaba al concluir; el cura, que era un viejo de cara tostada y de cabellos blancos, alto, fornido, con aspecto de cabecilla carlista, dió la bendición al pueblo.

Las mujeres apagaron las luces, y las guardaron con el paño blanco en los cestillos; se acercaron a la pila de agua bendita y fueron saliendo.

"I'm coming, I'm coming!"
"Were you really afraid I would run off without paying?" Fernando said to him.
"No, but anything is possible."
Ossorio wasn't looking for a quarrel; he paid the bill, which came to one *peseta*, and left town.

In the morning light, the castle wasn't what it had seemed to Fernando by night, to say the least; however, what it did have was a fine location: it was ideally situated, overlooking the valley.

In earlier times, it must have been a place for diversion rather than anything else; the noblemen of the Court would likely go there to play the bulls with lances, making passes with the cape, and their ladies, close by the windows, on stone benches in the towers, would contemplate the exploits of the lords of the castle.

Ossorio quickly lost sight of the small castle and started to skirt the edge of the meadows in which white and black bulls were grazing and looking attentively at him. Several famished-looking, filthy, disheveled herdsmen were contemplating him with the same indifference as the bulls. A young herdsman's helper was playing a primitive song on his shawm and it cut through the silent morning air.

The sky was turning darkish, leaden and violet in a number of places; a large, dark cloud kept advancing. It was beginning to rain, and Ossorio quickened his step. He was approaching a small wood luxuriant with poplars, bright green in color. A tiny hamlet with only a few houses, with a church with a tower shaped like a pyramid, topped by an enormous stork's nest, was hidden within that small wood. The bells were tolling for Mass. It was Sunday.

Fernando went into the church and found it to be in a ruinous condition, its walls covered over with lime and ingrained with dirt and flaking away.

When you entered, you could perceive nothing more than a few lit candles on the ground, placed on squares of white cloth; then you were able to see the high altar, the priest in his chasuble embroidered with red and green flowers; after that, you could distinguish the outlines of kneeling women, their black mantillas thrown over their foreheads, their rough faces darkened and tanned by the sun, praying in a posture of fervent mysticism; in the rear part of the church, under the choir, a silvery brilliance was pouring through a window with dust-covered panes, illuminating the heads of the men who were seated in a row on a long bench.

From the altar, the priest was intoning the Mass in a harsh voice that sounded like bleating; the organ resounded in the choir with a sound also like that of an old man. The Mass was coming to an end; the priest, who was an old man with a tanned face and white hair, tall and robust, with the appearance of a Carlist rebel leader,[24] gave his benediction to the people.

The women put out the candles and stored them away in their small baskets together with the white cloths; they went over to the holy water font and then they started walking out.

Y la iglesia quedó negra, vacía, silenciosa...

Fernando salió también, se sentó en un banco de la plaza, debajo de un álamo grande y frondoso frente al pórtico de la iglesia y contempló la gente que iba dispersándose por los caminos y senderos en cuesta.

Eran tipos clásicos: viejas vestidas de negro, con mantones verdosos, tornasolados; las mantillas con guarniciones de terciopelo roñoso, prendidas al moño. Las caras terrosas, las miradas de través, hoscas y pérfidas. Salieron todas las mujeres, viejas y jóvenes, al atrio, y fueron bajando las cuestas del pueblo, hablando y murmurando entre ellas.

En derredor de la torre, chillaban y revoloteaban los negros vencejos...

Fernando salió de la plaza y después del pueblo, siguiendo una vereda. Había cesado de llover; trozos de nubes blancas algodonosas se rompían y quedaban hechos jirones al pasar por entre los picachos de un monte formado por pedruscos, sin árboles ni vegetación alguna.

Cruzó cerros llenos de matas de tomillo violadas, campos esmaltados por las flores blancas de las jaras y con las amarillas brillantes de retama. Por entre el boscaje y las zarzas de ambos lados del camino levantaba su vuelo alguna urraca negra; una bandada de cuervos pasaba graznando por el aire.

A las cuatro o cinco horas de salir de Manzanares, Fernando estaba a poca distancia de otra aldea.

El camino, al acercarse al pueblo aquél, trazaba una curva bordeando un barranco.

En el fondo corría un arroyo de agua espumosa entre grandes álamos y enormes peñas cubiertas de musgo y en lo más bajo había un molino. Enfrente se recortaban y se contorneaban en el cielo, uno a uno, los riscos de un monte. Llegó Ossorio al pueblo, dió una vuelta por él y en la posada esperó a que le dieran de comer, sentándose en un banco que había al lado del portal.

Junto a una tapia de adobe color de tierra jugaban los chiquillos en un carro de bueyes; un burro tumbado en el suelo, patas arriba, coceaba alegremente. En el umbral de la casa frontera, de miserable aspecto, una vieja con refajo de bayeta encarnada, puesto como manto sobre la cabeza, espulgba a un chiquillo dormido en sus piernas, que llevaba una falda también de bayeta amarillenta. Era una mancha de color tan viva y armónica, que Fernando se sintió pintor y hubiera querido tener lienzo y pinceles para poner a prueba su habilidad.

Le llamaron para comer, y entró en una sala con el techo bajo cruzado de vigas, las paredes pintadas de blanco, con varios cromos, y el suelo embaldosado con ladrillos rojos y bastos. En la ventana, con las maderas entreabiertas, había una

And the church remained dark, empty, silent...

Fernando also went out, sat down on a bench in the square under a big, leafy poplar tree in front of the portico of the church, and he contemplated the people who were dispersing along the sloping roads and footpaths.

They were classic types: old women dressed in black, with greenish, iridescent shawls; mantillas trimmed with grimy velvet, pinned to the topknots in their hair. Their faces were earth-colored; their expressions were oblique, sullen and treacherous. All of the women, the old and the young, went out onto the paved terrace in front, and started walking down the slopes of the town, talking and gossiping among themselves.

Black swifts were shrieking and fluttering all around the tower...

Fernando left the square and then the town itself, making his way along a footpath. It had stopped raining; shreds of white, cotton-like clouds were breaking up and tearing into fragments as they passed between the sharp peaks of a mountain made of rough boulders, with no trees nor vegetation of any kind.

He crossed over hills covered with violet-colored bushes of thyme, through fields sprinkled with the white blossoms of rockrose and the brilliant yellow flowers of Spanish broom. Amid the thickets and blackberry bushes on either side of the road, an occasional magpie would raise its wings in flight; a flock of crows was flying about through the air, cawing as they passed.

About four or five hours after leaving Manzanares, Fernando was within a short distance of another town.

The road, as it approached that town, circled around it in an arc, running along the edge of a ravine.

At the bottom, a small stream with frothy water ran between big poplars and enormous boulders covered with moss, and at the very lowest part, there was a mill. In front of him, the crags of a mountain were outlined, one by one, contoured against the sky. Ossorio reached the town, strolled around there, and sat down on a bench on one side of the entryway to the inn, while he waited for them to prepare something for him to eat.

Some small children were playing in an oxcart near an earth-colored adobe wall; a donkey, stretched out on the ground with its feet in the air, was playfully kicking. At the threshold of the wretched-looking house opposite it, an old woman with a skirt of flesh-colored baize, placed over her head like a shawl, was cleaning the lice from a small child asleep on her legs, who was also wearing a skirt of yellowish baize. It was a patch of color that was so vivid and harmonious that Fernando felt his painter's instinct aroused anew and would have liked to have canvas and brushes so he could put his talent to the test.

They called him in to eat and he entered a room with a low ceiling with beams crossing over it, with walls painted white, with several chromolithographs, and the floor paved with rough, red bricks. There was a red curtain over the window, with

cortina roja, y al pasar la luz por ella, matizaba los objetos con una tonalidad de misterio y de artificio al mismo tempo, algo que a Fernando le parecía como su vida en aquellos momentos, una cosa vaga y sin objeto.

Concluyó de comer, y después de un momento de modorra, se levantó y no quiso preguntar nada de caminos ni de direcciones, y se marchó del pueblo.

Comenzó a subir un barranco lleno de piedras sueltas. Al terminar, tomó un sendero, y después, veredas y sendas hechas por los rebaños.

Se dirigió hacía una quiebra que hacían dos montañas desnudas, rojizas; se tendió en el suelo, y miró las nubes que pasaban por encima de su cabeza.

¡Qué impression de vaguedad producían el cansancio y la contemplación en su alma!

Su vida era una cosa tan inconcreta como una de aquellas nubes sin fuerza que se iba esfumando en el seno de la naturaleza.

Cuando hubo descansado, siguió adelante y atravesó el puerto. Desde allá, el paisaje se extendía triste, desolado. Enfrente se veía Somosierra como una cortina violácea y gris; más cerca se sucedían montes desnudos con altas cimas agudas, en cuyas grietas y oquedades blanqueaban finas estrías de nieve. Bajó Fernando hacia un valle, por una escarpada ladera, entre tomillares floridos y oloroses, matas de espinos y de zarzas. Al anochecer, un carbonero que encontró en el camino le indicó la dirección fija de una aldea.

XII

Siguiendo las instrucciones que le dieron, Fernando alquiló un caballo y se dirigió a buscar la carretera de Francia. El caballo era un viejo rocín cansado de arrastrar diligencias, que tenía encima de los ojos unos agujeros en donde podrían entrar los puños. Las ancas le salían como si le fueran a cortar la piel. Su paso era lento y torpe, y cuando Ossorio quería hacerle andar más de prisa, tropezaba el animal y tomaba un trote que, al sufrirlo el jinete, parecía como le estremecieran las entrañas.

A paso de andadura llegó al mediodía a un pueblecillo pequeño con unas cuantas casuchas cerradas; sobre los tejados terreros sobresalían las cónicas chimeneas. Llamó en una puerta.

Como no contestaba nadie, ató el caballo por la brida a una herradura incrustada en la pared, y entró en un zaguán miserable, en donde una vieja, con un refajo amarillo, hacía pleita.

– Buenos días – dijo Fernando –. ¿No hay posada?

–¿Posada? – preguntó con asombro la vieja.

its shutters half open, and as the light passed through, it shaded all the objects with a tonality of mystery and artifice at the same time, something that seemed to Fernando like his own life at those moments, something vague and purposeless.

He finished eating and after sleeping for a moment, he got up, decided not to inquire at all about roads or directions, and departed from town.

He began to make his way up a ravine covered with loose stones. When he finished, he took a footpath and then the tracks and trails made by the flocks.

He headed for a hollow formed by two barren, reddish-colored mountains; he stretched out on the ground and looked up at the clouds that were passing overhead.

What a sense of aimlessness his weariness and contemplation were producing in his spirit!

His life was something as indefinite as one of those forceless clouds that were fading away into the bosom of Nature.

When he had rested for a while, he started forward again and crossed over the pass. From there, the landscape stretched out, sad and desolate. Before him, he could make out Somosierra, like a violaceous, gray curtain; even closer, naked mountains with tall, sharp summits followed one another, and slender grooves of snow glistened white in their fissures and hollows. Fernando descended toward a valley along a precipitous slope between flowering, fragrant fields of thyme and bushes of hawthorn and blackberry. As night fell, a coal dealer he met on the road pointed out the exact direction of a village.

XII

Following the instructions given to him, Fernando rented a horse and set out to look for the road to France. The horse was an old nag, worn out with pulling stagecoaches, and it had a pair of cavities above the eyes into which you could fit your fists. The haunches protruded so sharply that you would think they were going to cut through the skin. Its gait was slow and sluggish, and when Ossorio wanted to make it move more rapidly, the animal would stumble and take off at a trot that made the rider enduring it feel as if his insides were being shaken up.

Moving along at this ambling gait, he reached a small village at noon, which was made up of a few shanties that were all closed; cone-shaped chimneys projected over the low-lying roofs. He knocked at one of the doors.

Since no one answered, he tied his horse by the reins to a horseshoe that was incrusted in the wall and entered a wretched-looking vestibule where an old lady in a yellow skirt was weaving plaited strands of esparto grass.

"Good day," said Fernando. "Is there an inn around here?"

"An inn?" the old lady asked in astonishment.

- Sí, posada o taberna.
- Aquí no hay posada ni taberna.
- ¿No podría usted venderme pan?
- No vendemos pan.
- ¿Hay algún sitio en donde lo vendan?
- Aquí cada uno hace el pan para su casa.
- Sí. Será verdad; pero yo no lo puedo hacer. ¿No me puede usted vender un pedazo?

La vieja, sin contestar, entró en un cuartucho y vino con un trozo de pan seco.
- ¿Cuántos días tiene? preguntó Fernando.
- Catorce.
- ¿Y qué vale?
- Nada, nada. Es una limosna.

Y la vieja se sentó sin hacer caso de Fernando.

Aquella limosna le produjo un efecto dulce y doloroso al mismo tiempo. Subió en el jamelgo; fué cabalgando hasta el anochecer, en que se acercó a un pueblo. Una chiquilla le indicó la posada; entró en el zaguán y se sentó a tomar un vaso de agua.

En un cuarto, cuya puerta daba al zaguán, había algunos hombres de mala catadura bebiendo vino y hablando a voces de política. Se habían verificado elecciones en el pueblo.

En esto llegó un joven alto y afeitado, montado a caballo; ató el caballo a la reja, entró en el zaguán, hizo restallar el látigo y miró a Fernando desdeñosamente.

Uno de los que estaban en el cuarto salió al paso del jaque y le hizo una observación, respecto a Ossorio; el joven entonces, haciendo un mohín de desprecio, sacó una navaja del bolsillo interior de la americana y se puso a limpiarse las uñas con ella.

Al poco rato entró en el zaguán un hombre de unos cincuenta años, chato, de cara ceñuda, cetrino, casi elegante, con una cadena de reloj, de oro, en el chaleco. El hombre, dirigiéndose al tabernero, preguntó en voz alta señalando con el índice a Ossorio:
- ¿Quién es ese?
- No sé.

Fernando, inmediatamente, llamó al tabernero, le pidió una botella de cerveza, y, señalando con el dedo al de la cadena de reloj, preguntó:
- Diga usted, ¿Quién es ese chato?

El tabernero quedó lívido; el hombre arrojó una mirada de desafío a Fernando, que le contestó con otra de desprecio. El chato aquel entró en el cuarto donde estaban reunidos los demás. Hablaban todos a la vez, en tono unas veces amenazador y otras irónico.

"Yes, an inn or a tavern."
"There are no inns or taverns here."
"Could you sell me some bread then?"
"We don't sell bread."
"Is there some place where they might sell it?"
"Everyone here makes their own bread for their own home."
"Yes. That's probably true; but I can't do it. Couldn't you sell me just one piece?"

Without answering, the old lady went into a squalid little room and came back with a piece of dry bread.

"How many days old is it?" asked Fernando.
"Fourteen."
"How much is it?"
"Nothing. Nothing. It's charity."

And the old lady sat down, paying no attention whatsoever to Fernando.

That charitable offering produced an effect on Fernando that was both sweet and painful at the same time. He climbed back on the nag: he kept riding until nightfall, at which time he came near a town. A little girl pointed out the inn to him; he went into the vestibule and sat down to have a glass of water.

In a room with a door leading into the vestibule, several nasty-looking men were drinking wine and talking in loud voices about politics. Elections had just taken place in the town.

At this moment, a young man, tall and clean-shaven, arrived, riding a horse; he tied his horse to the grating, walked into the vestibule, cracked his whip and looked at Fernando disdainfully.

One of the men who was in the room went out to meet the bully and made some observation to him concerning Ossorio; then the young fellow, with a scowl of contempt, pulled out a jackknife from the inside pocket of his jacket and began to clean his fingernails with it.

After a short while, a man came into the vestibule; he was about fifty years old, had a pug nose, a frown on his face, a sallow complexion, almost stylishly dressed, with a golden watch chain on his vest. The man addressed the tavern keeper and asked in a loud voice as he pointed at Ossorio with his index finger:

"Who is that fellow?"
"I don't know."

Immediately, Fernando called the tavern keeper, asked him for a bottle of beer, pointed his finger at the man with the watch chain and asked:

"Tell me, who is that fellow with the pug nose?"

The tavern keeper turned livid; the man cast a challenging look at Fernando, who in turn answered him with a look of contempt. That pug-nosed fellow went into the room where all the others were gathered. They were all talking at the same time in a tone sometimes menacing and at other times ironic.

– Y si no se gana la elección, hay puñaladas.

Fernando se olvidó de que era demócrata, y maldijo con toda su alma al imbécil legislador que había otorgado el sufragio a aquella gentuza innoble y miserable, sólo capaz de fechorías cobardes.

Hallábase Ossorio embebido en estos pensamientos cuando el joven jaque, seguido de tres o cuatro, salió al zaguán; primeramente se acercó al caballo que había traído Fernando y comenzó a hacer de él una serie de elogios burlones; después, viendo que esto no le alteraba al forastero, cogió una cuerda y empezó a saltar como los chicos, amagando dar con ella a Fernando. Éste, que notó la intención, palideció profundamente y cambió de sitio; entonces el joven, creyendo que Ossorio no sabría defenderse, hizo como que le empujaban, y pisó a Fernando. Lanzó Ossorio un grito de dolor; se levantó, y, con el puño cerrado, dió un golpe terrible en la cara de su contrario. El jaque tiró de cuchillo; pero, al mismo tiempo, Fernando, que estaba lívido de miedo y de asco, sacó el revólver y dijo con voz sorda:

– Al que se acerque, lo mato. Como hay Dios que lo mato.

Mientras los demás sujetaban al joven, el tabernero le rogó a Fernando que saliera. El pagó, y con la brida del caballo en una mano y en la otra el revólver, se acercó a un guardía civil que estaba tomando el fresco en la puerta de su casa, y le contó lo que había pasado.

– Lo que debe usted hacer es salir inmediatamente de aquí. Ese joven con el que se ha pegado usted es muy mala cabeza, y como su padre tiene mucha influencia, es capaz de cualquier cosa.

Ossorio siguió el consejo que le daban y salió del pueblo.

A las once de la noche llegó al inmediato, y, sin cenar, se fue a dormir.

En el cuarto que le destinron había colgadas en la pared una escopeta y una guitarra; encima, un cromo del Sagrado Corazón de Jesús.

Ante aquellos símbolos de la brutalidad nacional comenzó a dormirse cuando oyó una rondalla de guitarras y bandurrias que debía de pasar por delante de la casa. Oyó cantar una jota, y después otra y otra, a cual más estúpidas y más bárbaras, en las cuales celebraban a un señor que había debido salir diputado, y que vivía enfrente. Cuando concluyeron de cantar y se preparaba Ossorio a dormirse, oyó murmullos en la calle, silbidos, fueras, y después, cristales rotos en la casa vecina.

Era encantador; al poco rato volvía la rondalla.

Desesperado Fernando, se levantó y se asomó a la ventana. Precisamente en aquel momento pasaban por la calle, montados a caballo, el joven jaque de la riña del día anterior, con dos amigos.

"And if we don't win the elections, there will be blood flowing."

Fernando forgot he was a democrat and he cursed that imbecile of a legislator with all his soul for having granted suffrage to that ignoble, miserable rabble, who were only capable of cowardly villainy.

Fernando was completely absorbed in such thoughts when the young bully, followed by three or four others, came out into the vestibule; first of all, he went over to the horse Fernando had brought and proceeded to make a series of mocking praises about it; then, seeing that all this didn't seem to upset the stranger, he grabbed a piece of rope and started to jump just as children do, all the while threatening to strike Fernando with it. The latter, who noticed his intention, turned profoundly pale and moved to another place; then the young man, believing that Ossorio wouldn't know how to defend himself, pretended that he had been pushed and stepped on Fernando's foot. Ossorio cried out in pain; he stood up, his fist clenched, and struck his adversary a terrible blow in the face. The bully pulled out his knife, but at the same time, Fernando, livid with fear and loathing, drew his revolver and said in a muffled voice:

"I'll kill the first one who comes near me. As there's a God in heaven, I'll kill him."

While the others were restraining the young fellow, the tavern keeper begged Fernando to leave. He paid, and with the reins of the horse in one hand and the revolver in the other, he went over to a rural policeman who was taking some fresh air in the doorway of his house and recounted what had happened.

"What you'd better do is get out of here immediately. That young fellow you had a fight with is very hot-headed, and since his father has a lot of influence around here, he is capable of doing anything."

Ossorio followed the advice given him and left town.

At eleven that night, he reached the next town and went to bed without eating any supper.

In the room they gave him, a shotgun and a guitar were hanging on the wall; above them was a chromolithograph of the Sacred Heart of Jesus.

He was starting to fall asleep before these symbols of the national brutishness,[25] when he heard a group of serenaders with guitars and *bandurrias* who must have been passing in front of the house. He heard them singing a jota, then another and another, each one more stupid and barbaric, in which they were celebrating a man who must have been elected a deputy and who lived just across the way. When they finished singing and just as Ossorio was preparing to go back to sleep, he heard muttering in the street, whistling and shouts of "Get out of there," and then the sound of broken window panes in the house next door.

It was delightful; in a little while, the serenaders returned.

In desperation, Fernando got out of bed and peered out of the window. At exactly that moment, the young bully from the previous day's fight passed by along the street with two friends, riding on horseback.

Fernando avisó al posadero de que si preguntaban por él dijese que no estaba allí; y cuando el grupo de los tres, después de preguntar en la posada, entraron en otra calle, Fernando se escabulló, y, volviendo grupas, echó a trotar, alejándose del camino real hasta internarse en el monte.

XIII

Después de algunas horas de andar a caballo se encontró en Rascafría, un pueblo que le pareció muy agradable, con arroyos espumosos que lo cruzaban por todos sitios.

Luego de echar un vistazo por el pueblo tomó el camino del Paular, que pasaba entre prados floridos llenos de margaritas amarillas y blancas y regatos cubiertos de berros que parecían islillas verdes en el agua limpia y bullidora.

Al poco rato llegó a la alameda del Paular, abandonada, con grandes árboles frondosos de retorcido tronco.

A un lado se extendía muy alta la tapia de la huerta del monasterio; al otro saltaba el río claro y cristalino sobre un lecho de guijarros.

Llegó al abandonado monasterio y en la portería le hospedaron. Ossorio creyó aquel lugar muy propio para el descanso.

Se sentía allí en aquellos patios desiertos un reposo absoluto. Sobre todo el cementerio del convento era de una gran poesía. Era huerto tranquilo, reposado, venerable. Un patio con arrayanes y cipreses en donde palpitaba un recogimiento solemne, un silencio sólo interrumpido por el murmullo de una fuente que cantaba invariable y monótona su eterna canción no comprendida.

Las paredes que circundaban al huerto eran de granito azulado, áspero, de grano grueso; tenían góticas ventanas al claustro tapiadas a medias con ladrillos y a medias con tablas carcomidas por la humedad, negruzcas y llenas de musgo.

Entre ventana y ventana se elevaban desde el suelo hasta el tejado robustos contrafuertes de piedra terminados en lo alto en canecillos monstruosos; fantásticas figuras asomadas a los aleros para mirar al huerto, aplastadas por el peso de los chapiteles toscos, desmoronados, desgastados, rotos. Encima de algunas ventanas se veían clavadas cruces de madera carcomida. Masas simétricas de viejos y amarillentos arrayanes adornadas en los ángulos por bolas de recortado follaje, dividían el cementerio en cuadros de parcelas sin cultivar, bordeadas por las avenidas, cubiertas de grandes lápidas.

En medio del huerto había un aéreo pabellón con ventanas y puertas ojivales y en el interior una pila redonda con una gran copa de piedra, de donde brotaban por los caños, chorros brillantes de agua que parecían de plata.

Fernando told the innkeeper to say that he wasn't there if someone should ask for him; when the group of three men, after asking for him at the inn, went on to another street, Fernando slipped out, turned back the other way and started off at a trot, drawing away from the main road till he was deep into the mountain woodland.

XIII

After riding horseback for several hours, he found himself in Rascafría,[26] a town that seemed very pleasant to him, with foaming brooks running through it everywhere.

After taking a quick look around town, he took the road to El Paular,[27] which passed through blooming meadows filled with yellow and white daisies and pools of water covered with watercress, resembling little green islands in the clear, bubbling water.

In a short while, he reached the tree-lined lane of El Paular, which was neglected, with big, leafy trees with twisted trunks.

The high wall around the extensive monastery garden extended on one side; on the other side, the clear, crystalline river leaped over a bed of pebbles.

He reached the abandoned monastery and he was put up at the gatekeeper's lodge. Ossorio felt that this place was quite suitable for some peace and quiet.

There, in those deserted courtyards, you had an absolute feeling of repose. The monastery cemetery was especially poetic. It was a tranquil, peaceful and venerable garden. A courtyard with myrtles and cypresses, in which a solemn seclusion seemed to palpitate, a silence interrupted only by the murmur of a fountain that sang, invariably and monotonously, its eternal incomprehensible song.

The walls surrounding the garden were of bluish granite, rough and heavy-grained; they had Gothic windows opening into the cloister, walled up partly with bricks and partly with boards that had been eaten away by the dampness, blackish in color, covered with moss.

Between one window and the next, sturdy buttresses of stone rose up from the ground to the roof, terminating at the very top in monstrous modillions: fantastic shapes, peering over the eaves of the roof to look down into the garden, crushed by the weight of the rough, crumbling, eroded and broken capitals. You could see crosses made of worm-eaten wood nailed to the walls above several of the windows. Symmetrical masses of old, yellowish myrtle trees, garnished with balls of trimmed foliage in the corners, divided the cemetery into squares of uncultivated patches of ground, bordered by the lanes and covered with large gravestones.

There was an ethereal pavilion with ogival-shaped windows and doors in the middle of the garden, and in the interior was a round fountain basin with a large, stone bowl, and brilliant jets of water that looked like silver were gushing from its spouts.

A un lado, medio oculta por los arrayanes, se veía la tumba de granito de un obispo de Segovia muerto en el *cenobium*, y enterrado allí por ser ésta su voluntad.

¡Qué hermoso poema el del cadáver del obispo en aquel campo tranquilo! Estaría allá abajo con su mitra y sus ornamentos y su báculo, arrullado por el murmullo de la fuente. Primero, cuando lo enterraran, empezaría a pudrirse poco a poco: hoy se le nublaría un ojo, y empezarían a nadar los gusanos por los jugos vítreos; luego el cerebro se le iría reblandeciendo, los humores correrían de una parte del cuerpo a otra y los gases harían reventar en llagas la piel: y en aquellas carnes podridas y deshechas correrían las larvas alegremente...

Un día comenzaría a filtrarse la lluvia y a llevar con ella substancia orgánica, y al pasar por la tierra aquella substancia se limpiaría, se purificaría, nacerían junto a la tumba hierbas verdes, frescas y el pus de las úlceras brillaría en las blancas corolas de las flores.

Otro día esas hierbas frescas, esas corolas blancas darían su substancia al aire y se evaporaría ésta para depositarse en una nube...

¡Qué hermoso poema el del cadáver del obispo en el campo tranquilo! ¡Qué alegría la de los átomos al romper la forma que les aprisionaba, al fundirse con júbilo en la nebulosa del infinito, en la senda del misterio donde todo se pierde!

XIV

Al día siguiente de llegar, Fernando pensó que sería una voluptuosidad tenderse a la sombra en el cementerio, y fue allá.

Después de recorrer los claustros entró en el camposanto, buscó la sombra y vió que debajo de unos arrayanes estaba tendido un hombre alto, flaco y rubio. Ossorio se retiraba de aquel sitio, cuando el hombre, con acento extranjero le dijo:

–¡Oh! No encontrará usted mejor lugar que éste para tenderse.

– Por no molestarle a usted...

– No, no me molesta.

Se tendió a pocos pasos del desconocido y permanecieron los dos mirando el cielo.

El follaje de un *evonymus* nacido en medio de una parcela resplandecía con el sol al ser movido por el viento y rebrillaban las hojas con el tembleteo como si fueran laminillas de estaño.

Como contraste de aquel brillo y movimiento los cipreses levantaban las rígidas y altas pirámides de sus copas y permanecían inmóviles y obscuros, exaltados,

To one side, half hidden by the myrtles, you could see the granite tomb of a bishop of Segovia, who had died in the *cenobium* and had been buried there according to his wishes.

What a beautiful poem was that of the bishop's cadaver in that tranquil plot of land! He was probably down below, lulled by the murmur of the fountain, with his miter and his ornaments and his crosier. At first, when they buried him, he probably began to decay a little at a time: today, one of his eyes very likely grew cloudy and worms began to swim around in the vitreous juices; then, his brain would begin growing soft, the humors started to run from one part of the body to another, and the gases made the skin erupt in ulcers; and in all that decaying, dissolving flesh, the larvae merrily ran about...

One day the rain probably began to filter through and carry organic matter with it, and as that matter passed through the earth, it was cleansed and purified; fresh, green grass germinated near the tomb, and the pus from the ulcers glistened in the white corollas of the flowers.

On yet another day, those fresh grasses and those white corollas gave off their substance into the air and this evaporated in order to be deposited inside a cloud...

How beautiful the poem of the bishop's cadaver in that tranquil plot of land! What joy that of the atoms as they break from the form that has imprisoned them, as they jubilantly fuse with the nebulous entity of the infinite, along the path of mystery where everything is lost!

XIV

On the day after his arrival, Fernando thought it would be quite voluptuous to stretch out in the shade in the cemetery and so he went there.

After making the rounds of the cloisters, he went into the cemetery, looked around for some shade and saw that a tall, thin, blond man was stretched out under some myrtles. Ossorio started moving away from that place, when the man said to him in a foreign accent:

"Oh! You won't find any better place than this to stretch out."

"I just didn't want to bother you..."

"No, you're not bothering me."

He stretched out a few feet from the stranger and the two of them remained there looking at the sky.

The foliage of a *spindle tree* that had grown up in the middle of a nearby parcel of ground was shining in the sunlight as it was moved by the wind, and its leaves glistened as they trembled, as if they were thin sheets of tin.

In contrast to this brightness and movement, the cypresses raised their rigid, lofty, pyramid-shaped treetops and stood there, motionless, dark and exalted, as if

como si ellos guardasen el alma huraña de los monjes, y sus agudas cimas verdes, negruzcas, se perfilaban sobre la dulce serenidad del cielo inmaculado.

Se oía a veces vagamente un grito largo, lastimero, quizá el canto lejano de un gallo. En las avenidas, cubiertas de losas de granito, donde descansaban las viejas cenizas de los cartujos muertos en la paz del claustro, crecían altas hierbas y musgos amarillentos y verdosos. En medio del huerto, en el aéreo pabellón con puertas y ventanas ojivales, caían los chorros de agua en la pila redonda y cantaba la fuente su larga canción misteriosa.

El extranjero, sin abandonar su posición, dijo que se llamaba Max Schultze, que era de Nuremberg y que estaba en España por la simpatía y curiosidad que experimentaba por el país.

Fernando también se presentó a sí mismo.

Cambiaron entre los dos algunas palabras.

Cuando el sol estaba en el cenit, el alemán dijo:

– Es hora de comer. Vámonos.

Se levantaron los dos, y andando lentamente como bueyes cansinos, fueron a la portería del convento, en donde comieron.

– Ahora echaremos una siesta – dijo Schultze.

–¿Otra?

–Sí; yo por lo menos, sí.

Se tendieron en el mismo sitio, y como la reverberación del cielo era grande, se echaron el ala de los sombreros sobre los ojos.

– No es natural dormir tanto – murmuró Ossorio.

– No importa – replicó el alemán con voz confusa –. Yo no sé por qué hablan todos los filósofos de que hay que obrar conforme a la Naturaleza.

–¡Pchs! – murmuró Ossorio –; yo creo que será para que el mundo, los hombres, las cosas, evolucionen progresivamente.

–Y ese progreso, ¿para qué? ¿Qué objeto tiene? Mire usted qué nube más hermosa – dijo interrumpiéndose el alemán–; es digna de Júpiter.

Hubo un momento de silencio.

–¿Decía usted – preguntó Ossorio – que para qué servía el progreso?

– Sí; tiene usted buena memoria. Es indudable que el mundo ha de desaparecer; por lo menos en su calidad de mundo. Sí; su materia no desaparecerá, cambiará de forma. Algunos de nuestros alemanes optimistas creen que como la materia evoluciona, asciende y se purifica, y como esta materia no se ha de perder, podrá utilizarse por seres de otro mundo, después de la desaparición de la Tierra. Pero, ¿y si el mundo en donde se aprovecha esta materia está tan adelantado, que lo más alto

they were maintaining the withdrawn souls of the monks; and their sharp-pointed, green, blackish tops were profiled against the sweet serenity of the immaculate sky.

At times you could vaguely hear a long, doleful cry, perhaps the distant crowing of a cock. Tall grass and yellowish, greenish moss were growing in the lanes, that were covered with granite slabs, where were resting the venerable ashes of the Carthusian monks who had died in the peace of the cloister. In the middle of the garden, in the ethereal pavilion with ogival doors and windows, jets of water were falling into the round, stone basin, and the fountain kept singing its prolonged, mysterious song.

The foreigner, without changing his position, said that his name was Max Schultze,[28] that he was from Nuremburg and that he was living in Spain because of the affection and curiosity he felt for the country.

Fernando also introduced himself.

They both exchanged a few words.

When the sun was at its zenith, the German said:

"It's time to eat. Let's go."

They both stood up, and, walking slowly like weary oxen, they went back to the gatekeeper's lodge at the monastery where they ate their meal.

"We're going to take a nap now," said Schultze.

"Again?"

"Yes; at least I intend to do so."

They stretched out in the same place and, because the reverberation from the sky was extreme, they pulled the brims of their hats down over their eyes.

"It isn't natural to sleep so much," murmured Ossorio.

"It makes no difference," replied the German in a somewhat confused tone. "I don't know why all the philosophers keep saying that one ought to behave in accordance with Nature."

"Pshaw!" muttered Ossorio. "I suppose it must be that way so the world, mankind, everything, can evolve in a progressive way."

"And all that progress, what good is it? What purpose does it serve? Just look at that very beautiful cloud," the German said as he interrupted himself. "It's worthy of Jupiter."

There was a moment of silence.

"Were you saying that you didn't know what use there was for progress?" asked Ossorio.

"Yes, you have a good memory. There's no doubt that the world is going to disappear; at least as far as it exists as a world. Yes, its matter will not disappear, it will simply change in form. Some of our German optimists believe that as matter evolves, it ascends and is purified, and since this matter is not going to be lost, it might well be used by beings from another world after the disappearance of the Earth. But what if the world where they make use of this matter for their own purposes is

y refinado de la materia terrestre, el pensamiento de hombres como Shakespeare o Goethe, no sirve más que para mover molinos de chocolate?

– A mí todo esto me produce miedo; cuando pienso en las cosas desconocidas, en la fuerza que hay en una planta de éstas, me entra verdadero horror, como si me faltara el suelo para poner los pies.

– No parece usted español – dijo el alemán –; los españoles han resuelto todos esos problemas metafísicos y morales que nos preocupan a nosotros, los del Norte, en el fondo mucho menos civilizados que ustedes. Los han resuelto, negándolos; es la única manera de resolverlos.

– Yo no los he resuelto – murmuró Ossorio –. Cada día tengo motivos nuevos de horror; mi cabeza es una guarida de pensamientos vagos, que no sé de dónde brotan.

– Para esa misticidad – repuso Schultze –, el mejor remedio es el ejercicio. Yo tuve una sobreexcitación nerviosa, y me curé andando mucho y leyendo a Nietzsche. ¿Lo conoce usted?

– No. He oído decir que su doctrina es la glorificación del egoísmo.

–¡Cómo se engaña usted, amigo! Crea usted que es difícil de representarse un hombre de naturaleza más ética que él; dificilísimo hallar un hombre más puro y delicado, más irreprochable en su conducta. Es un mártir.

– Al oírle a usted, se diría que es Budha o que es Cristo.

–¡Oh! No compare usted a Nietzsche con esos miserables que produjeron la decadencia de la humanidad.

Fernando se incorporó para mirar al alemán, vió con asombro que hablaba en serio, y volvió a tenderse en el suelo.

Comenzó a anochecer; el viento silbaba dulcemente por entre los árboles. Un perfume acre, adusto, se desprendía de los arrayanes y de los cipreses; no piaban los pájaros, ni cacareaban los gallos... y seguía cantando la fuente, invariable y monótona, su eterna canción no comprendida...

XV

–¿Conque sube usted a ese monte o no? – le dijo el alemán –. Creo que le conviene a usted castigar el cuerpo, para que las malas ideas se vayan.

–¿Pero piensa usted pasar la noche allá arriba?

– Sí; ¿por qué no?

– Hará frío.

so very advanced that what is the highest, the most refined terrestrial matter, like the thought of men like Shakespeare and Goethe, serves no other purpose than to move chocolate grinders?"

"All this makes me terribly afraid; when I think of unknown things, of the force that exists in a plant like that, I am overcome by a veritable horror, as if I lacked the solid ground on which I could set my feet."

"You don't seem very Spanish to me," said the German. "You Spanish have resolved all these metaphysical and moral problems that seem to preoccupy us, the people of the North, who are fundamentally much less civilized than you. You have resolved them by denying their existence; that's the only way to resolve them."

"I haven't resolved them," murmured Ossorio, "Every day I have new reasons to be terrified; my head is a retreat for all manner of vague thoughts and I do not know where they originate."

"The best remedy for such mystical tendencies is exercise," Schultze replied. "I once had an attack of nervous over-stimulation and I cured myself by walking a great deal and reading Nietzsche. Are you familiar with him?"

"No. I've heard it said that his doctrine is no more than a glorification of egotism."

"Oh, how you are deceiving yourself, my friend! Believe me, it is difficult to imagine a man with a more ethical temperament than his; it would be most difficult to find a man more pure and delicate, more irreproachable in his conduct. He is a martyr."

"Listening to you speak, one might think that he's a Buddha or a Christ."

"Oh! Don't you compare Nietzsche to those scoundrels who produced nothing but decadence for Humanity."[29]

Fernando sat up to look at the German, and, to his great surprise, saw that he was speaking quite seriously, and he stretched out on the ground again.

It began to grow dark; the wind was whistling gently between the trees. An acrid, harsh perfume was coming from the myrtles and cypress trees; the birds weren't chirping and the cocks weren't crowing..., and the fountain kept singing, invariably and monotonously, its eternal, incomprehensible song...

XV

"Well, are you going to climb up that mountain or not?" the German said to him.[30] "I think it would be good for you to inflict some punishment on your body, so that all those bad ideas will go away."

"But, do you really intend to spend the night up there?"

"I do. Why not?"

"It will probably be very cold."

– Eso no importa. Encenderemos fuego, y llevamos mantas.
– Bien. Pero yo le advierto a usted que cuando me canse me tiro al suelo y no sigo,
– Es natural. Yo haré lo mismo. Conque vamos a comer y en seguida, ¡arriba!

Comieron, prepararon algunas viandas, para el día siguiente, y cada uno con su manta al hombro y la escopeta terciada se encaminaron hacia un pinar de la falda de Peñalara.

El alemán se sentía movedizo y jovial; había hecho indudablemente provisión de energía mientras pasaba los días tendido en el suelo.

Al llegar al pinar, la cuesta se hizo tan pendiente que se resbalaban los pies. Fernando tenía que pararse a cada momento fatigado. Schultze le animaba gesticulando, gritando, cantando a voz en grito, con entusiasmo irónico, una canción patriótica que tenía por estribillo:

Deutschland, Deutschland über alles.

Fernando sentía una debilidad como no lo había sentido nunca, y tuvo que hacer largas paradas. Schultze se detenía junto a él de pie, y charlaban un rato.

De pronto oyeron un ladrido lejano, más agudo que el de un perro.

–¿Será algún lobo? – preguntó Ossorio.

–¡Ca! Es un zorro.

El gañido del animal se oía cerca, o lejos.

– Voy a ver si lo encuentro; esté usted preparado por si acaso viene por aquí – dijo Schultze, y cargó la escopeta con grandes postas y desapareció por entre la maleza. Poco después se oyeron dos tiros.

Fernando se sentó en el tronco de un árbol.

Al poco rato oyó ruido entre los árboles. Preparó la escopeta, y al terminar de hacer esto, vió a diez o doce pasos el zorro, alto, amarillo, con su hermosa cola como un plumero, Sin saber por qué, no determinó a disparar, y el zorro huyó corriendo y se perdió en la espesura.

Al llegar Schultze, le dijo que había visto al zorro.

–¿Por qué no ha disparado usted?

– Me ha parecido la distancia larga y creí que no le daría.

– Sin embargo, se dispara. Dice Turgeneff que hay tres clases de cazadores: unos que ven la pieza, disparan en seguida, antes de tiempo, y no le dan; otros apuntan, piensan qué momento será el mejor, disparan, y tampoco le dan, y, por último, hay los que tiran a tiempo. Usted es de la segunda clase de cazadores, y yo, de la primera.

Charlando iban subiendo el monte, se internaban por entre selvas de carrascas espesas con claros en medio. A veces cruzaban por bosques, entre grandes árboles

"That makes no difference. We'll light a fire and bring some blankets."

"All right. But I must warn you that when I get tired, I just fall down on the ground and go no further."

"That's only natural. I'll do the same. So let's go eat and right after that, up we go!"

They ate, prepared some food supplies for the following day and each one, with his blanket over his shoulders and his shotgun slung diagonally across his back, they made their way toward a pine grove on the lower slope of the Peñalara.

The German felt agile and jovial; he had undoubtedly been storing up his energy during the days he had spent stretched out on the ground.

When they reached the pine grove, the slope became so steep that their feet kept slipping. Fernando had to stop every so often due to fatigue, and Schultze kept encouraging him by gesticulating, shouting and singing a patriotic song in a loud voice, with ironic enthusiasm, which had as its refrain:

Deutschland, Deutschland, über alles.[31]

Fernando was overcome by a weakness such as he had never experienced before, and he had to make extended stops. Schultze would stop and stand beside him and they would chat for a while.

Suddenly they heard a barking in the distance, shriller than that of a dog.

"Could that be a wolf?" asked Ossorio.

"Oh, no, it's a fox."

The howling of the animal was sometimes nearby and sometimes far away.

"I'll go see if I can find it; you be ready in case it comes this way," said Schultze as he loaded his shotgun with buckshot and disappeared in the underbrush. Shortly afterward, two shots were heard.

Fernando sat down on a tree trunk.

In a little while, he heard a noise among the trees. He readied his shotgun and, just as he finished doing this, he saw the fox ten or twelve paces away, tall and yellow, with a beautiful tail like a feather duster. Without knowing why, he couldn't make up his mind to fire, and the fox fled, running swiftly, and was lost in the thicket.

When Schultze returned, he told him he had seen the fox.

"Why didn't you shoot?"

"The distance seemed too great for me and I thought I wouldn't hit it."

"You should fire anyway. Turgenev says there are three kinds of hunters: those who see their quarry, shoot right away, before the proper moment, and miss; others, who aim, consider the best possible moment, fire and don't hit it either, and finally, there are those who shoot at the right time. You belong to the second class of hunters and I, to the first."

They continued conversing as they kept moving up the mountain and found themselves deep within the small forests thick with kermes oaks, with clearings between them. Occasionally, they would cross through woodlands, between large,

secos, caídos, de color blanco, cuyas retorcidas ramas parecían brazos de un atormentado o tentáculos de un pulpo. Comenzaba a caer la tarde. Rendidos, se tendieron en el suelo. A su lado corría un torrente, saltando, cayendo desde grandes alturas como cinta de plata. Pasaban nubes blancas por el cielo, y se agrupaban formando montes coronados de nieve y de púrpura; a lo lejos, nubes grises e inmóviles parecían islas perdidas en el mar del espacio con sus playas desiertas. Los montes que enfrente cerraban el valle tenian un color violáceo con manchas verdes de las praderas; por encima de ellos brotaban nubes con encendidos núcleos fundidos por el sol al rojo blanco. De las laderas subían hacia las cumbres, trepando, escalando los riscos, jirones de espesa niebla que cambiaban de forma, y al encontrar una oquedad hacían allí su nido y se amontonaban unos sobre otros.

– A mí, esos montes – murmuró Ossorio – no me dan idea de que sean verdad; me parece que están pintados, que eso es una decoración de teatro.

– No creo eso de usted.

– Pues, sí; créalo usted.

– Para mí esos montes – dijo Schultze – son Dios.

Comenzó a anochecer.

–¿Qué hacemos? ¿Subimos más? ¿Vamos a ver si encontramos esa laguna?

– Vamos.

Anochecido llegaron a la laguna y anduvieron reconociendo los alrededores por todas partes a ver si encontraban alguna cueva o socavón donde meterse. Era aquello un verdadero páramo, lleno de piedras, desabrigado; el viento, muy frío, azotaba allí con violencia. Como no encontraron ni un agujero, se cobijaron en la oquedad que formaban dos peñas, y Fernando trató de cerrar una de las aberturas amontonando pedruscos, lo que no pudo conseguir.

– Yo voy por leña – dijo Schultze –. Sin fuego aquí nos vamos a helar.

Se marchó el alemán, y Ossorio quedó allá envuelto en la manta, contemplando el paisaje a la vaga luz de las estrellas. Era un paisaje extraño, un paisaje cósmico, algo como un lugar de planeta inhabitado, de la Tierra en las edades geológicas del ichthiosauros y plesiosauros. En la superficie de la laguna larga y estrecha no se movía ni una onda; en su seno, obscuro, insondable, brillaban dormidas miles de estrellas. La orilla, quebrada e irregular, no tenia a sus lados ni arbustos ni matas; estaba desnuda.

En la cima de un monte lejano se columbraba la luz de la hoguera de algunos pastores.

Hasta que llegó Schultze, Fernando tuvo tiempo de desesperarse.

dried up, fallen trees, white in color, with twisted branches that resembled the arms of some tormented being or the tentacles of an octopus. The afternoon was coming to a close. Completely exhausted, they stretched out on the ground. Beside them, a torrent was rushing by, leaping, falling from great heights like a silvery ribbon; white clouds kept passing in the sky and they grouped together, forming mountains crowned snow-white and purple; in the distance, the gray, motionless clouds seemed like islands lost in a sea of space, their beaches deserted. The mountains that closed off the valley in front of them were of a violet hue, with green patches of meadows; clouds with flame-colored cores, fused by the sun to a reddish-white, were erupting above them. Shreds of dense fog were rising from the slopes toward the summits, climbing upward, scaling the crags, and they kept changing form, and whenever they would come upon a hollow, they would make their nest there and pile up, one on top of the other.

"As for me, those mountains don't leave me with the impression that they are real," murmured Ossorio; "it seems to me that they are painted, that it is all theatrical scenery."

"I find it hard to believe you think that."

"Well, I do. You can believe me."

"To me," said Schultze, "those mountains are God."

Night began to fall.

"What shall we do? Shall we continue climbing? Shall we go see if we can find that tarn?"

"Let's go."

They reached the tarn after night had fallen, and they began walking around, reconnoitering all over the surrounding area to see if they could find some cave or an excavation, where they could take refuge. That place was nothing but a barren expanse, covered with rocks and open to the elements; the bitter, icy wind kept whipping violently all around them. Since they couldn't even find a hole anywhere, they took shelter in a hollow formed by two boulders, and Fernando tried to close off one of the two openings by piling up some large stones, but his efforts were in vain.

"I'm going to look for wood," said Schultze. "Without a fire here, we're going to freeze."

The German went off and Ossorio remained there, wrapped in his blanket, contemplating the landscape by the faint light of the stars. It was a strange landscape, a cosmic landscape, like some place on an uninhabited planet, or on Earth during the geological age of the ichthyosaurs and the plesiosaurs. Not a single wave was moving over the surface of the long, narrow tarn; thousands of sleeping stars were shining in its dark, unfathomable depths. The broken, irregular shoreline had neither shrubs nor bushes at the sides; it was barren.

You could barely make out the light of some shepherds' bonfire at the summit of a distant mountain.

While he waited for Schultze to return, Fernando had adequate time to grow desperate.

Tardó más de media hora y vino con su manta llena de ramas sujeta en la cabeza.

Llegó sudando.

– Hay que andar mucho para encontrar algo combustible – dijo Schultze –. Hemos subido demasiado. A esta altura no hay más que piedras.

Tiró la manta, en donde traía ramas verdes de espino, de retama y de endrino. El encenderlas costó un trabajo ímprobo: ardían y se volvían a apagar al momento.

Cuando después de muchos ensayos pudo hacerse una mediana hoguera, ya no quedaban más ramas que quemar, y a medida que avanzaba la noche hacía más frío; el cielo estaba lechoso, cuajado de estrellas. Fernando se sentía aterido, pero dulcemente, sin molestia.

– Vamos a traer más leña – dijo Schultze.

–¿Para qué? – murmuró vagamente Fernando –. Yo estoy muy bien.

Schultze vió que Ossorio estaba tiritando y que tenía las manos heladas.

–¡Vamos! ¡A levantarse! – gritó agarrándole del brazo.

Ossorio hizo un esfuerzo y se levantó. Inmediatamente empezó a temblar.

– Tome usted mi manta – dijo el alemán –, y ahora, andando a buscar leña.

Fueron los dos hasta una media hora de camino; echaron las mantas en el suelo y las fueron cargando de ramas, que cortaban por allí cerca. Después, con la carga en las espaldas, volvieron hacia el sitio de donde habían salido.

Sobre el rescoldo de la apagada hoguera pudieron encender otra fácilmente.

Ya, como había combustible en gran cantidad, a cada paso echaban más ramaje, que crepitaba al ser devorado por las llamas. Cuando aún creían que era media noche, comenzaron a correr nubes plomizas por el cielo. Se destacaron sobre el horizonte las cimas de algunas montañas; las nubes obscuras se aclararon; más lejos fueron apareciendo otras nubes estratificadas, azules, como largos peces; se dibujaron de repente las siluetas de los riscos cercanos.

A lo lejos, el paisaje parecía llano, y que terminaba en una sucesión de colinas.

El humo espeso y negro de la hoguera iba rasando la tierra y subía después en el aire, por la pared pedregosa del monte.

De pronto apareció sobre las largas nubes azules una estría roja, el horizonte se illuminó con resplandores de fuego, y por encima de las lejanas montañas el disco del sol miró a la tierra y la cubrió con la gloria y la magnificencia de los rayos de su inyectada pupila. Los montes tomaron colores; el sol brilló en la superficie tersa y sin ondas de la laguna.

– El buen papá de arriba es un gran escenógrafo – murmuro Schultze–. ¿Verdad?

He took more than half an hour and came back with his blanket full of branches made fast to his head.

He came back sweating.

"You have to walk quite far to find something combustible," said Schultze. "We climbed up too high. At this altitude, there's nothing but stones."

He threw down the blanket in which he had brought unseasoned branches of hawthorn, Spanish broom and blackthorn. It took a strenuous effort to set fire to them: they would catch fire and go out right away.

When, after many efforts, a decent fire could be started, there were no more branches left to burn, and it kept getting colder as the night wore on; the sky was milky and laden with stars. Fernando felt stiff with cold, but pleasantly so, without any discomfort.

"Let's go bring more wood," said Schultze.

"What for?" Fernando murmured somewhat incoherently. "I'm fine the way I am."

Schultze saw that Ossorio was shivering and that his hands were frozen.

"Let's go! On your feet!" he shouted, grabbing him by the arm.

Ossorio made a supreme effort and got to his feet. He immediately began to tremble.

"Take my blanket," said the German, "and now, let's be on our way to look for wood."

The two men kept walking for almost half an hour; they threw their blankets on the ground and started loading up with branches, which they cut nearby. Then, with the loads on their backs, they made their way back to the place they had just left.

Over the embers of the extinguished fire, they succeeded in lighting another one easily.

Now that there was fuel in great quantity, they kept throwing more branches on the fire at every opportunity, and the branches crackled as the flames consumed them. While they thought that it was still the middle of the night, leaden clouds started racing through the sky. The summits of a number of mountains stood out against the horizon; the dark clouds grew brighter; farther in the distance, other clouds were now appearing, stratified, blue, like long fish; suddenly the silhouettes of the nearby crags took shape.

In the distance, the landscape seemed flat and ended in a series of hills.

The thick, black smoke from the bonfire was skimming the ground and then rising into the air, along the rocky wall of the mountain.

Suddenly a red groove appeared above the elongated, blue clouds, the horizon was illuminated with bursts of fire and, above the distant mountains, the disc of the sun looked down upon the earth and covered it with the glory and magnificence of its fiery red pupil. The mountains took on coloring; the sun shone on the smooth surface of the tarn with no waves.

"The good Father up above is a good scenographer," murmured Schultze. "Don't you think so?"

—¡Oh! Ahora no siento haber venido – respondió Ossorio.
Después de admirar el espectáculo de la aurora se decidieron los dos a subir a la cumbre del monte.
Fernando se detuvo en el camino, al pie de uno de los picachos.
Desde allá se veían los bosques de El Espinar, La Granja, que parecía un cuartel, y más lejos Segovia, en una inmensa llanura amarilla, a trechos manchada por los pinares. No se advertía ningún otro pueblo en la llanura extensísima.
Por la mañana, Schultze y Fernando se internaron en lo más áspero de la sierra, sin dirección fija; durmieron y almorzaron en la cabaña de un cabrero, el cual les indicó como pueblo más cercano el de Cercedilla; y al divisar los tejados rojos de éste, como no tenían gana de llegar pronto, tendiéronse en el suelo en una pradera que en el claro de un pinar se hallaba.
Hacía allí un calor terrible; la tarde estaba pesada, de viento Sur.
Con los ojos entornados por la reverberación de las nubes blancas, veían el suelo lleno de hierba, salpicado de margaritas blancas y amarillas, de peonías de malsano aspecto y tulipanes de purpúrea corola.
Una ingente montaña, cubierta en su falda de retamares y jarales florecidos, se levantaba frente a ellos; brotaba sola, separada de otras muchas, desde el fondo de una cóncava hondonada, y al subir y ascender enhiesta, las plantas iban escaseando en su superficie y terminaba en su parte alta aquella mole de granito como muralla lisa o peñón tajado y desnudo, coronado en la cumbre por multitud de riscos, de afiladas aristas, de pedruscos rotos y de agujas delgadas como chapiteles de una catedral.
En lo hondo del valle, al pie de la montaña, veíanse por todas partes grandes piedras esparcidas y rotas, como si hubieran sido rajadas a martillazos; los titanes, constructores de aquel paredón ciclópeo, habían dejado abandonados en la tierra los bloques que no les sirvieron.
Sólo algunos pinos escalaban, bordeando torrenteras y barrancos, la cima de la montaña.
Por encima de ella, nubes algodonosas, de una blancura deslumbrante, pasaban con rapidez.
A Fernando le recordaba aquel paisaje alguno de los sugestivos e irreales paisajes de Patinir.
Dando la espalda a la montaña se veía una llanura azulada, y la carretera, cruzándola en ziszás, serpenteando después entre obscuros cerros hasta perderse en la cima de un collado.
Le parte cercana de la llanura estaba en sombra; una nube plomiza le impedía reflejar el sol; la parte lejana, iluminada pefectamente, se alejaba hasta confundirse con la sierra de Gredos, faja obscura de montañas oculta a trozos por nubecillas grises y rojizas.

"Oh! Now I'm not sorry that I came," Ossorio replied.

After admiring the spectacle of the dawn for some time, the two men decided to climb to the top of the mountain.

On the way, Fernando stopped at the foot of one of the peaks.

From there you could see the forests of El Espinar as well as La Granja,[32] which looked like a barracks, and farther off in the distance, Segovia, on an immense, yellow plain, which was spotted in places by pine groves. You couldn't make out any other town on the incredibly vast plain.

In the morning, Schultze and Fernando made their way deep into the roughest part of the mountain range, with no fixed direction in mind; they slept and had some lunch in a goatherd's cabin, and he pointed out Cercedilla as the nearest town;[33] and when they caught sight of the red roofs of the town, and since they didn't feel very much like arriving in town too soon, they stretched out on the ground in a meadow that was located in the clearing of a pine grove.

It was terribly hot there; the afternoon was sultry and the wind was blowing from the south.

With their eyes half-closed because of the reverberation from the white clouds, they could see the ground, covered with grass, with white and yellow daisies scattered here and there, with sickly-looking peonies and tulips with purple corollas.

A huge mountain, its lower slope covered with blooming Spanish broom and rockrose, rose up in front of them; it sprang up from the bottom of a concave depression, all alone, separated from many others, and as it rose and climbed straight upward, the plants on its surface became scarcer, and that mass of granite ended at the very summit as a smooth wall or a steep naked spire, crowned at the very top by a multitude of crags, sharpened arrises, broken boulders and slender, needle-like pinnacles like the spires of a cathedral.

At the bottom of the valley, at the foot of the mountain, large stones could be seen everywhere, scattered and broken, as if they had been cracked by hammer blows; the Titans, builders of that mighty Cyclopean wall, had left the blocks they couldn't use abandoned on the ground.

Only a few pine trees, skirting the edges of the gullies and ravines, made their way up to the summit of the mountain.

Above it, cotton-like clouds of dazzling whiteness were swiftly passing.

That landscape recalled to Fernando some of the suggestive and unreal landscape paintings of Patinir.[34]

When you turned your back to the mountain, you could see a bluish plain and the road crossing over it zigzag, then winding through dark hills until it was lost at the top of a rise.

The nearer part of the plain was in shadow; a lead-colored cloud prevented it from reflecting the sun; the more distant part, perfectly illuminated, receded until it blended with the Sierra de Gredos[35], a dark band of mountains, hidden in places by gray and reddish little clouds.

Aquella tierra lejana e inundada de sol daba la sensación de un mar espeso y turbio; y un mar también, pero mar azul y transparente, parecía el cielo, y sus blancas nubes eran blancas espumas agitadas en inquieto ir y venir: tan pronto escuadrón salvaje, como manada de tritones melenudos y rampantes.

Con los cambios de luz, el paisaje se transformaba. Algunos montes parecían cortados en dos; rojos en las alturas, negros en las faldas, confundiendo su color en el color negruzco del suelo. A veces, al pasar los rayos por una nube plomiza, corría una pincelada de oro por la parte en sombra de la llanura y del bosque, y bañaba con luz anaranjada las copas redondas de los pinos. Otras veces, en medio del tupido follaje, se filtraba un rayo de sol, talladrándolo todo a su paso, coloreando las hojas en su camino, arrancándolas reflejos de cobre y de oro.

Fué anocheciendo. Se levantó un vientecillo suave que pasaba por la piel como una caricia. Los cantuesos perfumaron el aire tibio de un aroma dulce, campesino. Piaron los pájaros, chirriaron los grillos, rumor confuso de esquilas resonó a lo lejos. Era una sinfonía voluptuosa de colores, de olores y de sonidos.

Brillaban a intervalos los pedruscos de la alta muralla, enrojecidos de pronto por los postreros resplandores del sol, como sí ardieran por un fuego interior; a intervalos también, al nublarse, aquellas rocas erguidas, de formas extrañas, parecían gigantescos centinelas mudos o monstruosos pajarracos de la noche preparados para levantar el vuelo.

De pronto, por encima de un picacho comenzaron a aparecer nubes de un color ceniciento y rojizo que incendiaron el cielo y lo anegaron en un mar de sangre. Sobre aquellos rojos siniestros se contorneaban los montes ceñudos, impenetrables.

Era la visión algo de sueño, algo apocalíptico; todo se enrojecía como por el resplandor de una luz infernal; las piedras, las matas de enebro y de jabino, las hojas verdes de los majuelos, las blancas flores de jara y las amarillas de la retama, todo se enrojecía con un fulgor malsano. Se experimentaba horror, recogimiento, como sí en aquel instante fuera a cumplirse la profecía tétrica de algún agorero del milenario.

Graznó una corneja; la locomotora de un tren cruzó a lo lejos con estertor fatigoso. Llegaban ráfagas de niebla por entre las quebraduras de los montes; poco después empezó a llover.

Fernando y el alemán bajaron al pueblo. Se había levantado la luna sobre los riscos de un monte, roja, enorme, como un sol enfermizo e iba ascendiendo por el cielo. La vaga luz del crepúsculo, mezclada con la de la luna, iluminaba el valle y sus campos, violáceos, grises, envueltos en la blanca esfumación de la niebla.

Por delante de la luna llena pasaban nubecillas blancas, y el astro de la noche parecía atravesar sus gasas y correr vertiginosamente por el cielo.

That far off countryside, inundated with sunlight, gave one the sensation that it was a dense, turbid sea; and the sky too seemed to be a sea, but a blue, transparent sea, and its white clouds were the white foam, stirred up in a restless movement to and fro: now a savage squadron, then a horde of long-haired and rampant Tritons.

With the changes of light, the landscape was being transformed. Several mountains seemed as if they were cut in two; red at the summit and dark along the slopes, blending their colors into the darkish hues of the ground. At times, when the rays of the sun would pass through a lead-colored cloud, a touch of gold would run through the shaded part of the plain and the forest and bathe the rounded tops of the pines with its orange-colored light. At other times, a sunbeam would filter through the midst of the dense foliage, piercing everything in its way, coloring the leaves in its path, snatching reflections of copper and gold from them.

Night was falling. A soft, gentle breeze arose and passed over the skin like a caress. The tepid air was perfumed with the sweet and rustic aroma of French lavender. The birds twittered, the crickets chirped, the indistinct sound of cowbells resounded in the distance. It was a voluptuous symphony of colors, scents and sounds.

At various points along the high wall of the mountain, the rough stones would glow, suddenly turned red by the dying splendor of the sun, as if burning from an inner fire; in numerous places as well, as the clouds passed over, those rising cliffs with strange forms would resemble gigantic, silent sentinels or monstrous, ugly birds of night, preparing to rise up in flight.

Suddenly, ashen and reddish clouds began to appear above a peak and they lit up the sky and flooded it in a sea of blood. Scowling, impenetrable mountains were outlined above those sinister red hues.

The vision was like something out of a dream, somewhat apocalyptic; everything was turning red, as if by the radiance of an infernal light; the stones, the shrubs of juniper and savin, the green leaves of the English hawthorn, the white flowers of the rockrose and the yellow ones of the Spanish broom, everything was turning red with an unwholesome brilliance. One was overwhelmed by a feeling of horror and confinement, as if at that very instant the gloomy prophesy of some foreteller of the millennium were going to be fulfilled.

A crow began to caw; a train locomotive crossed by in the distance with a weary stertor. Bursts of mist were coming in from amid the gaps in the mountains; soon afterward, it began to rain.

Fernando and the German descended to the town. The moon had risen over the crags of one of the mountains, red, enormous, like a sickly sun, and it kept moving upward in the sky. The faint light of twilight blended with that of the moon and illuminated the valley and its fields, which were now purplish, gray, wrapped in the white blurring of the mist.

Little white clouds were passing in front of the full moon and the nocturnal celestial body seemed to pierce their gauzelike textures and race vertiginously through the sky.

XVI

Al día siguiente, Schultze volvió al Paular; Fernando se despidió de él y en un carro salió para Segovia.

Llegó a Segovia con un calor bochornoso. El cielo estaba anubarrado, despedía un calor aplastante; sobre los campos, abrasados y secos, se agitaba una gasa espesa de la calina.

Se paró el carro en la Posada del Potro, en donde entraban y salían arrieros y chalanes.

Llamó Ossorio a la dueña de la casa, una mujer gruesa, la cual le dijo que allá no daban de comer, que cada uno comía lo que llevaba.

Era costumbre ésta añeja de mesones y posadas del siglo XVII.

Le llevaron a su cuarto y se tendió en la cama. A las doce fué a la fonda de Caballeros a comer, y después salió a dar una vuelta por el pueblo, que no conocía.

Paseó por dentro de la catedral, grande, hermosa, pero sin suma de detalles que regocijase el contemplarlos; vió la iglesia románica de San Esteban, que estaban restaurando; después se acercó al Alcázar.

Desde allá, cerca de la verja del jardín del Alcázar, se veían a lo lejos lomas y tierras amarillas y rojizas; Zamarramala sobre una ladera, unas cuantas casas mugrientas apiñadas y una torre; y la carretera blanca que subía el collado; a la derecha, la torre de la Lastrilla, y abajo, junto al río, en una gran hondonada llena de árboles macizos de follaje apretado, el ruinoso monasterio del Parral. Se le ocurrió a Fernando verlo; bajó por un camino, y después por sendas y vericuetos llegó a la carretera, que tenía a ambos lados álamos altísimos. Pasó el río por un puente que había cerca de una presa y de una fábrica de harinas.

Al lado de ésta, en un remanso del río, se bañaban unos cuantos chicos. Se acercó al monasterio; el pórtico estaba hecho trizas, sólo quedaba su parte baja. En el patio crecían viciosas hierbas: ortigas y yezgos en flor.

Hacía un calor pegajoso; rezongueaban los moscardones y las abejas; algunos lagartos amarillos corrían por entre las piedras.

Del claustro, por un pasillo, salió a un patio con corredores de una casa que debía estar adosada al monasterio; unas cuantas viejas negruzcas charlaban sentadas en el suelo; dos o tres dormían con la boca abierta. Salió del monasterio y bajó a una

XVI

On the following day, Schultze returned to El Paular. Fernando bade him farewell and departed for Segovia in a cart.

He arrived in Segovia in a suffocating heat. The sky was filled with clouds and emitted an unbearable heat; a heavy veil of haze was wavering over the dry, scorched fields.

The cart stopped at the Posada del Potro, where mule drivers and horse dealers were arriving and leaving.

Ossorio called to the landlady, a heavy woman, who told him that they did not serve any food there, and that each person ate whatever he had brought along.

This was a timeworn custom in the hostelries and wayside inns of the XVIIth century.

They showed him to his room and he stretched out on the bed. At twelve o'clock, he went over to the Fonda de Caballeros to eat and then went out to take a stroll through the town, which he didn't know very well.

He wandered about inside the Cathedral,[36] which was big and beautiful, but didn't have the totality of detail which could offer a delight to anyone contemplating it; he saw the Romanesque church of San Esteban,[37] which was being restored; then he made his way to the Alcázar.[38]

Standing there, near the iron grille of the garden of the Alcázar, you could see low hills and yellow and reddish tracts of land in the distance; Zamarramala, on a hillside, several squalid houses crammed together and a tower; and the white road that climbed up the hill; to the right, the tower of La Lastrilla,[39] and down below, alongside the river, in a large depression filled with massive trees with dense foliage, the ruins of the monastery of El Parral.[40] It occurred to Fernando that it would be nice to see it; so he made his way down a narrow road, then continued along footpaths and rugged trails until he reached the main road, which had very tall poplars growing on both sides. He crossed the river over a bridge that was located near a dam and a flourmill.

Beside it, in a backwater of the river, several young boys were bathing. He approached the monastery; the portico was falling to pieces and only the lower part remained. Pernicious weeds were growing in the courtyard: nettles and blooming danewort.

The heat was clammy; botflies and bees were buzzing around everywhere; some yellow lizards were running between the stones.

From the cloister, he walked along a passageway and came out into a patio with corridors belonging to a house that must have been pushed right up against the monastery; several very dark old women were chatting as they sat on the ground; two or three were sleeping with their mouths open. He went out of the monastery and descended to a poplar grove on the right bank of the river. The ground there was

alameda de la orilla derecha del río. El suelo allí estaba cubierto de hierba verde, florecda; el follaje de los árboles era tan espeso que ocultaba el cielo.

El río se desilzaba con rapidez; los álamos en flor de las márgenes dejaban caer sobre él un polvillo algodonoso que corría por la superficie lisa, verde y negruzca del agua en copos blancos.

Fernando se sentó en la alameda.

Enfrente, sobre la cintura de follaje verde de los árboles que rodeaban la ciudad, aparecían los bastiones de la muralla y encima las casas, de paredes obscuras y grises, y las espadañas de las iglesias. Como la corola sobre el cáliz verde veíase el pueblo, soberbia floración de piedra, y sus torres y sus pináculos se destacaban, perfilándose en el azul intenso y luminoso del horizonte.

Se oían las campanas de la Catedral que retumbaban, llamando a vísperas.

Empezó a llover; Fernando se encaminó hacia el pueblo; cruzó un puente, y tomando una senda, fué hasta pasar cerca de una iglesia gótica con una portada decadente. Llegó a la plaza; había dejado de llover. Se sentó en un café. A un lado, en otra mesa, había una tertulia de gente triste, viejos con caras melancólicas y expresión apagada echando el cuerpo hacia adelante, apoyados en los bastones; señoritillos de pueblo que cantaban canciones de zarzuela madrileña, con los ojos vacíos, sin expresión ni pensamiento; caras hoscas por costumbre, gente de mirada siniestra y hablar dulce.

En aquellos tipos se comprendía la enorme decadencia de una raza que no guardaba de su antigua energía más que gestos y ademanes, el cascarón de la gallardía y de la fuerza.

Se respiraba allí un pesado aburrimiento; las horas parecían más largas que en ninguna parte. Fernando se levantó preso de una invencible tristeza y comenzó a andar sin dirección fija. El pueblo, ancho, silencioso, sin habitantes, parecía muerto.

En una calle que desembocaba en la plaza vio una iglesia románica con un claustro exterior. Estaba pintada de amarillo; el pórtico tenía a los lados dos imágenes bizantinas, de esas figuras alargadas, espirituales que admiran y hacen sonreir al mismo tiempo, como si en su hierática postura y en su ademán petrificado hubiese tanto de exaltación mistica, como de alegría y de candidez.

El interior de la iglesia estaba revocado con una torpeza e ignorancia repulsivas.

Molduras de todas clases, ajedrezadas y losanjeadas; filigranas de los capiteles, grecas y adornos habían quedado ocultos bajo una capa de yeso.

Estaban desesterando la iglesia; reinaba en ella un desorden extravagante. Encima de un sepulcro de alabastro se veía un montón de sillas y de palos; sobre la mesa del altar habían dejado un fardo de alfombras arrolladas. Ossorio salió al claustro

covered with green grass, in full bloom; the foliage of the trees was so thick that it concealed the sky.

The river was gliding by swiftly; the flowering poplar trees on its banks kept dropping a fine, cotton-like dust onto it, which ran along the smooth, green and blackish surface of the water in white flakes.

Fernando sat down in the poplar grove.

Opposite him, the bastions of the ramparts appeared above the band of green foliage of the trees surrounding the city, and above it, you could see the houses with their dark, gray walls and the belfries of the churches. The town could be seen like the corolla over a green calyx, a splendid flowering of stone, and its towers and pinnacles were outlined in profile against the intense, luminous blue of the horizon.

You could hear the bells of the Cathedral resounding as they called the faithful to Vespers.

It started to rain; Fernando took the road toward town; he crossed over a bridge, walked along a path, continued till he passed quite close to a Gothic church with a decaying façade. He reached the square; it had stopped raining. He sat down in a café. Beside him, at another table, there was a social gathering of sad-looking people, old men with melancholy faces and listless expressions, bending their bodies forward as they leaned on their canes; young, spoiled young men with small-town ways, who were singing tunes from a Madrilenian *zarzuela*, their eyes vacant, without any expression or inner thought; faces that were sullen out of habit, people with sinister looks and mellifluous voices.

The extraordinary decadence of a race that maintained nothing of its former energy but the gestures and manners, the shell of its courage and strength, could be grasped in those individuals.[41]

You could breathe the overpowering tedium there; the hours seemed longer than anywhere else. Fernando was seized by an overwhelming sadness and he stood up and began to walk with no particular direction in mind. The town, spacious and silent, without inhabitants, seemed dead.

On a street that came out onto the square, he saw a Romanesque church with an outer cloister.[42] It was painted yellow; the portico had two Byzantine images at its sides, those elongated, spiritual figures that astonish you and make you smile at the same time, as if there were as much mystic exaltation in their hieratic postures and their petrified gestures as there was gaiety and candor.

The interior of the church was plastered over with repulsive clumsiness and ignorance.

Moldings of all types, checkered and lozenge-shaped designs, filigrees on the capitals, Grecian frets and adornments, had all been obliterated under a coating of plaster.

They were removing the mats from the floor of the church; extravagant disorder reigned everywhere. A pile of chairs and some sticks could be seen on top of an alabaster sepulcher; a bundle of rolled-up rugs had been left on top of the altar

y se entretuvo en contemplar los capiteles románicos: aquí se veían guerreros con espadas en la mano haciendo una matanza de chicos; allá luchas entre hombres y animales fantásticos; en otro lado, la perdiz con cabeza humana de tan extraña leyenda arqueológica.

Como ya no llovía, Fernando volvió a salir en dirección a las afueras del pueblo por un camino en cuesta que bajaba hacia el barranco por donde corre uno de los arroyos que bordean Segovia: el arroyo de los Clamores. El camino pasaba cerca de un convento ruinoso con el campanario ladeado. Desde el raso del convento partía una fila de cruces de piedra que iba subiendo por colinas verdes las unas, amarillentas y rapadas las otras, rotas o cortadas en algunas partes, mostrando sus entrañas sangrientas de ocre rojo. Cerca de las colinas se alargaba una muralla de tierra blanca llena de hendeduras horizontales.

Era un paisaje de una desolación profunda; las cruces de piedra se levantaban en los áridos campos, rígidas, severas; desde cierto punto no se veían más que tres. Fernando se detuvo allí. Componía con la imaginación el cuadro del Calvario. En la cruz de en medio, el Hombre Dios que desfallece, inclinando la cabeza dolorida sobre el desnudo hombro; a los lados, los ladrones luchando con la muerte, retorcidos en bárbara agonía; las santas mujeres que se van acercando lentamente a la cruz, vestidas con túnicas rojas y azules; los soldados romanos con sus cascos brillantes; el centurión, en brioso caballo, contemplando la ejecución, impasible, altivo y severo, y a lo lejos un camino tallado en roca, que sube serpeando por la montaña, y en la cumbre de ésta, rasgando el cielo con sus mil torres, la mística Jerusalén, la de los inefables sueños de los santos...

Le faltaban los medios de representación para fijar aquel sueño.

Fernando siguió bordeando el barranco hasta llegar a un pinar en donde se tendió en la hierba. Desde allí se dominaba la ciudad, Enfrente, tenía la catedral, altísima, amarillenta, de color de barro, con sus pináculos ennegrecidos; rodeada de casas parduzcas, más abajo corría la almenada muralla, desde el acueducto, que se veía únicamente por su parte alta, hasta un risco frontero, a aquel en el cual se levantaba el Alcázar. Se oía el ruido del arroyo que murmuraba en el fondo del barranco.

Se nublaba; de vez en cuando salía el sol e iluminaba todo con una luz de oro pálido.

Ossorio se levantó del suelo; a medida que andaba veía el barranco más macizo de follaje; el Alcázar, sin el aspecto de repintado que tenía al sol, se ensombrecía: semejaba un castillo de la Edad Media.

El arroyo de los Clamores, al acercarse al río, resonaba con mugido más poderoso.

table. Ossorio went out into the cloister and amused himself in the contemplation of the Romanesque capitals: here you could see warriors, their swords in their hands, engaged in the slaughter of children; there, struggles between men and fantastic animals; in another place, the partridge with a human head, from a very strange archaeological legend.

As it was no longer raining, Fernando went out again, heading toward the outskirts of town, along a sloping road which descended toward the ravine through which flowed one of the streams that run along the edge of Segovia: the Arroyo de los Clamores. The road passed close by a convent in ruins, with a bell tower leaning to one side. A row of stone crosses started up from the level ground of the convent and kept rising upward through the hills, some green, others yellowish and shaven away, broken or cut off in some places, revealing their blood-colored innards, red and ochre in color. Near the hills stretched a white earthen wall, filled with horizontal cracks.

The landscape was profoundly desolate; the stone crosses rose up, rigid and austere, in the arid fields; if you stood in a certain place, you could only see three of them. Fernando stopped right there. He was reconstructing the picture of Calvary with his imagination. On the cross in the middle, the Man-God, growing ever weaker, leaning his suffering head on his naked shoulder; on either side, the thieves, struggling with death, contorted in barbaric agony; the saintly women, dressed in red and blue tunics, who are slowly approaching the cross; the Roman soldiers in their shining helmets; the centurion, impassive, haughty and severe, contemplating the execution on his spirited horse; and in the distance, a road carved in rock, that winds its way upward through the mountain, and at its summit, rending the sky with its thousand towers, mystic Jerusalem, the place of the ineffable dreams of the saints...

All his resources of representation were inadequate to sustain that dream.

Fernando continued skirting the edge of the ravine, till he reached a pine grove, where he stretched out on the grass. From there, you had a commanding view of the city. Before him, he had the Cathedral, so very tall, yellowish, the color of clay, with its blackened pinnacles, surrounded by drab, grayish houses; farther down, ran the great crenelated wall, from the aqueduct, with only the upper part visible, to a crag that faced the one on which the Alcázar rose up into the sky. You could hear the sound of the stream as it murmured at the bottom of the ravine.

It was clouding up; from time to time, the sun would emerge and illuminate everything with a pale, golden light.

Ossorio got up from the ground; as he kept walking along, he could see that the ravine was more and more thick with foliage; the Alcázar, now that it didn't have the blurred appearance it had in the sunlight, was covered with shadows: it looked like a castle of the Middle Ages.

The Arroyo de los Clamores echoed with a very powerful roar as it drew closer to the river.

En una hendedura del monte, unas mujeres andrajosas charlaban sentadas en el suelo; una de ellas, barbuda, de ojos encarnados, tenía una sartén sobre una hoguera de astillas, que echaba un humo irrespirable.

Fernando pasó un puente; siguio por una carretera próxima a un convento y subió al descampado de una iglesia que le salió al camino, en donde había una cruz de piedra. Se sentó en el escalón de ésta.

La iglesia, que tenía en la puerta en azulejos escrito *Capilla de la Veracruz*, era románica y debía de ser muy antigua; tenía adosada una torre cuadrada, y en la parte de atrás tres ábsides pequeños.

Para Fernando, ofrecía más encanto que la contemplación de la capilla, la vista del pueblo que se destacaba sobre la masa verde de follaje, contorneándose, recortándose en el cielo gris de acero y de ópalo.

Había en aquel verdor que servía de pedestal a la ciudad, una infinita gradación de matices: el verde esmeralda de los álamos, el de sus ramas nuevas, más claro y más fresco, el sombrío de algunos pinos lejanos, y el amarillento de las lomas cubiertas de césped.

Era una sinfonía de tonos suaves, dulces; una gradación finísima que se perdía y terminaba en la faja azulada del horizonte.

El pueblo entero parecía brotar de un bosque, con sus casas amarillentas, ictéricas, de maderaje al descubierto, de tejados viejos, roñosos como manchas de sangre coagulada, y sus casas nuevas con blancos paredones de mampostería, persianas verdes y tejados rojizos de color de ladrillo recién hecho.

Veíanse a espaldas del pueblo lomas calvas, bajas colinas, blancas, de ocre, violáceas, de siena...alguna que otra mancha roja.

El camino, de un color violeta, subía hacia Zamarramala; pasaban por él hombres y mujeres, ellas con el refajo de color sobre la cabeza, ellos llevando del ronzal las caballerías.

A la puesta del sol, el cielo se despejó; nubes fundidas al rojo blanco aparecieron en el poniente.

Sobre la incandescencia de las nubes heridas por el sol, se alargaban otras de plomo, inmóviles, extrañas. Era un cielo heroico; hacia el lado de la noche el horizonte tenía un matiz verde espléndido.

Los pináculos de la catedral parecían cipreses de algún cementerio.

Obscureció más; comenzaron a brillar los faroles en el pueblo.

El verde de los chopos y de los álamos se hizo negruzco; el de las lomas, cubiertas de césped, se matizó de un tono rojizo al reflejar las nubes incendiadas del horizonte, las lomas, rapadas y calvas, tomaron un tinte blanquecino, cadavérico.

Sonaron campanas en una iglesia; le contestaron al poco tiempo las de la Catedral con el retumbar de las suyas.

In a cleft in the mountain, some tattered women were chatting as they sat on the ground; one of them, with a slight beard and bloodshot eyes, was holding a frying pan over a fire of wooden chips, and it gave off a smoke that was unfit to be breathed.

Fernando crossed a bridge; he continued along a road that ran close to a convent and ascended to the open ground of a church that suddenly appeared before him, where there was a stone cross. He sat down on its footstone.

The church, which had *Capilla de la Veracruz* inscribed on the door in glazed tiles, was Romanesque and must have been very old; pushed right up against it was a square tower, and there were three small apses in the rear part.

For Fernando, the sight of the town, that stood out, with its contours outlining themselves against the steel-gray and opal sky, over the green mass of foliage, offered a greater attraction than the contemplation of the chapel.

In all that verdure, that served as a pedestal for the city, there was an infinite gradation of shades: the emerald green of the poplars, the lighter and fresher green of the new branches, the somber green of some distant pine trees and the yellowish green of the grass-covered hills.

It was a symphony of soft, mild tones, an extremely fine gradation that was lost as it ended in the bluish band of the horizon.

The entire town seemed to spring up from out of a forest, with its jaundice-yellow houses, with their open framework, old roofs that were rust-colored like stains of coagulated blood, and its new houses, with white, heavy walls of rubble masonry, green, slatted shutters and reddish roofs the color of recently-made brick.

In back of the city, you could see barren hillocks, low hills, white, ochre-colored, purplish, sienna-colored..., a red patch of color here and there.

The violet-colored road rose up toward Zamarramala;[44] men and women kept passing along it, the women, with colored underskirts worn over their heads, the men, leading their mounts by the halters.

When the sun set, the sky cleared; clouds, blended to a reddish-white, now appeared in the west.

Other clouds, leaden-colored, motionless and strange, stretched out over the incandescence of the clouds that were pierced by the sun. It was an heroic sky; toward the night side, the horizon took on a splendid green tint.

The pinnacles of the Cathedral resembled cypresses in some cemetery.

It grew even darker and the streetlamps in the town began to shine.

The green of the black poplars and the white poplars turned blackish; the green of the grass-covered hillocks blended to a reddish tone as it reflected the glowing clouds on the horizon; the hillocks, smoothly shaven away and barren, took on a whitish, cadaverous tint.

The bells of a church resounded; in a little while, those of the Cathedral replied with a resonant sound of their own.

Era la hora del *Angelus...*
El Alcázar parecía, sobre su risco afilado, el castillo de proa de un barco gigantesco...
Por la noche, en la puerta de la posada del Potro, un arriero joven cantaba malagueñas, acompañándose con la guitarra:

Cuando yo era criminal
en los montes de Toledo,
lo primero que robé
fueron unos ojos negros.

Y al rasguear de la guitarra se oían canciones lánguidas, de muerte, de una tristeza enfermiza, o jotas brutales, sangrientas, repulsivas como la hoja brillante de una navaja.

XVII

A la mañana siguiente, de madrugada, salió Fernando de casa. Había en el aire matinal del pueblo, además de su frescura, un olorcillo a pajar muy agradable. Pasó por la calle de San Francisco a preguntar en la posada de Vizcaínos por un arriero llamado Polentinos, que iba a Madrid en su carro; y como la posada de Vizcaínos estuviese cerrada, siguió andando hasta la plaza del Azoguejo.

Volvió al poco rato calle arriba, entró en la posada y preguntó por Polentinos. Estaba ya preparando el carro para salir.

Nicolás Polentinos era un hombre bajo, fornido, de cara ancha, con un cuello como un toro, los ojos grises, los labios gruesos, belfos. Llevaba un sombrero charro de tela, de esos sombreros que, puestos sobre una cabeza redonda, parecen el planeta Saturno rodeado de su anillo. Vestía traje pardo y botas hasta media pierna.

—¿Es usted el señor Polentinos?
— Para servirle.
— Me han dicho en la posada del Potro que va usted a Madrid en carro.
— Sí, señor.
— ¿Quiere usted llevarme?
— ¿Y por qué no? ¿Es un capricho?
— Sí.
— Pues no hay inconveniente. Yo salgo ahora mismo.
— Bueno. Ya arreglaremos lo del precio.
— Cuando usted quiera.
—¿Por dónde iremos?
— Pues de aquí a la Granja, y por la venta de Navecerrada a salir hacia Torrelodones, y de allá, pasando por Las Rozas y Aravaca, a Madrid. Es posible

It was the hour of the *Angelus*.
The Alcázar, on its sharp-pointed crag, seemed to be the forecastle of some gigantic ship...
That night, in the doorway of the Posada del Potro, a young mule driver sang malagueñas, accompanying himself with a guitar:

When I was a criminal
in the mountains of Toledo,
The first thing I stole
were a pair of dark eyes.

And to the strumming of the guitar, you could hear languid songs about death, that had a sickly sadness about them, or *jotas*, brutal, bloodthirsty, and repulsive, like the gleaming blade of a clasp knife.

XVII

The following morning, at daybreak, Fernando left the inn. In addition to the coolness, there was a slight, very pleasant smell of hay in the early morning air of the town. He went by the Calle de San Francisco to ask at the Posada de Vizcaínos for a mule driver named Polentinos, who was going to Madrid in his cart; as the Posada de Vizcaínos was closed, he kept walking till he reached the Plaza del Azoguejo.

A short while later, he came back up the street, went into the inn and asked for Polentinos. He was already preparing the cart for his departure.

Nicolás Polentinos was a short, robust man, with a wide face, a neck like a bull, gray eyes and thick, blobber lips. He was wearing a wide-brimmed felt hat, one of those hats that, when worn on a round head, look very much like the planet Saturn surrounded by its rings. He was wearing a brown suit and knee-high boots.

"Are you Señor Polentinos?"
"At your service."
"They told me at the Posada del Potro that you're going to Madrid by cart."
"Yes, sir."
"Would you mind taking me?"
"And why not? Is it just a whim?"
"Yes."
"Well, it'll be no trouble at all. I'm leaving right now."
"Good. We can arrange the price later."
"Whenever you wish."
"Which way will we go?"
"Well, from here to La Granja, then by the Venta de Navacerrada,[43] so we come out near Torrelodones;[44] and from there, we'll pass through Las Rozas[45] and

que yo no entre en Madrid – añadió Polentinos –; tengo que ir a Illescas a ver a una hija.

–¿Y por qué no va usted en tren?

–¿Para qué? No tengo prisa.

–¿Cuántas leguas tenemos de aquí a Madrid?

– Trece o catorce.

–¿Y de Madrid a Illescas?

– Unas seis leguas.

Pusieron unas tablas en el carro, y, sentado en ellas Fernando, con los pies dentro de la bolsa del carro, y Polentinos en el varal, bajaron por la calle de San Francisco hasta tomar la carretera.

– Va a hacer mucho calor – dijo Polentinos.

–¿Sí?

–¡Vaya!

– Maldito sea. Y eso será malo para el campo, ¿eh?

– En esta época, pues, ya no le hace daño al campo.

– Y la cosecha, ¿qué tal es? – preguntó Fernando por entrar en conversación.

– Por aquí no es como pensábamos en el mes de mayo y hasta mediados de junio, por causa de las muchas lluvias y fuertes vientos, que nos tumbó el pan criado en tierra fuerte antes de salir la espiga, y no ha podido criarse el grano; y a lo que no le ha sucedido esto, los aires lo han arrebatado.

Era el hablar de Polentinos cachazudo y sentencioso.

Parecía un hombre que no se podía extrañar de nada.

A poco de salir vieron una cuadrilla de segadores que venían por un camino entre las mieses.

–¿Estos serán gallegos? – preguntó Ossorio.

– Sí.

– Qué vida más horrible la de esta gente.

–¡Bah! Todas las vidas son malas – dijo Polentinos.

– Pero la del que sufre es peor que la del que goza.

–¡Gozar! ¿Y quién es el que goza en la vida?

– Mucha gente. Creo yo...

–¿Usted lo cree?...

– Yo, sí. ¿Usted no?

– Le diré a usted. Y no es que yo quiera enseñarle a usted nada, porque usted ha estudiado y yo soy un rústico; pero, también a mi modo, he visto y observado algo, y creo, la verdad, que cuanto más se tiene más se desea, y nunca se encuentra uno satisfecho.

– Sí, eso es cierto.

– Es que la vida – prosiguió el señor Nicolás –, después de todo, no es nada. Al

Aravaca,[46] and on into Madrid. It's possible that I may not even go into Madrid," added Polentinos. "I have to go to Illescas[47] to see one of my daughters."
"Then why don't you go by train?"
"What for? I'm in no hurry."
"How many leagues is it from here to Madrid?"
"Thirteen or fourteen."
"And from Madrid to Illescas?"
"Some six leagues."
They placed some boards in the cart and Fernando sat down on them, his feet inside the matting that hung down below the cart, and with Polentinos seated on the side pole, they rode down the Calle de San Francisco till they got to the main road.
"It's going to be very hot," said Polentinos.
"Really?"
"You can bet on it."
"That's rotten luck. And that will probably be bad for the crops, won't it?"
"Actually, at this time of the year, it doesn't harm the crop any more."
"And how is the harvest?" asked Fernando just to make conversation.
"Around here, it isn't what we thought it would be during the month of May and even the middle of June, and that's because of the heavy rains and the strong winds that knocked over the wheat they were growing in the hard soil, even before the spikes could come out, and so the grain hasn't been able to grow; and where this didn't happen, the winds took it all away anyway."
Polentinos's manner of speaking was phlegmatic and sententious.
He seemed to be a man who couldn't be surprised by anything.
Shortly after departing, they saw a gang of harvesters coming along a road through the grain fields.
"Can those people be Galicians?" Ossorio asked.
"Yes."
"What a terrible life those people must lead."
"Nonsense! All lives are bad," said Polentinos.
"But the one who suffers is worse off than the one who enjoys."
"Enjoyment! And who of us has any enjoyment in this life?"
"Many people. I believe..."
"You really believe so...?"
"I do. Don't you?"
"I'll tell you. And it isn't that I want to teach you anything, because you have studied a lot and I'm just a country bumpkin; but in my own way, I've also seen and observed things, and to tell the truth, I believe that the more one has, the more one wants, and one never feels satisfied."
"Yes, that's true."
"The fact of the matter is," Señor Nicolás continued, "that life, after all, is

fin y al cabo, lo mismo da ser pobre que ser rico; ¿quién sabe? puede ser que valga más ser pobre.

 –¿Cree usted? – pregunto con suave ironía Ossorio, y se tendió sobre las maderas del carro, apoyó la cabeza en un saco y se puso a contemplar el fondo del toldo.

 – Pues qué, ¿los ricos no tienen penas? Yo, algunas veces, cuando vengo a Segovia de Sepúlveda, que es donde vivo, y voy al teatro, arriba, al paraíso, suelo pensar: Y qué bien deben de encontrarse las señoras y los caballeros de los palcos, y después se me ocurre que también ellos tienen sus penas como nosotros.

 – Pero, por si acaso, todo el mundo quiere ser rico, buen amigo.

 – Sí, es verdad, porque todo el mundo quiere gozar de los placeres, y siempre se desea algo. A mí me pasó lo mismo; hasta los veinticinco años fui pastor, y en mi pequeñez y en mi miseria, pues ya ve usted, vivía bien. De vez en cuando tenía tres o cuatro duros para gastarlos; pero se me metió en la cabeza que había de hacer dinero, y empecé a comprar ganado aquí y a venderlo allá; primero en Sepúlveda y en Segovia, después en Valencia. en Sevilla y en Barcelona, y ahora mi hijo vende ganado ya en Francia; tengo mi casa y algunos miles de duros ahorrados, y no crea usted que soy más feliz que antes. Hay muchos disgustos y muchas tristezas.

 – Sí, ¿eh?

 – Vaya. Mire usted, cuando se casaron mis hijas me hice yo este cargo. Si les doy su parte es posible que se olviden de mí; pero si no se la doy es posible que lleguen a encontrar que tardo en morirme. Hice las reparticiones, y a cada hija su parte. Bueno, pues por unas cercas que entraron en la repartición, y porque a un arrendador le perdonaba yo veinticinco o cuarenta reales al año, este yerno de Illescas, ¿sabe usted lo que hace?, pues nada; despide al que estaba en la cerca, a un viejo que era un buen pagador y amigo mío, y pone allí a uno que quiso ser verdugo y ha sido carcelero en la villa de Santa María de Nieva. Figúrese usted qué hombre será el tal, que el viejo al tener que dejar la cerca le advierte que el fruto de los huertecillos, unas judías y unas patatas son suyas, como la burra que dejó en el corral, y el hombre que quiso ser verdugo le arranca toda la fruta y todas las hortalizas. Le escribo esto a mi yerno, y dice él que tiene razón, y mi hija se pone a su favor en esta cuestión y en todas. Y la otra hija, lo mismo. Después de haber hecho lo que he podido por ellas. La única que me quiere es la menor, pero la pobre es desgraciada.

 – Pues ¿qué la pasa?

 – Es jorobada. Tuve de niña una enfermedad.

nothing at all. In the long run, it's just the same whether you're poor or whether you're rich; who knows?, it may be that it's better to be poor."

"Do you really believe so?" Ossorio asked with mild irony, and he stretched out on the boards in the cart, leaned his head on a sack and started contemplating the bottom of the canvas awning over the cart.

"Well, what do you think, that the rich don't have any troubles? When I come to Segovia from Sepúlveda,[48] which is where I live, I sometimes go to the theater, way up in the top gallery, and I often think to myself, 'What a nice feeling those ladies and gentlemen must have as they sit down there in their reserved boxes,' and then it occurs to me that they too have their troubles, just as we do."

"But, my dear friend, it so happens that everyone wants to be rich."

"Yes, that's true, because everyone wants to enjoy pleasures, and there's always something we want to have. The same thing happened to me; until I was twenty-five years old, I was a shepherd, and in all my insignificance and misery, well to tell the truth, I lived well. Sometimes I would have three or four *duros* to spend; but I got it into my head that I had to make money, and I began to buy cattle here and sell them there; first in Sepúlveda and in Segovia, later in Valencia, in Sevilla and in Barcelona, and now, my son even sells cattle in France; I have my house and I have thousands of *duros* saved up, and don't believe I am any happier than I was before. There are many misfortunes and many sad things."

"Oh, really?"

"You can be sure of it. Look here, when my daughters got married, I came to this reckoning. If I give them their share now, it's possible they'll forget all about me; but if I don't give it to them, it's possible they may end up finding that I'm taking too long to die. So I divided it all up, and each daughter got her share. Well, all because of a few fenced in pieces of land that were part of the distribution and just because I waived the rent of twenty-five or forty *reales* per year for one of my tenants, this son-in-law of mine from Illescas, do you know what he goes and does? Well, no more than this: he gets rid of the man who was on this fenced in property, an old man who paid on time and was a friend of mine, and he sets up someone else there, who once tried to be an executioner and served as a jailer in the village of Santa María de Nieva. Just imagine what kind of man such a fellow must be if, when the old man, when he has to leave the property, lets him know that the produce from the small vegetable gardens, a few green beans and some potatoes, as well as the she-ass he left in the barnyard, belong to him; and the man, who tried to be an executioner, takes away all the fruit and vegetables from him. I write this to my son-in-law and he says that the man is right, and my daughter agrees with him, on this issue, as well as on all issues. And it's the same with the other daughter. After I did all that I could for them. The only one who loves me is the youngest, but the poor thing leads a wretched life."

"Why, what is the matter with her?"

"She's a hunchback. She had some illness as a child."

—¿Y vive con usted?
— No; ahora la tengo en Illescas. Voy a recogerla. La pobrecilla... Nada, que la vida es una mala broma.
— Es que usted, señor Nicolás, y dispénseme usted que se lo diga, es usted insaciable.
— Y todos los hombres lo son, créalo usted, y como no se pueden saciar todos los deseos, porque el hombre es como un gavilán, pues vale más no saciar ninguno. ¿Usted no cree que se puede vivir en una casa de locos encerrado y ser más feliz con las ilusiones que tenga uno, que no siendo rico y viviendo en un palacio?
— Sí. Es posible.
— Claro. Si la vida no es más que una ilusión. Cada uno ve el mundo a su manera. Uno lo ve de color de rosa, y otro negro. ¡Vaya usted a saber cómo será! Es posible que no sea también más que una mentira, una figuración nuestra, de todos.

Y el señor Nicolás hizo una mueca de desdén con sus labios gruesos y belfos y siguió hablando de la inutilidad del trabajo, de la inutilidad de la vida, de lo grande y niveladora que es la muerte.

Fernando miraba con asombro a aquel rey Lear de la Mancha, que había repartido su fortuna entre sus hijas y había obtenido como resultado el olvido y el desdén de ellas. La palabra del ganadero le recordaba el espíritu ascético de los místicos y de los artistas castellanos; espíritu anárquico cristiano, lleno de soberbias y de humildades, de austeridad y de libertinaje de espíritu.

XVIII

Llegaron antes del mediodía a La Granja y comieron los dos en una casa de comidas. Por la tarde fueron a ver los jardines, que en el filosófico arriero no hicieron impresión alguna.

A Fernando, todas aquellas fuentes de gusto francés; aquellas estatuas de bronce de los Padres ríos, con las barbas rizadas; aquellas imitaciones de Grecia, pasadas por el filtro de Versalles; aquellas esfinges de cinc blanqueado, peinadas a lo Madame Pompadour, le parecieron completamente repulsivas, de un gusto barroco, antipático y sin gracia.

Salieron de La Granja y por la noche llegaron a un pueblo; durmieron en la posada, y a la mañana siguiente, antes de que se hiciese de día, aparejaron las mulas, las engancharon y salieron del pueblo.

La luz eléctrica brillaba en los aleros de las casuchas negruzcas, débil y descolorida; la luna iluminaba el valle y plateaba el vaho que salía de la tierra húmeda.

"And she lives with you?"

"No; I keep her in Illescas now. I'm going to pick her up. The poor little thing... There's no doubt about it, life is a bad joke."

"The trouble with you, Señor Nicolás, and forgive me for saying this to you, is that you are insatiable."

"And so are all men, believe me, and since all our desires can't be satisfied, because man is like a sparrow hawk, it's better not to satisfy any of them. Don't you think that one can live, locked up in a madhouse, and be happier there with all his illusions than if he were rich and living in a palace?"

"Yes. It's possible."

"Of course. Because life is nothing but an illusion. Each person sees the world in his own way. One sees it pink-colored and another sees it black. Just go and try to find out what it's really like! It's possible that it may be nothing more than a lie, a figment of our imagination, of all of us."

And Señor Nicolás made a disdainful grimace with his thick blobber lips and went on speaking of the futility of work, of the uselessness of life, of how Death is so powerful and puts us all at the same level.

Fernando looked with astonishment at that King Lear of La Mancha, who had distributed his fortune among his daughters and had obtained oblivion and their disdain as a result. The words of the cattle dealer reminded him of the ascetic spirit of the mystics and of the Castilian artists, an anarchic, Christian spirit, filled with presumptuous and humble feeling at the same time, with austerity and spiritual libertinism.

XVIII

They arrived at La Granja before midday and the two men had a meal in a cheap eating house. In the afternoon, they went to see the gardens, which made absolutely no impression whatsoever on the philosophical mule driver.

For Fernando, all those fountains in the French style, those bronze statues of river-gods, with their curly beards, those imitations of the Greek filtered through Versailles, those sphinxes of blanched zinc, with their hair done à la Mme. Pompadour, all seemed utterly repulsive, baroque in taste, unpleasant and with no charm whatsoever.

They departed from La Granja and came to a town at nightfall; they slept at the inn, and the following morning, even before daybreak, they harnessed the mules and hitched them to the cart and left town.

The electric lights were shining, weak and lifeless, on the eaves of the dark-looking hovels; the moon illuminated the valley and tinted the vapor rising from the humid earth to a silvery hue.

En el campo obscuro rebrillaban como el azogue charcos y regueros que corrían como culebrillas.

En un redil, veíase un rebaño de ovejas blanquinegras, y cubiertos con un gran manta los pastores, a quienes se veía rebullir debajo...

El camino trazaba una curva. Desde lejos se veía el pueblo con sus casas en montón y las paredes blancas por la luz de la luna.

Pasando por Torrelodones y Las Rozas, llegaron a Aravaca por la tarde, y de aquí por la Puerta de Hierro, decidieron seguir por el paseo de los Melancólicos, que pasa por entre el Campo del Moro y la Casa de Campo, sin parar en Madrid.

El día era domingo. A la caída de la tarde, entre dos luces, llegaron a la Puerta de Hierro. Hacía un calor sofocante...

En el cielo, hacia El Pardo, se veía una faja rojiza de color de cobre.

En la Casa de Campo, por encima de la tapia blanca, aparecían masas de follaje, que en sus bordes se destacaban sobre el cielo con las ramitas de los árboles como las filigranas esculpidas en las piedras de una catedral.

En el río, sin agua, con dos o tres hilillos negruzcos, se veían casetas hechas de esparto y se levantaba de allí una peste del cieno imposible de aguantar.

En los merenderos de la Bombilla se notaba un movimiento y una algarabía grandes.

El camino estaba lleno de polvo. Cuando llegaron en el carro, cerca de la estación del Norte, había anochecido.

No se veía Madrid, envuelto como estaba en una nube de polvo. A largos trechos brillaban los faroles rodeados de un nimbo luminoso.

La gente tornaba de pasear, de divertirse, de creer, por lo menos, que se había divertido, pasando la tarde aprisionado en un traje de domingo, bailando al compás de las notas chillonas de un organillo.

En los tranvías, hombres, mujeres y chicos, sudorosos, llenos de polvo, luchaban a empujones, a brazo partido, para entrar y ocupar el interior o las plataformas de los coches, y cuando éstos se ponían en movimiento, rebosantes de carne, se perdían de vista pronto en la gasa de calor y de polvo que llenaba el aire.

La atmósfera estaba encalmada, asfixiante; la multitud se atropellaba, gritaba, se injuriaba, quizá sintiendo los nervios irritados por el calor.

Aquel anochecer, lleno de vaho, de polvo, de gritos, de mal olor; con el cielo bajo, pesado, asfixiante, vagamente rojizo; aquella atmósfera, que se mascaba al respirar; aquella gente endomingada, que subía en grupos hacia el pueblo, daba una sensación abrumadora, aplastante, de molestia desesperada, de malestar, de verdadera repulsión.

In the dark countryside, still pools and irrigation ditches that raced along like small snakes, sparkled like quicksilver.

You could see a flock of whitish-black sheep in a sheepfold, and you could see the shepherds, covered by a large blanket, stirring beneath it...

The road turned in a curve. From a distance, you could see the town with its houses all bunched together and its walls white in the moonlight.

After passing through Torrelodones and Las Rozas, they reached Aravaca in the afternoon, and from here, by way of the Puerta de Hierro, they decided to continue along the Paseo de los Melancólicos, which passes between the Campo del Moro and the Casa de Campo, without stopping in Madrid.

It was Sunday. As the afternoon came to an end, they reached the Puerta de Hierro at twilight. The heat was stifling.

A reddish band, the color of copper, could be seen in the sky toward El Pardo.

In the Casa de Campo, masses of foliage appeared above the white earthen wall, and they were outlined against the sky at the edges, with the slender tree branches, like filigrees sculptured on the stones of a cathedral.

You could see huts made of esparto grass in the dried up river, with only two or three blackish trickles, and a stench of muck rose up from it that was all but impossible to bear.

A great deal of movement and uproar could be noted in the roadside eating places of La Bombilla.

The road was covered with dust. When they drew near the Estación del Norte in their cart, night had fallen.

You couldn't see Madrid, wrapped as it was in a cloud of dust. The widely separated street lamps were shining, surrounded by a luminous halo.

The people were returning from their strolling, from their diversions, believing, at the least, that they had enjoyed themselves, after spending the afternoon imprisoned in their Sunday clothes, dancing to the beat of the shrill notes of a barrel organ.

On the street cars, men, women and children, sweating, covered with dust, were struggling and shoving at close quarters, trying to board and occupy the interior or the platforms of the cars, and when these were set in motion, overflowing with flesh, they were quickly lost from sight in the veil of heat and dust that filled the air.

The atmosphere was overheated, asphyxiating; the masses of people kept pushing one another, shouting and insulting one another, perhaps because they felt their nerves irritated by the heat.

That hour of twilight, filled with the fumes, dust, shouting and bad odors, with the low, heavy sky, stifling and vaguely reddish; that atmosphere that you almost had to chew in order to breathe it; all those people dressed in their Sunday best, going up toward the city in groups, gave one an oppressive, overwhelming sensation, filled with a desperate feeling of discomfort, malaise and true repulsion.

XIX

−¿Es Illescas? – preguntó Fernando.
– Sí, es Illescas – contestó Polentinos.
Se veía desde lejos el Hospital de la Caridad y la alta torre de la Asunción, recortándose sobre el cielo azul blanquecino luminoso, y a los pies de la torre un montón pardusco de tejados.

Un camino polvoriento, con álamos raquíticos, subía hacia la iglesia.

Tomaron por la alameda y fueron acercándose al pueblo, que parecía dormido profundamente bajo un sol ardiente, abrasador; las puertas de las casas estaban cerradas; sus paredes reflejaban una luz deslumbradora, cruda, que cegaba; entre los hierros de las rejas, terminadas en la parte alta por cruces, brillaban rojos geranios y claveles.

Atontados por el calor, que caía como un manto de plomo, siguieron andando hasta llegar a casa de la hija de Polentinos.

Entraron en la casa.

Fernando pudo notar la frialdad con que recibieron al señor Nicolás, excepto la jorobadita, que le abrazó con efusión.

El yerno miró a Fernando con desconfianza, y éste dijo que se iba. Como habían comido ya en la casa, decidieron el señor Nicolás y Ossorio ir a la fonda del pueblo, y enviaron a una muchacha a que encargara la comida.

Fernando, con el pretexto de que quería ver la iglesia, salió de la casa, diciéndole a Polentinos que le esperaría en la fonda.

Fernando salió, y al ver el Hospital de la Caridad abierto, entró en la iglesia; pasó primero por un patio con árboles.

La iglesia estaba desierta. Se sentó en un banco a descansar. Enfrente, en el altar mayor, ardían dos lamparillas de aceite: una muy alta, otra junto al suelo. Había un silencio de esos que parecen sonoros; del patio llegaba a veces el piar de los pájaros; al paso de alguna carreta por la calle, retemblaba el suelo. De la bóveda central de la iglesia colgaban, suspendidas por barras de hierro, dos lámparas grandes, envueltas en lienzos blancos, como dos lagrimones helados; de vez en cuando crujía, por el calor, alguna madera.

Fernando se acercó a la gran verja central, pintarrajeada, plataresca, que dividía el templo, y vió en el fondo unas viejas vestidas de negro que andaban de un lado a otro. Salió de allá, y en el patio se encontró con Polentinos.

Entraron a comer en la confitería, que era al mismo tiempo fonda. El comedor era un cuartucho empapelado con papel amarillo, con unas banquetas de percalina roja.

XIX

"Is this Illescas?" Fernando asked.

"Yes, it's Illescas," answered Polentinos.

From afar, you could see the Hospital de la Caridad[49] and the lofty tower of La Asunción,[50] outlined against the luminous, whitish-blue sky, and you could make out a brownish heap of roofs at the foot of the tower.

A dusty road, with stunted poplars, rose up toward the church.

They moved along the lane lined with poplars, and kept drawing closer to the town, which seemed sound asleep under the blazing, burning sun; the doors of the houses were closed; their walls reflected a dazzling, harsh, blinding light; red geraniums and carnations were glistening between the iron bars of the grillwork, which terminated in crosses at the upper part.

Overcome by the heat, which fell on them like a leaden mantle, they continued on their way until they reached the house where Polentinos's daughter was staying.

They went into the house.

Fernando could notice the coolness with which Señor Nicolás was received, with the exception of the little hunchback, who embraced him effusively.

The son-in-law looked at Fernando mistrustfully and the latter said that he was leaving. Since those in the house had already eaten, Señor Nicolás and Ossorio decided to go to the restaurant in town and they sent a girl ahead to order their meal.

Under the pretext that he wanted to see the church, Fernando left the house, telling Polentinos to wait for him at the restaurant.

Fernando left and when he saw that the Hospital de la Caridad was open, he went into its church; he first passed through a courtyard with trees.

The church was deserted. He sat down on a bench to rest. Opposite him, on the high altar, two small oil lamps were burning: one very high up, the other quite close to the floor. The silence prevailing there was of the kind that seemed sonorous; the sound of birds chirping would occasionally come in from the courtyard; the floor would shake whenever a cart would pass along the street. Two large lamps, wrapped in white linen, like two enormous, frozen tears, were hanging, suspended from iron bars, from the central vault of the church; from time to time, a floor board would creak because of the heat.

Fernando approached the large center grille, which was daubed with paint and plateresque in style, and which divided the temple, and he saw some old women dressed in black at the rear, walking from one side to the other. He left and came across Polentinos in the courtyard.

They went into the confectioner's, which also served as a restaurant, to have something to eat. The dining area was a small, humble room with yellow wallpaper and several long benches covered with red percaline.

Por entre las cortinas se veía un trozo de tapia blanca que reverberaba por el sol. Una nube de moscas revolteaban en el aire y se depositaban en masas negras sobre la mesa.

Polentinos hablaba con tristeza de su hija la jorobadita, ¡que era más buena la pobre...!

La infeliz comprendía que no se podría casar, y todo su ideal era ir a Segovia y poner allí una cacharrería. Se despidieron afectuosamente Polentinos y Fernando.

—¿Qué va usted a hacer? – le dijo Polentinos.
— Me voy a Toledo.
— Tiene usted más de treinta kilómetros desde aquí.
— No me importa.
—¿Pero va usted a ir a pie?
— Sí.

Salió a eso de las cuatro.

El paisaje de los alrededores era triste, llano. Estaban en los campos trillando y aventando. Salió del pueblo por una alameda raquítica de árboles secos.

Al acercarse a la estación vió pasar el tren; en los andenes no había nadie.

Comenzó a andar; se veían lomas blancas, trigales rojizos, olivos polvorientos; el suelo se unía con el horizonte por una línea recta.

Bajo el cielo de un azul intenso, turbado por vapores blancos como salidos de un horno, se ensanchaba la tierra, una tierra blanca calcinada por el sol, y luego campos de trigo, y campos de trigo de una entonación gris parduzca, que se extendían hasta el límite del horizonte; a lo lejos, alguna torre se levantaba junto a un pueblo; se veían los olivos en los cerros, alineados como soldados en formación, llenos de polvo; alguno que otro chaparro, alguno que otro viñedo polvoriento...

Y a medida que avanzaba la tarde calurosa, el cielo iba quedándose más blanco.

Sentíase allí una solidificación del reposo, algo inconmovible, que no pudiera admitir ni la posibilidad del movimiento. En lo alto de una loma, una recua de mulas tristes, cansadas, pasaban a lo lejos levantando nubes de polvo; el arriero, montado encima de una de las caballerías, se destacaba agrandado en el cielo rojizo del crepúsculo, como gigante de edad prehistórica que cabalgara sobre un megaterio.

El aire era cada vez más pesado, más quieto.

En algunas partes estaban segando.

Eran de una melancolía terrible aquellas lomas amarillas, de una amarillez cruda calcárea, y la ondulación de los altos trigos.

Pensar que un hombre tenía que ir segando todo aquello con un sol de plano, daba ganas, sólo por eso, de huir de una tierra en donde el sol cegaba, en donde los ojos no podían descansar un momento contemplando algo verde, algo jugoso,

Through the curtains, you could see a section of white, earthen wall, which reverberated in the sunlight. A swarm of flies flitted around in the air and settled on the table in black masses.

Polentinos spoke sadly about his daughter, the little hunchback, who was so good, the poor thing...!

The unfortunate girl understood that she couldn't get married, and her great ambition was to go to Segovia and set up a crockery shop there. Polentinos and Fernando took leave of one another with warm affection.

"What are you going to do?" Polentinos said to him.

"I'm going off to Toledo."

"It's more than thirty kilometers from here."

"I don't really care."

"But do you really intend to go there on foot?"

"Yes."

He started out at about four o'clock.

The landscape all around was sad and flat. They were threshing and winnowing in the fields. He left town along a sorry-looking poplar-lined lane with withered trees.

As he approached the station, he saw the train pass by; there was nobody on the platforms.

He began to walk; you could see low, white hillocks, reddish-colored wheat fields, dust-covered olive trees; the ground joined with the horizon in a straight line.

Under the intensely blue sky, stirred up by white vapors like those that pour out of an oven, the land broadened, a white land that was scorched by the sun, and beyond it, wheat fields and more wheat fields, drab grayish-brown in tone, and they extended to the very limits of the horizon; in the distance, an occasional tower would rise up alongside a town; you could see olive trees on the hills, lined up like soldiers in formation, covered with dust; here and there, a holm oak, every so often, a dusty vineyard...

And as the hot afternoon wore on, the sky kept turning even whiter.

One could feel a solidification of quiescence there, something unyielding, that couldn't even admit the possibility of movement. A drove of sad, weary mules was passing by at the top of a hill in the distance, raising clouds of dust; you could see the mule driver, astride one of his mounts, outlined and magnified against the reddish twilight sky, like a giant from a prehistoric age, mounted on a megathere.

The air was getting heavier and heavier, ever more still.

In some places they were reaping the wheat.

Those low, yellow hills, of a yellow that was harsh and calcareous, and the undulation of the tall wheat, seemed so terribly melancholy.

To think that a man had to go on reaping all that under a sun that kept shining straight down upon him, made you feel, for that reason alone, like running away from a land where the sun was blinding, where the eyes couldn't rest for even a

en donde la tierra era blanca, y blancos también y polvorientos los olivos y las vides...

Fernando se acercó a un pueblo rodeado de lomas y hondonadas amarillas, ya segadas.

En uno de aquellos campos pastaban toros blancos y negros.

El pueblo se destacaba con su iglesia de ladrillo y unas cuantas tapias y casas blancas que parecían huesos calcinados por un sol de fuego.

Veíanse las eras cubiertas de parvas doradas; trillaban, subidos sobre los trillos arrastrados por caballejos, los chicos, derechos, sin caerse, gallardos como romanos en un carro guerrero, haciendo evolucionar sus caballos con mil vueltas; a los lados de las eras se amontonaban las gavillas en las hacinas, y, a lo lejos, se secaba el trigo en las amarillentos tresnales.

Por las sendas, entre rastrojos, pasaban siluetas de hombres y de mujeres denegridos; venían por el camino carretas cargadas hasta el tope de paja cortada.

Nubes de polvo formaban torbellinos en el aire encalmado, inmóvil, que vibraba en los oídos por el calor.

Las piedras blanquecinas, las tierras grises, casi incoloras, vomitaban fuego.

Fernando, con los ojos doloridos y turbados por la luz, miraba entornando los párpados. Le parecía el paisaje un lugar de suplicio, quemado por un sol de infierno.

Le picaban los ojos, estornudaba con el olor de la paja seca, y se le llenaba de lágrimas la cara.

Un rebaño de ovejas grises, también polvorientas. se desparramaba por unos rastrojos.

Fue obscureciendo.

Fernando dejó atrás el pueblo.

A media noche, en un lugarón tétrico, de paredes blanqueadas, se detuvo a descansar; y al día siguiente, al querer levantarse, se encontró con que no podía abrir los ojos, que tenía fiebre y le golpeaba la sangre en la garganta.

Pasó así diez días enfermo en un cuarto obscuro, viendo hornos, bosques incendiados, terribles irradiaciones luminosas.

A los diez días, todavía enfermo, con los ojos vendados, en un carricoche, al amanecer, salió para Toledo.

XX

Llegó a la imperial ciudad por la mañana, a las ocho.

Entró por el puente de Alcántara.

El día era fresco, hermoso, tranquilo. El cielo azul, limpio, con nubes

moment in the contemplation of something green, something succulent, where the land was white and the olive trees and grapevines also white and dusty...

Fernando approached a town surrounded by low, yellow hills and hollows, which had already been reaped.

Several white and black bulls were grazing in one of those fields.

The town stood out with its brick church and a number of earthen walls and white houses that looked like bones burned dry by a fiery sun.

You could see the threshing floors covered with golden heaps of grain yet to be threshed; young boys were threshing, standing upright, without ever falling, as gallant as Romans in a war chariot, standing on the threshing machines, which were drawn by nags, and they were making their horses turn round and round in endless evolutions; the sheaves of wheat were being piled up in stacks along the sides of the threshing floors, and in the distance, the wheat was drying, heaped in yellowish shocks.

The silhouettes of blackened men and women were passing along the paths between the stubble; carts were coming along the road, loaded to the very top with cut straw.

Clouds of dust kept forming whirlwinds in the still, motionless air, which vibrated in one's ears because of the heat.

The whitish stones, the almost colorless, gray earth, were spewing fire.

Fernando, his eyes aching and disturbed by the light, kept looking around with half-closed eyelids. The landscape seemed to him like a place of torture, scorched by an infernal sun.

His eyes were stinging, he kept sneezing from the odor of dry straw and his face was covered with tears.

A flock of gray sheep, also covered with dust, was spreading out amid the grain stubble.

It was growing dark.

Fernando left the town behind him.

At midnight, he stopped to rest in a large, gloomy town with whitewashed walls; on the following day, when he tried to get up, he found that he was unable to open his eyes, that he had a fever and the blood was pounding in his throat.

He spent ten days like that, sick, in a darkened room, seeing ovens, burning forests, terrifying, luminous irradiations.

After ten days, although he was still sick, he departed for Toledo at daybreak in a canvas-covered cart, with a bandage over his eyes.

XX

He reached the imperial city at eight o'clock in the morning.

He came in by the Puente de Alcántara.

The day was cool, beautiful and calm. The sky was blue, limpid, filled with small,

pequeñas, redondeadas, negruzcas en su centro, adornadas con un reborde blanco reverberante.

El cochero le recomendó una casa de huéspedes de la plaza de las Capuchinas que él conocía; pero Fernando prefería ir a un mesón.

El cochero paró el coche en una posada a la entrada de Zocodover, enfrente de un convento.

Era el mesón modernizado, con luz eléctrica, pero simpático en su género. Un pasillo en cuesta, con el suelo recubierto de cascajo, conducía a un patio grande, limpio y bien blanqueado, con techumbre de cristalería en forma de linterna.

En el patio se abrían varias puertas: la de las cuadras, la de la cocina y otras, y desde él subía la escalera para los pisos altos de la casa. Era el patio el centro de la posada; allí estaba la artesa para lavar la ropa, el aljibe con su pila para que bebiese el ganado; allí aparejaban los arrieros los caballos y las mulas, y allí se hacía la tertulia en el verano al anochecer.

En aquella hora el patio estaba desierto; llamó Ossorio varias veces, y apareció el posadero, hombre bajo y regordete, que abrió una de las puertas, la del comedor, e hizo pasar a Fernando a un cuarto largo, estrecho, con una mesa también larga en medio, dos pequeñas a los lados, y en el fondo dos armarios grandes y pesadotes, llenos de vajilla pintarrajeada de Talavera.

Desayunóse Fernando y salió a Zocodover.

La luz del sol le produjo un efecto de dolor en los ojos, y algo mareado se sentó en un banco.

Una turba de chiquillos famélicos se acercó a él.

– ¿Quiere usted ver la Catedral, San Juan de los Reyes, la Sinagoga?
– No, no quiero ver nada.
– Una buena fonda, un intérprete.
– No, nada.
– *Musiú, musiú,* deme usted un *sú* – gritaban otros chiquillos.

Fernando volvió a la posada y se acostó pronto. Al día siguiente se despertó con que no podía abrir los ojos de inflamados que nuevamente los tenía, y se quedó en la cama.

La gente del mesón le dejaba solo, sin cuidarse más que de llevarle la comida.

En aquel estado era un flujo de pensamientos el que llegaba a su cerebro.

De optimista pensaba que aquella enfermedad, los días horribles que estaba pasando, podían ser dirigidos para él por el destino, con un móvil bueno, a fin de que se mejorase su espíritu. Después, como no admitía una voluntad superior que dirigiera los destinos de los hombres, pensaba que aunque las desgracias y las

rounded clouds, somewhat blackish at the core, decorated with white, reverberant borders.

The cart driver recommended a boarding house with which he was familiar on the Plaza de las Capuchinas; but Fernando preferred to go to an inn.

The driver stopped the vehicle at an inn right at the entrance to the Plaza de Zocodover, opposite a convent.

The inn had been modernized with electric lighting, but it was quite pleasant in its own way. A sloping passageway, with its surface covered with broken gravel, led to a large, clean and nicely whitewashed courtyard, with glasswork roofing in an open lantern style.

Several doors opened into the courtyard: the ones to the stables, one to the kitchen and other places, and a stairway ascended from there to the upper floors of the house. The courtyard was the very heart of the inn; the trough where the clothes were washed was located there, and a cistern with its basin, where the cattle could drink; the mule drivers would harness their horses and mules there, and they would hold their social get-togethers there at nightfall during the summer.

The courtyard was deserted at that hour; Ossorio called out several times and the innkeeper, a short, chubby man, finally appeared, opened one of the doors, the one to the dining room, and had Fernando go into a long, narrow room, with an equally long table in the middle, two smaller ones at the sides, and two large, very ponderous cupboards in the back filled with gaudily bedaubed Talavera dishware.

Fernando had breakfast and went out onto the Zocodover.

The sunlight produced a painful effect on his eyes, and feeling somewhat dizzy, he sat down on a bench.

A horde of famished-looking little children came running over to him.

"Would you like to see the Cathedral,[51] San Juan de los Reyes,[52] the Synagogue?"[53]

"No, I don't want to see anything."

"A good restaurant, an interpreter."

"No, nothing."

"*Musiú, musiú,* give me a *su,*" some other youngsters kept shouting.

Fernando returned to the inn immediately. When he awoke the next day, he found that he couldn't open his eyes, because they had become inflamed again, and so he stayed in bed.

The people at the inn left him alone, taking only the responsibility for bringing him his meals.

While he was in this state, a flux of thoughts kept reaching his brain.

From an optimistic point of view, he felt that his illness and the horrible days he was enduring might be directed against him by destiny, with a favorable motive, in order to improve the state of his spirit. Afterwards, since he was unwilling to admit the possibility that a superior will might be directing the destinies of men, he thought that, although the misfortunes and maladies in themselves had no moral

enfermedades en sí no tuviesen un objeto moral, el individuo podía dárselos, puesto que los acontecimientos no tienen más valor que aquel que se les quiere conceder.

Otras veces hubiera deseado dormir. Pasar toda la vida durmiendo con un sueño agradable, ¡qué felicidad! ¡Y si el sueño no tuviera ensueños! Entonces, aún felicidad mayor. Pero como el sueño está preñado de vida, porque en las honduras de esa muerte diaria se vive sin conciencia de que se vive, al despertar Ossorio y al no hacer gasto de su energía ni de su fuerza, esta energía se transformaba en su cerebro en un ir y venir de ideas, de pensamientos, de proyectos, en un continuo oleaje de cuestiones, que salían enredadas como las cerezas cuando se tira del rabito de una de ellas.

Decía, por ejemplo, inconscientemente, en voz alta, quejándose:

– ¡Ay, qué vida ésta!

Y el cerebro, automáticamente, hacía el comentario.

– ¿Qué es la vida? ¿Qué es vivir? ¿Moverse, ver, o el movimiento anímico que produce el sentir? Indubablemente es esto: una huella en el alma, una estela en el espíritu, y entonces, ¿qué importa que las causas de esta huella, de esta estela, vengan del mundo de adentro o del mundo de afuera? Además, el mundo de afuera no existe; tiene la realidad que yo le quiero dar. Y, sin embargo, ¡qué vida ésta más asquerosa!

XXI

Cuando comenzó a sentirse mejor, compró unas antiparras negras que le tapaban por completo los ojos, y con ellas puestas paseaba todos los días en Zocodover, a la sombra, entre empleados, cadetes y comerciantes de la ciudad; veía a los chiquillos que llegaban por el Miradero, voceando los periódicos de Madrid, y como no le interesaban absolutamente nada las noticias que pudieran tener, no los compraba.

El primer día que se encontró ya bien, decidió marcharse de la posada e ir a la casa de huéspedes que le había recomendado el hombre en compañía del cual fué a Toledo. Se levantó de madrugada, como casi todos los días, se desayunó con un bartolillo que compró en una tienda de allí cerca, salió a Zocodover, y callejeando, llegó a la plaza de las Capuchinas, cerca de la cual le habían indicado que se hallaba la casa de huéspedes; la encontró, pero estaba cerrada. Volvió de aquí para allá, a fin de matar el tiempo, hasta encontrarse en una plaza en donde se veía una iglesia grandona y churrigueresca con dos torres a los lados, portada con tres puertas y una gradería, en la que estaban sentadas una porción de mujeres y de chicos.

object, the individual was capable of giving this to them, since events have no other meaning than that which we wish to concede to them.

At other times, he would have simply wanted to sleep. To spend his whole life sleeping in a most pleasant slumber. What a joy! And if only that sleep would have no dreams! Then, even greater joy. But since sleep is impregnated with life, because we live without realizing that we are living within the recesses of that daily death, when Ossorio would wake up, without having used up any of his energy or vital force, this very energy would be transformed within his brain into a continuous movement back and forth of ideas, thoughts and projects, in a continuous flow of questions that came out all entangled, like cherries, when you pull one out of the bunch by the stem.

As an example, he would often say aloud unconsciously, as a kind of complaint:

"Oh, what a life this is!"

And his brain would automatically make this commentary:

"What is life? What is living? Moving, seeing, or is it the psychic movement produced by this sensation? It is undoubtedly this: an impression left upon a soul, a trail left upon the spirit, and if this is so, then what difference does it make if the causes of this impression or of this trail come from the world within or the world without? Besides, the world outside doesn't exist; it only has the reality that I want to give to it. And nevertheless, what a disgusting life this is!"

XXI

When he started feeling better, he bought a pair of dark glasses that completely covered his eyes, and he would stroll around the Zocodover every day, wearing them and staying in the shade, among the clerks, the military cadets and the merchants of the city; he would see the small boys as they came along the Miradero, hawking the Madrid newspapers, and since he had absolutely no interest whatsoever in the news they might contain, he would never buy them.

The first day that he felt completely well, he decided to leave the inn and go to the boarding house recommended to him by the man in whose company he had come to Toledo. He arose at sunrise, as he did almost every day, made a breakfast of a small, triangular cream tart he purchased in a store nearby, went out onto the Zocodover and walked along the streets until he reached the Plaza de las Capuchinas, near where he had been informed the boarding house was located; he found it, but it was closed. He walked in one direction or the other in order to kill some time, until he found himself in a square where you could see a rather large, Churrigueresque[54] church with two towers at the sides and a façade with three doors and a flight of steps, upon which a number of women and children were sitting.

Entre aquellas mujeres había algunas que llevaban refajos y mantos de bayeta de unos colores desconocidos en el mundo de la civilización, de un tono tan jugoso, tan caliente, tan vivo, que Fernando pensó que sólo allí pudo el Greco vestir sus figuras con los paños espléndidos con que las vistió.

En medio de la plaza había una fuente y un jardinillo con bancos. En uno de éstos se sentó Fernando.

En la acera de una callejuela en cuesta, que partía de la plaza, se veía una fila de cántaros sosteniéndose amigablemente, como buenos camaradas; unos hacían el efecto de haberse dormido sobre el hombro de los compañeros; otros, apoyándose en la pared, tan gordos y tripudos, parecían señores calmosos y escépticos, completamente convencidos de la inestabilidad de las cosas humanas.

A un lado de la plaza, por encima de un tejado, asomaba la gallarda torre de la Catedral.

Ossorio miraba a los cántaros y a las personas sentadas en las gradas de la iglesia, preguntándose qué esperarían unos y otras.

En esto, vino un hombre con un látigo en la mano, se acercó a la fuente, hizo una serie de manipulaciones con unos bramantes y unas cañas, y al poco rato el agua empezó a manar.

Entonces el hombre restalló el látigo en el aire.

Inmediatamente, como una bandada de gorriones, toda la gente apostada en las gradas bajó a la plaza; cogieron mujeres y chicos los cántaros en la acera de la callejuela, y se acercaron con ellos a la fuente.

Después de contemplar el espectáculo, pensó Fernando que estaría ya abierta la casa.

A pesar de que sabía que estaba cerca de las Capuchinas, de la calle de las Tendillas y de otra que pasa por Santa Leocadia y Santo Domingo el Antiguo, se perdió a pocos metros de distancia y tuvo que dar muchas vueltas para encontrarla.

Entró Fernando en el obscuro zaguán, llamó la campanilla, y abierta la puerta, pasó a un patio, no muy grande, con el suelo de baldosa encarnada.

En el centro había unos cuantos *evonymus*, y en un ángulo un aljibe. En uno de los lados estaba la puerta del piso bajo, que daba a una galería estrecha o pasillo con ventanas, en una de las cuales se sujetaba la cuerda que al tirar de ella abría la puerta del zaguán; del pasillo partía la escalera, que era clara, con una gran linterna de cristales en el techo, que dejaba pasar la claridad del sol.

En el piso alto vivía la patrona; el bajo lo tenía alquilado a otra familia.

La casa era grande y bastante obscura, pues aunque daba a una calle y tenía un patio en medio, estaba rodeada de casas más altas que no la dejaban recibir el sol.

Among those women, there were several wearing baize skirts and shawls in colors unknown to the civilized world, of shades so moist, so warm, so vivid in tone, that Fernando concluded that only in such a place could El Greco have been able to dress his figures in the splendid fabrics with which he clothed them.

There was a fountain in the middle of the square and a small garden with benches. Fernando sat down on one of them.

Along the sidewalk of a sloping side-street, which started at the square, you could see a row of earthen pitchers, amicably supporting one another like good comrades; some gave you the impression that they'd fallen asleep on the shoulders of their companions; others, leaning against the wall, so fat and pot-bellied, looked like tranquil, skeptical gentlemen, completely convinced of the instability of human affairs.

On one side of the square, the graceful tower of the Cathedral peered out over a roof.

Ossorio looked at the pitchers and at the people sitting on the steps of the church and wondered what hopes the one group or the other might have.

Just then, a man with a whip in his hand came on the scene, went over to the fountain, made a series of manipulations with some hemp twine and cane sticks, and in a very short while, the water began to flow.

Then the man snapped his whip in the air.

Immediately, all the people who had taken a position on the steps came down into the square like a flock of sparrows; women and children grabbed the pitchers on the sidewalk of the side street and went over to the fountain with them.

After contemplating the spectacle, Fernando concluded that the house would probably be open by now.

In spite of the fact that he knew he was near Las Capuchinas, the Calle de las Tendillas and another one that passes by the Church of Santa Leocadia and of Santo Domingo el Antiguo,[55] he had walked only a few meters before he realized he was lost and he had to walk round and round before he could find the house.

Fernando went into the darkened vestibule, rang the bell and, when the door was opened, he made his way into a patio which wasn't very large and which was paved with incarnadine tiles.

There were several spindle trees in the middle and a water tank in a corner. On one side was the door to the lower floor, which led into a narrow gallery or corridor with windows, on one of which was fastened the rope which, when pulled, opened the door to the vestibule; the stairway ran up from the corridor and was very bright, with a large, glass lantern roof which let the sunlight pass through.

The landlady lived on the upper floor; the lower floor was rented to another family.

The house was large and quite dark, because, even though it faced the street and had a patio in the middle, it was surrounded by taller houses and was unable to receive the sunlight.

Desde que se entraba, olíase a una planta rústica, quemada, que recordaba los olores de las sacristías.

Fernando preguntó en el piso bajo por la casa de doña Antonia, y le indicaron que subiera al principal.

Allí se encontró con la patrona, una mujer gruesa, frescota, de unos treinta y cinco a cuarenta años, de cara redonda y pálida, ojos negros, voluptuosos, y modo de hablar un tanto libre.

Su marido era empleado en el Ayuntamiento, un hombre bajito, charlatán y movedizo, al que vió salir Fernando para ir a la oficina.

No tuvieron que discutir ni condiciones ni precio, porque a Ossorio le pareció todo muy barato; y por la tarde abandonó la posada y fue a instalarse en la casa nueva.

El cuarto que ocupó Fernando era un cuarto largo, para entrar en el cual había que subir unos escalones; estaba blanqueado y tenía más alto el techo que las demás habitaciones de la casa. El balcón, de gran saliente, daba a una callejuela estrechísima, y parecía que se podía dar la mano con el vecino de enfrente, un cura viejo, alto y escuálido, que por las tardes salía a una azotea pequeña, y paseando de un lado a otro y rezando, se pasaba las horas muertas.

En el cuarto había una cómoda grande, y sobre ella, en medio, una Virgen del Pilar de yeso, y a los lados, fanales de cristal, y dentro de ellos, ramilletes hechos de conchitas pequeñas pegadas unas a otras, imitando margaritas, rosas, siemprevivas, abiertas o en capullo, en medio de un follaje espeso, formado por hojas de papel verde, descoloridas por la acción del tiempo.

El cuarto de Fernando estaba frente a una escalera de ladrillo que conducía a la cocina y a otros dos cuartos grandes, y que seguía después hasta terminar en un terrado.

La cama era de varias tablas sostenidas por dos bancos pintados de verde.

Indudablemente doña Antonia, viendo a Fernando tan preocupado y distraído, le había puesto en el peor cuarto de la casa.

Comía Ossorio casi siempre solo, mucho más temprano que los demás huéspedes.

En aquellas horas no solía haber en el comedor más que una vieja ciega y chocha, que tenía un aspecto de bruja de Goya, con la cara llena de arrugas y la barba de pelos, que hacía muecas y se reía hablando a un niño recién nacido que llevaba en brazos; la vieja solía venir con una muchachita, hija de la casa, de aspecto monjil, aunque muy sonriente, que muchas veces le servía la comida a Fernando.

Se sentaba la abuelita en una silla, la muchacha traía el niño, se lo entregaba a la vieja, y ésta pasaba horas y horas con él.

¡Qué de cosas se dirían sin hablarse aquellas dos almas! – pensaba Fernando – y

As soon as you came in, you noticed that it had a smell like a rustic, burnt plant, reminding you of the odors of sacristies.

Fernando inquired on the lower floor where Doña Antonia's lived and he was told to go up to the second floor.

There he met the landlady, a heavy, buxom woman who was about thirty-five or forty years old, with a pale, round face, black, voluptuous eyes and a somewhat outspoken way of talking.

Her husband was a clerk at the City Hall and was a smallish, garrulous and fidgety man, whom Fernando saw just as he was leaving to go to the office.

They didn't find it necessary to discuss either conditions or price, because it all seemed quite cheap to Ossorio, and he abandoned the inn that afternoon and came over and settled in the new house.

The room Fernando occupied was a long room, and you had to go up a few steps to go inside; it was painted white and had a higher ceiling than the other rooms in the house. The balcony, which projected quite far, faced a very narrow little side street and it seemed that you could almost shake hands with the neighbor living across the way, an old priest, tall and emaciated, who would come out onto a small flat roof every afternoon and while away the lifeless hours walking back and forth praying.

There was a large bureau in his room and a Virgen del Pilar made of plaster on top of it, in the middle, as well as some glass bell jars on both sides, and inside them, small bouquets made of little shells, all stuck together, imitations of daisies, roses, immortelles, some open and others budding, all surrounded by thick green foliage formed by leaves made of green paper, discolored by the ravages of time.

Fernando's room faced a brick staircase that led to the kitchen and to two other large rooms, and it continued up till it came out on a roof terrace.

The bed was made of several boards supported by two benches painted green.

There was little doubt that Doña Antonia, when she saw that Fernando seemed so preoccupied and distracted, had given him the worst room in the house.

Ossorio would almost invariably eat alone, much earlier than all the other guests.

At that hour, there would be nobody in the dining room but a blind, doddering old woman who had the appearance of a witch from a work of Goya; her face was filled with wrinkles and her chin covered with hairs, and she would make faces and laugh to herself as she spoke to a recently-born child she held in her arms; the old lady would come in with a sweet young girl, the daughter of the house, who had the appearance of a nun, though she was always smiling, and who would often serve Fernando his meal.

The kindly old grandmother used to sit down in a chair and the girl would bring the baby, hand him over to the old woman, and she would spend hours and hours with him.

What remarkable things those two souls must have said to one another without

si efectivamente las almas primitivas son las que mejor pueden comunicarse sin la palabra, ¡qué de cosas no se dirían aquéllas!
Un día, mientras estaba comiendo, Fernando habló con la vieja:
– ¿Es usted de Toledo? – le preguntó.
– No. Soy de Sonseca.
– ¿Pero vive usted aquí?
– Unas veces aquí con mi hijo, otras con mi hija en Sonseca.
– ¿Esa criatura es su nieto?
– Sí, señor.
Entró la muchachita, la hija de la patrona, que servía algunas veces la mesa, y, dirigiéndose a la anciana, murmuró:
– Abuela, ¡a ver si no pone usted así al chico, que lo va a tirar al suelo!
– ¿Es su abuela? – preguntó Ossorio a la muchacha.
– Sí. Es la madre de mi padre.
– ¿Madre del dueño de la casa? Entonces ¿tendrá muchos años?
– Figúrese usted – contestó riendo –. Yo no sé los que tiene. Se lo voy a preguntar. Abuela, ¿cuántos años tiene usted?
– Más de setenta...y más de ochenta.
– No sabe – dijo la muchacha, volviéndose a reír. Al reírse, sus ojos estaban llenos de guiños cándidos, enseñaba los dientecillos blancos y, a veces, entornaba los ojos, que entonces casi no se veían.
– ¿Y usted cuántos años tiene? – le preguntó Fernando.
– ¿Yo? Diez y ocho.
– Tiene usted un hermano, ¿verdad?
– Un hermano y una hermana.
– A la hermana no la he visto.
– Está en el colegio de Doncellas Nobles.
– ¡Caramba! Y el hermano ¿estudia?
– Sí. Estudió para cura.
– ¿Y ha dejado la carrera?
– No le gustaba. Mi padre quería que mi hermano fuese cura y nosotras monjas; pero no queremos.
– Usted se querrá casar, claro.
– Sí; cuando tenga más años.
– Pero ya tiene usted edad de casarse. ¡A los diez y ocho años!
– ¡Bah! A los diez y ocho años dice mi madre que sólo se casan las locas que no saben ni el arreglo de la casa.
– Pero usted ya lo sabe.
– Yo, sí; pero, ¿para qué me voy a casar tan pronto? – Y miró a Fernando con una expresión de alegría, de dulzura, de serenidad.

speaking a single word!– Fernando would think– and if primitive souls are truly those which can best communicate without the use of words, what wonderful things those two must have told one another!
   One day, while he was eating, Fernando spoke to the old woman:
   "Are you from Toledo?" he asked her.
   "No, I'm from Sonseca."
   "But you live here?"
   "Sometimes I'm here with my son; other times with my daughter in Sonseca."
   "That little baby is your grandchild?"
   "Yes, indeed."
   The landlady's daughter, the young girl who occasionally served at the table, came in, and, addressing the old woman, murmured:
   "Grandmother, you ought not to hold the baby this way; if you do, you're liable to drop him on the floor!"
   "Is she your grandmother?" Ossorio asked the girl.
   "Yes, she's my father's mother."
   "The landlord's mother? Then she must be very old?"
   "You can say so," she answered with a laugh, "I don't know how old she is. I'm going to ask her. Grandmother, how old are you?"
   "Over seventy...and over eighty."
   "She doesn't know," the girl said laughing again. As she laughed, her eyes winked candidly, she revealed her small, white teeth and she half-closed her eyes every so often and then you could hardly see them.
   "And how about you, how old are you?" Fernando asked her.
   "Me? Eighteen."
   "You have a brother, don't you?"
   "A brother and a sister."
   "I haven't seen your sister."
   "She's away at the Colegio de Doncellas Nobles."
   "You don't say! And your brother, is he a student too?"
   "Yes. He studied to be a priest."
   "And he gave up studying for that?"
   "He didn't like it. My father wanted my brother to be a priest and for us to be nuns, but we don't want to."
   "You'll probably want to get married, of course."
   "Yes, when I'm older."
   "But you're old enough to get married now. At eighteen years of age!"
   "Nonsense! My mother says that only silly girls get married when they're eighteen, when they don't even know how to take care of a home."
   "But you already know that."
   "Yes, I do, but why should I get married so soon?" And she looked at Fernando with an expression full of happiness, sweetness and serenity.

Para la muchacha aquella, lo único importante para casarse era saber el arreglo de la casa.

Era interesante la niña; sobre todo, muy mona. Se llamaba Adela.

A primera vista no parecía una preciosidad; pero fijándose bien en ella, iban notándose perfecciones. Su cabeza rubia, de tez muy blanca, hubiera podido ser de un ángel de Rubens, algo anémico.

El cuerpo, a través del vestido, daba la impresión de ser blanco, linfático, perezoso en sus movimientos.

Era la chica hacendosa por gusto, y se pasaba el día haciendo trabajos y diligencias, porque no le gustaba estar sin hacer nada.

No conocía las calles de Toledo. Se había pasado la vida sin salir de casa.

La mayor parte de los días, de las Capuchinas a casa y de casa a las Capuchinas, era su único paseo. De vez en cuando, algún día de fiesta, iba con su padre por el camino de la Fábrica, bajaban por cerca de la Diputación, tomaban por el presidio antiguo, a salir al paseo de Merchan, y volvían a casa. Esta era su vida.

Quizá aquel aislamiento le permitía tener un carácter alegre.

Fernando, que había notado que comiendo temprano le servía la comida Adela, porque la criada vieja solía estar ocupada, iba a casa antes de las doce. En la comida hablaba con la abuela de Sonseca y con Adela, y para disimularse el placer que esto le daba, se decía a sí mismo seriamente:

– Aprendo en las palabras de la vieja y de la niña la sencillez y la piedad.

XXII

A las dos o tres semanas de estar en casa de doña Antonia, comenzó Fernando a conocer y a intimar con los demás huéspedes.

Había dos curas en la casa, un muchacho teniente y un registrador de un pueblo inmediato, con su madre.

De los dos curas, el uno, don Manuel, tenía una cara ceñuda y sombría, abultada, de torpes facciones. Era hombre de unos cuarenta y cinco años, de cuerpo alto y robusto, de pocas palabras, y éstas con frecuencia acres y mal humoradas; parecía estar distraído siempre.

La patrona, en el seno de la confianza, suponía que estaba enamorado. Quizá

For that girl, the only important requirement for marriage was to know how to take care of a home.

The young girl was quite interesting and especially attractive. Her name was Adela.

At first sight, she didn't much look like a beauty, but if you looked at her carefully, you began to notice her perfections. Her blond head and her very white complexion could have belonged to a somewhat anemic angel by Rubens.

Under her dress, her body left an impression of being white, lymphatic and indolent in its movements.

The girl was hard working for the very pleasure of it, and she spent the day doing small tasks and running errands because she didn't like to be inactive.

She hardly knew the streets of Toledo. She had spent her life without leaving the house.

Most days, her only walk was from Paseo de las Capuchinas to her house and from her house to Las Capuchinas. From time to time, on some holiday, she would go for a walk with her father along the Camino de la Fábrica de Armas; they would go down somewhere near the Provincial Council Building, take the road by the old prison and come out on the Paseo de Merchan, and then return home. This was her life.

Perhaps it was that isolation that permitted her to have such a cheerful disposition.

Fernando, who had noticed that Adela would serve him his meal when he ate early, because the old housemaid was generally busy, started going to the house before twelve. During the meal, he would speak to the grandmother from Sonseca and to Adela, and in order to conceal the pleasure this would bring him, he would say to himself quite seriously:

"I am learning simplicity and compassion in the words of the old woman and the young girl."

XXII

After he had been in Doña Antonia's house for two or three weeks, Fernando began to get acquainted and become friendlier with the other guests.

In the house, there were two priests, a young fellow who was a lieutenant, and a recorder of deeds in a nearby town, with his mother.

Of the two priests, the one, Don Manuel, had a face that was frowning, somber and bulky, with coarse features. He was a man about forty-five years of age, with a tall, robust body; he was sparing with words and these were frequently biting and ill humored; he always seemed to be distracted.

The landlady, in the very strictest confidence, implied that he was in love.

estaba enamorado de alguien o de algo, porque se hallaba continuamente fuera de la realidad. Sin embargo, no tenía nada de místico.

Se contaba en la casa que, aunque cumplía siempre su misión escrupulosamente, no era muy celoso. Además, no confesaba nunca.

– Un día me tiene usted que confesar, don Manuel – le dijo la patrona.

– No, señora – le contestó don Manuel con violencia– ; no tengo ganas de ensuciarme el alma.

El otro cura, don Pedro Nuño, era todo lo contrario de don Manuel: amable, sonriente, aficionado a la arqueología, pero aficionado con verdadero furor.

Ossorio fue a visitar una vez a este cura, y viendo que le acogía muy bien, después de comer echaba con él un párrafo, tocando de paso todos los puntos humanos y divinos de la religión y de la ciencia.

El despacho de don Pedro Nuño daba por dos ventanas a la calle y era el mejor de la casa.

El suelo era de una combinación de ladrillos encarnados y blancos; en las paredes había un zócalo de azulejos árabes.

Guardaba don Pedro en su gabinete un monetario completo de monedas romanas que había coleccionado en Tarragona, y una porción de libros viejos encuadernados en pergamino.

A pesar de su afición por las cosas artísticas, tenía una noción clara, aunque un tanto desdeñosa, de las actuales. Sin darse cuenta, era un volteriano. La idea de arte había substituído en él toda idea religiosa.

Si le dejaba hablar, y habiaba con mucha gracia, con acento andaluz, duro, aspirando mucho las haches, se delizaba hasta considerar la Iglesia como la gran institución protectora de las artes y de las ciencias, y se permitía bromas sobre las cosas más santas. Si se trataba de atacar las ideas religiosas, que él debía tener, aunque no las tenía, entonces se le hubiera tomado por un fanático completo.

Más que la irreligiosidad – que en algunos no le molestaba por completo, el *Diccionario Filosófico* de Voltaire lo citaba mucho en sus escritos – , le indignaban algunas cosas nuevas; el neocristianismo de Tolstoi, por ejemplo, del cual tenía noticias por algunas críticas de revistas, le sacaba de quicio.

Para él, aquel noble señor ruso era un infatuado y un vanidoso que tenía talento, él no lo negaba; pero que el zar debía de obligarle a callar, metiéndolo en una casa de locos.

El mismo odio sentía por los autores del Norte, a quien no conocía, y le molestaba que periodistas y críticos españoles, en las revistas y en los periódicos supieran que aquellos rusos y noruegos y dinamarqueses valieran más que los franceses, que los españoles e italianos.

Las mixtificaciones y exageraciones graciosas de los historiadores, le encantaban.

Perhaps he was in love with someone or something, because he always seemed to be beyond reality. Nevertheless, there was nothing mystical about him.

It was rumored around the house that, although he fulfilled his duties quite scrupulously, he wasn't very zealous. Besides that, he never heard Confession.

"One of these days, you're going to have to hear my Confession, Don Manuel," the landlady said to him.

"No, señora," Don Manuel replied violently. "I have no desire to besmirch my soul."

The other priest, Don Pedro Nuño, was just the opposite of Don Manuel: amiable, smiling, an enthusiast of archaeology, but one who took to it with true fervor.

Ossorio once went to visit the priest and when he saw that he was well received, he would chat with him after dinner, in the course of which they touched on all the human and divine aspects of both religion and science.

Don Pedro Nuño's study had two windows that faced the street and was the best room in the house.

The floor was a combination of red and white tiles and there was a skirting board of Arabic glazed tiles around the walls.

In his display case, Don Pedro kept a complete collection of Roman coins that he had gathered together in Tarragona, and a number of old books bound in vellum.

In spite of his fondness for artistic things, he had a clear, though somewhat disdainful attitude toward present-day things. Without realizing it, he was a Voltairian. His conception of art had supplanted all religious ideas in him.

If you let him speak, and he spoke with considerable charm, with a harsh Andalusian accent, aspirating the sound h exaggeratedly, he would inadvertently go so far as to consider the Church the great protective institution of the arts and sciences, and he would permit himself jests concerning the most sacred of things. But if you tried to attack the religious ideas, which he was supposed to have, though he didn't really have them, then you would have taken him for a complete fanatic.

Even more than being irreligious – which absolutely didn't distress him in certain individuals, for he would frequently cite Voltaire's *Philosophical Dictionary* in his own writing – certain new ideas would fill him with indignation; the neo-Christianity of Tolstoy, for example, concerning which he had gained information from a number of critiques published in magazines, drove him frantic.

For him, that Russian nobleman was a self-opinionated and vain individual, with a great deal of talent, he didn't deny that; but, nonetheless, the czar ought to have forced him into silence by putting him in a madhouse.

He felt the same hatred for the authors from the North, whom he really didn't know, and it disturbed him that Spanish journalists and critics, in their magazines and their newspapers, should maintain that those Russians, Norwegians and Danes had more merit than the French, the Spanish and the Italians.

He was delighted by the hoaxes and witty exaggerations of the historians.

Uno de los párrafos que le leyó a Fernando el primer día, sonriendo maliciosamente, era éste, de una *Historia de Toledo*, que estaba consultando:

"Vió que para albergar a la gran Casa de Austria en la ostentación magnífica que se porta, era su Real Alcázar nido estrecho; y así en lo más salutífero de su territorio, y adonde con más anchura pudiese ostentar su Corte, le fabricó palacio. De suerte, que Madrid es como nuevo Alcázar de Toledo, un arrabal, un barrio, un retiro suyo, donde, como a desahogarse, se ha retirado toda la Grandeza y Nobleza de Toledo."

De los otros huéspedes, el militar joven se pasaba la mayor parte del día en la Academia, en donde estaba destinado.

El otro, el registrador, don Teodoro, era un hombre humilde y triste. Su padre, minero de Cartagena, había prometido con cierto fervor religioso en algún momento de mala suerte que si una mina le daba resultado dotaría un asilo o una casa de beneficencia.

Efectivamente le dio resultado la mina, y en vez de dotar el hospital, empezó a gastar dinero a troche y moche, tuvo tres o cuatro queridas, se arregló además con la criada de su casa, y como ésta quedara embarazada, quiso que su hijo se casara con ella.

Don Teodoro protestó, y con su madre se fue a Madrid, hizo oposiciones y las ganó.

Muchos de estos detalles le contaban a Fernando por la tarde en el cuarto en donde cosían las mujeres de la casa, incluso la vieja criada.

De aquellas conversaciones comprendía Ossorio claramente que Toledo no era ya la ciudad mística soñada por él, sino un pueblo secularizado, sin ambiente de misticismo alguno.

Sólo por el aspecto artístico de la ciudad podía colegirse una fe que en las conciencias ya no existía.

Los caciques, dedicados al chanchullo; los comerciantes, al robo; los curas, la mayoría de ellos con sus barraganas, pasando la vida desde la iglesia al café, jugando al monte, lamentándose continuamente de su poco sueldo; la immoralidad, reinando; la fe, ausente, y para apaciguar a Dios, unos cuantos canónigos cantando a voz en grito en el coro, mientras hacían la digestión de la comida abundante, servida por alguna buena hembra.

XXIII

Comenzó a andar sin rumbo por las callejuelas en cuesta.

Se había nublado; el cielo, de color plomizo, amenazaba tormenta. Aunque Fernando conocía Toledo por haber estado varias veces en él, no podía orientarse

One of the paragraphs that he read to Fernando the first day, as he smiled maliciously, was this one from a *History of Toledo*, which he was consulting:
"He saw that in order to accommodate the great House of Austria in the magnificent ostentation with which it conducts itself, his Royal Alcázar was too narrow a nest; and so he had a palace built for himself in the most salutary part of his territory, where his Court could be shown off with greater ease. The result is that Madrid is like a new Alcázar of Toledo, a suburb, a quarter, a retreat, where all the Grandees and the Nobility of Toledo have retired, so to speak, in order to unburden themselves."

As for the other guests, the young officer spent the greater part of his day at the Academy, to which he had been appointed.

The other man, the recorder of deeds, Don Teodoro, was a humble, sad man. His father, a miner from Cartagena, in an ill-fated moment, had promised with a certain religious fervor that he would endow a poorhouse or a hospital if a certain mine he owned turned out to be profitable.

As a matter of fact, the mine turned out to be lucrative, and instead of endowing the hospital, he began to spend his money helter-skelter, kept three or four paramours, established a relationship with his housemaid, and when it turned out that she was pregnant, he made up his mind that his son should marry her.

Don Teodoro protested, went off to Madrid with his mother, and took competitive examinations for a post and won it.

Many of these details were related to Fernando during the afternoon in the room where the women of the house, including the old maid servant, were sewing.

From these conversations, Ossorio clearly understood that Toledo was no longer the mystical city he dreamed of, but rather a secularized town without any atmosphere of mysticism whatsoever.

Only in the artistic aspect of the city could one infer a faith that no longer existed in the consciences of the people.

The political bosses, dedicated to pettifogging; the merchants, to theft; the priests, the majority of them with their concubines, spending their lives flitting back and forth from the church to the café, playing *monte*, constantly bemoaning their pitiful salaries; immorality, reigning everywhere; faith, totally absent, and in order to pacify God, a handful of canons, singing in the choir at the top of their voices, while they digested the ample meal served them by some fine-looking woman.[56]

XXIII

He began to walk along the sloping side streets with no particular direction in mind.

It had turned cloudy; the sky, the color of lead, was threatening a storm. Although Fernando was familiar with Toledo because he had been there several times before,

nunca; así que fue sin saber el encontrarse cerca de Santo Tomé, y una casualidad hallar la iglesia abierta. Salían en aquel momento unos ingleses. La iglesia estaba obscura. Fernando entró. En la capilla, bajo la cúpula blanca, en donde se encuentra *El Enterramiento del Conde de Orgaz*, apenas se veía; una luz débil señalaba vagamente las figuras del cuadro. Ossorio completaba con su imaginación lo que no podía percibir con los ojos. Allá en el centro del cuadro veía a San Esteban, protomártir, con su áurea capa de diácono, y en ella, bordada la escena de su lapidación, y San Agustín, el santo obispo de Hipona, con su barba de patriarca blanca y ligera como humo de incienso, que rozaba la mejilla del muerto.

Revestidos con todas sus pompas litúrgicas, daban sepultura al conde de Orgaz y contemplaban la milagrosa escena, monjes, sacerdotes y caballeros.

En el ambiente obscuro de la capilla el cuadro aquel parecía una oquedad lóbrega, tenebrosa, habitada por fantasmas inquietos, immóviles, pensativos.

Las llamaradas cárdenas de los blandones flotaban vagamente en el aire, dolorosas como almas en pena.

De la gloria, abierta al romperse por el Angel de la Guarda las nubes macizas que separan el cielo de la tierra, no se veían más que manchones negros, confusos.

De pronto, los cristales de la cúpula de la capilla fueron heridos por el sol, y entró un torrente de luz dorada en la iglesia. Las figuras del cuadro salieron de su cueva.

Brilló la mitra obispal de San Agustín con todos sus bordados, con todas sus pedrerías; resaltó sobre la capa pluvial del santo obispo de Hipona la cabeza dolorida del de Orgaz, y su cuerpo, recubierto de repujada coraza milanesa, sus brazaletes y guardabrazos, sus manoplas, que empuñaron el fendiente.

En hilera colocados, sobre las rizadas gorgueras españolas, aparecieron severos personajes, almas de sombra, almas duras y enérgicas, rodeadas de un nimbo de pensamiento y de dolorosas angustias. El misterio y la duda se cernían sobre las pálidas frentes.

Algo aterrado de la impresión que le producía aquello, Fernando levantó los ojos, y en la gloria abierta por el ángel de grandes alas, sintió descansar sus ojos y descansar su alma en las alturas donde mora la Madre rodeada de eucarística blancura en el fondo de la Luz Eterna.

Fernando sintió como un latigazo en sus nervios, y salió de la iglesia.

....

he was never able to orient himself; so it was that he found himself near the Church of Santo Tomé, without his being aware of it, and it was also a coincidence that he found the church open. Some English visitors were coming out at that moment. The church was dark. Fernando went in. In the chapel, under the white cupola where *The Burial of the Count of Orgaz*[57] can be found, it was virtually impossible to see; a faint light dimly illuminated the figures of the painting. Fernando completed what he wasn't able to see with his eyes with his imagination. There, in the center of the painting, he saw Saint Stephen, the protomartyr, in his golden deacon's cloak, with the scene of his lapidation embroidered on it, and Saint Augustine, the sainted Bishop of Hippo, with his patriarchal beard, as white and delicate as incense smoke, that was just grazing the dead man's cheek.

Invested in all their liturgical pomp, they were laying the Count of Orgaz to rest, and monks, clerics and noblemen were contemplating the miraculous scene.

In the darkened atmosphere of the chapel, that painting appeared to be a lugubrious, shadowy cavity, inhabited by restless, motionless, pensive phantoms.

The purple flashes from the large wax tapers floated vaguely in the air, as afflicted as the souls in purgatory.

Of the glory that had opened when the Guardian Angel had cleaved the massive clouds that separate heaven from earth, you could see nothing more than large, confused patches of black.

Suddenly, the panes of glass forming the cupola in the chapel were struck by the sun's rays and a torrent of golden light entered the church. The figures in the painting emerged from their cave.

Saint Augustine's episcopal miter shone with all its embroidery, with all its precious stones; the dolorous head of the lord of Orgaz stood out against the pluvial cope of the sainted Bishop of Hippo, as did his body, covered over with a Milanese repoussé cuirass, his vambraces and brassarts, and his gauntlets which once clasped the down-stroking sword.

Austere personages, shadowy souls, harsh and vigorous souls, surrounded by a nimbus of meditation and mournful afflictions, all appeared arranged in a line, over the crimpled Spanish ruffs. Mystery and doubt hovered over their pale foreheads.

Somewhat terrified by the impression all this produced in him, Fernando raised his eyes and, in the glory opened by the angel with the great big wings, he felt his eyes come to rest and his soul come to rest in the heavens where the Mother dwells, surrounded by Eucharistic whiteness, in the bosom of the Eternal Light.

Fernando felt something like a lash upon his nerves and left the church.

XXIV

Un domingo por la mañana, al levantarse, vió Fernando en casa a la otra hija de su patrona y hermana de Adela. Iba Teresa, la educanda del Colegio de Doncellas Nobles, todos los domingos a pasar el día con sus padres.

Mientras Ossorio se desayunaba, doña Antonia le explicó cómo logró conseguir una beca para su hija en el Colegio de Doncellas Nobles, por medio de don Pedro Nuño, que había hablado al secretario del arzobispo, y lo que había pagado por el equipo y la manera de vivir y demás condiciones de la fundación del Cardenal Siliceo.

El tener la chica en este Colegio halagaba a doña Antonia en extremo. Para ella era un bello ideal realizado.

Mientras doña Antonia daba todas estas explicaciones, que creía indispensables, entraron sus dos hijas, Adela y Teresa, la colegiala, la cual en seguida adquirió confianza con Ossorio.

– Tienen que ser hijas de Toledo para ir al colegio – seguía diciendo doña Antonia –; si salen para casarse, las dan una dote, y si no se pueden casar, pasan allí toda su vida.

– No seré yo la que pase la vida allá con esas viejas – replicó Teresa, la colegiala –. ¡Que las den morcilla a todas ellas!

– Esta hija...es más repicotera. ¿Pues qué vas a hacer si no te casas?

– ¡Cómo me casaré!

Teresa, la colegiala, era graciosa; tenía la estatura de Adela, la nariz afilada, los labios delgados, los ojos verdosos, los dientes pequeños y la risa siempre apuntando en los labios, una risa fuerte, clara, burlona; sus ademanes eran felinos. Repetía una porción de gracias que sin duda corrían por el colegio, y las repetía de tal manera, que hacía reir.

A las primeras palabras que le dijo Fernando, le interrumpió ella, diciéndole:

– ¡Ay, que risa con usted y con su suegra!

Teresa contó lo que pasaba en el colegio.

La superiora era perrísima; la rectora también tenía más mal genio. Entre las mayores había una que dirigía la cocina; otras, las labores.

– Pero, ¿viven ustedes todas juntas, o en cuartos?

– Cada una en su cuarto, y no nos reunimos más que para comer y rezar. ¡Es más aburrido!... Cada cuatro jóvenes tienen una mayor que las dirige, a la que llamamos tía.

– Y usted, ¿qué piensa hacer? ¿Salir del colegio para casarse o meterse monja?

XXIV

One Sunday morning, when he was getting up, Fernando saw the landlady's other daughter, Adela's sister, in the house. Teresa, the schoolgirl at the Colegio de Doncellas Nobles, used to come every Sunday to spend the day with her parents.

While Ossorio was having breakfast, Doña Antonia explained to him how she had succeeded in acquiring a scholarship for her daughter at the Colegio de Doncellas Nobles, through the intervention of Don Pedro Nuño, who had spoken to the archbishop's secretary, and she told him how much she had spent for her outfit, and the way they lived there and the other circumstances concerning this institution founded by Cardinal Siliceo.[58]

Doña Antonia was extremely flattered at having her daughter at this School. To her it was a beautiful ideal that had been realized.

While Doña Antonia was giving him all these explanations, which she thought were indispensable, her two daughters, Adela and Teresa, the schoolgirl, came into the room and the latter immediately took Ossorio into her confidence.

"You have to be a daughter of Toledo in order to go to the School," Doña Antonia continued; "if they leave to get married, they are given a dowry, and if they can't get married, they spend their whole life there."

"I won't be one of those who spends her whole life there with those old biddies," answered Teresa, the schoolgirl. "They can all go to blazes, for all I care!"

"This child. . . is such a chatterbox. So what are you going to do if you don't get married?"

"Oh, I'll get married all right!"

Teresa, the schoolgirl, was quite charming; she was the same height as Adela, had a pointed nose, thin lips, greenish eyes, small teeth and a laugh always ready to break out on her lips, a loud, clear, mocking laugh; her movements were catlike. She was forever repeating a number of clever expressions which were undoubtedly circulating at the School, and she would repeat them in such a way that it made you laugh.

At the very first words that Fernando spoke to her, she interrupted him, saying: "Oh, how funny you are!"

Teresa recounted everything that was going on at the school.

The mother superior was a mean old thing and the head mistress also had a terribly nasty nature. Among the older girls, there was one in charge of the kitchen; others took care of the needlework.

"Tell me, do you all live together or in separate rooms?"

"Each one in her own room and we don't get together except to eat and to pray. It's all so boring!... Every four younger girls has an older girl who is in charge of them, and we all call her auntie."

"And how about you, what do you intend to do? To leave the School to get married or become a nun?"

— Sí, monja...de tres en celda — replicó Adela, creyendo que la frase debía de tener mucha malicia.

— Yo quisiera casarme — dijo Teresa — con un hombre muy rico. A mí me entusiasman las batas de color de rosa, y las perlas y los brillantes —. Luego, riéndose añadio: — ¡Ya sé que no me casaré sino con un pobretón! ¡Que les zurzan a los ricos con hilo negro!

— Pues yo — manifestó Adela — quisiera una casita en un cigarral y un marido que me quisiera muchísimo y que yo le quisiera muchísimo y que...

— Hija, qué perrísima eres — repuso la colegiala, y rodeó el cuello de Adela con su brazo y la atrajo hacia sí.

— Déjame, muchacha.

— No quiero, de castigo.

— ¿A que no puede usted con ella? — preguntó Fernando a Teresa señalando a su hermana.

— ¿Qué no? ¡Vaya! Y la estrechó entre sus brazos, sujetándola y besuqueándola.

Era aquella Adelita muy decidida y muy valiente, no callaba nada de lo que la pasaba por la imaginación. Volvieron a hablar Teresa y Adela de novios y de amoríos.

— ¿Pero qué? — dijo Fernando — ¿dos muchachas tan bonitas como ustedes no tienen ya sus respectivos galanes..., algún gallardo toledano; alguno de Sonseca?...

— ¿Los de Sonseca...? Son más *cazuelos* — contestó Teresa.

Durante todo el día oyó Fernando la charla de las dos, interrumpida por carreras que daban por los pasillos de la casa, y por no pocas discusiones y riñas. Sobre todo Adela, aquella muchacha tan valiente y decidida, era muy agradable y simpática.

— Yo no he estado en Madrid — le decía a Fernando antes de marcharse al colegio, con los ojos verdes brillantes — . Debe ser más bonito! — añadía juntando las manos y sonriendo.

XXV

A los dos meses de estar en Toledo, Fernando se encontraba más excitado que en Madrid.

En él influían de un modo profundo las vibraciones largas de las campanas, el silencio y la soledad que iba a buscar por todas partes.

En la iglesia, en algunos momentos, sentía que se le llenaban los ojos de lágrimas;

"Sure, a nun...living three in a cell; you can count on it," Adela replied, believing that the expression sounded quite malicious.

"I would like to get married to a very rich man," said Teresa. "I am crazy about pink-colored dressing gowns, pearls and diamonds." Then she added with a laugh, "But I know for sure that I'll only marry some poor devil! The rich can all go croak, as far as I'm concerned!"

"As for me," Adela declared, "I would like a little house in a nice little plot of land near Toledo, and a husband who would love me very much and whom I could love just as much, and who..."

"You're so wicked, you little ninny," the schoolgirl replied as she threw her arm around Adela's neck and pulled her toward herself.

"Let me go, you silly girl."

"I don't want to. It's a punishment."

"I'll bet you can't get the better of her?" Fernando asked Teresa, pointing to her sister.

"You don't think so? We'll see about that!" And she squeezed her in her arms, holding her tight and covering her with kisses.

That Teresita was really very determined and very bold, and never suppressed anything that might come into her imagination. Teresa and Adela began talking again about sweethearts and love affairs.

"But how is it possible?" Fernando asked. "Two girls as pretty as you and you still don't have your respective beaus..., some handsome Toledan; someone from Sonseca?"

"Those fellows from Sonseca... ? They're just a bunch of sissies," Teresa replied.

During the course of the whole day, Fernando heard the chatter of the two girls, interrupted by their running along the corridors of the house and by endless arguments and squabbles. Teresa, that bold and determined girl, was especially pleasant and congenial.

"I haven't been to Madrid," she said to Fernando, her green eyes shining, just before she started back to school. "It must be very lovely!" she added, joining her hands together and smiling.

XXV

After he had been in Toledo for two months, Fernando found that he was more emotionally stimulated than he'd been in Madrid.

The prolonged vibrations of the bells and the silence and solitude he would go seek out everywhere were exerting a profound influence upon him.

At certain moments, while he was in church, he would feel his eyes filling with

en otros seguía murmurando por lo bajo, con el pueblo, la sarta de latines de una letanía o las oraciones de la misa.

Él no creía ni dejaba de creer. Él hubiese querido que aquella religión tan grandiosa, tan artística, hubiera ocultado sus dogmas, sus creencias y no se hubiera manifestado en el lenguaje vulgar y frío de los hombres, sino en perfumes de incienso, en murmullos del órgano, en soledad, en poesía, en silencio. Y así, los hombres, que no pueden comprender la divinidad, la sentirían en su alma, vaga, lejana, dulce, sin amenazas, brisa ligera de la tarde que refresca el día ardoroso y cálido.

Y, después pensaba que quizá, esta idea era de un gran sensualismo y que en el fondo de una religión así, como él la señalaba, no había más que el culto de los sentidos. Pero ¿por qué los sentidos habían de considerarse como algo bajo, siendo fuentes de la idea, medios de comunicación del alma del hombre con el alma del mundo?

Muchas veces, al estar en la iglesia, le entraban grandes ganas de llorar, y lloraba.

– ¡Oh! Ya estoy purificado de mis dudas – se decía a sí mismo – . Ha venido la fe a mi alma.

Pero al salir de la iglesia a la calle se encontraba sin un átomo de fe en la cabeza. La religión producía en él el mismo efecto que la música: le hacía llorar, le emocionaba con los altares espléndidamente iluminados, con los rumores del órgano, con el silencio lleno de misterio, con los borbotones de humo perfumado que sale de los incensarios.

Pero que no le explicaran, que no le dijeran que todo aquello se hacía para no ir al infierno y no quemarse en lagos de azufre líquido y calderas de pez derretida; que no le hablasen, que no le razonasen, porque la palabra es el enemigo del sentimiento; que no trataran de imbuirle un dogma; que no le dijeran que todo aquello era para sentarse en el paraíso al lado de Dios, porque él, en su fuero interno, se reía de los lagos de azufre y de las calderas de pez, tanto como de los sillones del paraíso.

La única palabra posible era amar. ¿Amar qué? Amar lo desconocido, lo misterioso, lo arcano, sin definirlo, sin explicarlo. Balbuciar como un niño las palabras inconscientes. Por eso la gran mística Santa Teresa había dicho: *El infierno es el lugar donde no se ama.*

En otras ocasiones, cuando estaba turbado, iba a Santo Tomé a contemplar de nuevo el *Enterramiento del conde de Orgaz,* y le consultaba e interrogaba a todas las figuras.

Una mañana, al salir de Santo Tomé, fué por la calleja del Conde a una explanada con un pretil.

Andaban por allí unos cuantos chiquillos que jugaban a hacer procesiones: habían hecho unas andas y colocado encima una figurita de barro, con manto de papel y

tears; at other times, he would keep murmuring the string of Latin words of a litany or the prayers of the Mass in a low voice, along with the other people.

He neither believed nor did he stop believing. He would have wished that this religion, so grandiose, so artistic, could have hidden its dogmas, its creeds, and would not have manifested itself in the common and cold language of men, but rather in the perfumes of the incense, in the murmurs of the organ, in solitude, in poetry, in silence. And in this way, men, who can not understand divinity would feel it in their souls, vague, distant, sweet, without any threats, like a gentle afternoon breeze that cools the blazing, hot day.

And afterward, he would think that this idea was perhaps extremely sensual, and that there was little more than the worship of the senses at the core of a religion as he conceived it. But why did one have to consider the senses as something base, considering the fact that they were the sources of ideas, the means of communication between the soul of a man and the soul of the world?

Many times, while he was in church, he would be overcome by a great desire to weep and he would weep.

"Oh! Now I have been cleansed of my doubts," he would say to himself. "Faith has come to my soul."

But when he went out of the church into the street, he found himself without a single atom of faith in his head. Religion produced in him the same effect as music: it made him cry, and it moved him with its splendidly illuminated altars, with the sounds of the organ, with the silence filled with mystery, with the bubbling up of perfumed smoke rising from the censers.

But let them not explain, let them not tell him that all that was being done in order not to go to Hell and not to burn in lakes of liquid sulfur and cauldrons of melted pitch; let them not talk to him, let them not reason with him, because the word is the enemy of feeling; let them not try to imbue him with dogma; let them not tell him that all that was just to be able to sit beside God in Paradise, because, in his innermost heart, he laughed at the lakes of sulfur and the cauldrons of pitch, just as much as he did at the armchairs in Paradise.

The only possible word was love. To love what? To love the unknown, the mysterious, the arcane, without defining it, without explaining it. To babble the unconscious words like a child. For that reason, the great mystic Saint Teresa had said: *Hell is the place where one doesn't love.*[59]

On other occasions, when he was upset, he would go to Santo Tomé to look at *The Burial of the Count of Orgaz* again, and he would consult with all the figures and question them.

One morning, as he left Santo Tomé, he walked along the Calleja del Conde to an esplanade with a parapet.

Several small children were running about there, playing at making processions: they had made a portable platform and placed a little figure made of clay, with a cloak made of paper and a crown made of tinplate on top of it. They were carrying

corona de hoja de lata. Llevaban las microscópicas andas entre cuatro chiquillos; por delante iba el pertiguero con una vara con su contera y sus adornos de latón, y detrás, varios chicos y chicas con cerillos y otras con cabos de vela.

Fernando se sentó en el pretil.

Enfrente de donde estaba, había un gran caserón adosado a la iglesia, con balcones grandes y espaciados en lo alto, y ventanas con rejas en lo bajo.

Fernando se acercó a la casa, metió la mano por una reja y sacó unas hojas rotas de papel impreso. Eran trozos de los ejercicios de San Ignacio. En la disposicion de Fernando, aquello le pareció una advertencia.

Callejeando salió a la puerta del Cambrón, y desde allá, por la Vega Baja, hacia la puerta Visagra.

Era una mañana de octubre. El paisaje allí, con los árboles desnudos de hojas, tenía una simplicidad mística. A la derecha veía las viejas murallas de la antigua Toledo; a la izquierda, a lo lejos, el río con sus aguas de color de limo; más lejos, la fila de árboles que lo denunciaban, y algunas casas blancas y algunos molinos de orillas del Tajo. Enfrente, lomas desnudas, algo como un desierto místico; a un lado, el hospital de Afuera, y partiendo de aquí, una larga fila de cipreses que dibujaba una mancha alargada y negruzca en el horizonte. El suelo de la Vega estaba cubierto de rocío. De algunos montones de hojas encendidas salían bocanadas de humo negro que pasaban rasando el suelo.

Un torbellino de ideas melancólicas giraba en el cerebro de Ossorio, informes, indefinidas. Se fué acercando al hospital de Afuera, y en uno de los bancos de la Vega se sentó a descansar. Desde allá se veía Toledo, la imperial Toledo, envuelta en nieblas que se iban disipando lentamente, con sus torres y sus espadañas y sus paredones blancos.

Fernando no conocía de aquellas torres más que la de la Catedral; las demás las confundía; no podía suponer de dónde eran.

Acababan de abrir la puerta del hospital de Afuera.

Fernando recordaba que allí dentro había algo, aunque no sabía qué.

Atravesó el zaguán y pasó a un patio con galerías sostenidas por columnas a los lados, lleno de silencio, de majestad, de tranquilo y venerable reposo. Estaba el patio solitario; sonaban las pisadas en las losas, claras y huecas. Enfrente había una puerta abierta, que daba acceso a la iglesia. Era ésta grande y fría. En medio, cerca del presbiterio, se destacaba la mesa de mármol blanco de un sepulcro. A un lado del altar mayor, una hermana de la Caridad, subida en una escalerilla, arreglaba una lámpara de cristal rojo. Su cuerpo, pequeño, delgado, cubierto de hábito azul, apenas se veía; en cambio, la toca, grande, blanca, almidonada, parecía las alas blancas e inmaculadas de un cisne.

the microscopic platform between four small children; the verger came in front, carrying a staff with a metal tip at the end and bronze ornaments, and behind him were several boys and girls with small wax tapers and others carrying candle ends.

Fernando sat down on the parapet.

Opposite the place where he was seated, there was a large, rambling house, leaning against the church, with big, widely separated balconies in the upper part, and windows with grillwork on the lower part.

Fernando walked over to the house, put his hand through one of the grills and removed some torn pages of imprinted paper. They were fragments of the exercises of Saint Ignatius. In Fernando's state of mind, that seemed to him to be a warning.

He kept walking along the streets until he came out at the Puerta del Cambrón, and from there, he kept going along the Vega Baja toward the Puerta Visagra.

It was an October morning. The landscape there, with the trees bare of any leaves, had a mystical simplicity about it. To the right, he could see the old walls of ancient Toledo; to the left, in the distance, the river with its waters the color of silt; even farther away, the row of trees that defined the river, and several white houses and a number of mills along the banks of the Tajo. Opposite him, barren hills, somewhat like a mystical desert; to one side, the Hospital de Afuera, and starting there, a long line of cypress trees that traced a lengthy, blackish patch on the horizon. The ground of La Vega was covered with dew. Puffs of black smoke were rising from several piles of burning leaves, and they passed by, just skimming the ground.

A whirlwind of melancholy ideas kept revolving in Ossorio's brain, formless and indefinite. He kept nearing the Hospital de Afuera, and he sat down to rest on one of the benches of La Vega. From there, you could see Toledo, imperial Toledo, wrapped in slowly dissipating mists, with its towers, its belfries and thick, white walls.

Of all those towers, the only one Fernando could recognize belonged to the Cathedral; he confused all the others; he couldn't even guess to which buildings they belonged.

They had just opened the door to the Hospital de Afuera.[60]

Fernando recalled that there was something interesting inside, although he didn't know what it was.

He crossed the vestibule and made his way into a courtyard with galleries supported by columns at the sides, filled with silence, majesty and tranquil, venerable repose. The courtyard was deserted; his footsteps resounded on the flagstones, clear and hollow. There was an open door at the opposite end, which gave access to the church. Inside, it was dark and cold. In the middle, near the chancel, the white marble base of a sepulcher was plainly visible. On one side of the high altar, a Sister of Charity was standing on a small ladder, adjusting a red, cut glass lamp. You could barely see her small, slender body, covered by a blue habit; on the other hand, her headdress, large, white and starched, looked like the white, immaculate wings of a swan.

A la derecha del altar mayor, en uno de los colaterales, había un cuadro del Greco, resquebrajado; las figuras, todas alargadas, extrañas, con las piernas torcidas.

A Fernando le llamó la atención; pero estaba más impresionado por el sepulcro, que le parecía una concepción de los más genial y valiente.

La cara del muerto, que no podía verse más que de perfil, producía verdadera angustia. Estaba indubablemente sacada de un vaciado hecho en el cadáver; tenía la nariz curva y delgada, el labio superior hinchado, el inferior hundido; el párpado cubría a medias el ojo, que daba la sensación de ser vidrioso.

La hermana de la Caridad se le acercó, y con acento francés le dijo:

— Es el sepulcro del cardenal Tavera. Ahí está el retrato del mismo, hecho por el Greco.

Fernando entró en el presbiterio.

Al lado derecho del altar mayor estaba: era un marco pequeño que encerraba un espectro, de expresión terrible, de color terroso, de frente estrecha, pómulos salientes, mandíbula afilada y prognata. Vestía muceta roja, manga blanca debajo; la mano derecha extendida junto al birrete cardenalicio; la izquierda, apoyada despóticamente en un libro. Salió Fernando de la iglesia y se sentó en un banco del paseo. El sol salía del seno de las nubes, que lo ocultaban.

Veíase la ciudad destacarse lentamente sobre la colina en el azul puro del cielo, con sus torres, sus campanarios, sus cúpulas, sus largos y blancos lienzos de pared de los conventos, llenos de celosías, sus tejados rojizos, todo calcinado, dorado por el sol de los siglos y de los siglos; parecía una ciudad de cristal en aquella atmósfera tan limpia y pura. Fernando soñaba y oía el campaneo de las iglesias que llamaban a misa.

El sol ascendía en el cielo; las ventanas de las casas parecían llenarse de llamas. Toledo se destacó en el cielo lleno de nubes incendiadas..., las colinas amarillearon y se doraron, las lápidas del antiguo camposanto lanzaron destellos al sol... Volvió Fernando hacia el pueblo, pasó por la puerta Visagra y después por la del Sol. Desde la cuesta del Miradero se veía la línea valiente formada por la iglesia mudéjar de Santiago del Arrabal, dorada por el sol; luego la puerta Visagra con sus dos torres, y al último, el hospital de Afuera.

XXVI

Aquella misma tarde, en una librería religiosa de la calle del Comercio, compró Fernando los ejercicios de San Ignacio de Loyola.

Sentía al ir a su casa verdadero terror y espanto, creyendo que aquella obra iba a concluir de perturbarle la razón.

There was a painting by El Greco, with cracks all over it, to the right of the high altar, at one of the side altars, the figures, all elongated, strange, with twisted legs.

It attracted Fernando's attention; but he was even more impressed by the sepulcher, which seemed to him of an inspired, bold conception.

The dead man's face, which could only be seen in profile, filled you with a real sense of anguish. It was undoubtedly taken from a plaster cast made of the corpse; the nose was curved and thin, the upper lip swollen, the lower one sunken; the eyelid half-covered the eye, which gave the impression that it was glassy.

The Sister of Charity came over to him and said with a French accent:

"This is the tomb of Cardinal Tavera.[61] The portrait of him done by El Greco is in there."

Fernando went into the chancel.

There it was on the right side of the high altar: it consisted of a small frame enclosing a specter, with a terrifying expression on his face, which had an earthy color, a narrow forehead, prominent cheekbones and a pointed, prognathous jaw. He was wearing a red mozzetta with a white manga underneath; his right hand, extended close to his cardinal's biretta, the left hand, resting despotically on a book. Fernando went out of the church and sat down on a bench along the promenade. The sun was coming out from behind the inner recesses of the clouds that were concealing it.

The city slowly began to be visible, outlined upon the hill in the pure blue of the sky, with its towers, its belfries, its cupolas, its long, white stretches of convent walls, filled with lattices; its reddish roofs, the whole of it burned white, gilded by the sun of century upon century; it seemed like a city made of crystal in that very limpid, pure atmosphere. Fernando was dreaming and he could hear the ringing of the church bells calling the faithful to Mass.

The sun was climbing up into the sky; the windows of the houses seemed to be filled with flames. Toledo stood out in a sky filled with fiery clouds...; the hills turned yellow and changed to gold, the gravestones in the old cemetery cast their flashes of light upward toward the sun... Fernando started back toward town, passed through the Puerta Visagra, and then through the Puerta del Sol. From the slope of the Miradero, you could see the bold line formed by the mudejar church of Santiago del Arrabal,[62] gilded by the sun, then, the Puerta Visagra, with its two towers, and finally, the Hospital de Afuera.

XXVI

That very afternoon, Fernando bought a copy of the exercises of Saint Ignatius of Loyola in a religious bookstore on the Calle del Comercio.

As he returned to the house, he felt a genuine terror and dread, because he thought that this work was ultimately going to end up upsetting his rationality.

Llegó a casa y en su cuarto se puso a leer el libro con detenimiento.

Creía que cada palabra y cada frase estampadas allí debían de ser un latigazo para su alma.

Poco a poco, a medida que avanzaba en la lectura, viendo que la obra no le producía el efecto esperado, dejó de leer y se propuso reflexionar y meditar en todas las frases aquellas, palabra por palabra.

Al día siguiente reanudó la lectura, y el libro siguió pareciendo la producción de un pobre fanático ignorante y supersticioso.

A Fernando, que había leído el *Eclesiastes*, le parecían los pensamientos del obscuro hidalgo vascongado sencillas vulgaridades.

El infierno, en aquel librito, era el lugar tremebundo pintado por los artistas medievales, por donde se paseaba el demonio con su tridente y sus ojos llameantes y en donde los condenados se revolvían entre el humo y las llamas, gritando, aullando, en calderas de pez hirviente, lagos de azufre, montones de gusanos y de podredumbre.

Una página de Poe hubiera impresionado más a Fernando que toda aquella balumba terrorífica. Pero, a pesar de esto, había en el libro, fuera del elemento intelectual, pobre y sin energía, un fondo de voluntad, de fuerza; un ansia para conseguir la dicha ultraterrena y apoderarse de ella, que Ossorio se sintió impulsado a seguir las recomendaciones del santo, si no al pie de la letra, al menos en su espíritu.

– ¿Habré nacido yo para místico? – se preguntaba Fernando algunas veces. – Quién sabe si estas locuras que he tenido no eran un aviso de la Providencia. Debo ser un espíritu religioso. Por eso, quizá, no me he podido adaptar a la vida. Busquemos el descubrir lo que hay en el fondo del alma; debajo de las preocupaciones; debajo de los pensamientos; más allá del dominio de las ideas.

Y a medida que iban pasando los días, tenía necesidad de sentir la fe que le atravesara el corazón como con una espada de oro.

Tenía, también, la necesidad de humillarse, de desahogar su pecho llorando, de suplicar a un poder sobrenatural, a algo que pudiera oírle, aunque no fuera personalizado.

XXVII

Un día que Fernando paseaba en el Zocodover, vió venir hacia él un muchacho teniente, amigo suyo, que se le acercó, le alargó la mano y se la apretó con efusión.

– Fernando, ¿tú por aquí?

Ossorio conocía desde niño al teniente Arévalo, pero no con gran intimidad.

He arrived at the house and started reading the book in his room with great thoroughness.

He thought that each word and each sentence imprinted there would likely be like a lashing of his soul.

Little by little, as he moved ahead with his reading, when he began to see that this work wasn't producing the effect he'd hoped for, he stopped reading and made up his mind to reflect and meditate on all those sentences, word by word.

On the following day, he renewed his reading and the book continued to appear to be the work of a pathetic, ignorant and superstitious fanatic.

For Fernando, who had read Ecclesiastes, the thoughts of this obscure Basque hidalgo seemed to be simple banalities.[63]

In that little book, hell was the terrifying place painted by the medieval artists, through which the Devil traveled about with his trident and his flaming eyes, and where the damned twisted about amid the smoke and the flames, shouting and howling in cauldrons of boiling pitch, lakes of sulfur, heaps of worms and putrefaction.

A page out of Poe would have impressed Fernando more than all that frightful hodgepodge. But in spite of all this, there was something in the book, outside of an intellectual content that was poor and lacking in vitality, a certain fund of will and latent power, a yearning to achieve happiness beyond this earth and to seize control of it, which made Ossorio feel compelled to follow the recommendations of the saint, if not to the letter, then at least in their spirit.

"Is it possible that I was born to be a mystic?" Fernando asked himself a number of times. "Who knows if these crazy ideas which I've had were not a warning from Providence. I must really be a religious spirit. Perhaps that is why I've been unable to adapt to life. Let's try to discover what there is in the depths of the soul; beneath our preoccupations; beneath our thoughts; beyond the realm of ideas."

And as the days kept passing, he felt a need to have faith cross through his heart as if it were a golden sword.

He also felt the need to humble himself, to unburden his heart by weeping, to plead with a supernatural power, to something that could hear him, even though it need not be personalized.

XXVII

One day, as Fernando was strolling on the Zocodover, he saw a young lieutenant, a friend of his, coming toward him, and who then walked over to him, took his hand and shook it warmly.

"Fernando, what are you doing around here?"

Ossorio had known Lieutenant Arévalo since childhood, but not very intimately.

Se pusieron a charlar, y al irse para casa, Fernando dijo al teniente:
– No te convido a comer, porque aquí se come bastante mal.
– Hombre, no importa; vamos allá.

A Fernando le molestaba Arévalo, porque pensaba que quería darse tono entre la gente bonachona y silenciosa de la casa de huéspedes. Se sentaron a la mesa. El teniente habló de la vida de Toledo; de los juegos de ajedrez en el café Imperial; de los paseos por la Vega. En el teatro de Rojas no se sostenían las compañías.

Había ido una que echaba dos dramas por función; pusieron el precio de la butaca a seis reales y no fué nadie.

Sólo los sábados y los domingos había una buena entrada en el teatro. En el pueblo no había sociedad, la gente no se reunía, las muchachas se pasaban la vida en su casa.

Se interrumpió el teniente para hacer una pregunta de doble intención a Adela, la hija de la casa, que le contestó sin malicia alguna.

– Deja ya a la muchacha – le dijo irritado Fernando.
– ¡Ah! Vamos. Te gusta y no quieres que otro la diga nada. Bueno, hombre, bueno; por eso no reñiremos – y el teniente siguió hablando de la vida de Toledo con verdadera rabia.

Salieron Arévalo y Ossorio a pasear. Arévalo quería llevar a Fernando a cualquier café y pasarse allí la tarde jugando al dominó. Fueron bajando hasta la Puerta del Sol. Junto a ésta había una casita pequeña de color de salmón, con las ventanas cerradas, y el teniente propuso entrar allí a Fernando.

– ¿Qué casa es ésta? – dijo Ossorio.
– Es una casa de muchachas alegres. La casa de la Sixta. Una mujer que baila la danza del vientre que es una maravilla. ¿Vamos?
– No.
– ¿Has hecho voto de castidad?
– ¿Por qué no?
– Chico, tú no estás como antes – murmuró el teniente –. Has variado mucho.
– Es posible.
– ¿Y quieres que pasemos la tarde andando por callejuelas en cuesta? Pues es un porvenir, chico.

Fernando estuvo por decirle que le dejara y se fuese; pero se calló, porque Arévalo creía que era una obligación suya impedir que Fernando se aburriera.

– ¡Hombre! – dijo el teniente – tengo un proyecto; vamos al Gobierno civil.
– ¿A qué?
– Veremos al gobernador. Es un hombre muy *barbián*.

Fernando trató de oponerse, pero Arévalo no dio su brazo a torcer. Habían de ir donde decía él o si no, se incomodaba.

They began to chat and when Fernando started back to his house, he said to the lieutenant:

"I won't invite you over to eat, because people eat rather badly here."

"Oh, that doesn't make any difference, old fellow; let's go to your place anyway."

Arévalo's presence troubled Fernando, because he thought his friend would try to put on airs among the good-natured, silent people at the boarding house. They sat down at the table. The lieutenant spoke of life in Toledo; of the chess matches at the Café Imperial; of strolling along La Vega. At the Teatro de Rojas, they were barely able to support performances by theatrical companies.

One company had come there that offered two dramas at each performance; they set the price of an orchestra seat at six *reales* and nobody came.

Only on Saturdays and Sundays was there a decent audience in the theater. There was no real social life in the town, people didn't get together and girls spent their lives in their houses.

The lieutenant interrupted himself to ask Adela, the daughter of the house, a question with a double entendre, and she answered him without any malice whatsoever.

"Why don't you leave the girl alone," Fernando said to him very irritably.

"Oh, I see! You like her and you don't want anyone else to say anything to her. Very well, my dear fellow, very well; let's not fight over that," and the lieutenant went on speaking quite vehemently about life in Toledo.

Arévalo and Ossorio left the house to take a stroll. Arévalo wanted to take Fernando to some café and spend the afternoon playing dominoes. They kept walking down toward the Puerta del Sol. Just next to it was a small unimpressive salmon-colored house with all its windows closed, and the lieutenant suggested to Fernando that they go inside.

"What house is that?" said Ossorio.

"It's a house of *filles de joie*. It's La Sixta's house. A woman who can do a belly dance that is really marvelous to behold. Shall we go in?"

"No."

"Have you taken a vow of chastity?"

"Why not?"

"My dear boy, you aren't like you were before," the lieutenant muttered. "You've changed a great deal."

"That's possible."

"And you expect us to spend the afternoon strolling up and down these steep back streets? Well, there's a great future in that, my boy."

Fernando was about to tell him to leave him alone and go away, but he kept silent, because Arévalo probably thought that it was his duty to prevent Fernando from getting bored.

Se fueron acercando al Gobierno civil. Atravesaron un corredor que daba la vuelta por una escalera ruinosa y preguntaron por el gobernador.

No se había levantado aún.

– Sigue madrileño – murmuró el teniente sonriendo.

Podían pasar al despacho; Arévalo hizo algunas consideraciones humorísticas acerca de aquel gobernador refinado, amigo de placeres, gran señor en sus hábitos y costumbres, que dormía a pierna suelta en el enorme y destartalado palacio a las tres de la tarde.

El despacho del gobernador era un salón grande, tapizado de rojo, con dos balcones. En el testero principal había un retrato al óleo de Alfonso XII; unos cuantos sillones y divanes, una mesa de ministro debajo del retrato y dos o tres espejos en las paredes.

En medio de la sala zumbaba una estufa encendida. Como hacía mucho calor, Arévalo abrió un balcón y se sentó cerca de él. Desde allá se veía un entrelazamiento de tejados con las tejas cubiertas de musgos que brillaban con tonos amarillentos, verdosos y plateados. Por encima de las casas, como si fueran volando por el aire, se presentaban las blancas estatuas del remate de la fachada del Instituto. Se oían las campanas de alguna iglesia que retumbaban lentamente, dejando después de sonar una larga y triste vibración.

– Esto me aplasta – dijo Arévalo irritado–. ¡Qué silencio más odioso!

Fernando no le contestó.

Al poco rato entró un señor flaco, de bigote gris, en el despacho.

El teniente y él se saludaron con afecto, y después Arévalo se lo presentó a Fernando como escritor, sociólogo y pedagogo.

– ¿No se ha levantado el gobernador? – preguntó el pedagogo.

– No; todavía no. Sigue tan madrileño.

– Sí; conserva las costumbres madrileñas. Yo ahora me levanto a las siete. Antes, en Madrid, me levantaba tarde.

Después, encarándose con Fernando, le dijo:

– ¿A usted le gusta Toledo?

– ¡Oh! Sí. Es admirable.

– ¡Ya lo creo!

Y el pedgogo fué barajando palabras de arquitectura y de pintura con un entusiasmo fingido.

"Well, now!" said the lieutenant. "I have a proposal; let's go to the Provincial Government Palace."

"Where?"

"We'll see the Governor. He's a very easy-going fellow."

Fernando tried to resist, but Arévalo wouldn't let his mind be changed. They were going to go where he wanted or else he would be very upset.

They kept drawing closer to the Provincial Government Palace. They crossed through a corridor that ran all around a courtyard; they went up a dilapidated staircase and asked for the governor.

He hadn't gotten up yet.

"He's just as Madrilenian as ever," the lieutenant murmured with a smile.

They were permitted to go into his office; Arévalo made some humorous observations about that refined governor, a friend of all pleasures, a grand gentleman in his habits and customs, who was sleeping like a log in the enormous, ramshackle palace at three in the afternoon.

The governor's office was a large room with red carpeting and two balconies. On the front wall there was an oil portrait of Alfonso XII[64]; there were several easy chairs and divans, a ministerial table underneath the portrait and two or three mirrors on the walls.

In the middle of the room, a stove had been lit and it kept on buzzing. As it was very warm, Arévalo opened one of the balcony windows and sat down nearby. From there, you could see an interlacing of roofs with moss-covered tiles that were shining with yellowish, greenish and silver-colored tints. The white statues on the pinnacle of the façade of the Instituto[65] appeared above the houses, as if they were flying through the air. You could hear the bells of some church as they slowly resounded, leaving behind a prolonged, sad vibration after they stopped pealing.

"All this simply overwhelms me," Arévalo said very irritably. "What an odious silence!"

Fernando didn't answer him.

In a little while, a skinny man with a gray mustache came into the office. The lieutenant and he greeted one another cordially, and then Arévalo introduced him to Fernando as a writer, a sociologist and a pedagogue.

"Hasn't the Governor gotten up yet?" asked the pedagogue.

"No, not yet. He's as Madrilenian as ever."

"Yes, he preserves his Madrilenian habits. I now get up at seven. Before, in Madrid, I used to get up late."

Then, turning to face Fernando, he said to him:

"Do you like Toledo?"

"Oh! Yes! It's a wonderful place."

"I should say so!"

And the pedagogue started throwing around words about architecture and painting with feigned enthusiasm.

En esto entró el gobernador, vestido de negro.

Era un hombre de mediana estatura, de barba negra, ojos tristes, morunos, boca sonriente y voz gruesa.

Saludó a Arévalo y al otro señor, cambió unas cuantas frases amables con Fernando, se sentó a la mesa, hizo sonar un timbre, y al conserje que se presentó le dijo:

– Que vengan a la firma.

Se presentaron unos cuantos señores, con un montón de expedientes debajo del brazo, y el gobernador empezó a firmar vertiginosamente.

– ¿Ve usted ese retrato de Alfonso XII? – dijo a Fernando el pedagogo –. Pues es todo un símbolo de nuestra España.

– ¡Hombre! Y ¿cómo es eso?

– Es un retrato que tiene su historia. Fué primitivamente retrato de Amadeo, vestido de capitán general; vino la República; se arrinconó el cuadro y sirvió de mampara en una chimenea; llegó la Restauración, y el gobernador de aquella época mandó borrar la cabeza de Amadeo y substituirla por la de Alfonso. Es posible que ésta de ahora sea substituida por alguna otra cabeza. Es el símbolo de la España.

No había acabado de decir esto, cuando entró el secretario en la sala y habló al oido del gobernador.

– Que esperen un poco, y cuando concluya de firmar, que pasen – dijo éste.

Se retiraron los empleados con sus mamotretos debajo del brazo, y entraron en la sala los individuos de una comisión del Ayuntamiento de un pueblo que venían a quejarse del cura de la localidad.

El gobernador, volteriano en sus ideas, engrosó la voz y les dijo que él no podía hacer nada en aquel asunto.

¿Creían que el cura había faltado? Pues le procesaban, instruían expediente y le llevaban a presidio.

Los del Ayuntamiento, que comprendían que nada de aquello se podía hacer, marcharon cabizbajos y cariacontecidos.

Al salir éstos, entró un señor grueso, bajito, muy elegante, con botas de charol y chaleco blanco, que habló a media voz y riéndose con el gobernador.

Concluyó diciendo:

– Usted hace lo que quiera, a mí me los han recomendado las monjas.

El gobernador hizo sonar el timbre, entró su secretario y le dijo:

– Diga usted a esos señores que pasen.

Aparecieron dos curas en una puerta y saludaron a todos haciendo grandes zalemas.

– ¿Cómo está su excelencia?

The governor came in at this point, dressed in black.

He was a man of average height, with a black beard, sad Moorish eyes, a smiling mouth and a deep-sounding voice.

He greeted Arévalo and the other gentleman, exchanged a few friendly words with Fernando, sat down at the table, rang a bell, and when the porter appeared, he said to him:

"Have them come in for the signatures."

A number of men appeared with piles of documents under their arms and the governor began signing them with vertiginous speed.

"Do you see that portrait of Alfonso XII?" the pedagogue said to Fernando. "Well, it is the perfect symbol of our Spain."

"You don't say! And how is that?"

"It's a portrait that has a history. Originally it was a portrait of King Amadeo,[66] dressed as a field marshal; along came the Republic[67] and they stored the painting away in some corner and it was even used as a screen for a fireplace; then came the Restoration[68] and the governor at that time ordered Amadeo's head to be removed and that of Alfonso to be substituted for it. It's possible that this one we now have may someday have another head substituted for it. It's the symbol of Spain."

He had hardly finished saying this when the secretary came into the room and said something in the governor's ear.

"Let them wait a while, and have them come in when I finish signing," the governor said.

The clerks withdrew with their thick sheaves of papers under their arms and the members of a committee of a nearby Town Council came into the room with a complaint about the priest of their community.

The governor, a Voltairian in his ideas, made his voice huskier and told them he couldn't do anything in that matter.

Did they really think the priest had committed some offense?

Well, then let them indict him, open an inquiry concerning him and send him off to prison.

The representatives of the Town Council, who understood that none of this could be done, went away with their heads lowered and looking down in the mouth.

When they had departed, a stout man, quite short and very elegantly dressed, with patent leather shoes and a white vest, came into the room and spoke with the governor in a low voice as he laughed.

He ended by saying:

"You can do whatever you wish; the nuns have recommended them to me."

The governor rang the bell, his secretary came in and he said to him:

"Tell those gentlemen to come in."

Two priests appeared in the doorway and they greeted everyone bowing very deeply.

"How is Your Excellency?"

– No me den ustedes tratamiento – dijo el gobernador, después de estrechar las manos a los dos– . Vamos aquí.

Y se fué a hablar con ellos al hueco de uno de los balcones.

El grupo del teniente Arévalo, el pedagogo y Fernando, se había engrosado con el señor gordo de las botas de charol y del chaleco blanco.

Ossorio, interrogado por el pedagogo, contó la impresión que le había producido un convento al amanecer.

El señor bajo y gordo, que dijo que era médico, al oir que Ossorio creía en la espiritualidad de las monjas, dijo con una voz impregnada de ironía:

– ¡Las monjas! Sí; son casi todas zafias y sin educación alguna. Ya no hay señoritas ricas y educadas en los conventos.

– Sí. Son mujeres que no tienen el valor de hacerse lavanderas – afirmó el pedagogo – y vienen a los conventos a vivir sin trabajar.

– Yo las insto – continuó el señor grueso – para que coman carne. ¡Ca! Pues no lo hacen. Mueren la mar; como chinches. Luego ya no tienen ni dinero, ni rentas; viven diez o doce en caserones grandes como cuarteles, en unas celdas estrechas, mal olientes, con el piso de piedra, sin que tengan ni una esterilla, ni nada que resguarde los pies de la frialdad.

– A mi me gustaría verlas – dijo el teniente – . Debe de haber algunas guapas.

– No, no lo crea usted. Si no estuviéramos en *Adviento* – replicó el médico – yo les llevaría a ustedes; pero ya no tiene interés.

De pronto se oyó la voz de uno de los curas que, en tono de predicador, decía:
– Todo el mundo tiene derecho a ser libre menos la Iglesia, y ¿ésa es la libertad tan decantada?

El gobernador le dijo que hiciera lo que quisiese, que él no había de tomar cartas en el asunto, y les acompañó a los dos curas hasta la puerta.

El teniente y Fernando se despidieron del gobernador; y éste les invitó a comer con él dos días después.

XXVIII

Entraron en el comedor provisionalmente alhajado. Era ya el anochecer. Se sentaron a la mesa, además del anfitrión, el médico grueso, el teniente Arévalo y Fernando.

La conversación revoloteó sobre todos los asuntos, hasta que fué a parar en los atentados anarquistas.

"No need to rely on ceremony here," the governor said after shaking hands with the two of them. "Let's go over here."

And he walked off to talk with them in the recess of one of the balconies.

The group consisting of Lieutenant Arévalo, the pedagogue and Fernando had now been enlarged to include the fat gentleman with the patent leather shoes and the white vest.

Ossorio, when the pedagogue questioned him, recounted the impression the sight of a convent at daybreak had left with him.

When the short, fat gentleman, who said he was a doctor, heard Ossorio say that he believed in the spirituality of nuns, he said in a voice impregnated with irony:

"The nuns! Yes, indeed, they're almost all coarse, without any breeding or education whatsoever. There are no longer any rich, well bred young ladies in the convents."

"Yes. They are women who don't have the courage to become laundresses," the pedagogue affirmed," and so they come to the convents to live without having to work."

"I urge them to eat meat," the stout gentleman continued. "But it's no use! Because they don't do it. They die in droves; like flies. Besides that, they have neither money nor income any more; so ten or twelve of them live in great big houses like army barracks, in narrow, foul-smelling cells, with stone floors, without even a straw mat or anything else to protect their feet from the cold."

"I would really like to see them," said the lieutenant. "There must be some pretty ones."

"No, don't you believe it. If it weren't Advent," the doctor replied, "I would take you to see them; but there's no point to it now."

Suddenly, the voice of one of the priests was heard saying in the tone of a preacher:

"Everybody has the right to be free except the Church, and so this is what your exalted idea of liberty is like?"

The governor told him that he could do whatever he wanted, but that he himself wasn't going to intervene in the matter, and he accompanied the two priests to the door.

The lieutenant and Fernando took leave of the governor, and he invited them to dine with him two days afterward.

XXVIII

They went into the dining room that had been furnished just for the occasion. It was already dark. Seated at the table, in addition to the host, were the stout doctor, Lieutenant Arévalo and Fernando.

The conversation flitted back and forth on all manner of questions until it ended up on the violent attacks by the anarchists.[69]

Arévalo senaló a Ossorio como uno de tantos demagogos partidarios de la destrucción en el terreno de las ideas.

El pedagogo se sintió indignado, y entonces el gobernador le dijo:
– Pero si aquí todos somos anarquistas.

El pedagogo anunció que iba a hacer un libro en el cual plantearía, como única base de la sociedad, ésta: El fin del hombre es vivir.

Los cuatro comensales, en vez de encontrar la base social hallada por el pedagogo firme y sólida, la creyeron digna de la chacota y de la broma.

– Pues, sí, señor; es la única base social: El fin del hombre es vivir. Es verdad que esta frase puede representar lo más egoísta y mezquino si se dice: El fin de cada hombre es vivir.

A pesar del distingo, todos rieron a costa de la base social tan importante y trascendentalísima.

De esta cuestión, mezclada con ideas políticas y sociales, se pasó a hablar del arzobispo de Toledo.

Uno decía que era un hereje, otro que un modernista. Arévalo se encogió de hombros; él creía que el cardenal arzobispo era un majadero; se aseguraba que creía en la sugestión a distancia y en el hipnotismo, y que deseaba que el clero español estudiara y se instruyese.

Con este objeto enviaba a algunos curas jóvenes al extranjero.

Había tenido la idea de fundar un gran periódico demócrata y católico al mismo tiempo; pero ninguno de los obispos y arzobispos le secundó, y el de Sevilla dijo que aquél era el camino de la herejía.

Se empezaron a contar anécdotas del arzobispo.

A uno le había dicho:
– ¡Ríase usted de los masones! Eso es un espantajo que inventan los reaccionarios.

A un conónigo muy ilustrado le dijo, en confianza, que entre San Pablo y San Pedro él hubiera elegido a San Pablo.

Era un hombre demócrata que hablaba con las mujeres de la calle. Arévalo seguía encogiéndose de hombros y creyendo que era un majadero.

El pedagogo dijo que el anterior arzobispo, conociendo los instintos ambiciosos del actual, decía:

– Si él es *Lagartijo*, yo soy *Frascuelo*.

Se celebró la anécdota tanto como la exposición de la base social.

– En tiempo de agitación – concluyó diciendo el médico – este arzobispo sería capaz de hacer independiente de Roma la Iglesia española y erigirse Papa.

Se habló de las ventajas que esto tendría para Toledo, y después se discutió si esta ciudad tenía verdadero carácter místico.

Arévalo indicated that Ossorio was one of so many demagogues who supported the destructive approach in the sphere of ideas.

The pedagogue grew indignant and then the governor said to him:

"But really, we are all anarchists here."

The pedagogue announced that he was going to write a book in which he would establish that the only foundation for society was this: The goal of man is to live.

His four table companions, instead of finding that the social foundation discovered by the pedagogue was firm and solid, thought it worthy of nothing more than ridicule and jest.

"But yes, indeed; it is the only social foundation: The goal of man is to live. It's true that this phrase can represent the most selfish and mean-minded aspect in us, if you say: The goal of each man is to live."

In spite of this distinction, they all laughed at the cost of so very important and so transcendental a social foundation.

From this question, which was mixed with political and social concepts, they moved on to speak of the archbishop of Toledo.

One of them said that he was a heretic and another said he was a modernist. Arévalo shrugged his shoulders: he thought the cardinal-archbishop was a fool; it was said with some certainty that the archbishop believed in telepathic suggestion and hypnotism, and that he wanted the Spanish clergy to study and be educated.

With this objective in mind, he was sending several young priests abroad.

He had gotten the idea of founding a great newspaper, democratic and Catholic at the same time, but none of the bishops or archbishops supported him, and the archbishop of Seville said that this was the road to heresy.

They began telling anecdotes about the archbishop.

He had once said to someone:

"All that business of the Masons is laughable! All that is a bugaboo invented by the reactionaries."

He once said to a very illustrious canon, in confidence, that between Saint Paul and Saint Peter, he would have chosen Saint Paul.

He was a democratic man who even spoke to the women of the street.

Arévalo kept shrugging his shoulders and still insisting that he was a fool.

The pedagogue said that the previous archbishop, aware of the ambitious instincts of the present one, used to say:

"If he is *Lagartijo*, then I am *Frascuelo*."[70]

The anecdote was celebrated as much as the exposition of the social foundation.

"In time of agitation," the doctor said in conclusion, "this archbishop would be capable of declaring the independence of the Spanish Church from Rome and setting himself up as Pope."

They spoke of the advantages this would have for Toledo and then they discussed the question of whether or not this city had a true mystical character.

El gobernador aseguró que el pueblo castellano no era un pueblo artista. Decía que Toledo, lo mismo que está puesto en medio de la Mancha, podía estar en medio de Marruecos, repleto de obras artísticas de maestros alemanes, italianos, griegos, o de discípulos de éstos, sin que el pueblo las admirase, proviniendo aquel arte del instinto de lujo de los cabildos.

Así en Toledo se advertía un arte de aluvión, sin raíz en la tierra manchega, adusta, seca, antiartística.

Arévalo no veía en Toledo más que una ciudad aburrida, una de las muchas capitales de provincia española donde no se puede vivir.

El pedagogo la llamaba la ciudad de la muerte: era el título que, según él, mejor cuadraba a Toledo.

Después se citó al Greco. Alguien contó que dos pintores impresionistas, uno catalán y el otro vascongado, habían ido a ver el *Entierro del conde de Orgaz* de noche, a la luz de los cirios.

– ¿Vamos nosotros a ver qué efecto hace? – dijo Arévalo.

– Vamos – repuso el gobernador – . Que le avisen al sacristán para que nos abra.

Hizo sonar el timbre, dió recado a un portero, se levantaron todos de la mesa y se pusieron los gabanes.

Fernando se estremeció sin saber por qué. Le parecía una irreverencia monstruosa ir a ver aquel cuadro con el cerebro enturbiado por los vapores del vino. Pensaba en aquella ciudad de sus sueños, llena de recuerdos y de tradiciones, poblada por la burguesía estúpida, gobernada espiritualmente por un cardenal *baudeleresco* y un gobernador volteriano.

Al salir del Gobierno era de noche. Se dirigieron por las callejuelas tortuosas hacia Santo Tomé.

La puerta de la iglesia estaba entornada; fueron entrando todos. El sacristán tenía encendidos los dos ciriales, y, entre él y su hijo los levantaron hasta la altura del cuadro.

Fuera por excitación de su cerebro o porque las llamaradas de los cirios iluminaban de una manera tétrica las figuras del cuadro, Ossorio sintió una impresión terrible, y tuvo que sentarse en la obscuridad, en un banco, y cerrar los ojos.

Salieron de allá; fueron al Gobierno civil, y en la puerta se despidieron.

Fernando tenía la seguridad de que no podría dormirse, y comenzó a dar vueltas y vueltas por el pueblo. Se encontró en los alrededores de la cárcel. Bordeó el Tajo por un camino alto. En el fondo de ambas orillas brillaba el río como una cinta de acero a la luz vaga del anochecer, unida a la luz de la luna.

Al seguir andando se veía ensancharse el río y se divisaban las casitas blancas

The governor assured them that the Castilians were not an artistic people.

He said that Toledo, in spite of the fact that it was located in the heart of La Mancha, could just as well be in the middle of Morocco, replete with the artistic works of German, Italian and Greek masters or their disciples, and still the people wouldn't admire them, because that kind of artistic creation originated from the instinct of luxury of the town councils.

Thus, in Toledo, you could observe an art of alluvion, with no roots in the Manchegan soil, austere, arid, anti-artistic.

Arévalo could see nothing more in Toledo than a boring city, one of so many provincial capitals in Spain where it is impossible to live.

The pedagogue called it the city of death: according to him, it was the name that best depicted Toledo.

Then someone cited El Greco. Someone recounted how two impressionist painters, one Catalan and the other Basque, had once gone to see *The Burial of the Count of Orgaz* at night, by the light of wax candles.

"Why don't we go and see what effect it has on us," said Arévalo.

"Let's go," replied the governor. "Have them notify the sacristan so that he can open up for us."

He rang the bell, gave the message to a porter, and they all arose from the table and put on their overcoats.

Fernando trembled without knowing why. It seemed to him a monstrous lack of reverence to go see that painting with one's brain muddled by the vapors of wine. He kept thinking of that city of his dreams, full of memories and traditions, now populated by a stupid bourgeoisie and spiritually governed by a *Baudelairesque* Cardinal and a Voltairian governor.

When they left the Provincial Palace, it was night. They made their way along the winding side streets toward Santo Tomé.

The door of the church was partly open; they all started going in. The sacristan had lit two large processional candlesticks and both he and his son raised them up to the height of the painting.

Either because of the stimulation in his brain or because the bursts of flame from the wax candles illuminated the figures in the painting in a gloomy way, Ossorio was overcome by a terrifying sensation and had to sit down on a bench in the darkness and close his eyes.

They all went out; they went back to the Provincial Governor's Palace and took leave of one another in the doorway.

Fernando was certain he wouldn't be able to fall asleep, and so he began to walk round and round through the town. He found himself in the environs of the prison. He made his way along the banks of the Tajo along a high road. At the bottom, between both banks, the river was shining like a band of steel, by the dim light of late evening, combined with the light of the moon.

As he kept walking, the river could be seen to widen, and you could make out

de los molinos; después, cerca de las presas, las orillas del Tajo se estrechaban entre paredones amarillentos cortados a pico.

Se hizo de noche, y la luna se levantó en el cielo, iluminando los taludes pedregosos de las orillas, e hizo brillar con un resplandor de azogue el río estrecho, encajonado en una angosta garganta, y que luego se veía extenderse por la vega.

Fernando sentía el vértigo al mirar para abajo al fondo del barranco, en donde el río parecía ir limando los cimientos de Toledo.

Siguió hacia el puente de Alcántara. El agua saltaba en la presa, tranquila, sin espuma; brillaban luces rojas en el fondo del río; más lejos, parpadeaban las luces en la barriada baja de las Covachuelas.

Sobre un monte, a la luz de la luna, se perfilaba escueta y siniestra la silueta de una cruz que Fernando creyó que le llamaba con sus largos brazos.

XXIX

Un día, muy de mañana, fue al convento de Santo Domingo el Antiguo, *Divo Dominicus Silaecensis.*

La puerta de la iglesia se encontraba todavía cerrada. Enfrente había una casa de un piso y en el balcón una mujer con una niña en brazos. Preguntó a ésta cuándo abrían la iglesia, y la mujer le dijo que no tardarían mucho, que lo preguntara en la portería del convento, al otro lado.

Dió Fernando la vuelta, y en un portal, sobre cuyo dintel se veía una imagen en una hornacina y en un azulejo el nombre del convento en letras azules; entró y llamó en la portería.

Una mujer que salió le dijo:

– Llame usted por el torno y pida usted permiso a las monjas para entrar.

Fernando se acercó al torno y llamó. Al poco tiempo oyóse la voz de la hermana tornera que le preguntaba qué quería.

Fernando expresó su deseo.

– Se lo preguntaré a la madre superiora – contestó la monja.

Mientras esperaba, Fernando paseó por el zaguán, en donde sonaban sus pisadas como en hueco.

Por el montante de una puerta se veía parte del jardín del convento.

Al poco tiempo se oyó la voz de la monja que preguntaba:

– ¿Está usted ahí?

the small white houses of the mills; then, near the dams, the banks of the Tajo narrowed between the very steep, thick, yellowish walls.

Night fell, and the moon rose into the sky, illuminating the rocky slopes of the banks, and it made the river, squeezed into a contracted gorge, shine with the brilliance of quicksilver; then it could be seen stretching out over the fertile plain.

Fernando felt quite dizzy as he looked downward into the bottom of the ravine, where the river seemed to move along, filing down the very foundations of Toledo.

He continued toward the Puente de Alcántara. The water was leaping into the dam, tranquil, without foam; red lights were shining on the bottom of the river; further away, the lights in the lower district of Las Covachuelas were blinking.

On top of a mountain, the silhouette of a cross could be seen in profile, unadorned and sinister, by the light of the moon, and Fernando was convinced that it was beckoning to him with its long arms.

XXIX

One day, very early in the morning, he went to the Convent of Santo Domingo el Antiguo, *Divo Dominicus Siloecensis*.[71]

He found that the door to the church was still closed. There was a one-story house directly opposite and a woman with a little girl in her arms was on the balcony. He asked her when they opened the church and the woman told him that it wouldn't be very long and that he should inquire at the porter's lodge on the other side of the convent.

Fernando went around to the other side to a portal, where you could see a religious statue in a niche over the lintel, and the name of the convent inscribed in blue letters on a glazed tile; he went inside and knocked at the door to the porter's lodge.

A woman who came out said to him:

"Just call out at the revolving server at the wall and ask the sisters for permission to enter."

Fernando went over to the revolving server and called out. In a little while, you could hear the voice of the sister on duty at the server asking him what he wanted.

Fernando expressed his wishes.

"I'll go ask the mother superior," the nun replied.

While he was waiting, Fernando strolled around the vestibule and his footsteps resounded as though he were in an empty space.

You could see part of the convent garden through the transom of one of the doors.

In a little while, you could hear the nun's voice asking:

"Are you still there?"

— Sí, hermana.
— La madre superiora dice que puede usted pasar, siempre que entre en la iglesia con el respeto debido y haga todas las reverencias ante el Santísimo Sacramento.
— Descuide usted, hermana, las haré.
— Se separó del torno al decir esto; advirtió a la portera la respuesta afirmativa de la monja; tomó ésta la llave grande y le dijo a Fernando:
— Bueno, vámonos.
Salieron a dar la vuelta al convento.
— ¿Cuántas monjas hay aquí? — preguntó Fernando.
— No hay más que trece desde hace muchísimo tiempo.
— ¿Es que no viene ninguna nueva a profesar?
— Sí, han venido varias; pero ha dado la casualidad de que cuando se han reunido catorce ha muerto alguna y han vuelto a ser trece.
— Es extraño.
Dieron vuelta al convento hasta llegar a la plaza en la cual estaba colocada la iglesia.
Fernando tomó el agua bendita y se arrodilló delante del altar.
Fué mirando los cuadros.
En el retablo mayor, tallado y esculpido por el Greco, en el intercolumnio, se veía, medio oculto por un altarcete de mal gusto, un cuadro del Greco, con figuras de más de tamaño natural, firmado en latín.
Recordó que le habían dicho que aquel cuadro no era del Greco, sino la copia de otro que había estado en aquel lugar, y que se lo había llevado, con el asentimiento de las monjas, un infante de España.
Admiró después, en los retablos colaterales, dos cuadros que le parecieron maravillosos; una *Resurrección* y un *Nacimiento*, y se acercó al púlpito de la iglesia a ver una *Verónica* pintada al blanco y negro.
Al acercarse al púlpito vió frente al altar mayor, en la parte de atrás de la iglesia, dos rejas de poca altura, y, a través de ellas, el coro, con una sillería de madera tallada y el techo lleno de artesonados admirables.
En el ambiente obscuro se veían tres monjas arrodilladas, con el manto blanco como el plumaje de una paloma y la toca negra sobre la cabeza. A la luz tamizada y dulce que entraba cernida por las grandes cortinas del coro, aquellas figuras tenían la simetría y el contraste fuerte de claroscuro de un cuadro impresionista.
Haciendo como que contemplaba el cuadro de la *Verónica*, Ossorio se fué acercando a una de las rejas distraídamente, y cuando estaba cerca, miró hacía el interior del coro.

"Yes, sister."

"The mother superior says that you can come in, provided that you go into the church with the proper respect and make all the genuflections in front of the Blessed Sacrament."

"You needn't worry, sister, I'll do it."

He withdrew from the revolving server as he said this; he informed the woman at the porter's lodge that the nun had replied affirmatively; she took a large key and said to Fernando:

"Very well, then, let's go."

They went out in order to walk around the convent.

"How many nuns are there here?"

"There have been no more than thirteen for a very long time."

"Is it that nobody new has come here to profess?"

"Yes, several have come; but as chance would have it, whenever fourteen have come together here, one of them has died and there are thirteen again."

"That's strange."

They walked all around the convent till they reached the square on which the church was located.

Fernando took some holy water and knelt in front of the altar.

He began looking at the paintings.

On the retable behind the high altar, which had been fashioned and sculpted by El Greco, in the intercolumniation, you could see, half-hidden by a small altar done in very poor taste, a painting by El Greco, with figures larger than natural size, signed in Latin.[72]

He remembered that he'd been told that this painting wasn't an original El Greco, but rather a copy of another one that had once been in that place and had been removed by a Spanish infante with the consent of the nuns.

Then, in the collateral retables, he admired two paintings that seemed quite marvelous to him: a *Resurrection* and a *Nativity*, and then he went over to the pulpit of the church to see a *Veronica* painted in black and white.

As he approached the pulpit, he saw opposite the high altar, in the rear part of the church, two gratings that weren't very high, and through them, he could make out the choir with its stalls made of finely carved wood and a ceiling covered with admirable caissoned paneling.

You could see three nuns kneeling in the dark surroundings, with robes as white as the plumage of a dove and black coifs over their heads. By the sifted, gentle light that entered and was filtered by the large curtains of the choir, those figures took on the symmetry and the strong contrast of the chiaroscuro of an Impressionist painting.

Pretending that he was contemplating the painting of the *Veronica*, Ossorio kept moving closer to one of the gratings in a nonchalant manner, and when he was quite close, he looked toward the interior of the choir.

Las tres monjas le lanzaron una ojeada escrutadora.

La abadesa tuvo una mirada de desdén observador, otra de las monjas miró con curiosidad, y la tercera lanzó a Fernando una mirada con sus ojos negros llenos de pasión, de tristeza y de orgullo. No fué más que un momento, pero Fernando sintió aquella mirada en lo más intimo de su alma.

La superiora se levantó de su sillón y extendió los brazos para colocar bien su hábito, como un pájaro blanco que extiende las alas; las otras dos monjas la siguieron sin volver el rostro.

Después, en los días posteriores, iba Fernando por la mañana temprano a oir la misa del convento.

En la iglesia, que solía oler a cerrado, no había más que algunas viejas enlutadas y algunos ancianos.

Fernando oía la misa, se colocaba cerca de la doble reja del coro y veía a la monja a poca distancia suya, rezando, con la toca negra, que servía de marco a una cara delgada, fina, de ojos brillantes, valientes y orgullosos. Sus manos eran huesudas, con los dedos largos, delgados, que, al cruzarse los de una mano con la otra para rezar, formaban como un montón blanco de huesos.

Un día Fernando se decidió a escribir a la monja. Lo hizo así, y fué a la portería del convento a convencer a la portera para que entregase la carta a la monja.

Por la conversación que tuvo con la portera, comprendió que no haría nunca lo que él deseaba.

Lo único que averiguó fue que la monja pálida, de ojos negros, alta y delgada, se llamaba la hermana Desamparados, y que era la que tocaba el órgano y el armonium en las fiestas.

Todos los días Ossorio iba dispuesto a entregarle una carta rabiosa, proponiéndola escaparse de allá con él, que estaba dispuesto a todo.

Se sentía a veces con fuerza para hacer un disparate muy grande; otras, se sentía débil como un niño.

Le indignaba pensar que aquella mujer, en cuyos ojos se leía el orgullo, la pasión, tuviera que vivir encerrada entre viejas imbéciles, sufriendo el despotismo de la superiora, atormentada por pensamientos de amor, sin ver el cielo azul.

Una mañana, después de misa, Fernando vió a la hermana Desamparados rezando en un reclinatorio cerca de la verja. En el coro no había más que otra monja. La superiora no estaba.

Fernando, haciendo como que miraba a un altar, con la mano izquierda introdujo la carta por la reja.

La hermana Desamparados, al notar el movimiento, indicó con los ojos a Fernando algo como una señal de alarma. Entonces, de pronto Ossorio vió levantarse

The three nuns cast a scrutinizing glance at him.

The Abbess had an expression of watchful disdain, another one of the nuns looked at him curiously, and the third one cast a glance at Fernando with her dark eyes, filled with passion, sadness and pride. It took no more than a moment, but Fernando felt that glance in the innermost part of his soul.

The mother superior stood up from her armchair and extended her arms so she could set her habit right, like a white bird extending its wings; the other two nuns followed her without turning their faces.

Subsequently, on the days that followed, Fernando would go to hear Mass at the convent very early in the morning.

There were only a few old women, dressed in black mourning, and several old men in the church, which smelled as if it had been shut up for some time.

Fernando would hear the Mass, station himself near the double grating that led to the choir and see the nun only a short distance from him, as she prayed, in her black coif, which served as a frame for her fine, thin face, with her shining eyes, courageous and proud. Her hands were bony, with long, slender fingers, which, when she crossed the fingers of one hand with the other to pray, would form what appeared to be a white pile of bones.

One day, Fernando decided to write to the nun. He did so and went to the porter's lodge of the convent and tried to convince the woman serving there to hand over the letter to the nun.

From the conversation he had with the woman, he understood that she would never do what he wanted.

The only thing he did find out was that the pale, dark-eyed, tall, slender nun was named Sister Desamparados, and that she was the one who played the organ and the harmonium on holy days.

Ossorio would go there every day, prepared to hand over a reckless letter to her, in which he proposed that she escape with him from the convent and that he was prepared for any contingency.

Sometimes he felt that he was strong enough to commit any foolish act; at other times, he felt as weak as a child.

It made him indignant to think that this woman, in whose eyes you could read both pride and passion, should have to live in this way, locked up with these imbecilic old women, suffering the despotism of the mother superior, tormented by thoughts of love, without ever seeing the blue sky.

One morning after Mass, Fernando saw Sister Desamparados as she prayed on the prie-dieu near the grating. There was only one other nun in the choir. The Mother Superior wasn't there.

Fernando, pretending that he was looking at an altar, inserted the letter through the grating with his left hand.

Sister Desamparados, when she noticed this movement, indicated something akin to a sign of alarm to Fernando with her eyes. Then, Ossorio suddenly saw the

a la otra monja, una vieja negruzca de cara terrosa, y acercarse a la reja con una expresión tan terrible en la mirada, que quedó perplejo. A pesar de esta perplejidad, tuvo tiempo para meter la mano entre las rejas y recoger la carta. Después miró tranquilamente a la vieja, que parecía un espectro, una cara de loca, alucinada y furiosa, y volviéndose hacia la puerta, huyó con rapidez.

Al día siguiente, Fernando ya no vió a la hermana Desamparados, y en los días posteriores tampoco. A veces el armonium cantaba, y en sus notas creía ver Fernando las quejas de aquella mujer de la cara pálida, de los ojos negros llenos de fuego y de pasión.

XXX

Días después, Fernando buscó por todas partes al teniente Arévalo hasta que lo encontró.

– Chico – le dijo – necesito de ti. Tengo un aburrimiento mortal. Llévame a alguna parte que tú conozcas.

– Veo que vuelves al buen camino. Comeremos hoy en casa de Granullaque platos regionales, nada más que platos regionales. Te presentaré dos muchachas que conozco muy amables. Si quieres las convidamos a comer, ¿eh?

– Bueno. Entonces yo preparo todo y tú me esperas en tu casa adonde iré a recogerte.

A las tres de la mañana se retiraron los dos amigos.

Al otro día se levantó Fernando a las doce y no pudo asistir como acostumbraba a la misa del convento.

Se encontraba débil, turbado, sin fuerzas.

Apenas pudo comer, y después de levantarse de la mesa se dirigió en seguida al convento por ver si la iglesia estaba abierta, como domingo; pero viendo que no lo estaba, comenzó a pasearse por las callejuelas próximas.

Cerca había una plaza, triste, solitaria, a la cual se llegaba recorriendo dos estrechos pasadizos, obscuros y tortuosos.

A un lado de la plaza se veía la fachada de una iglesia con pórtico bajo, sostenido por columnas de piedra y cubierto con techumbres de tejas llenas de musgos.

En los otros lados, altas paredes de ladrillo, con una fila de celosías junto al alero, puertas hurañas, ventanucas con rejas carcomidas en la parte baja... Un silencio de campo reinaba en la plazoleta; el grito de algún niño o las pisadas del caballo de algún aguador, que otras veces turbaban el callado reposo, no sonaban en el aire

other nun, a darkish-looking old woman with an earthen-colored face, rise up and walk over to the grating, with an expression on her face that was so terrifying that he was left completely perplexed. In spite of this perplexity, he had enough time to put his hand through the iron bars and retrieve the letter. He then looked tranquilly at the old woman, who seemed like a specter, with the face of a mad woman, hallucinated and enraged, and he turned toward the door and quickly fled.

On the following day, Fernando didn't see Sister Desamparados any more, and he didn't see her on the days that followed either. Sometimes, the harmonium would sing out, and he thought he could hear in its notes the laments of that woman with the pale face, with the dark eyes, full of fire and passion.

XXX

A few days afterward, Fernando looked for Lieutenant Arévalo everywhere until he found him.

"I really need you, old friend," he said to him. "I'm overcome by a deadly boredom. Take me somewhere you know"

"I see that you're getting back on the right track. We'll eat some regional dishes today at Granullaque's place, nothing but regional dishes. I'll introduce you to two girls I know who can be quite friendly. If you wish, we can invite them to dinner, all right?"

"Yes."

"Good. Then I'll arrange everything, and you can wait for me at your house and I'll come by there and pick you up."

The two friends retired at three in the morning.

On the following day, Fernando got up at twelve and was unable to attend Mass at the convent, as was his custom.

He found that he was weak, upset and without any strength at all.

He could hardly eat, and after getting up from the table, he immediately made his way to the convent to see if the church was open, since it was Sunday; but when he saw that it wasn't, he began to walk along the nearby side streets.

There was a sad, lonely square nearby and you reached it by making your way along two narrow, dark and winding alleys.

On one side of the square, you could see the façade of a church with a low portico that was supported by stone columns and covered with roofing made of moss-filled tiles.

On the other sides, high brick walls with rows of latticework next to the eaves, forbidding doors, ugly, grating-covered windows with the lower parts eaten away... A silence like that of the countryside reigned in the little square; in the tranquil air of that placid, sad Sunday afternoon, you could hear neither the shout of a child

tranquilo de aquella tarde dominguera, plácida y triste. El cielo estaba azul, limpio, sereno; de vez en cuando llegaba de lejos el murmullo del río, el cacareo estridente de algún gallo.

Mecánicamente Ossorio volvía hacia el convento y le daba vueltas. Una de las veces advirtió un rumor a rezo que salía de las celosías y después el tintineo de una campanilla.

Una impresión de tristeza y de nostalgia acometió su espíritu, y escuchó durante algún tiempo aquellos suaves murmullos de otra vida.

Inquieto e intranquilo sin saber por qué, con el corazón encogido por una tristeza sin causa, sintió una gran agonía en el espíritu al oir las vibraciones largas de las campanas de la catedral, y hacia la santa iglesia encaminó sus pasos.

Era la hora de vísperas. La gran nave estaba negra y silenciosa. Fernando se arrodilló junto a una columna. Sonó una hora en el gran reloj y comenzaron a salir curas y canónigos de la sacristía y a dirigirse al coro.

Resonó el órgano; se vieron brillar en la obscuridad, por debajo de los arcos de la sillería, tallados por Berruguete, luces y más luces.

Después, precedidos por un pertiguero con peluca blanca, calzón corto y la pértiga en la mano, que resonaba de un modo metálico en las losas, salieron varios canónigos con largas capas negras, acompañando a un cura revestido de capa pluvial.

A los lados iban los monaguillos; en el aire obscuro de la iglesia se les veía avanzar a todos como fantasmas, y las nubes de incienso subían al aire.

Toda la comitiva entró en la capilla mayor; se arrodillaron frente al altar, y el que estaba revestido con la capa pluvial, de líneas rígidas como las de las imágenes de las viejas pinturas bizantinas, tomó el incensario e incensó varias veces el altar.

Luego se dirigieron todos a la sacristía; desaparecieron en ella, y al poco rato volvieron a salir para entrar en el coro. Y empezaron los cánticos, tristes, terribles, sobrehumanos... No había nadie en la iglesia; sólo de vez en cuando pasaba alguna negra y tortuosa sombra.

Al salir Ossorio a la calle recorrió callejuelas buscando en el silencio, lleno de misterio, de las iglesias, emoción tan dulce que hacía llegar las lágrimas a los ojos, y no la encontró.

Callejeando apareció en la puerta del Cambrón, después de pasar por cerca de Santa María la Blanca, y desde allá, por la Vega, fué a la puerta Visagra y paseó por la explanada del hospital de Afuera. Al anochecer, desde allá, aparecía Toledo severo, majestuoso; desde la cuesta del Miradero tomaba el paisaje de los alrededores un

nor the sound of the hoofs of a water vender's horse, which usually disturbed the silent repose at other times. The sky was blue, limpid, serene; from time to time, the murmur of the river or the shrill crowing of some rooster could be heard from afar.

Ossorio was returning toward the convent mechanically and kept walking all around it. At one of those times, he noted the sound of praying coming from behind the shutters, and then the jingling of a small bell.

An impression of sadness and nostalgia overcame his spirit and he listened for some time to those soft murmurs of another life.

Uneasy and restless, without really knowing why, his heart contracted by an inexplicable sadness, he felt a great agony within his spirit as he heard the prolonged vibrations of the Cathedral bells, and then he directed his steps toward the holy church.

It was the hour of Vespers. The great nave was dark and silent. Fernando knelt beside a column. An hour tolled on the large clock and the priests and canons started to emerge from the sacristy and make their way to the choir.

The organ resounded; you could see lit candles and more lit candles shining in the darkness, under the arches of the choir stalls, which had been carved by Berruguete.[73]

After that, several canons, wearing long black capes came out, preceded by a verger in a white wig, wearing knee breeches, carrying a staff in his hand, which resounded with a metallic sound on the flagstones, accompanying a priest invested with his pluvial cope.

The acolytes walked along the sides; in the dark atmosphere of the church, you could see them all advance like phantoms, and clouds of incense kept rising into the air.

The whole retinue went into the chapel behind the high altar; they knelt in front of the altar and the one invested with the pluvial cope, with rigid lines like those of images in old Byzantine paintings, took the incensory and sprinkled incense over the altar several times.

Then they all made their way to the sacristy; they disappeared inside and came out again in a short while in order to enter the choir. And the canticles began, sad, terrifying, superhuman.,, There was nobody in the church; only occasionally would some dark, tortuous shadow pass by.

When Ossorio came out into the street, he made his way through the narrow streets, searching in the mystery-filled silence of the churches for that incredibly sweet emotion that had once brought tears to his eyes, but he didn't find it.

After passing close by Santa María de Blanca, he kept roaming through the streets and found himself at the Puerta del Cambrón, and from there, along La Vega, he moved on to the Puerta Visagra and walked along the esplanade of the Hospital de Afuera. When night fell, Toledo appeared severe and majestic from where he was standing; from the slope of the Miradero, the landscape of the surrounding area took

tono amarillo, cobrizo, como el de algunos cuadros del Greco, que terminaba al caer la tarde en un tinte calcáreo y cadavérico.

En un café descansó un momento; pero impulsado por la excitación de los nervios, salió en seguida a la calle. Era de noche. Había niebla, y el pueblo tomaba, envuelto en ella, unas proporciones gigantescas.

Las calles subían y bajaban, no tenían algunas salida. Era aquello un laberinto; la luz eléctrica, tímida de brillar en la mística ciudad, alumbraba débilmente, rodeada cada lámpara por un nimbo espectral.

En la calle de la Plata, Fernando solía ver en un mirador una muchacha pálida, carirredonda, con grandes ojos negros. No debía de salir aquella muchacha más que a rezar en las iglesias.

Fernando pensaba en que su piel blanca y exangüe debía haber compenetrado el perfume del incienso.

Ossorio fué a ver si la veía. La casa estaba cerrada; no había ni luz.

¡Qué bien se debía vivir en aquellas grandes casas! Se debía de pasar una vida de convento saboreando el minuto que transcurre. Fernando pasaba de una calle a otra, sin saber por dónde iba, como si fuera andando con la fantasía por un pueblo de sueños. En algunas casas se veían desde fuera semiiluminados patios enlosados con una fuente en medio.

Con la cabeza llena de locuras y los ojos de visiones anduvo; por una calle, que no conoció cuál era, vió pasar un ataúd blanco, que un hombre llevaba al hombro, con una cruz dorada encima.

La calle estaba en el mismo barrio por donde había pasado por la tarde.

A un lado debía estar Santo Tomé; por allá cerca, Santa María la Blanca, y abajo de la calle, San Juan de los Reyes.

A pesar del cono de luz que daban las lámparas incandescentes, brillaban la cruz y las listas doradas de la caja de una manera siniestra, y al entrar en la zona de sombra, la caja y el hombre se fundían en una silueta confusa y negra. El hombre corría dando vueltas rápidamente a las esquinas.

Fernando pensaba:

— Este hombre empieza a comprender que le sigo. Es indudable.

Y decía después:

— Ahí van a enterrar una niña. Habrá muerto dulcemente, soñando en un cielo que no existe. ¿Y qué importa? Ha sido feliz, más feliz que nosotros que vivimos.

Y el hombre seguía corriendo con su ataúd al hombro, y Fernando detrás.

Después de una correría larga, desesperada, en que se iba sucediendo a ambos lados tapias blanqueadas, caserones grandes, obscuros, con los portales iluminados

on a yellowish, coppery tone, like that in some of El Greco's paintings, and at dusk it finally assumed a calcareous, cadaverous tint.

He stopped to rest for a moment in a café; but, impelled by the stimulation of his nerves, he immediately went out into the street. It was night. There was a mist covering the town that made it assume gigantic proportions.

The streets sloped up and down and some of them came to a dead end. It was all a huge labyrinth; the electric lights, reticent to shine in the mystical city, gave off a very weak light and each lamp was surrounded by a ghostly halo.

On the Calle de la Plata, Fernando used to see a pale girl with a round face and big, black eyes, in a windowed balcony. That girl probably never went out except to pray in the churches.

Fernando kept thinking that her white, exsanguine skin must have been permeated with the perfume of the incense.

Fernando walked over to see if he could see her. The house was closed up; there wasn't even a light.

How well people must live in those grand houses! They must live a kind of monastic life, savoring each minute that passes by. Fernando kept going from one street to the next without knowing where he was going, as if he were walking along in his fantasy through a city of dreams. In some of the houses, you could see partially illuminated patios from outside that were paved with flagstones, with a fountain in the middle.

He kept on walking, his head full of wild ideas and his eyes with visions; along one of the streets, he didn't know which one it was, he saw a white coffin with a golden cross on top pass by, which a man was carrying on his shoulder.

The street was in the same neighborhood where he had passed that afternoon.

Santo Tomé was probably on one side; Santa María de la Blanca not far away, in that direction, and San Juan de los Reyes, down the street.

In spite of the cone of light given off by the incandescent street lamps, the cross and the golden strips on the coffin were shining in a sinister way, and the coffin and the man merged into a confused, black silhouette as they moved into an area of shadow. The man was running along, turning the corners very rapidly.

Fernando was thinking:

"This man is beginning to understand that I'm following him. There's no doubt about it."

And then he said:

"They're going to bury a little girl there. She must have died sweetly, dreaming of a heaven that doesn't exist.[74] But what difference does that make? She was happy, happier than those of us who are still alive."

And the man kept running with the coffin on his shoulder and Fernando ran behind him.

After running for a desperately long time, during which low, whitewashed, earthen walls kept appearing one after another on both sides, and big, dark, rambling houses, with vestibules illuminated by stairway lights, with doors trimmed with

por una luz de la escalera, puertas claveteadas, grandes escudos, balcones y ventanas floridas, el hombre se dirigió a una casa blanca que había a la derecha, que tenía unos escalones en la puerta; y mientras esperaba, bajó el ataúd desde su hombro hasta apoyarlo derecho en uno de los escalones, en donde sonó a hueco.

Llamó, se vió que se abría la madera de una ventana, dejando al abrirse un cuadro de luz, en donde apareció una cabeza de mujer.

– ¿Es para aquí esta cajita? – preguntó el hombre.
– No; es más abajo: en la casa de los escalones – le contestaron.

Cogió el ataúd, lo colocó en el hombro y siguió andando de prisa.

– ¡Qué impresiøn más tremenda habrá sido la de esta mujer al ver la caja! – pensó Fernando.

El hombre con su ataúd miraba vacilando a un lado y a otro, hasta que vió próximo a un arco una casa blanca con la puerta abierta vagamente iluminada. Se dirigió a ella y bajó la caja sin hacer ruido.

Dos mujeres viejas salieron de un portal y se acercaron al hombre.
– ¿Es para aquí esa caja?
– Sí debe ser. Es para una chiquilla de seis a siete años.
– Sí, entonces es aquí. Se conoce que se ha muerto la mayor. ¡Pobrecita! ¡Tan bonita que era!

Se escabulleron las viejas. El hombre llamó con los dedos en la puerta y preguntó con voz alta:

– ¿Es para aquí una cajita de muerto, de una niña?

De dentro debieron de contestarle que sí. El hombre fué subiendo la caja que, de vez en cuando, al dar un golpe, hacía un ruido a hueco terrible. Fernando se acercó al portal. No se oía adentro ni una voz ni un lloro.

De pronto, el misterio y la sombra parecieron arrojarse sobre su alma, y un escalofrío recorrió su espalda y echó a correr, hacia el pueblo. Se sentía loco, completamente loco; veía sombras por todas partes. Se detuvo. Debajo de un farol estaba viendo el fantasma de un gigante en la misma postura de las estatuas yacentes de los enterramientos de la Catedral, la espada ceñida a un lado y en la vaina, la visera alzada, las manos juntas sobre el pecho en actitud humilde y suplicante, como correspondía a un guerrero muerto y vencido en el campo de batalla. Desde aquel momento ya no supo lo que veía: las paredes de las casas se alargaban, se achicaban; en los portones entraban y salían sombras; el viento cantaba, gemía, cuchicheaba. Todas las locuras se habían desencadenado en las calles de Toledo. Dispuesto a luchar a brazo partido con aquella ola de sombras, de fantasmas, de cosas extrañas que iban a tragarle, a devorarle, se apoyó en un muro y esperó... A lo lejos oyó el rumor de un piano; salía de una de aquellas casas solariegas; prestó atención: tocaban *Loin du bal*.

....

nails, large escutcheons, balconies and windows covered with flowers, the man made his way toward a white house located on the right, which had several steps leading to the door; while he waited, he lowered the coffin from his shoulder till he could lean it upright against one of the steps, and it gave off a hollow sound.

He knocked; you could see one of the window shutters open, and as it opened, it left a square of light in which a woman's head appeared.

"Is this little coffin for here?" the man asked.

"No; it's further down, in the house with the steps," came the reply.

He picked up the coffin, put it on his shoulder and hurriedly kept walking.

"What a terrifying impression this woman must have had when she saw the coffin!" Fernando thought.

The man with his coffin kept looking hesitantly to one side and the other, until he saw a white house next to an arch, its door open and very dimly lit. He made his way there and lowered the coffin without making any noise.

Two old women came out of the vestibule and approached the man.

"Is that coffin for here?"

"It must be. It's for a little girl six or seven years old."

"Yes, then it is here. Everyone knows that the older girl died. The poor little thing! And she was so pretty!"

The old women scurried away. The man knocked at the door with his fingers and asked in a loud voice:

"Are you expecting a small coffin here for a little girl?"

They must have answered yes from inside. The man started taking the coffin upstairs, and from time to time, as it struck something, it would make a terrible, hollow sound. Fernando approached the vestibule. Inside the house, you could hear neither voices nor weeping.

Suddenly the mystery and the shadows seemed to hurl themselves upon his spirit and a chill ran down his spine, and he started to run toward the town. He felt he was mad, completely mad; he kept seeing ghosts everywhere. He stopped. Under a streetlight, he could see an apparition that was a giant, in the same posture as the recumbent statues in the tombs at the Cathedral, their swords in their scabbards, girded at one side, their visors raised, their hands joined together over their breasts in a humble and supplicant manner, as befitted a warrior killed and conquered on the field of battle. From that moment on, he no longer knew what he was seeing: the walls of the houses kept growing longer, then shrinking; ghosts kept entering and leaving through the large front doors; the wind kept singing, moaning and whispering. All manner of madness had broken loose in the streets of Toledo. Prepared to fight hand to hand with that surge of spirits and ghosts and fanciful things that were going to swallow him, to devour him, he leaned against a wall and waited... In the distance, he heard the sound of a piano; it was coming from one of the ancestral houses; he listened attentively: they were playing *Loin du bal*.[75]

Rendido, sin aliento, entró a descansar en un café grande, triste, solitario. Alrededor de una estufa del centro se calentaban dos mozos. Hablaban de que en aquellos días iba a ir al teatro de Rojas una compañía de teatro.

El café, grande, con sus pinturas detestables y ya carcomidas y sus espejos de marcos pobres, daba una impresión de tristeza desoladora.

XXXI

– Y usted, ¿dónde duerme? – preguntó Ossorio a Adela.
– En el segundo piso.
– ¿Sola, en su cuarto?
– Sí.
– ¿Y no tiene usted miedo?
– Miedo, ¿de que?
– Figúrese usted que dejara la puerta abierta y entrara alguno...
– ¡Ca!

Fernando sintió una oleada de sangre que afluía a su cara.

Adela estaba también roja y turbada, no tenía el aspecto monjil de los demás días, sonreía forzadamente y sus mejillas estaban coloreadas con grandes chapas rojas.

Hablaban de noche en el comedor iluminado por la lámpara de aceite que colgaba del techo.

Doña Antonia y la vieja criada habían salido a la novena.

La abuela, con el niño en brazos, dormía en una silla. Adela y Ossorio estaban solos en la casa. Habían hablado tanto de los deseos y aspiraciones de cada uno, que se habían quedado ambos turbados al mismo tiempo. Adela escuchaba atentamente por si se oía llamar a la puerta, quizá deseando, quizá temiendo que llamaran.

Tenían que decirse muchas cosas; pero si las palabras pugnaban por brotar de sus labios, la prudencia lo impedía. No se conocían, no se podían tener cariño, y sin embargo, temblaban y el corazón latía en uno y en otro como un martillo de fragua.

– ¿Y si yo?... – le dijo Fernando.
– ¿Qué? – preguntó la muchacha penosamente.
– Nada, nada.

Estuvieron mirándose de reojo largo tiempo.

De pronto oyeron llamar a la puerta. Era doña Antonia y la criada.

Fernando se levantó de la mesa, miró a la muchacha y ésta le miró también

Exhausted, breathless, he went into a large, sad, lonely café to rest. Two young fellows were warming themselves around a stove in the middle of the room. They were speaking of the fact that a theatrical company was coming to the Teatro de Rojas one of these days.

The café, quite big, with its detestable pictures, already worn away, and its mirrors in their shabby frames, gave one an impression of desolate sadness.

XXXI

"And how about you, where do you sleep?" Ossorio asked Adela.
"On the second floor."
"Alone, in your own room?"
"Yes."
"And you're not afraid?"
"Afraid, of what?"
"Well, let's say you left your door open and someone came in..."
"Nonsense!"
Fernando felt a surge of blood that rose up into his face.

Adela also blushed and seemed upset; she didn't have the appearance of a nun that she had on other days, her smile was forced and her cheeks took on color with big, red blotches.

They were talking one night in the dining room, which was lit up by the oil lamp that was hanging from the ceiling.

Doña Antonia and the old maidservant had gone out to a Novena.

The grandmother was asleep in a chair with the child in her arms. Adela and Ossorio were alone in the house. They had spoken so much about their desires and aspirations that they had both felt troubled at the same time. Adela kept listening attentively in case someone might knock at the door, perhaps desiring and perhaps fearing that someone might knock.

They had many things to tell one another; but if the words were struggling to emerge from their lips, prudence held them back. They didn't really know one another, and nevertheless, they were trembling and both their hearts were beating like a forge hammer.

"And what if I...?" Fernando said to her.
"What?" the girl asked with considerable distress.
"Nothing. Nothing at all."

They kept looking at one another out of the corners of their eyes for a long time.

Suddenly they heard a knocking at the door. It was Doña Antonia and the maid.

Fernando got up from the table, looked at the girl, and she looked at him too,

sofocada y temblorosa. Fernando salió a la calle abrumado por deseos agudos; no encontraba ninguna idea moral en la cabeza que le hiciese desistir de su proyecto.
– La muchacha era suya – pensaba él– . Es indudable. ¡Afuera escrúpulos! La moral es una estupidez. Satisfacer un ansia, dejarse llevar por un instinto, es más moral que contrariarlo.
El aire frío de la noche, en vez de calmar su excitación, la agrandaba. Parecía que tenía el corazón hinchado.
– Es la vida – decía él– que quiere seguir su curso. ¿Quién soy yo para detener su corriente? Hundámonos en la inconsciencia. En el fondo es ridícula, es vanidosa la virtud. Yo siento un impulso que me lleva a ella, como ella siente hoy impulso que la empuja hacia mí. Ni ella ni yo hemos creado este impulso. ¿Por qué vamos a oponernos a él?
Recorría mientras tanto las calles obscuras, los pasadizos...
La noche estaba fresca y húmeda.
– Es verdad que puede haber consecuencias para ella que para mí no existen. Estas consecuencias pueden truncar la vida a esa pobre muchacha de aspecto monjil. ¿Y qué? Nada, nada. Hay que cegarse. Esta preocupación por otro es una cobardía. Esperaré en un café.
Estuvo más de una hora allí, sin poder coordinar sus pensamientos, hasta que se levantó decidido.
– Voy a casa – murmuró– y salga lo que salga.
Se acercó a la plaza de las Capuchinas, abrió la puerta, subió las escaleras, entró en su cuarto y apagó la luz.
El corazón le latía con fuerza, se agitaban en su cerebro, en una ebullición loca, pensamientos embrionarios, ideas confusas de un idealismo exaltado, y recuerdos intensos gráficos de una pornografía monstruosa y repugnante.
Oyó cómo se cerraban las puertas de los cuartos; vió que se apagaba la luz.
Al poco rato, Adela pasó por el corredor a su cuarto. Luego de esto, Fernando, sin zapatos, salió de su alcoba. Recorrió el pasillo, llegó a la cocina y empezó a subir la escalera.
Llegó al descansillo del cuarto de la muchacha. La alcoba era muy pequeña, y tenía un ventanillo alto, que daba a la escalera.
Por él vió Fernando a la muchacha, que se persignaba y rezaba ante un altarillo formado por una virgen de yeso, puesta sobre una columna encima de una cómoda grande y antigua. Fernando, que en su turbación discurría con frialdad, pensó:
– Reza con fe. Esperemos.
La muchacha commenzó a desnudarse, mirando de vez en cuando hacia la puerta. Se veía que estaba intranquila. A veces miraba al vacío.

choked and trembling. Fernando went out into the street, overcome by keen desires; he could find no moral precept in his head that might force him to turn away from his intentions.

"The girl was his," he kept thinking. "There is no doubt about it. Away with all scruples! Morality is just stupid. Satisfying a desire, letting oneself be carried away by an instinct, this is far more moral than thwarting it."[76]

The cold night air, instead of calming his arousal, only increased it. It seemed that his heart was swelling with emotion.

"It is life," he said, "trying to follow its natural course. Who am I to stop its flow? We must submerge ourselves in insensibility. Basically, virtue is ridiculous, it is vain. I feel an impulse that draws me toward her, just as she feels an impulse that pushes her toward me. Neither she nor I have created this impulse. Why should we try to oppose it?"

In the meantime, he kept walking through dark streets and alleys...

The night was cool and humid.

"It is true that there can be consequences for her that don't exist for me. These consequences can cut short the life of that poor girl who has the appearance of a nun. But what of it? Nothing, nothing at all. You have to blind yourself. This preoccupation for another is a show of cowardice. I'm going to wait in a café."

He remained there for more than an hour without being able to coordinate his thoughts until he finally got to his feet, full of determination.

"I'm going to the house," he murmured, "and whatever happens can happen."

He approached the Plaza de las Capuchinas, opened the door, went up the stairs, entered his room and put out the light.

His heart was beating violently; embryonic thoughts, confused ideas of an exalted idealism and intense, graphic memories of monstrous and repugnant pornography kept swirling around in his brain in a mad ferment.

He heard the doors to the rooms being closed; he saw that they were putting out the lights.

In a little while, Adela passed along the corridor on her way to her room. Shortly thereafter, Fernando left his bedroom without his shoes. He went down the passageway, reached the kitchen and started to climb the stairs.

He reached the landing where the girl's room was located. The bedroom was very small and had a little window high up that opened onto the stairway.

Looking through it, Fernando saw the girl as she made the sign of the cross and prayed in front of a small altar formed by a plaster figure of the Virgin placed on a column on top of a large old bureau. Fernando, who was able to reason quite coldly even in his present state of confusion, thought to himself:

"She is praying with faith. We'll just wait."

The girl started to undress, looking toward the door from time to time. You could see she was uneasy. At times she would stare into space.

De pronto, la mirada de los dos debió cruzarse. Fernando, sin pensar ya en nada, se acercó a la puerta y empujó. Estaba cerrada.
– ¿Quién? – dijo ella con voz ahogada.
– Yo, abre – contestó Fernando.
La puerta cedió.

Ossorio entró en el cuarto, cogió a la muchacha en sus brazos, la estrujó y la besó en la boca. La levantó en el aire para dejarla en la cama, y al mirarla la vió pálida, con una palidez de muerto, que doblaba la cabeza como un lirio tronchado.

Entonces Fernando sintió un estremecimiento convulsivo, y le temblaron las piernas y le castañatearon los dientes. Vió ráfagas de luz, círculos luminosos y espadas de fuego. Temblando como un enfermo de la medula, salió del cuarto, cerró la puerta y bajó a la cocina; de allí salió al pasillo y entró en su alcoba. Se puso las botas y salió a la calle, siempre temblando, con las piernas vacilantes.

La noche estaba fría, brillaban las estrellas en el cielo. Trataba de coordinar sus movimientos, y sus miembros no respondían a su voluntad. Empezaba a sentir un verdadero placer por no haberse dejado llevar por sus instintos. No, no era sólo el animal que cumple una ley orgánica: era un espíritu, era una conciencia.

¿Qué hubiese hecho la pobre muchacha tan buena, tan apacible, tan sonriente?

El hubiera podido casarse con ella, pero hubiesen sido desgraciados los dos.

En aquel momento se acordó de una muchacha de Yécora, a quien había seducido, aunque en sus relaciones ni cariño ni nada semejante hubo.

Nunca se había acordado de ella con tanta intensidad como entonces. Lo que no comprendía es cómo estuvo tanto tiempo sin que el recuerdo de aquella muchacha le viniese a la mente.

Al pensar en la otra, la figura de Adela se perdía, y en cambio se grababa con una gran fuerza la imagen de la muchacha de Yécora.

Recordaba como nunca hasta entonces la hubiera recordado, a Ascensión, la hija de Tozenaque. Cuando comenzó a pretenderla estaba entonces en una época de furor sexual.

A ella, que era bastante bonita, le gustaba coquetear con los muchachos.

Durante un período de vacaciones, la persiguió Fernando, rondó su casa, y una tarde consiguió de la muchacha que saliera a pasear con él solo por entre los trigos, altos para ocultar una persona.

Fueron los dos hacia una ermita abandonada; oculta en una umbría formada por altos olmos, cercando el bosque por un lado, había un montón de piteras que escalaban un alto ribazo con sus palas verdes, brillantes, erizadas de espinas.

Al llegar a la unbría, comenzaba a caer la tarde.

Sin frases de amor, casi brutalmente, se consumó el sacrificio.

Suddenly their gaze must have met. Fernando, without thinking about anything now, went over to the door and pushed. It was locked.

"Who is it?" she said in a choked voice.

"It is I. Open up," Fernando replied.

The door yielded.

Ossorio went into the room, took the girl in his arms, pressed her against his body and kissed her on the mouth. He lifted her into the air in order to set her on the bed, and when he looked at her, he saw that she was pale, with the pallor of a corpse, that her head was bent over like a cut iris.

Then Fernando felt a convulsive shuddering and his legs began to tremble and his teeth started to chatter. He saw flashes of light, luminous circles and flaming swords. Trembling like a man with a disease of the medulla, he left the room, closed the door and went down to the kitchen; from there he went out into the corridor and entered his bedroom. He put on his boots and went out into the street, still trembling, with unsteady feet.

The night was cold and the stars were shining in the sky. He kept trying to coordinate his movements, but his limbs wouldn't respond to his will. He was beginning to feel a real sense of pleasure at not having allowed himself to be carried away by his instincts. No, he wasn't just an animal that fulfills an organic law; he was a spirit, he was a conscience.

What would that poor girl, so kind, so gentle, so smiling, have done?

He could have married her, but the two of them would have been wretched.

At that moment, he recalled a girl in Yécora,[77] whom he had seduced, even though there had been neither affection nor anything resembling it in their relationship.

He'd never remembered the girl with such intensity as at that moment. What he couldn't understand was how he had been able to go on so long without bringing the memory of that girl back into his mind.

As he thought of the other girl, Adela's face was lost and the image of the girl from Yécora was powerfully engraved in its place.

He remembered Ascensión, Tozenaque's daughter, as he'd never remembered her until then. He had been going through a period of sexual frenzy at the time and he began to court her.

She was quite pretty and liked to play the coquette with the boys.

During one vacation period, Fernando pursued her and prowled around her house, until one afternoon, he succeeded in persuading her to go for a walk alone with him in the wheat fields, which were high enough to conceal a person.

The two of them walked toward an abandoned hermitage: hidden in a shaded spot formed by tall elm trees, that surrounded the wood, there were a considerable number of pita plants on one side, with brilliant green blades, bristling with thorns, rising up on a high incline.

When they reached this shady spot, night was beginning to fall.

Without any words of love, almost brutally, the sacrifice was consummated.

Al principio, la muchacha opuso resistencia, se defendió como pudo, se lamentó amargamente; después se entregó, sin fuerzas, con el corazón hinchado por el deseo, en medio de aquel anochecer de verano ardiente y voluptuoso.

XXXII

Al día siguiente, con el pretexto de un viaje corto, Fernando se marchó de Toledo.
Tomó el tren al mediodía y trasbordó en Castillejo.
Tendido en el banco de un coche de tercera, pasó horas y horas contemplando ensimismado el techo del vagón, pintado de amarillo, curvo como camarote de barco, con su farol de aceite, que se encendió al anochecer, y que apenas daba luz.
Se hizo de noche; pasaban por delante de la ventanilla sombras de árboles, pedruscos de la pared de una trinchera.
Salió la luna en menguante. De vez en cuando, al pasar cerca de una estación, se veía vagamente un molino de viento que, con sus aspas al aire, parecía estar pidiendo socorro.
Cerca de Albacete entró un labriego con una niña, a la que dejó tendida sobre un banco. La niña se durmió en seguida.
Su padre se puso a hablar con otro aldeano. De vez en cuando la niña abría los ojos, sonreía y llamaba a su mamá.
– Ahora viene – le decía Fernando, y la chica volvía a dormirse otra vez.
El vagón presentaba un aspecto extraño: hombres envueltos hasta la cabeza en mantas blancas y amarillas, aldeanos con sombrero ancho y calzón corto, cestas, líos, jaulas, viejas dormidas con el refajo puesto encima de la cabeza... todo envuelto en una atmósfera brumosa empañada por el humo del tabaco.
Sólo en un compartimiento en donde iban unas muchachas, se hablaba y se reía.
Llegó el tren al apeadero donde Fernando tenía que bajar. Cogió su lío de ropa y saltó del coche. La estación estaba completamente desierta, iluminada por dos faroles clavados en una tapia blanca.
– ¡Eh, el billete! – gritó un hombre envuelto en un capote. Ossorio le dió el billete.
– ¿Por dónde se sale de la estación? – le preguntó.
– ¿Va usted a Yécora?
– Sí.
– Ahí tiene usted dos coches.

At first the girl put up some resistance, defended herself as best she could and lamented bitterly; then she gave herself to him, with no force left in her, with her heart swollen with desire, in the midst of that ardent and voluptuous summer twilight.

XXXII

On the following day, on the pretext that he was taking a short trip, Fernando departed from Toledo.

He took the train at midday and changed trains at Castillejo.[78] Stretched out on a seat in the third-class coach, he spent hour upon hour absorbed in his thoughts, contemplating the overhead of the coach, painted yellow, curved like the stateroom on a ship, with its oil lamp that was lighted toward nightfall and which gave virtually no light at all.

Night fell; the shadows of trees, the rough stones of the wall of a deep railway cut kept passing in front of the window.

The waning moon appeared. From time to time, as they passed near some station, you could vaguely see a windmill, which seemed to be asking for help with its arms reaching up into the air.

Near Albacete[79], a farmer came in with a little girl and he had her stretch out on one of the benches. The little girl fell asleep right away.

Her father started to speak with a countryman. From time to time, the little girl would open her eyes and call for her mama.

"She'll be right here," Fernando would say to her and the little girl would go back to sleep.

The coach presented a strange impression: men wrapped up to their heads in white and yellow traveling blankets, rustic men with wide-brimmed hats and knee-length pants, baskets, bundles, cages, old women asleep, with a skirt thrown over their head..., everything bathed in a hazy atmosphere, clouded by tobacco smoke.

There was conversation and laughter in only one compartment, one in which several girls were traveling.

The train arrived at the stop where Fernando was supposed to get off. He picked up his bundle of clothes and jumped down from the coach. The station was completely deserted, illuminated by two lanterns attached to a white wall.

"Hey, how about your ticket!" shouted a man all wrapped up in a capote. Ossorio gave him his ticket.

"How does one get out of the station?" he asked him.

"Are you going to Yécora?"

"Yes."

"The coaches are over there."

Pasó Fernando por la puerta de la tapia blanca a una plazoleta que había delante de la estación, y vió una diligencia casi ocupada y una tartana. Se decidió por la tartana.

Hallábase ésta alumbrada por una linterna que daba más humo que luz. Subió Ossorio en el carricoche. De los dos cristales de delante, uno estaba roto, y en su lugar había un trapo sucio y lleno de agujeros.

Cerraban por detrás la tartana tres fajas de lona; el interior del coche estaba ocupado por unas cuantas maletas, dos o tres fardos, una perdiz en su jaula, y encima del montón que formaban estas cosas, dos hermosos ramos de flores de papel.

– Aquí viene alguna muchacha bonita – pensó Fernando, y no había acabado de pensarlo cuando apareció un hombre con trazas de salteador de caminos, envuelto hasta la cabeza, como si saliera del baño, en una manta a cuadros que no dejaba ver más que dos ojos amenazadores, una nariz aguileña y un bigotazo de carabinero.

El hombre subió a la tartana, se sentó sin dar las buenas noches, y se puso a observar a Fernando con una mirada inquisitorial. Éste, viendo que persistía en mirarle, cerró los ojos pidiéndose a sí mismo paciencia para soportar a aquel imbécil.

– ¿Pero no salimos? – dijo Fernando como dirigiéndose a una tercera persona.

Creyó que al decir esto su compañero de viaje le aniquilaba con sus ojos siniestros, y todas las ideas humildes de Ossorio se le marcharon al ver la insistencia del hombre en observarle; estuvo por decirle algo, pero se contuvo.

Poco después, una voz de tiple salió de entre los bigotes formidables:
– Vamos, Frasquito, echar a andar.

Si Fernando no hubiera estado seguro de la procedencia de la voz, hubiese creído que era una broma. Estudió con una curiosidad impertinente de arriba abajo y de abajo arriba al hombre de aspecto tan fiero y de voz tan ridícula.

El de la manta contestó mirándole con una mueca de desdén. Fué aquello un duelo de miradas a la luz de una linterna.

El cochero, a quien el hombre de la manta había llamado Frasquito, no hizo ningún caso de la advertencia; sin duda no tenía prisa y no se apresuraba a arrancar; pero en cambio hablaba con una volubilidad extraordinaria, y por lo que oyó Fernando, desafiaba al cochero de la diligencia a ver quién llegaba antes a Yécora; así que sólo cuando vió que el otro se subía al pescante, montó él para que las condiciones fuesen iguales y salieran los dos coches a la vez; ya arriba Frasquito, azotó los caballos, que arrancaron hacia un lado, y la tartana salió botando, dando tumbos y más tumbos, y a poco estuvo que no se hiciera pedazos en una tapia. El carricoche avanzaba y tomaba ventaja a la diligencia.

Fernando passed through the door in the white wall into a small square located in front of the station, and he saw a diligence that was almost full and a *tartana*, a two-wheeled round-top carriage. He decided in favor of the *tartana*.

A lantern used to light up this coach gave off more smoke than light. Ossorio climbed into the rickety, old coach. One of the two front window panes was broken and there was a filthy, tattered piece of cloth in its place.

Three strips of canvas closed off the *tartana* in the back; the interior of the coach was occupied by a number of suitcases, two or three bundles, a partridge in its cage and two beautiful bouquets of paper flowers on top of the pile formed by all the other things.

"Here comes a pretty girl," Fernando thought, and he had hardly finished thinking this when a man appeared, looking very much like a highwayman, bundled right up to his head, as if he were coming out of a bath, in a large, checkered traveling blanket, which only permitted you to see two menacing eyes, an aquiline nose and a heavy mustache like that of an armed revenue guard.

The man climbed up into the *tartana*, sat down without saying a word of greeting and began to observe Fernando with an inquisitorial look. The latter, when he saw that the fellow persisted in staring at him, closed his eyes, asking himself for enough patience to put up with that imbecile.

"Well, aren't we going to start?" Fernando said as if he were addressing a third party.

He believed that when he said this, his traveling companion was going to annihilate him with his sinister eyes and all of Ossorio's ideas of humility left him when he saw the persistence with which that man kept observing him; he was about to say something to him, but he restrained himself.

A little later, a soprano voice came from behind the formidable mustache:

"Come on Frasquito, let's be on our way."

If Fernando hadn't been certain of the source of the voice, he would have thought that it was a joke. With impertinent curiosity, he studied the man with so fierce an appearance and so ridiculous a voice, from head to toe and then back up gain.

The man in the traveling blanket responded by looking at him with a sneer of disdain. It was a duel of stares by the light of a lantern.

The coach driver, whom the man in the traveling blanket had called Frasquito, paid no attention whatsoever to the remark; he was obviously in no hurry and didn't seem pressed to pull out; in fact, quite the contrary; he was speaking with extraordinary volubility, and from what Fernando could hear, he was challenging the driver of the diligence to see who could arrive in Yécora first; so that only when he saw the other one getting up on the coach box, did he climb up so that the conditions should be equal, and so that the two coaches should depart at the same time; once Frasquito was up there, he whipped the horses and they pulled to one side, and the *tartana* departed, bouncing, lurching one way and the other, and was all but dashed to pieces against a wall. The rickety, old coach started moving forward and gaining over the diligence.

Por la ventana sin cristales empezó a entrar un viento helado que cortaba como un cuchillo, y al mismo tiempo hinchaba el trapo lleno de agujeros, puesto para remediar la falta del cristal, como una vela.

– ¿Por qué no lleva *faró, Fraquito*? – preguntó el de la manta sacando la cabeza por la ventana sin cristales.

– ¿*Pa qué*? –dijo el cochero volviendo la cabeza hacia atrás.

– *Pa* que no vaya a *volcá*.

– *Agora* ha *hablao uté* como quien *é* – replicó descaradamente Frasquito –. ¿*He volcao alguna ve*?

– No te incomodes, Frasquito, no lo digo por tanto.

Al oír en boca de aquel hombre de aspecto furibundo una explicación tan humilde, Fernando, que se había olvidado de sus buenos propósitos, se creyó en el caso de lanzar una mirada de absoluto desdén a su compañero de viaje.

Como allá no se podía dormir por el frío, Ossorio se puso a contemplar el campo por la ventana. Se veía una llanura extensa, sombría, con matorrales como puntos negros y charcos helados en los cuales rielaba la claridad de la noche; a lo lejos se distinguía un encadenamiento de colinas que se contorneaban en el cielo obscuro, iluminado por la luna rota torpemente.

Pronto la diligencia, que había quedado detrás de la tartana, comenzó a acercarse a ella; se vió la luz de su reverbero por entre las rendijas de la lona que cerraba el carricoche; se oyó el campanilleo de las colleras de los caballos que se fueron acercando, y, por último, un toque de bocina; el cochero dirigió la tartana a un lado del camino, y la diligencia pasó por delante, iluminando con su luz la carretera. No fué chica la indignación de Frasquito. Latigazos, gritos, juramentos, pintorescas blasfemias. Trotaron los caballos, chirriaron las ruedas, y la tartana, al golpear con las piedras de la carretera, saltó y rechinó y pareció que iba a romperse en mil pedazos.

La diligencia, en tanto, iba ganando terreno, alejándose, alejándose cada vez más. El aire entraba por la ventanilla y dejaba a los viajeros ateridos. Fernando trataba de sujetar el trapo que cerraba la ventana sin cristal, y viendo que no lo podía conseguir, se ponía la capa por encima del sombrero.

Y mientras tanto la diligencia iba alejándose cada vez más, y en la revuelta de una carretera se perdió de vista. Al poco rato el carricoche se detuvo.

– ¿Qué te pasa, *Fraquito*? – preguntó el de la manta.

– *Na*, que se me ha *perdío* el látigo.

Bajó Frasquito del pescante, volvió a subir breve tiempo después, y la tartana siguió dando tumbos y tumbos, siguiendo las vueltas de la carretera solitaria. La

An icy wind that cut through you like a knife started to come through the window without the pane, and at the same time the tattered cloth, which had been put in place to make up for the missing glass, swelled out like a sail.

"How come you don't have a *hea'light, Fraquito?*" the man in the traveling blanket asked, as he put his head outside the window with no pane.

"*Wha*' for?" said the coach driver, turning his head to the rear.

"So we don' end up tippin' over."

"*Now you're talkin' like the fool y' are*," Frasquito replied impudently. "*Hav' I eva' tip' ova'*."

"Don't get upset, Frasquito, I didn't mean anything by it."

When he heard such a humble explanation from the mouth of that man with the fierce appearance, Fernando, who had forgotten about his good intentions, thought this an opportune time to cast a glance of absolute disdain at his traveling companion.

Since it was impossible to sleep there because of the cold, Ossorio started to contemplate the countryside through the window. You could see a somber expanse of plain, with thickets resembling black spots, and frozen pools of water in which the light of the night was glistening; in the distance, you could make out a string of hills outlined against the dark sky, crudely illuminated by a fragment of moon.

Soon the diligence, which had remained behind the *tartana* till now, started to draw closer; you could see the light of its reflecting lamp between the cracks in the canvas enclosing the rickety, old coach; you could hear the tinkle of the bells on the horses' collars as they kept drawing nearer, and finally, the sound of a horn; the coach driver moved the *tartana* off to one side of the road and the diligence passed in front of them, illuminating the road with its light. Frasquito's indignation was by no means small. There was a cracking of a whip, shouts, oaths, picturesque blasphemies. The horses kept trotting along, the wheels squeaked and the *tartana*, as it struck the stones in the road, bounced and creaked and it seemed as if it were going to break into a thousand pieces.

In the meantime, the diligence kept gaining ground, drawing away, moving further and further ahead. The air kept coming in through the small window and left the travelers stiff with cold. Fernando kept trying to fasten down the cloth that covered the window with no pane, and when he saw he couldn't accomplish this, he pulled his cloak completely over his hat.

And all the while, the diligence kept drawing further ahead and was soon lost from sight at a turn in the road. Shortly thereafter, the rickety, old coach came to a stop.

"What's the matter, *Fraquito?*" asked the man in the traveling blanket.

"Nothin', just that I *los*' my whip."

Frasquito got down from the driver's seat, climbed back up a short while later and the *tartana* went on its way, bouncing and lurching, following the turns in the

linterna se apagó y se quedaron en el interior del carricoche a obscuras.

Se veía así más claramente el campo, los cerros negruzcos bombeados, las estrellas que iban palideciendo con la vaga e incierta luz del alba. El frío era cada vez más intenso; Ossorio comenzó a dar taconazos en el suelo del coche y notó que el piso se hundía bajo sus pies; el suelo de la tartana era de tablillas unidas con esparto, encima de las cuales había una estera de paja. Con los golpes de Ossorio, una de las tablillas se había roto, y por el agujero entraba más frío aún.

De pronto Frasquito volvió a parar el coche, se bajó del pescante y echó a correr hacia atrás. Se le había caído nuevamente el látigo. Era para matarlo.

Pasó tiempo y más tiempo. Frasquito no parecía; de improviso sonó en el interior de la tartana ese ruido característico que hacen las navajas de muelle al abrirse.

Al oírlo, Fernando se estremeció. Pensó que el cochero les había dejado allá intencionadamente. El tío de la voz atiplada se iba a vengar de las miradas desdeñosas de Fernando.

– No va a encontrar el látigo – dijo el de la manta al poco rato – . Aquí le he cortado yo una cuerda.

Ossorio respiró. Al cabo de un cuarto de hora vino Frasquito sudando a mares sin el látigo. Ató la cuerda que le dio el de la manta a un sarmiento que cogió de una viña, se subió al pescante y echó la tartana a andar de nuevo.

El cielo iba blanqueando; a un lado, al ras del suelo, sobre unas colinas redondas, se veía una faja rojo anaranjada en la que se destacaban, negros y retorcidos, algunos olivos centenarios y pinos achaparrados.

Poco a poco la tierra fue aclarándose; primero apareció como una cosa gris, indefinida, luego ya más distinta con matas de berceo y de retama; fueron apareciendo a lo lejos formas confusas de árboles y de casas. Comenzaban a pasar por la carretera hombres atezados envueltos en capotes pardos; otros, con anguarinas de capucha, que iban bromeando, siguiendo a las caballerías cargadas de leña, y mujeres vestidas con refajos de bayeta arreando a sus borriquillos.

La luz fué llegando lentamente, brillaba en los campos verdes, centelleaba con blancura deslumbradora en las casas de labores, enjalbegadas con cal.

El pueblo iba apareciendo a lo lejos con su caserío agrupado en las estribaciones de un cerro desnudo, con sus torres y su cúpula redonda, de tejas azules y blancas.

La tartana se iba acercando al pueblo.

Aparecieron en el camino una caseta de peón caminero, una huerta cerrada, un parador...

secluded road. The lantern went out and they were left in darkness inside the rickety old coach.

In this way, you could see the countryside more clearly, the blackish, bulging hills, the stars growing faint with the coming of the dim, uncertain light of the dawn. The cold grew more and more intense; Ossorio started to kick against the floor of the coach with his heels and he noticed that the flooring was giving way under his feet; the floor of the *tartana* was made of boards held together by esparto grass, with a matting of straw on top. Under Ossorio's blows, one of the boards had broken and even more cold air was coming in through the hole.

Suddenly Frasquito stopped the coach again, he got down from the driver's seat and began to run back, away from the coach. His whip had fallen down once more. He was fit to be tied.

More and more time kept passing. Frasquito was nowhere to be seen; suddenly there was a sound inside the coach that is the characteristic noise switchblade knives make when they are opened.

When he heard it, Fernando shuddered. He thought that the coach driver had left them alone there intentionally. The fellow with the high-pitched voice was going to take revenge for Fernando's scornful glances.

"He isn't going to find the whip," the man in the traveling blanket said after a while. I've cut a length of rope for him here."

Ossorio breathed easier. Frasquito came back after a quarter hour, sweating profusely, but without the whip. He took the rope given him by the man in the traveling blanket and tied it to a vine shoot he fetched from a vineyard, and then he climbed back on the driver's seat and the *tartana* started to move again.

The sky was turning white; to one side, level with the ground, you could see a reddish-orange band of color over some rounded hills, and, black and twisted, stumpy, century-old olive trees and pines were outlined against it.

Little by little, the countryside was getting lighter; at first it appeared somewhat gray and indefinite, then considerably more distinct, with matweed bushes and Spanish broom; the confused forms of trees and houses started appearing in the distance. Men with sun-tanned faces, wrapped in brown cloaks, were beginning to pass along the road; others, in sleeveless, hooded coats, who were walking along, joking, following their mounts, which were loaded down with wood, and women who were dressed in baize skirts, urging on their small donkeys.

Slowly it started to grow light, and it shone on the green fields and it sparkled with dazzling whiteness on the farmhouses whitewashed with lime.

The town was beginning to appear in the distance, with its cluster of houses grouped together on the spur of a barren hill, with its towers and round dome made of blue and white tiles.

The *tartana* was coming closer to town.

A road laborer's shack appeared on the road, an enclosed vegetable garden, a wayside inn...

El carricoche entró en el pueblo levantando nubes de polvo.

El sol arrancaba destellos a los cristales de las ventanas; parecían las casas presas de un incendio que se corría por todos los cristales y vidrieras de aquel lugarón.

Cacareaban los gallos, ladraban los perros; alguna que otra beata cruzaba la solitaria calle; despertaba la ciudad manchega para volverse a dormir en seguida aletargada por el sol...

XXXIII

Yécora es un pueblo terrible; no es de esas negrísimas ciudades españolas, montones de casas viejas, amarillentas, derrengadas con aleros enormes sostenidos por monstruosos canecillos, arcos apuntados en las puertas y ajimeces con airosos parteluces; no son sus calles estrechas y tortuosas como obscuras galerías ni en sus plazas solitarias crece la hierba verde y lustrosa.

No hay en Yécora la torre ojival o románica en donde hicieron hace muchos años su nido de ramas las cigüeñas, ni el torreón de homenaje del noble castillo, ni el grueso muro derrumbado con su ojiva o su arco de herradura en la puerta.

No hay allá los místicos retablos de los grandes maestros del Renacimiento español, con sus hieráticas figuras que miraron, en éxtasis, los ojos, llenos de cándida fe, de los antepasados; ni la casa solariega de piedra sillar con su gran escudo carcomido por la acción del tiempo; ni las puertas ferradas y claveteadas con clavos espléndidos y ricos; ni las rejas con sus barrotes como columnas salomónicas tomadas por el orín; ni los aldabones en forma de grifos y de quimeras; ni el paseo tranquilo en donde toman el sol, envueltos en sus capas pardas, los soñolientos hidalgos. Allí todo es nuevo en las cosas, todo es viejo en las almas. En las iglesias, grandes y frías, no hay apenas cuadros, ni altares, y éstos se hallan adornados con imágenes baratas traídas de alguna fábrica alemana o francesa.

Se respira en la ciudad un ambiente hostil a todo lo que sea expansión, elevación de espíritu, simpatía humana. El arte ha huído de Yécora, dejándolo en medio de sus campos que rodean montes desnudos, al pie de una roca calcinada por el sol, sufriendo las inclemencias de un cielo africano que vierte torrentes de luz sobre las casas enjalbegadas, blancas, de un color agrio y doloroso, sobre sus calles rectas y monótonas y sus caminos polvorientos; le ha dejado en los brazos de una religión áspera, formalista, seca; entre las uñas de un mundo de pequeños caciques, de leguleyos, de prestamistas, de curas, gente de vicios sórdidos y de hipocresías miserables.

Los escolapios tienen allí un colegio y contribuyen con su educación a embrutecer lentamente el pueblo. La vida en Yécora es sombría, tétrica, repulsiva; no se siente

The rickety old coach entered the town raising clouds of dust.

The sun was snatching reflected gleams from the window panes; the houses seemed to have been set afire with a flame that ran over all the panes of window glass and all the glass doors of that somber town.

Roosters were crowing, dogs were barking; every so often some zealously pious woman would cross the deserted street; this Manchegan city was awakening, only to go back to sleep again almost immediately, lulled into lethargy by the sun...

XXXIII

Yécora is a terrible town; it isn't one of those extremely dark Spanish cities, heaps of old houses, yellowish and contorted, with enormous eaves supported by monstrous corbels, with pointed arches over the doors and arched windows with graceful mullions in the middle; its streets aren't narrow and winding like darkened galleries, nor does bright, green grass grow in its secluded squares.

There is no ogival or Romanesque tower in Yécora, where the storks made their nest of branches many years before, nor the keep of a noble castle, nor the thick, crumbling wall with its ogive or horseshoe-shaped arch at the gate.

There are no mystical retables of the great masters of the Spanish Renaissance there, with their hieratic figures which the eyes of our ancestors, eyes filled with candid faith, contemplated with ecstasy; nor the ancestral mansion built of ashlars, with its great coat-of-arms eaten away by the passage of time; nor doors trimmed with iron and garnished with splendid, exquisite nails; nor grillwork with bars like wreathed columns, eaten away by rust; nor door knockers in the shape of griffins and chimeras; nor that tranquil promenade, where somnolent hidalgos take the sun, wrapped in their drab-colored capes. Everything that deals with material things there is new, everything dealing with the spirit is old. There are hardly any paintings or altars in the spacious, cold churches, and what there is, is adorned with cheap images brought from some German or French factories.

In the city, you breathe an atmosphere hostile to all that might be expansive, have elevation of spirit or human congeniality. Art has fled from Yécora, leaving it in the midst of its fields, surrounded by barren mountains, at the foot of a rock burned white by the sun, suffering the inclement effects of an African sky that pours torrents of light onto the bleached, whitewashed houses, acrid and doleful in color, and onto its straight, monotonous streets and its dust-covered roads; it has been left in the arms of a harsh, formalistic and arid religion; in the clutches of a world of petty political bosses, pettifoggers, moneylenders, priests, people with sordid vices and despicable hypocrisies.

The Piarists have a school there, and they contribute to the gradual brutalizing of the people with their education.[80] Life in Yécora is somber, gloomy and repulsive;

la alegría de vivir; en cambio pesan sobre las almas las sordideces de la vida.
No se nota en parte alguna la preocupación por la comodidad, ni la preocupación por el adorno. La gente no sonríe.
No se ven por las calles muchachas adornadas con flores en la cabeza; ni de noche los mozos pelando la pava en las esquinas. El hombre se empareja con la mujer con la obscuridad en el alma, medroso, como si el sexo fuera una vergüenza o un crimen, y la mujer, indiferente, sin deseo de agradar, recibe al hombre sobre su cuerpo y engendra hijos sin amor y sin placer, pensando quizá en las penas del infierno con que le ha amenazado el sacerdote, legando al germen que nace su mismo bárbaro sentimiento del pecado.
Todo allí, en Yécora, es claro, recortado, nuevo, sin matiz, frío. Hasta las imágenes de las hornacinas que se ven sobre los portales están pintadas hace pocos años.

XXXIV

La casa del administrador de la familia de Ossorio era espaciosa; estaba situada en una de las principales calles de la ciudad.
Se entraba por el zaguán a un vestíbulo estucado, con las paredes llenas de malos cuadros. Del vestíbulo, en donde había una chimenea con el hueco de más altura que la de un hombre, se pasaba por un corredor a un patio muy chico, con una gradería en su fondo, en la cual se veían en hileras filas de tiestos con plantas muertas por los hielos del pasado invierno.
De un extremo del patio, cerca de la pared, una escalera daba acceso a la parte alta de la gradería, que era una ancha plataforma enladrillada, en uno de cuyos rincones se veía un aljibe recubierto de cal adonde iba a dar el agua de todas las cañerias del tejado. Desde la plataforma aquella se pasaba por una puerta embadurnada de azul a cuartos obscuros, bajos de techo, llenos de gavillas y de haces de sarmientos y de leña de vid.
Al recorrer la casa, Fernando recordó con placer alguno que otro rincón; el gabinete, la alcoba suya, la cocina, el despacho del administrador le hicieron el mismo efecto de antipatía que cuando era muchacho. Estaba todo dispuesto y arreglado de un modo insoportable; los malos cuadros de iglesia abundaban; el piano de la sala tenía una funda de hilo crudo con ribetes rojos; las sillas y sillones se hallaban envueltos en idénticos envoltura gris. En las puertas de cada cuarto, cruzándolas, había gruesas cadenas de hierro.
Después de descansar del viaje, la primera idea que tuvo Fernando fué ir a casa de Tozenaque. Salió a la calle y se dirigió por una alameda polvorienta, y luego

nobody feels the joy of living; quite the contrary, the sordid aspects of life weigh heavily upon their spirits.

Nowhere can you notice a preoccupation with comfort or a preoccupation with adornment of any kind. The people do not smile.

On the streets, you don't see girls with flowers adorning their hair, or young men carrying on flirtations on street corners at night. A man couples with a woman with darkness in his soul, fearful, as if sex were a shame or a crime, and the woman, indifferent, without any desire to please, receives the man upon her body and begets children, without love and without pleasure, thinking perhaps of the torments of hell with which the priest has threatened her, bequeathing to the seed that is being created her own barbaric feeling of sin.

Everything there in Yécora is bright, clear cut, new, with no nuances, cold. Even the images in the niches seen over the vestibules were painted only a few years ago.

XXXIV

The house belonging to the administrator of the Ossorio family estate was spacious; it was located on one of the principal streets in the city.

You went in through an entryway into a stuccoed vestibule, with walls covered with paintings in poor taste. From the vestibule, where there was a fireplace with a recess higher than the height of a man, you made your way along a corridor to a very small patio with a series of steps at the far end, on which you could see lines of flower pots with plants that had been killed by the frost of the past winter.

Near the wall at one end of the patio, a stairway gave access to the upper part of the series of steps, which consisted of a wide platform paved with bricks, with a lime-covered cistern in one corner, into which the water from all the rainspouts would pour down from the roof. From that platform, you went through a door, daubed with blue paint, into several dark rooms with low ceilings, full of bundles of vine shoots and fagots of vine kindling wood.

As he made his way through the house, Fernando remembered some corner here and there with pleasure; the sitting room, his own bedroom, the kitchen, the administrator's office, all gave him the same feeling of aversion as they had when he was a boy. Everything was laid out and arranged in an insufferable manner; there was an abundance of church pictures in poor taste; the piano in the drawing room had a slipcover made of coarse linen with red trimming; the chairs and armchairs were covered in an identical gray material. On the doors of each room, there were heavy iron chains crossing over them.

After resting from his trip, the first idea Fernando had was to go visit Tozenaque's house. He went out into the street and made his way along a dusty, tree-lined walk,

cruzando unos viñedos hacia la casa de labor en donde antes vivía la muchacha. Llegado allí, contempló largo rato desde muy lejos el paraje, y a un hombre que se cruzó en el camino le preguntó por la familia de Ascensión.

Hacía much tiempo que se habían marchado, le dijo. Se fueron primeramente a vivir a las Cuevas, porque andaban al parecer mal de dinero; después emigraron todos a Argel, excepto una de las chicas que casó en el pueblo.

Fernando preguntó cuál de las hijas era la que se había casado en Yécora; el hombre no le supo dar razón. Cruzó Ossorio por los viñedos y en la alameda se sentó sobre un ribazo, al borde del polvoriento camino.

¡Qué silencio por todas partes!

De aquella enorme ciudad no brotaba más que el canto estridente de los gallos, que se interrumpían unos a otros desde lejos. El cielo estaba azul, de un azul profundo, y sobre él se destacaba, escueto y pelado, un monte pedregoso con una ermita en lo alto.

Ossorio pensaba en Ascensión, sin poder separar de la muchacha su recuerdo. ¿Qué sería de ella? ¿Cómo sería antes? Porque no había llegado a formarse una idea de si era buena o mala, inteligente o no. Nunca se preocupó de esto.

Si en aquella época él hubiera sospechado las decepciones, las tristezas de la vida, quizá se hubiera casado con Ascensión; ¿por qué no? Pero cómo en aquel lugarón atrasado, hostil a todo lo que fuese piedad, caridad, simpatía humana? Allí no se podían tener más que ideas mezquinas, bajas, ideas esencialmente católicas. Allí, de muchacho, le habían enseñado, al mismo tiempo que la doctrina, a considerar gracioso y listo al hombre que engaña, a despreciar a la mujer engañada y a reírse del marido burlado.

Él no había podido sustraerse a las ideas tradicionales de un pueblo tan hipócrita como bestial. Había conseguido a la muchacha en un momento de abandono; no se paró a pensar si en ella estaría su dicha; se contentó con oír las felitaciones de sus amigos y con esconderse al saber que el padre de la Ascensión le andaba buscando.

XXXV

Apenas cambió algunas palabras con el administrador, su mujer y sus hijos.

Al día siguiente, por la mañana, subió a las Cuevas, que estaban en la falda del Castillo, a preguntar de nuevo por la familia de Ascensión, a ver si se enteraba de

and he then crossed over some vineyards toward the farmhouse in which the girl had lived at that time. When he arrived there, he stood at a considerable distance contemplating the place for a long time, and he asked a man whom he ran across on the road about Ascensión's family.

He was told that they had gone away a long time ago. At first they went off to live in Las Cuevas, because they were apparently having serious financial problems; then they all emigrated to Algiers, except for one of the girls, who got married and lived in town.

Fernando asked him which one of the girls it was who had gotten married in Yécora; the man was unable to give him this information. Fernando crossed through the vineyards and sat down on an embankment on the tree-lined walk, beside the dusty road.

How silent it was everywhere!

The only sound that emanated from that horrible city was the shrill crowing of the roosters, interrupting one another from afar. The sky was blue, a deep blue, and a rocky mountain, unadorned and barren, with a hermitage at the summit, was outlined against it.

Ossorio kept thinking about Ascensión and he couldn't separate his memories from the girl. What could have become of her? What was she really like before? The fact is that he really hadn't been able to develop a clear idea of whether she was good or bad, intelligent or not. He never troubled himself with this.

If at that time he had suspected the deceptions, the sad events of life, perhaps he would have married Ascensión; why not? But how could he put up with this backward, gloomy town, which was hostile to anything that might relate to compassion, charity or humane feeling? All you could have there were petty, base, essentially Catholic ideas. There, as a boy, they had taught him, along with his Catechism, to consider the man who seduces a woman to be accomplished and clever, to look down on the woman seduced and to ridicule the cuckolded husband.

He wouldn't have been able to resist the traditional ideas of a town that was as hypocritical as it was bestial. He had seduced the girl in a moment of abandonment; he didn't stop to wonder whether his happiness could be with her; he was content to hear the congratulations of his friends and hide when he found out that Ascensión's father was going around looking for him.

XXXV

He hardly exchanged a single word with the administrator, his wife and their children.

On the following day, early in the morning, he went up to Las Cuevas, which was on the lower slope of El Castillo, to ask about Ascensión's family again, to see

algo más, y si podía saber cuál de las muchachas era la que se había casado.

El Castillo era un monte lleno de pedruscos, árido, seco, con una ermita en la cumbre. El sol de siglos parecía haberle tostado matizándole del color de yesca que tenía; daba la impresión de algo vigoroso y ardiente, como el sabor de un vino centenario.

La senda que escalaba el cerro subía en ziszás; era una calzada cubierta de piedras puntiagudas que corrían debajo de los pies; a un lado y a otro del quebrado camino había capillas muy pequeñas, en cuyo interior, embutidos en la pared, se veían cuadros de azulejos que representaban escenas de la Pasión.

A lo largo de la calzada, sobre todo en su primera parte, veíanse filas de puertas azules, cada una con su número escrito con tinta obscura; eran aquellas puertas las entradas de las cuevas excavadas en el monte, tenían una chimenea que brotaba al ras del suelo y alguna, un corralillo con un par de higueras blancas.

Fernando se detuvo en una cueva que era al mismo tiempo cantina, pidió una copa, se sentó en un banco y gradualmente fué llevando la conversación con la mujer del mostrador hacia lo que a él le interesaba.

Tozenaque el Manejero y toda su família se había marchado a Argelia, le dijo la mujer, excepto una de las chicas casada en el pueblo y que vivía en el Pulpillo, en la misma labor que antes tuvo su padre.

– ¿Y por qué vino aquí el Manejero, cuando tenía su casa y sus tierras?

– ¡Pues ahí verá usted! Que resultaron que no eran suyas; que las tenía hipotecadas – repuso la tabernera– . Además, sabe usted, el hermano le engañó y le sacó muchos miles de pesetas.

– Y aquí en las Cuevas, ¿el hombre marchaba?

– No. Acostumbrados a otra manera de vivir, pues, no podía. Luego, la cueva suya, el ayuntamiento la mandó tirar, y entonces fué cuando el Manejero se decidió a irse.

– Y ¿cuál de las muchachas se casó?

– Pues no sé decirle a usted. Era una rubita; así pequeña de cuerpo, garbosa.

Salió Ossorio del tabernucho y fué subiéndo por el camino hacia la ermita de la cumbre. Se veía el pueblo desde allí a vista de pájaro, enorme, con sus tejados en hilera, simétricos como las casillas de un tablero de ajedrez, todos de un tinte pardo negruzco, y sus casas blancas unas, otras amarillentas de color de barro, y sus caminos blancos cubiertos de una espesa capa de polvo, con algunos árboles escasos, lánguidos y sin follaje.

Alrededor del pueblo se extendía la huerta como un gran lago siempre verde, cruzado por la línea de plata ondulante de la carretera. Más lejos, cerrando la vallada, montes pedregosos, plomizos, se destacaban con valentía en el cielo azul de Prusia,

if he could find out anything more and if he could learn which of the girls was the one who had gotten married.

El Castillo was a barren, arid mountain, covered with jagged rocks, with a hermitage at the summit. Through the long centuries, the sun seemed to have scorched it, blending it to the color of touchwood that it now had; it left you with the impression of something vigorous and burning, like the flavor of a century-old wine.

The road that led to the top of the hill rose in a zigzag fashion; it was a roadway covered with sharp-pointed stones that slid under your feet; there were very small chapels on either side of the rough road, and in their interiors, you could see pictures made of glazed colored tiles inlaid on the walls, representing scenes of the Passion.

All along the roadway, especially along the first part, you could see rows of blue doors, each one with its number written in dark ink; those doors were the entrances to the caves that had been excavated in the mountain; they had chimneys that emerged at ground level, and a number of them had a little fenced in yard with a couple of white fig trees.

Fernando stopped at a cave that served as a tavern at the same time; he asked for a glass of wine, sat down on a bench and gradually began leading the conversation with the woman behind the counter to the matter that interested him.

Tozenaque the Horse Trainer had gone off to Algeria along with his whole family, the woman told him, except for one of the girls who had married in town and was living in El Pulpillo, in the same farmhouse that her father had owned before.

"But why did the Horse Trainer come here when he had his house and his land?"

"Well, you'll see now! Because it turned out that they weren't his; that they were mortgaged," the tavern keeper's wife replied. "Besides, you know, his brother cheated him and took many thousands of *pesetas* from him."

"Was the man able to get by here, in Las Cuevas?"

"No. Since they were accustomed to another way of life, well, he couldn't make it. Also, as for his cave, the City Council gave orders to have it torn down, and it was then that the Horse Trainer decided to go away."

"And which one of the girls got married?"

"Well, I can't tell you exactly. She was a little blonde; sort of small in body, very attractive."

Ossorio left the squalid tavern and kept walking up the road toward the hermitage at the summit. From there, you had a bird's eye view of the enormous town, with its roofs all in rows, symmetrical like the squares on a chess board, all blackish-brown in tone, its houses, some white, others yellowish like the color of clay, and its white roads, covered with a thick coat of dust, and a few meager, languid, leafless trees.

The irrigated produce gardens extended all around the town like a great lake, eternally green, traversed by the line of undulating silver that was the main road. Further away, closing in the valley, rocky, lead-colored mountains projected boldly

ardiente, intenso como la plegaria de un místico. Y en aquel silencio de la ciudad y de la huerta, sólo se oía el estridente cacareo de los gallos que se contestaban desde lejos.

Salían delgadas y perezosas columnas de humo de las chimeneas de las cuevas y de las casas. Resonaba el silencio. De pronto, Fernando oyó el murmullo de un rezo o canción y se asomó a ver lo que era.

Venían de dos en dos, en fila, las muchachas de un colegio o de un asilo, uniformadas con un traje de color de chocolate; detrás de ellas iban dos monjas y cantaban las asiladas una triste y dolorosa salmodia...

XXXVI

Al día siguiente, Fernando se levantó muy temprano: estaba amaneciendo; por la ventana de su cuarto entraba la luz fría, mate, sin brillo, la luz deslustrada del amanecer.

Salió a la calle. Hallábase el pueblo silencioso; las casas grises, amarillentas, de color de adobe, parecían dormir con sus persianas y sus cortinas tendidas. El cielo estaba gris, como un manto de plomo; alguna que otra luz moribunda, parpadeaba sin fuerza ante el santo guardado en la hornacina de un portal. Corría un viento frío, penetrante.

Ossorio fué saliendo del pueblo hacia el campo, recorrió la alameda y comenzó a cruzar viñedos. Había aparecido ya el sol; brillaban los bancales verdes de trigo y alcacel, como trozos de mar, plateados por el rocío. El cielo estaba azul, claro y puro, de una claridad dulce y suave.

A la hora se halló Fernando en el Pulpillo. Todo estaba igual que antes. Se acercó a la casa y se asomó a la ventana de la cocina. Cerca del fuego, estaba ella, Ascensión, con un pañuelo de color en la cabeza, inclinada sobre la cuna de un niño.

Fernando dió la vuelta a la alquería y entró en la cocina. Saludó con una voz ahogada por la emoción. Al verle ella palideció; él se quedó admirado al encontrarla tan demacrada y tan vieja.

– ¿Qué quieres aquí? ¿A qué vienes? – preguntó ella.

Fernando no supo qué contestar.

– ¡Vete! – gritó la mujer con un gesto enérgico señalándole la puerta.

– ¿No está tu marido?

– No. Sabía que estabas en el pueblo, pero no creí que te atreverías a venir.

– Me porté mal contigo, pero has tenido suerte, más suerte que yo – murmuró Fernando.

into the Prussian-blue sky, fervent and intense, like the supplication of a mystic. And all you could hear in that silence of the city and the produce gardens was the shrill crowing of the roosters as they answered one another from afar.

Slender, indolent columns of smoke kept rising from the chimneys of the caves and houses. The silence reverberated. Suddenly, Fernando heard the murmur of a prayer or a song and he glanced over to see what it was.

Two by two, the girls from a school or an orphanage, were coming by in rows, dressed in chocolate-colored uniforms; two nuns were walking behind them and the girls from the orphanage were singing a sad and doleful psalmody...

XXXVI

On the following day, Fernando got up very early; dawn was just breaking; the cold, flat, lusterless light of early morning was coming in through the window of his room.

He went out into the street. The town was silent; the gray, yellowish, adobe-colored houses seemed to be asleep, with their window blinds and curtains drawn. The sky was gray, like a leaden mantle; here and there a moribund light was blinking weakly in front of the saint that stood in the vaulted niche of an entry door. A cold, penetrating wind was blowing.

Ossorio kept moving away from town toward the countryside, and he walked along the tree-lined promenade and started to cross through the vineyards. The sun had already appeared; the green, oblong fields of wheat and blooming barley were glistening like patches of sea, turned silvery by the dew. The sky was blue, clear and pure, with a sweet, delicate brightness.

After an hour, Fernando found himself in El Pulpillo. Everything was the same as before. He approached the house and peered in through the kitchen window. There she was, near the fire, Ascensión, with a colored scarf over her head, leaning over a child's cradle.

Fernando walked around the farmhouse and went into the kitchen. He greeted her in a voice choked with emotion. When she saw him, she turned pale; he stood there, astonished at finding her looking so emaciated and so old.

"What do you want here? Why have you come?" she asked.

Fernando didn't know what to answer.

"Go away!" the woman shouted with a forceful gesture as she pointed to the door.

"Your husband isn't here?"

"No. I knew that you were in town, but I didn't think you would dare come here."

"I behaved rather badly to you, but you've been fortunate, more fortunate than I," Fernando murmured.

— ¡Vete! No quiero oirte.
— ¿Por qué? De los dos quizá soy yo el más desgraciado.
— ¡Tú desgraciado! ¿Entonces yo?
— Tú tienes hijos; tienes un marido que te quiere.
— Vete, por favor, márchate; puede venir mi marido y entonces será peor para ti.
— ¿Por qué? ¿Qué iba a hacer? ¿Matarme? Me haría un favor. Además, que él no sabe lo que ha pasado entre los dos. Pero hablemos – dijo Ossorio apoyándose en el respaldo de una silla.
— No quiero oirte; no quiero oirte. ¡Vete!
— No. Sí, me voy. Pero quisiera antes hablarte.
— Te digo que no, que no y que no.
— ¿No quieres atender mis razones?
— No.
— Eres cruel.
— ¿No lo has sido tú más?
— Pero la suerte te ha vengado... Tú eres feliz.
— ¡Feliz! – murmuró ella con una sonrisa llena de amargura.
— ¿No lo eres?
— Vete, vete de una vez.

Fernando paseó la mirada por el cuarto, se fijó en la cuna y se acercó a ver al niño que allí dormía.

— No le toques, no le toques – gritó la mujer levantándose de su asiento.
— Tú no perdonas.
— No.
— Sin embargo, yo no tuve toda la culpa. Tú no lo creerás...
— No.
— Si quisieras oírme... un momento.
— Vete; no quiero oir nada.
— Adiós, pues – murmuró Fernando y salió de la casa pensativo –. Odiar tanto – se decía al marchar hacia el pueblo –. Si fuera buena, me hubiera perdonado. ¡Qué imbécil es la vida!

XXXVII

— A ver si sienta ya la cabeza – dijo el administrador al saber que Fernando se quedaba en el pueblo.

Ossorio quería permanecer algún tiempo en Yécora; esperaba que allí su voluntad

"Go away! I don't want to hear you."
"Why? Of the two of us, perhaps it is I who am the more unhappy."
"You unhappy! And how about me?"
"You have children, you have a husband who loves you."
"Go away, please; get out of here. My husband may come home and then it will be all the worse for you."
"Why? What could he do? Kill me? He'd be doing me a favor. Besides, he surely doesn't know what happened between us. But let's talk," said Ossorio, leaning on the back of a chair.
"I don't want to hear you, I don't want to hear you. Go away!"
"No. All right then, I'll go. But I'd like to speak to you first."
"I tell you no, no, absolutely no."
"You don't want to hear my explanations?"
"No."
"You're cruel."
"Weren't you even more so?"
"But destiny has avenged you... You are happy."
"Happy!" she muttered with a smile filled with bitterness.
"Aren't you?"
"Get out of here, get out once and for all."
Fernando glanced around the room, stared at the cradle and went over to see the child sleeping there.
"Don't touch him, don't touch him," the woman shouted as she got up from her chair.
"You don't forgive."
"No."
"Nevertheless, I wasn't wholly responsible. You probably don't believe it, but..."
"No."
"If you would only hear me out...for a moment."
"Go away. I don't want to hear anything."
"Goodbye then," Fernando murmured, and he went out of the house, rapt in thought. "To hate so much," he said to himself as he started to walk toward town. "If she were really good, she would have forgiven me. How idiotic life is!"

XXXVII

"Let's see if he will come to his senses now," said the administrator, when he found out that Fernando was remaining in town.

Ossorio wanted to remain in Yécora for some time; he was hoping that, in a

desmayada se rebelase y buscara una vida enérgica, o concluyera de postrarse aceptando definitivamente una existencia monótona y vulgar.

Le pareció que si podía resistir y aficionarse al pueblo aquel y sentirse religioso en Yécora, a pesar de las ideas sórdidas y mezquinas de la tal ciudad, era porque su alma se encontraba en un estado de postración y decadencia absolutos.

Los días siguientes de su llegada se sucedieron con una gran monotonía. Por las tardes, Fernando paseaba con algunos condiscípulos que habían ido a su casa a renovar con él su amistad...

Aquella tarde, después del paseo, entraron Fernando y dos amigos que le acompañaban en la sacristía de una iglesia destartalada del pueblo. Se sentaron los tres en una banqueta negra que había debajo de un cuadro grande y obscuro de las Ánimas.

En las paredes de la sacristía colgaban mugrientos carteles amarillos, escritos en latín con letras capitales rojas. Entraba la luz por una ventana pequeña e iluminaba el cuarto; a un lado se veía un armario roñoso y carcomido donde se guardaban casullas y ornamentos; encima de él, un busto de una santa o de una monja en madera pintada, que tenía una peana con vestigios de haber sido dorada y un agujero elíptico en el pecho que antes debió de servir para guardar las reliquias de la santa o monja que representaba la escultura.

En el cuarto iba y venía un sacristán viejo con cara de bandido. Comenzó a sonar una campana. A poco entró un cura joven en la sacristía, un muchacho fuerte y rollizo que parecía un toro, saludó a los dos amigos de Fernando y a éste también, tímidamente.

– ¿No te acuerdas de él? – preguntó uno de los amigos de Ossorio, señalándole al cura – . Sí, hombre; Pepico, un muchacho muy gordo, con cara de bruto, hijo del sastre. Es más joven que nosotros...

– Sí, algo recuerdo.

– Pues es éste; aquí lo tienes hecho un padre de almas.

– Oye, Pepico – le preguntó el otro de los amigos al cura joven – ¿cuándo te van a hacer más grande esa moneda que llevas en la cabeza?

– Cuando me ordene en mayores.

– ¿De modo que ahora estás en cuarto menguante?

El cura joven hizo un movimiento de hombros, como indicando que a él le tenían sin cuidado aquellas irreverencias. El amigo de Fernando volvió a la carga.

– Y oye, ese redondel tendrá un tamaño fijo, ¿verdad?

– No. Es *ad libitum*.

– Nada; hasta que no habláis latín no estáis satisfechos los curas.

El muchacho volvió a hacer otro gesto de indiferencia y siguió paseando a lo largo de la sacristía.

place like this, his apathetic will would rebel and make him search out a more energetic way of life, or else that he would end up prostrating himself and accepting a monotonous and routine existence once and for all.

It seemed to him that if he were truly able to put up with this town, and take a liking to it and feel religious here in Yécora, in spite of the sordid and petty ideas of a city like that, it was because his spirit had reached a state of absolute prostration and decay.

The days following his arrival succeeded one another with considerable monotony. In the afternoon, Fernando would stroll around with some of his former classmates, who had come to the house to renew their friendship with him...

That afternoon, after their stroll, Fernando and the two friends who were accompanying him went into the sacristy of a dilapidated church in town. The three of them sat down on a black bench that was located underneath a large, dark painting of Las Animas.

Grimy, yellow placards, written in Latin with red capital letters, were hanging on the walls of the sacristy. The light was coming in through a small window and illuminating the room; on one side, you could see a filthy, worm-eaten wardrobe where they kept the chasubles and ornaments; on top of it was a bust of a female saint or a nun, in painted wood, which had a pedestal, and it showed traces of once having been gilded and had an elliptical hole in the breast which must have once been used to store the relics of the saint or nun represented by the piece of sculpture.

An old sacristan with the face of a bandit kept coming and going. A bell began to ring. Shortly thereafter, a young priest, a strong, stocky young fellow, looking very much like a bull, came into the sacristy and timidly greeted Fernando and his two friends.

"Don't you remember him?" one of his friends asked Ossorio, pointing at the priest. "Yes, indeed, Pepico, a very fat boy with a brutish face, the tailor's son. He's younger than we are..."

"Yes, I somewhat remember him."

"Well, this is the same one; here you see him, turned into a father of souls."

"Hey, Pepico," the other friend asked the young priest, "when are they going to let you have a larger ring than the one you now have on your head?"

"When I'm ordained into major orders."

"Then you mean that for the time being you're only in the last quarter-moon stage?"

The young priest made a movement with his shoulders as if to indicate that those irreverent remarks were of no concern to him. Fernando's friend renewed the attack.

"And by the way, that circular tonsure probably has a fixed size, isn't that so?"

"No. It's *ad libitum* (to your own taste)."

"What's the use; you priests aren't satisfied unless you're speaking in Latin."

The young man again made a gesture of indifference and continued walking all around the sacristy.

Comenzó a sonar de nuevo la campana de la iglesia. Entró poco después un cura delgado, morenillo, de ojos negros y sonrisa irónica, que saludó a Fernando y a sus amigos de una manera exageradamente mundana. El cura joven fué a decir la novena a la iglesia en donde se habían reunido unas cuantas viejas; el otro, el morenillo, ofreció cigarros, encendió uno y se puso a fumar con el manteo desabrochado y las manos en los bolsillos del pantalón.

– Y usted, ¿no tiene trabajo hoy? – le preguntaron.
– Sí; yo estoy aquí para el *capeo*.
– Es que tiene que predicar – murmuró uno de los amigos al oído de Fernando.

Se habló después de capellanías, de pleitos, de mujeres; luego Ossorio y sus amigos salieron de la iglesia.

– ¿Quién es este cura?
– Es un *perdío*, que vive con dos sobrinas y se acuesta con las dos. ¿Qué hacemos ahora? ¿Vamos al colegio de escolapios?
– Vamos.

Fernando se dejó llevar; tenía una idea muy vaga de aquel caserón en donde había pasado dos años de su vida. Se acercaron al colegio, una especie de cuartel grande, y entraron por la senda central de un patinillo a un ancho zaguán que conducía a un corredor bajo de techo, adornado con cuadros y letreros. Fernando, al entrar, recordó de repente todo el colegio con todos sus detalles, como si le quitaran una venda de los ojos; reconocía uno a uno los mapas, los cuadros de las paredes, con medidas de capacidad, las figuras de anatomía, de zoología y de botánica.

Por el corredor paseaban dos escolapios fumando, con el bonete ladeado; a ellos se dirigieron los amigos de Ossorio para que les enseñara el colegio. Los dos padres les fueron mostrando a los tres amigos las clases, que olían a cuarto cerrado, con sus largas mesas negras y sus ventanas enrejadas. Aquí, recordaba Fernando, habían variado el piso; allá habían condenado una puerta.

En un patio jugaban los chicos a la pelota, vestidos con blusas grises. Al pasar Fernando y los demás, los muchachos les miraban con ansiedad. Subieron los visitantes al piso de arriba, en el cual había un corredor y, a los lados, celdas pequeñas, con el techo cubierto por una alambrera, ocupadas por la cama, el colgador y el lavabo; la puerta, con una persiana para espiar desde fuera al encerrado.

Fernando, al mirar el interior de aquellos cuartuchos, recordó los dos años de su vida pasados allí. ¡Qué tristes y qué lentos! Se veía por las mañanas, cuando tocaba la campana y palmoteaban los camareros, despertarse sobresaltado, salir de la cama, lavarse, y al volver a oír el aviso, se veía en el tétrico corredor, iluminado por un farol humeante de petróleo, colgado del techo por un garabato en forma de

The church bell started to ring again. Shortly afterward, a slender priest with an unpleasant, sallow face, with black eyes and an ironic smile, came in and greeted Fernando and his friends in an exaggeratedly worldly manner. The young priest went off to say the Novena in the church, where a few old women had come together; the other one, the unpleasantly dark one, offered them all cigarettes, lit one, and with his outer mantle unbuttoned and his hands in the pockets of his trousers, he started to smoke.

"How about you, you aren't working today?" they asked him.

"Yes, I'm here for the capeo (to pull the wool over their eyes)."[81]

"He means he has to preach," one of Fernando's friends murmured in his ear.

After that, they spoke of funds left for religious purposes, of litigations, of women. Then Ossorio and his friends left the church. "Who is this priest?"

"He's a reprobate, who's living with two of his nieces and going to bed with both of them.[82] Well, what should we do now? Why don't we go over to the Piarist School?"[83]

"Let's go."

Fernando permitted himself to be led along; he had a very vague recollection of that great big building where he'd spent two years of his life. They approached the school, a kind of large barracks, and they went inside along the central walk of a small courtyard into a vestibule that led to a corridor with a low ceiling, adorned with pictures and posters. When he entered, Fernando suddenly remembered the whole school with all of its details, as if they had removed a blindfold from his eyes; one by one, he recognized the maps, the charts on the walls with measurements of capacity, the drawings for anatomy, zoology and botany.

Two Piarist priests were walking along the corridor, smoking, their caps tilted to one side; Ossorio's friends walked over to them and asked if they could be shown around the school. The two fathers started showing the three friends the classrooms, which smelled as if they had been shut up for a time, with their long black tables and grill-covered windows. In one place, Fernando recalled, the flooring had been changed; in another, they had closed off a door.

The young boys, dressed in gray blouses, were playing ball in the courtyard. When Fernando and the others passed by, the boys looked at them anxiously. The visitors ascended to the upper floor, where there was a corridor with small cells on either side, with a ceiling covered by wire screening, that contained a bed, a clothes rack and a wash basin; the door had a slatted shutter, so that you could spy on the person enclosed there from the outside.

When he looked inside those small, wretched rooms, Fernando remembered the two years of his life spent here. How sad and slow moving! He could see himself on those early mornings, when the attendants would ring the bell and begin clapping their hands, and he would wake up quite startled, get out of bed, wash up, and when he would hear the warning bell again, he would find himself in the gloomy corridor, which was illuminated by a smoking oil lamp that was hanging from the ceiling

lira. Luego recordaba durante el invierno, cuando, después de rezar arrodillados, puestos en dos filas en el obscuro pasillo, capitaneados por uno de los padres, iban bajando todos las escaleras, medio dormidos, tiritando, envueltos en bufandas, y recorrían los corredores y entraban en el oratorio a cantar los rezos de la mañana y a oír misa. ¡Qué impresión de horrible tristeza daba el ver las ventanas iluminadas por la claridad blanca y fría del amanecer!

Al dirigirse a las clases, comenzaba el terror, pensando en las lecciones no aprendidas aún; y en la clase se leían y releían con desperación páginas y páginas de los libros, que pasaban por la memoria como la luz por un cristal; un aluvión de palabras que no dejaban ni rastro.

Y el tormento de dar la lección uno a uno se alargaba, y cuando éste daba una tregua, comenzaba el fastidio, que a Fernando se le metía en el alma de una manera aguda, dolorosa, insoportable.

Después de comer en el refectorio, que tenía largas mesas de mármol blanco, tristes, heladas, se volvía de nuevo al trabajo; lento suplicio interrumpido por las horas de recreo, en las que se jugaba a la pelota en un sitio cercado por paredes altas, que más que lugar de esparcimiento parecía patio de presidio.

Pero de noche... de noche era horroroso. Al subir después de cenar, a las nueve, desde el refectorio frío y triste, al pasillo donde desembocaban las celdas, al arrodillarse para rezar las oraciones de la noche y al encerrarse luego en el cuarto, entonces se sentía más que nunca la tristeza de aquel presidio. Por las hendeduras de la persiana, cuyo objeto era espiar a los muchachos, se veía el corredor apenas iluminado por un quinqué de petróleo; ya dentro de la cama, de cuando en cuando se oían sonar los pasos del guardián; del pueblo no llegaba ni un murmullo; sólo rompía el silencio de las noches calladas, el golpear del martillo del reloj de la torre, que contaba los cuartos de hora, las medias horas, las horas, que pasaban lentas, muy lentas, en la serie interminable del tiempo.

¡Qué vida! ¡Qué horrorosa vida! ¡Estar sometido a ser máquina de estudiar, a llevar como un presidiario un número marcado en la ropa, a no ver casi nunca el sol!

¡Qué comienzo de vida estar encerrado allí, en aquel odioso cuartel, en donde todas las malas pasiones tenían su asiento; en donde los vicios solitarios brotaban con la pujanza de las flores malsanas!

¡Qué vida! ¡Qué horrorosa vida! Cuando más se sufre, cuando los sentimientos son más intensos, se le encerraba al niño, y se le sometía a una tortura diaria, hipertrofiándole la memoria, obscureciéndole la inteligencia, matando todos los instintos naturales, hundiéndole en la obscuridad de la superstición, atemorizando su espíritu con las penas eternas...

by a hook in the shape of a lyre. Then he remembered how, during the winter, after praying on their knees, lined up in two rows in the dark passageway, led by one of the priests, they all started going down the stairs, half-asleep, shivering, wrapped in their mufflers, and how they made their way along the corridors, and how they entered the oratory to chant their morning prayers and hear Mass. What an impression of horrible sadness it must have given them to see the windows illuminated by the white, cold light of early morning!

The real terror would begin when they would make their way to their classes, thinking of the lessons they hadn't yet learned; in the class, they would read and reread pages and more pages from their books in desperation, and it would all pass through their memories like light through a pane of glass; an alluvion of words that didn't even leave a trace.

And the torment of having to recite the lesson, one by one, would be prolonged, and when this procedure would give him a moment of respite, the boredom would begin, and it would overwhelm Fernando's spirit in an acute, painful and unbearable way.

After eating in the refectory, which had long tables made of white marble which were sad and freezing cold, they would again return to their work; a slow torture, interrupted by periods for recreation, during which they would play ball in a place surrounded by high walls, which more resembled a penitentiary courtyard than a place for diversion.

But at night..., at night it was horrible. At nine o'clock, after they had eaten, when they would go upstairs, from the cold, sad refectory, into the passageway onto which their cells opened, when they would kneel down to say their evening prayers and they would then lock themselves in their rooms, it was then that you began to feel more than ever the sadness of that prison. Through the cracks in the shutter, the sole purpose of which was to spy on the boys, you could see the corridor, barely illuminated by an oil lamp; once in bed, you could hear the sound of the monitor's footsteps from time to time; not even a murmur came from the town; only the strokes of the hammer in the tower clock would break the silence of the still nights, as it counted the quarter hours, the half hours, the hours, as they slowly elapsed, very slowly, in the interminable succession of time.

What a life! What a horrible life! To be subjected to being a studying machine, to wearing a number marked on your clothing like a prisoner, almost never seeing the sunlight!

What a beginning to life to be locked up there, in that odious barracks, where all evil passions had their seat, where the solitary vices germinated with the vigor of noxious flowers!

What a life! What a horrible life! At a time when he suffers the most, when his feelings are most intense, they would lock up the child and submit him to a daily torture, hypertrophying his memory, beclouding his intelligence, killing all his natural instincts, burying him in the darkness of superstition, terrifying his spirit with the thought of eternal punishment...

De allí había brotado la anemia moral de Yécora; de allí había salido aquel mundo de pequeños caciques, de curas viciosos, de usereros; toda aquella cáfila de hombres que se pasaban la vida bebiendo y fumando en la sala de un casino.

Era el Colegio, con su aspecto de gran cuartel, un lugar de tortura; era la gran prensa laminadora de cerebros, la que arrancaba los sentimientos levantados de los corazones, la que cogía los hombres jóvenes, ya debilitados por la herencia de una raza enfermiza y triste, y los volvía a la vida convenientemente idiotizados, fanatizados, embrutecidos; los buenos, tímidos, cobardes, torpes; los malos, hipócritas, embusteros, uniendo a la natural maldad, la adquirida perfidia, y todos, buenos y malos, sobrecogidos con la idea aplastante del pecado, que se cernía sobre ellos como una gran mariposa negra.

XXXVIII

El teatro estaba lleno; verdad que era muy chico. Sólo el sábado se ocupaban las localidades. Representaban cuatro zarzuelas madrileñas, de ésas con sentimentalismos, celos y demás zarandajas.

En el palco del Ayuntamiento estaban el alcalde, pariente del administrador de Ossorio, Fernando y dos concejales jóvenes de los que acompañaban al alcalde, por ser de familias adineradas del pueblo.

El antepalco era muy grande; el teatro frío; el alcalde, un dictador a quien se le obedecía como a un rey, había mandado que pusieran allí un brasero. El alcalde asombraba a los dos concejales asegurando que aquellas obras que se representaban en Yécora las había visto en Madrid, en Apolo, nada menos.

– ¡Qué diferencia, eh! – le decía a Fernando. Éste escuchaba indiferente, aburrido, la representación, mirando a una parte y a otra.

El alcalde señaló a Ossorio en la sala algunas muchachas casaderas, ricas, con las que podía intentar un matrimonio ventajoso. De pronto, el hombre se calló y se puso a mirar con los gemelos al escenario. Lolita Sánchez había salido a escena; era la primera actriz y traía revuelto todo Yécora. Cuando terminó el acto, el alcalde invitó a Fernando a bajar a las tablas. Aquella Lolita Sánchez era cosa suya.

Fueron a los bastidores; el escenario era muy pequeño; los cuartos de los cómicos más pequeños todavía. El alcalde hizo entrar a Fernando en el cuarto de la primera actriz. Estaban allí sentados en un sofá roto, la hermana de Lola, Mencía Sánchez, con la cara afilada, llena de polvos de arroz y de lunares, el director artístico de la compañía, Yáñez de la Barbuda, un joven que a primera vista se comprendía que

All the moral anemia of Yécora had flowered in that place; that world of petty political bosses, vicious priests, usurers; that whole pack of individuals who spent their lives drinking and smoking in the lounge of a casino had emerged from there.

The School, with its appearance like that of a big barracks, was a place of torture; it was the great rolling mill for brains, one that rooted out all lofty feelings from the heart, one that took hold of young men, already weakened by what they had inherited from a sickly, sad race, and returned them to life conveniently converted into idiots, fanatics and brutes; the good ones, now timid, cowardly, dull-witted; the bad ones, now hypocrites and liars, combining the treacherous nature they had acquired with their natural wickedness, and all of them,, the good and the bad, in the clutches of the oppressive idea of sin, that hovered over them like a big, black butterfly.[84]

XXXVIII

The theater was full; it must be said that it was quite small. Only on Saturday were the seats filled. They were putting on four Madrilenian zarzuelas, of the kind that were filled with sentimentalism, jealousy and other such trivia.

In the box reserved for the Municipal Authorities, sat the Mayor, who was a relative of the Ossorio family's administrator, Fernando and two young councilmen who generally accompanied the Mayor, since they were members of the town's well-to-do families.

The antechamber to the box was very spacious; the theater, cold; the mayor, a dictator who was obeyed as if he were a king, had ordered them to set up a brazier there. The mayor was astonishing the two councilmen by assuring them that he had seen those plays now being performed in Yécora, when he was in Madrid, and at the Apolo, no less.

"What a difference, eh!" he said to Fernando. The latter, quite bored by it all, was listening to the performance indifferently, looking in one direction or another.

The mayor pointed out several rich, marriageable young women in the theater to Ossorio, with whom an advantageous marriage could be arranged. Suddenly the man fell silent and began to look at the stage with his opera glasses. Lolita Sánchez had come out onto the stage; she was the leading lady and all of Yécora was simply wild about her. When the act ended, the mayor invited Fernando to go down to the stage. That Lolita Sánchez belonged to him.

They went down to the wings; the stage was very small; the actors' dressing rooms were even smaller. The mayor invited Fernando to go into the leading lady's room. Seated there on a broken-down sofa was Lola's sister, Mencía Sánchez, who had a sharp-featured face covered with rice powder and beauty spots; Yáñez de la Barbuda, the artistic director of the company, a young man who at first glance

era imbécil, escritor aficionado al teatro, que se arruinaba contratando compañías para que representasen sus dramas; Lolita Sánchez, una mujer insignificante, muy pintada, con los ojos negros y la boca muy grande, y algunas personas más.

Como no cabían todos en el cuarto, Fernando se quedó de pie cerca de la puerta, sin aceptar los ofrecimientos que le hicieron de sentarse, y al ver que no se fijaban en él, se escabulló e iba a salir a la calle, cuando se encontró con dos amigos también del colegio, que no le permitieron escaparse. Eran ambos la única representación del intelectualismo en Yécora; hablaban de Bourget, de Prevost con el respeto que se puede tener por un fetiche.

– No creas, vale la pena de ver a Lola Sánchez – le dijo uno a Fernando.

– Es una mujer digna de estudio – aseguró el otro.

– Una voluptuosa – murmuró el primero.

– Una verdadera *demi-vierge* – añadió el segundo.

Ossorio miró a sus antiguos camaradas asombrado, y oyó que uno y otro barajaban nombres de escritores franceses que él nunca había oído y que trataban indubablemente de abrumarle con sus conocimientos. Pretextando que tenía que ver al alcalde, los dejó, y se fué a buscar de nuevo la puerta del escenario.

Abrió una que le salió al paso, entró pensando si daría al pasillo de salida, y se encontró en un cuarto pequeño a dos o tres cómicos, a la característica y al de la taquilla, que estaban sentados alrededor de una mesa desvencijada, de esas llenas de dorados, que sirven en las decoraciones de palacios para sostener dos copas de latón, con las cuales se envenenan el galán y la dama. Entonces sostenía una botella de vino y un vaso. Ossorio trató inmediatamente de salir de allí, después de haberse excusado; pero el gracioso, un hombre de nariz muy larga que sin duda le había visto con el alcalde, le invitó a tomar un poco de vino. Fernando dió las gracias.

– ¿Nos va usted a desairar porque somos unos pobres cómicos?

Ossorio tomó el vaso que le ofrecían y lo bebió.

– ¿No se sienta usted? – continuó el gracioso – . Sí, hombre, precisamente estamos riñendo y no sabe usted lo chuscas que son estas riñas entre cómicos tronados. Bueno. Cuando no hay bofetadas y golpes, que de todo suele haber. – Luego comenzó a presentar a los que estaban allí.

– Gómez Manrique, primer actor, un cómico, ahí donde lo ve usted, que si no fuera tan soberbio, y tan amanerado, podría ser con el tiempo algo.

El aludido, que parecía un hombre que estaba bajo el peso de una terrible catástrofe, lanzó una mirada de desdén al gracioso a través de sus lentes; luego se atusó la melena, mostrando la manga raída de su chaqueta, y después llevó la mano

could obviously be considered an imbecile, a writer with a taste for the theater who was ruining himself by engaging theatrical companies to perform his plays; Lolita Sánchez, an insignificant woman, heavily made up, with black eyes and a very large mouth, as well as a number of other persons.

Since they couldn't all fit in the room, Fernando remained standing near the door, refusing all offers made to him to sit down, and when he saw they were hardly paying any attention to him, he slipped out and was about to make his way into the street, when he ran into two friends of his, also from his school, who would not let him escape. The two of them were the only examples of intellectualism in Yécora; they talked of Bourget[85] and Prévost[86] with all the respect one might have for a fetish.

"Don't believe what you hear, Lola Sánchez is really worth seeing," one of them said to Fernando.

"She's a woman really worth studying," the other one assured him.

"A voluptuary," murmured the first one.

"A veritable *demi-vierge*," added the second one.

Ossorio looked at his former school companions with astonishment, and he heard the one and the other bandying about the names of French writers he'd never heard of, as they were undoubtedly trying to overwhelm him with their knowledge. On the pretext that he had to see the mayor, he left them and went off again in search of the stage door.

He opened one he happened to come upon, went in, thinking it would lead to the exit corridor, and he found himself in a small room with two or three actors, the actress who played parts of older ladies and the man from the ticket office, who were seated around a rickety table, of the kind that is covered with golden adornments and is used in a palace set to hold two brass goblets, with which the leading man and leading lady generally poison themselves. At that moment, a bottle of wine and a glass were resting on the table. After excusing himself, Ossorio immediately tried to get out of there, but the actor who played comic characters, a man with a very long nose, who had undoubtedly seen him with the mayor, invited him to have a little wine. Fernando thanked him.

"You aren't going to snub us just because we're only humble actors?"

Ossorio took the glass they offered him and drank it.

"Won't you sit down?" the comic actor continued. "Yes, indeed, we just happen to be quarreling right now and you have no idea how funny these fights among broken-down actors can be. Well, then. When we aren't slapping one another or coming to blows, then you're liable to have anything." Then he began to introduce those who were there.

"Gómez Manrique, the leading man, a real actor, there as you see him, and if he weren't so arrogant and affected, he might amount to something in time."

The one alluded to, who looked like a man living under the weight of a terrible catastrophe, cast a disdainful glance at the comic actor through his eyeglasses; then he smoothed back his long mane of hair, thereby showing the threadbare sleeve of

al bigote y trató de retorcerlo, pero como haría sólo diez o quince días que dejaba de afeitarse, no pudo.

– De la señora – anadió el de la nariz larga mostrando a la característica –, nada puedo decir; no la he conocido más que en su decadencia. En su tiempo...

– En mi tiempo – gritó la vieja – no se las tragaban como puños, como ahora en Madrid y en todas partes. ¡Re...pateta! Si no hay cómicos ya.

– Eso es cierto – repuso con voz borrosa uno de los que se hallaban sentados a la mesa.

– Este señor que ha hablado, o que ha mugido, no se sabe lo que hace – prosiguió el de la nariz larga – es don Dionis el Crepuscular, nuestro taquillero, nuestro contador, nuestro administrador, un hombre que no nos roba más que todo lo que puede.

– Y ustedes, ¿qué hacen? – preguntó don Dionis.

– Advertencia. Le llamamos el Crepuscular por esa voz tan agradable que tiene, como habrá usted podido notar. Yo soy Cabeza de Vaca, de apellido, bastante buen cómico.

– Si no fueras tan borracho – interrumpió don Dionis.

– Ahora, joven yecorano – siguió Cabeza de Vaca dirigiéndose a Ossorio – no creo que tendrá usted inconveniente en pagarnos una botella.

– Hombre, ninguna. ¿Quiere usted que al salir yo mismo la encargue?

– No. El mozo irá por ella.

– Bueno. Y usted hará el favor de enseñarme dónde está la puerta.

– Sí, señor, con mucho gusto. Por aquí, por aquí. Adiós.

XXXIX

– Ya que te aburres en Yécora, vente a Marisparza – le dijo un amigo.

– ¿Qué es eso de Marisparza?

– Una casa de labor que tengo ahí en el monte. Te advierto que te vas a aburrir.

– ¡Bah! No tengas cuidado.

A la mañana siguiente, después de comer, un día de fiesta, llegó el amigo en un carricoche, tirado por un caballejo peludo, a la puerta de la casa del administrador de Ossorio. Fernando montó y se acomodó sobre unos sacos; el amigo se sentó en el varal y echaron a andar.

his jacket, and he then raised his hand to his mustache and tried to twist it, but since he had most likely stopped shaving only ten or fifteen days before, he was unable to accomplish this.

"As for the lady," added the man with the long nose, pointing at the woman who played roles as older women, "I can say nothing; I haven't known her except during her period of decline. In her time..."

"In my time," the old woman shouted, " they didn't put up with them as if they were really something to rave about, as they now do in Madrid and everywhere else. The Devil can take them all! There aren't any real actors around any more."

"That's for sure," replied one of the men who happened to be seated at the table, in a bleary voice.

"This gentleman who has just spoken, or has bellowed, you can't tell what he really does," the man with the long nose continued, "is Don Dionis, *el Crepuscular*, our ticket seller, our bookkeeper, our manager, a man who only steals from us as much as he can get."

"And all of you, what do you do?" asked Don Dionis.

"One further observation. We call him *el Crepuscular* because of that very pleasant voice he has, as you probably have noticed. I am Cabeza de Vaca by name, a rather good actor."

"If you weren't so drunk," interrupted Don Dionis.

"Now my young Yecoran," Cabeza de Vaca continued, addressing himself to Ossorio, "I don't think you would consider it an imposition to repay us with a bottle."

"Not at all, my good man. Do you want me to take care of it myself when I go out?"

"No. The porter will go get it."

"All right. And you will be so kind as to show me where I can find the door."

"Yes, indeed, with great pleasure. This way, this way. Goodbye."

XXXIX

"Since you're so bored in Yécora, come to Marisparza," a friend said to him.

"What's all this about Marisparza?"

"It's a farm that I have up there on the mountain. But I must warn you that you're going to be bored."

"Nonsense! Don't worry about it."

The following morning, which happened to be a holiday, after he'd eaten, his friend came up to the door of the Ossorio's administrator's house in a two-wheeled covered cart, drawn by a shaggy nag. Fernando climbed up and made himself comfortable on top of some sacks; his friend sat down on the perch and they started off.

El camino estaba lleno de carriles hondos, que habían dejado las ruedas de los carros al pasar y repasar por el mismo sitio. El paisaje no tenía nada de bello. Iban por entre campos desolados, tierras rojizas de viña con alguna que otra mancha verde negruzca de los pinos, cruzando ramblas y cauces de ríos secos, descampados llenos de matorrales de brezo y de retama.

Al anochecer llegaron a Marisparza. La casa estaba aislada en medio de un pedrizal; hallábase unida a otra más baja y pequeña. Era de color de barro, amarillenta, cubierta de una capa de arcilla y de paja; tenía grandes ventanas, con rotas y desteñidas persianas verdes. Una chimenea alta, gruesa, cuadrada, parecía aplastar al tejado pardusco; encima de la puerta, alguien, quizá el dueño anterior, había pintado con yeso una cruz grande que se destacaba blanca en el fondo sucio de la pared.

Abrieron la casa y entraron; dos o tres murciélagos refugiados en el viejo caserón salieron despavoridos.

No había muebles en las habitaciones; las ventanas no tenían cristales; en todos los cuartos sonaba a hueco. En la parte de atrás de la casa, una cerca de adobe medio derruida, cubierta con bardas de césped, limitaba un jardín abandonado en donde crecían dos cipreses negros y tristes y un almendro florido.

Del zaguán de esta casa se pasaba al vestíbulo de otra más pequeña, en donde vivía el colono con su familia. Mientras el amigo se ocupaba en desenganchar el caballejo del carricoche, Fernando se asomó a una ventana. Corría un viento frío. Veíase enfrente un cerro crestado lleno de picos que se destacaba en un cielo de ópalo. Allá, a lo lejos, sobre la negrura de un pinar que escalaba un monte, corría una pincelada violeta y la tarde pasaba silenciosa mientras el cielo heroico se enrojecía con rojos resplandores. Unos cuantos miserables, hombres y mujeres, volvían del trabajo con las azadas al hombro; cantaban una especie de guajira triste, tristísima; en aquella canción debían concretarse en queja inconsciente las miserias de una vida animal de bestia de carga. ¡Tan desolador, tan amargo era el aire de la canción! Obscureció; del cielo plomizo parecían llegar rebaños de sombras; el horizonte se hizo amenazador...

De noche, en la cocina, quemando sarmientos, a la luz de las teas puestas sobre palas de hierro, pasaron Fernando y su amigo hasta muy tarde. Se acostaron y toda la noche estuvo el viento gimiendo y silbando.

The road was full of deep furrows that had been left by the wheels of the carts as they went back and forth over the same place. There was nothing very beautiful about the landscape. They kept traveling through desolate fields, reddish-colored vineyards with blackish-green patches of pine trees interspersed here and there, crossing sandy ravines and dried up river beds, clear, open tracts that were covered with thickets of heather and Spanish broom.

They arrived in Marisparza at nightfall. The house was isolated in the middle of a stony stretch of ground; it was joined to another structure that was lower and smaller. The house was the color of mud, yellowish, covered by a layer of clay and straw, it had large windows with broken and faded green shutters. A tall, heavy, square-shaped chimney seemed to be pressing down on the grayish roof; on top of the door, someone, perhaps the previous owner, had painted a big cross out of plaster, and it stood out white against the dirty background of the wall.

They opened up the house and went inside; two or three bats, which had taken refuge in the large, old house, were frightened and flew out.

There was no furniture in the rooms; the windows had no panes, and all the rooms echoed with a hollow sound. In the rear part of the house, an adobe wall, partly demolished, covered with thatches of grass, enclosed an abandoned garden, where two sad, black cypresses and an almond tree covered with blossoms were growing.

From the entryway of the house, you went into the vestibule of another, smaller one, where the tenant farmer lived with his family. While his friend was busy unhitching the nag from the covered cart, Fernando peered out of a window. A cold wind was blowing. Opposite him, you could see a crested hill covered with peaks, which was outlined in the opal-colored sky. Out there, in the distance, over the black of a pine grove that scaled a mountain, a violet-shaded touch of color ran through the sky, and the late afternoon passed silently, as the heroic sky turned crimson with red resplendence. Several wretched-looking people, men and women, were returning from their toils, with their hoes on their shoulders; they were singing a kind of sad *guajira*, so incredibly sad; the misery of their animal-like existence as beasts of burden must have taken form, as a somewhat unconscious lament, in that song. The spirit of that song was so desolate, so bitter! It grew dark; droves of shadows seemed to be coming from the lead colored sky; the horizon turned threatening...

That night, in the kitchen, where they were burning vine shoots, by the light of torches set onto iron shovels, Fernando and his friend stayed up till very late. They went to bed and the wind kept howling and whistling the whole night.

XL

El día siguiente era domingo. Fernando se levantó temprano y salió de la casa. Su amigo se había marchado antes a ver un cortijo de las inmediaciones.

Los alrededores de Marisparza eran desnudos parajes de una adustez tétrica, con cerros sin vegetación y canchales rotos en pedrizas, llenos de hendeduras y de cuevas.

En el raso desnudo, en donde estaban las dos viviendas reunidas, había un aljibe encalado, con su puerta azul y el cubo que colgaba por un estropajo de la garrucha; un poco más lejos, en los primeros taludes del monte, se veía una balsa derruida y cuadrada, en cuyo fondo brillaba el agua muerta, negruzca, llena de musgos verdes.

Eran los alrededores de Marisparza de una desolación absoluta y completa. Desde el monte avanzaban primero las lomas yermas, calvas; luego tierras arenosas, blanquecinas, como si fueran aguas de un torrente solidificado, llenas de nódulos, de mamelones áridos, sin una mata, sin una hierbecilla, plagadas de grandes hormigueros rojos. Nada tan seco, tan ardiente, tan huraño como aquella tierra; los montes, los cerros, las largas paredes de adobe de los corrales, las tapias de los cortijos; los portillos de riego, los encalados aljibes, parecían ruinas abandonadas en un desierto, calcinadas por un sol implacable, cubiertas de polvo, olvidadas por los hombres.

Bajo las piedras brotaban los escorpiones; en los vallados y en las cercas corrían las lagartijas. Los grandes lagartos grises y amarillo-verdosos, se achicharraban inmóviles al sol. Unicamente en las hondonadas había campos de verdura; grandes pantanos claros, con islas de hierbas llenos de trasparencias luminosas, en cuyo fondo se veían las imágenes invertidas de los árboles y el cielo azul cruzado por nubes blancas. En las alturas, la tierra era árida; sólo crecían algunos matorros de berceo y de retama.

Aquel día, Fernando, después de dar una vuelta y esperar a su amigo, entró en la cocina de la casa contigua. Como domingo, el labrador y su mujer habían ido a misa a un poblado próximo. No quedaba en casa más que el abuelo y tres muchachas casi de la misma edad, ataviadas con pañuelos blancos en la cabeza.

La cocina era grande, encalada, con una chimenea que ocupaba la mitad del cuarto. De algunas perchas de madera colgaban arreos para los caballos y las mulas; en un rincón había un arca y sobre un vasar una caja de alhelíes.

Fernando estuvo charlando con el viejo y con las mozas; después se puso a jugar a la bola con dos muchachos de la casa, y cuando se cansó subió a su cuarto a distraerse con sus propias meditaciones.

XL

The following day was Sunday. Fernando got up early and went out of the house. His friend had gone off some time before to look over a piece of farm property in the environs.

The area all around Marisparza consisted of bare terrain, gloomily austere, with hills devoid of vegetation and rocky ground with broken boulders scattered everywhere, full of crevices and caves.

There was a whitewashed cistern on the flat, barren ground where the two dwellings stood joined together, and it had a blue door and a wooden bucket that was hanging from the pulley by a rope of esparto grass; a little further away, on the lower slopes of the mountain, you could see a square-shaped pool of water with its sides crumbling, and stagnant, blackish water full of green moss shining at the bottom.

The surroundings of Marisparza were absolutely and completely desolate. Starting at the mountain, the uncultivated, barren hills were first to appear; then, sandy, whitish tracts of land, which might well have been waters of a torrent that had solidified, full of nodules, arid knolls the shape of teats, without a single shrub, without a single blade of grass, infested with large, red anthills. Nothing so dry, so fiery, so withdrawn as that terrain; the mountains, the hills, the long adobe walls of the enclosed yards, the low earthen walls of the farms, the gates of the irrigation ditches, the whitewashed cisterns, all seemed like abandoned ruins in a desert, burned white by an implacable sun, covered with dust, forgotten by men.

Scorpions emerged from under the rocks; small lizards scampered along the earthen walls and fences. Larger, gray and yellow-greenish lizards stood motionless as they toasted themselves in the sun. Only in the hollows were there any fields of greenery; large, clear marshes with islands of green herbage, filled with luminous transparencies, and at the bottom you could see the inverted images of the trees reflected, and the blue sky with white clouds crossing over it. On the heights, the earth was arid; only a few clumps of matweed and Spanish broom were growing there.

That day, after taking a walk and waiting for his friend, Fernando went into the kitchen of the adjoining house. As it was Sunday, the farmer and his wife had gone to Mass in a nearby town. Only the grandfather remained in the house with three girls, about the same age, all dressed up with white scarves on their heads.

The kitchen was spacious, whitewashed, with a fireplace that occupied half the room. Some harnesses for the horses and mules were hanging from a number of wooden pegs; there was a chest in the corner and a box of wallflowers on a kitchen shelf.

Fernando spent some time chatting with the old man and the young girls; then he began to play ball with the two boys from the house, and when he tired of this, he went up to his room to amuse himself with his own meditations.

Al medio día volvió el amigo de Fernando.

– Mira – le dijo a éste – yo aquí he terminado lo que tenía que hacer. Me voy; pero si tú quieres estar, te quedas el tiempo que te dé la gana.

– Pues me quedo.

– Muy bien.

Comieron y el amigo se marchó en seguida de comer en su carricoche.

Fernando, al verse solo, sin saber qué hacer, se tendió en la cama. Desde allí, por la ventana abierta, veía los crestones del monte, destacándose con todas sus aristas en el cielo; a un lado y a otro las vertientes parecían sembradas de piedras; más abajo se destacaban algunos olivos en hileras simétricas, algunos viñedos y después el camino blanco, lleno de polvo, que se alejaba hasta el infinito, en medio de aquella desolación adusta, de aquel silencio aplanador.

Al caer de la tarde, Fernando se levantó de la cama y se fué a jugar otra vez a la bola con los dos muchachos, y cuando obscureció, entró con ellos en la cocina. El labrador y su padre, ambos sentados en el banco de piedra, hablaban; la mujer hacía media; las mocitas jugueteaban.

El abuelo contó a Fernando las hazañas de Roche, un bandido generoso, como todos los bandidos españoles, y después describió las maravillas de una cueva del monte cercano, en la cual, según viejas tradiciones, se habían refugiado los moros. Se entraba en la cueva, decía el viejo, y a poco andar topaba uno con una puerta ferrada, que a los lados tenía hombres de piedra con grandes mazas; si alguno trataba de acercarse a ellos, levantaban las mazas y las dejaban caer sobre el importuno visitante.

Después de esta relación, el viejo le preguntó a Ossorio:

– ¿Y qué? ¿Se va usted a quedar aquí durante algún tiempo?

– Sí, me parece que sí.

– A ver si hace usted como Juan Sedeño.

– ¿Quién es? No le conozco.

– Juan Sedeño es un señorito de Yécora que se gastó todo el dinero en Madrid y vino hace ocho años y no quiso ir a vivir a la ciudad, y dijo que en la corte o en el campo, y vive en una choza. Eso sí, se pasea por la casa con traje negro y con *futraque*.

– ¿Pero qué hace? ¿Lee o escribe?

– No, no hace más que eso; pasearse vestido como un caballero.

– Pues es una ocupación.

– ¡Vaya!

Cuando dieron las diez se concluyó la reunión en la cocina, y se fueron todos a acostar. En los días posteriores, Fernando siguió haciendo las mismas cosas; aquella vida monótona comenzó a dar a Ossorio cierta indiferencia para sus ideas

Fernando's friend returned at midday.

"Look here," he said to his friend, "I've finished everything I had to do here. I'm leaving; but if you want to stay on, you can remain as long as you feel like staying."

"Then I'll stay."

"Very well."

They ate and as soon as they had finished, his friend left in his covered cart.

When Fernando found himself alone without knowing what to do, he stretched out on his bed. From there, he could see the mountain crests through the open window, profiled against the sky with all their arrises; the slopes seemed to be sown with rocks on one side and the other; lower down, several olive trees were outlined in symmetrical rows, as well as a number of vineyards, and beyond them, the white road, covered with dust, which stretched out into the infinite, in the midst of that austere desolation, of that oppressive silence.

As the afternoon came to an end, Fernando got up from the bed and went out to play ball with the two boys again, and when it grew dark, he went back into the kitchen with them. The farmer and his father were both seated on the stone bench talking; his wife was knitting; the young girls were romping about.

The grandfather told Fernando all about the exploits of Roche, a generous bandit, like all Spanish bandits, and then he described the wonders of a cave in the nearby mountain, in which, according to old traditions, the Moors had once taken refuge. You entered the cave, the old man said, and after walking a short distance, you came upon a door trimmed with iron, that had men of stone on either side, holding large maces; if someone tried to approach them, they would raise their maces and let them fall on the inopportune visitor.

After this narrative, the old man asked Ossorio:

"How about it? Are you going to stay here for some time?"

"Yes, I think I will."

"We'll see if you do just as Juan Sedeño did."

"Who is he? I don't know him."

"Juan Sedeño is a young gentleman of good family from Yécora who squandered all his money in Madrid, and came here eight years ago and decided he didn't want to live in the city, and he said it either had to be the court in Madrid or in the country, and so he lives in a shack. One thing he still does, he goes around the house in a black suit and a *frock coat*."

"But what does he do? Does he read or do any writing?"

"No, that's all he does; going around dressed as a gentleman."

"Well, that's one way to spend your time."

"I'll say!"

When it struck ten, the gathering in the kitchen broke up and they all went off to bed. During the days that followed, Fernando kept doing the same things; that monotonous existence started to give Ossorio a certain sense of indifference toward

y sensaciones. Allí comprendía como en ninguna parte la religión católica en sus últimas fases jesuíticas, seca, adusta, fría, sin arte, sin corazón, sin entrañas; aquellos parajes, de una tristeza sorda, le recordaban a Fernando el libro de San Ignacio de Loyola que había leído en Toledo. En aquella tierra gris, los hombres no tenían color; eran su cara y sus vestidos parduscos, como el campo y las casas.

XLI

Por las mañanas, Fernando se levantaba temprano, subía a los montes de los alrededores y se tendía debajo de algún pino.

Iba sintiendo por días una gran laxitud, un olvido de todas sus preocupaciones, un profundo cansancio y sueño a todas horas. Tenía que hacer un verdadero esfuerzo para pensar o recordar algo.

– Como las lagartijas echan cola nueva – se decía – , yo debo de estar echando cerebro nuevo.

Si después de hacer un gran esfuerzo imaginativo recordaba, el recuerdo le era indiferente y no quedaba nada como resultado de él; sentía la poca consistencia de sus antiguas preocupaciones. Todo lo que se había excitado en Madrid o en Toledo iba remitiendo en Marisparza. Al ponerse en contacto con la tierra, ésta le hacía entrar en la realidad.

Por días iba sintiéndose más fuerte, más amigo de andar y de correr, menos dispuesto a un trabajo cerebral. Se había hecho en el monte compañero del guarda de caza, un hombre viejo, chiquitín, con patillas, alegre, que había estado en Orán y Argelia, y contaba siempre historias de moros. Gaspar, así se llamaba el guarda, gastaba alpargatas de esparto, pantalón de pana, blusa azul, pañuelo encarnado en la cabeza y encima de éste un sombrero ancho. Gaspar tenía una escopeta de pistón, vieja, atada con unos bramantes, y no se podía comprender cómo disparaba y cazaba con aquello. Solía acompañar al guarda un perrillo de lanas muy chico, que, según decía su dueño, no había otro como él para levantar la caza.

En los paseos que daban el guarda y Fernando, hablaban de todo y resolvían entre los dos, de una manera generalmente radical, los más arduos problemas de la sociología, de la política y de lo que constituye la vida de los pueblos y de los individuos. Otras veces, Gaspar se constituía en maestro de Fernando, le contaba una porción de historias y le explicaba las virtudes curativas de las hierbas y algunos secretos médicos que sabía.

– Mire usted la verónica – le dijo una vez – . ¿Usted sabe por qué esa planta no tiene raíz?

his ideas and his sensations. There, in that place, he understood the Catholic religion as he could nowhere else, in its final Jesuitical stages, arid, austere, cold, without art, without heart, without humane feelings;[87] those isolated places, filled with mute sadness, reminded Fernando of the book by Saint Ignatius of Loyola he'd read in Toledo. In that gray terrain, men had no color; their faces and their clothes were the same drab color as the countryside and the houses.

XLI

Every morning, Fernando would get up early, climb the surrounding mountains and stretch out under some pine tree.

On some days he would feel an extraordinary laxity, forgetting all his preoccupations, feeling extremely weary and drowsy at all hours of the day. He had to make a supreme effort in order to think or remember anything.

"Just as small lizards grow a new tail," he would say to himself, "I must be growing a new brain."

If, after making a great effort with his imagination, he was able to remember something, he was totally indifferent to the recollection and nothing would remain as a result of it; he realized the limited consistency of his previous preoccupations. All the stimulation he had worked up in Madrid and in Toledo was now subsiding in Marisparza. As he came more in contact with the earth, it began to bring him closer to reality.

Over a period of days, he was feeling stronger, fonder of walking and running, less disposed to any intellectual effort. Up on the mountain, he had become a companion of the gamekeeper, an old man, quite small, with sideburns, very cheerful, who had been in Oran and Algeria, and who was always recounting stories about the Moors. Gaspar, for that was the gamekeeper's name, wore sandals made of esparto grass, corduroy pants, a blue blouse, a red kerchief over his head and a wide-brimmed hat on top of this. Gaspar had an old shotgun, tied together with hemp twine, and it was difficult to understand how he could shoot and hunt with that thing. A very small water spaniel used to accompany the keeper, and according to its master, there wasn't another like it to flush out game.

During the walks Fernando and the keeper would take, they would talk about everything, and, between the two of them, they would resolve the most arduous problems of sociology, politics and all that constitutes the life of peoples and individuals, generally in a radical way. On other occasions, Gaspar would set himself up as Fernando's teacher, and he would recount a whole lot of stories and explain to him the curative powers of herbs and a number of medical secrets that he knew.

"Just look at the speedwell," he once said to him. "Do you know why that plant has no roots?"

— No, señor.

— Pues le diré a usted: un día fué el diablo y arrancó la mata del suelo y la tiró; pasó por allá San Blas, y, viendo la planta tirada, la puso otra vez en tierra, y así siguió viviendo, aunque sin raíz.

— ¿Pero eso es histórico? — le preguntó Fernando.

— Pues no ha de serlo. Como que ahora es de día; lo mismo.

— ¿Usted cree en el diablo?

— Hombre. Aquí, en el monte, y de día, no creo... en nada; pero en mi casa, y de noche... ya es otra cosa.

Fernando, sin contestarle, tiró de una de las plantas de verónica, y, quizá por casualidad, salió llena de raíces, y se la enseñó a Gaspar.

— Usted sí que es el diablo — le dijo el guarda riéndose.

Muchas veces, andando por el monte o tendidos con la pipa en la boca entre los matorros de brezos, de romeros y de jaras, se olvidaban de la hora, y entonces, cuando tardaban mucho, solían avisarles desde Marisparza llamándoles con un caracol de mar, que producía un ruido bronco y triste.

Las tardes de los domingos, como Gaspar se marchaba a hacer recados al pueblo, Fernando las pasaba jugando en compañía de los dos chicos de la casa, con una bola de hierro, arrojándola lo más lejos posible. Cuando se cansaba, sentábase en un poyo de la puerta. Las gallinas picoteaban en el raso de la casa; los carromatos venían por el camino de la parte de Alicante hacia la Mancha alta, grises, llenos de polvo, de un color que se confundía con el del suelo.

XLII

Como todos los de la alquería iban a Yécora a ver las fiestas, fué también Fernando con ellos a casa del administrador.

Le recibieron allí fríamente.

Por la noche del Miércoles Santo los del pueblo subían al castillo por un camino en ziszás, que tenía a trechos capillas pequeñas de forma redonda, en cuyo fondo veíanse pasos pintados. Gente desharrapada y sucia subía a lo alto, tocando tambores y bocinas, en cuadrillas, deteniéndose en cada paso, subiendo y bajando al monte.

Al día siguiente por la tarde, Ossorio fué a ver la procesión de Jueves Santo. Se puso a esperarla en una calle ancha y en cuesta, que tenía a los lados tapias y paredones de corrales, casas bajas de adobe, cuyas ventanucas estaban iluminadas con tristes farolillos de aceite. Cuando pasó la procesión por allí, era ya al anochecer; había obscurecido; las lamparillas de aceite de los balcones y ventanas brillaban

"No, sir."

"Well, I'll tell you: one day the Devil went and pulled the shrub out of the ground and threw it away; San Blas[88] passed by there, and seeing the plant pulled out, he put it back in the ground again; that's how it went on living, even without roots."

"But is all that historically so?" Fernando asked him.

"Well, it doesn't really have to be. Just as true as it's daytime right now; just the same."

"Do you believe in the devil?"

"My good man! Here on the mountain, during the day, I don't believe...in anything like that; but in my house, at night..., that's another story."

Without answering him, Fernando pulled out one of the speedwell plants, and perhaps by chance, it came out full of roots, and he showed it to Gaspar.

"You are the very devil," the keeper said to him with a laugh.

Many times, as they walked about the mountain or stretched out with their pipes in their mouths, among the thickets of heath, rosemary and rockrose, they would forget the time, and then, when they would take too long, they would let them know from Marisparza with a seashell that produced a hoarse, sad sound.

On Sunday afternoons, since Gaspar would go off to the village to run some errands, Fernando would spend his time in the company of the two boys of the house, with an iron ball, throwing it as far as possible. When he tired of this, he would sit down on a stone bench next to the door. The hens were pecking away on the open ground around the house; the covered carts were coming along the road from the direction of Alicante heading toward La Mancha Alta, and they were gray, covered with dust, and their color was such that it blended with the color of the soil.

XLII

Since all the people from the farmstead were going to Yécora to see the celebrations, Fernando also went along with them to the administrator's house.

There he was received very coldly.

On the night of Holy Wednesday, the townspeople were going up to El Castillo along a zigzagging road that had small, round-shaped chapels along it, at intervals, with stages in the Passion of Christ painted on the back walls. Tattered, grubby people were walking up to the very top, in cohorts, beating drums and blowing horns, stopping at every step, going up and down the mountain.

On the afternoon of the following day, Ossorio went to see the procession for Holy Thursday. He found a place to wait for it on a wide, sloping street, which had, on both sides, earthen walls, thick barnyard walls, low houses made of adobe with ugly windows that were illuminated by sad little oil lanterns. When the procession

con más fuerza; por encima de un cerro iba apareciendo una luna enorme, rojiza, verdaderamente amenazadora.

La procesión era larguísima. Venían primero los estandartes de las cofradías, después dos largas hileras de soldados romanos, a ambos lados de la calle, con un movimiento de autómatas que hacían resonar las escamas plateadas de sus lorigas; tras ellos aparecieron judíos barbudos, negros, con la mirada terrible.

Luego fueron presentándose, todos en dos filas, grupos de veinte o treinta cofrades, vestidos con el hábito del mismo color, llevando en la mano faroles redondos colocados sobre altas pértigas; después aparecieron los disciplinantes, con sus túnicas y sus corazas rojas, verdes, blancas, en compañías que llevaban en medio los pasos, custodiándolos, entonando lúgubres plegarias, mientras algunos chiquillos desharrapados, delante de cada paso, iban marcando, con un rataplán sonoro, el ritmo de la marcha en sus tambores.

Se veía aparecer la procesión por la calle en cuesta, como un cortejo de sombras lúgubres y terribles. Ante aquellos pasos llenos de luces, ante aquella tropa de disciplinantes rojos, con su alta caperuza en la cabeza y el rostro bajo el antifaz, se sentía la amenaza de una religión muerta, que al revivir un momento y al vestirse con sus galas, mostraba el puño a la vida.

El pueblo, a los lados de la calle, se arrodillaba fervorosamente. Había un silencio grave, sólo turbado por el tañido de una campana.

De vez en cuando, algún hombre del pueblo aparecía en la procesión, descalzo, llevando atada al pie una cadena y sobre los hombros una pesada cruz.

Al último ya, al final de todos, cerrando la marcha, aparecieron dos filas larguísimas de disciplinantes vestidos de negro, que llevaban un ancho cinturón y un gran escapulario, amarillos, y un cirio, también amarillo, apoyado por el extremo en la cintura. Era el colmo de lo tétrico, de lo lúgubre, de lo malsano.

Fernando, que se había inclinado al pasar los otros grupos de cofrades, se irguió con intenciones de protestar de aquella horrible mascarada. Vió las miradas iracundas que le dirigían los disciplinantes al ver su acto de irreverencia, los ojos negros llenos de amenazador brillo a través de los antifaces, y sintió el odio; cubrió su cabeza, ya que no podía hacer más en contra, y volviendo la espalda a la procesión, se escabulló por una callejuela.

La gente rebullía por todas partes; pasaban como sombras, labriegos envueltos en capotes de capucha parda, mujeres con mantellinas de otra época, gente de rostro denegrido y mirar amenazador y brillante.

De noche era costumbre visitar las iglesias; Fernando entró en una. En el ámbito

passed by there, it was already dusk; it had grown dark; the small oil lamps on the balconies and in the windows were shining more brightly; an enormous, reddish, truly menacing moon was just beginning to appear over one of the hills.
The procession was very long.
First came the standards of the confraternities, then two long lines of Roman soldiers, along both sides of the street, moving with a step like that of automatons, which made the silvery scales of their *loricae* resound; behind them came long-bearded Jews, dark-looking, with terrifying expressions.
Then groups of twenty or thirty members of the confraternities started to appear, all of them in two lines, dressed in habits of the same color, carrying round lanterns placed on top of tall poles in their hands; then the disciplinants appeared, with their red, green and white tunics and cuirasses, walking in companies, carrying sculptured scenes from the Passion of Christ between them on the platforms, watching over them, intoning lugubrious prayers, while several ragged little boys, walking along in front of each platform, kept marking the rhythm of the march on their drums with a resounding rubadub.
You could see the procession appear along the sloping street like a cortège of lugubrious, terrifying shadows. Standing before those platforms full of lights, before that troupe of red disciplinants with their high-pointed hoods on their heads and their faces under their masks, you could feel the threat of a dead religion, which, on reviving for a moment and dressing up in all its trappings, was shaking its fist at life.
Along the sides of the streets, the people were fervently kneeling down. There was a grave silence, disturbed only by the tolling of a bell.
From time to time, some man from the town would appear in the procession, barefoot, wearing a chain attached to his foot and a heavy cross on his shoulders.
Finally, at the very end, after all the others, bringing up the rear, two very long rows of disciplinants appeared, dressed in black, wearing wide, yellow belts and large scapulars, with long wax tapers, also yellow, supported at the ends against their waists. It was the very height of all that was gloomy, lugubrious and unwholesome.
Fernando, who had bowed his head when the other groups of confraternity members had passed, now straightened up, with every intention of protesting against that horrible masquerade. He saw the angry stares directed at him by the disciplinants, when they saw his act of irreverence, their black eyes filled with menacing brilliance, even through their masks, and he felt their hatred; since he could no longer do anything in opposition to them, he covered his head, turned his back on the procession and slipped away down a narrow side street.
People were stirring about everywhere; peasants, wrapped in cloaks with brown hoods, women with mantillas from another period, people with darkened faces and menacing, shining glances, kept passing by like shadows.
At night, it was the custom to visit the churches; Fernando went inside one

anchuroso y negro, se veía el altar iluminado por unas cuantas velas que brillaban en la obscuridad; el órgano, después de sollozar por la agonía del Cristo, había enmudecido por completo. Un silencio lleno de horrores, resonaba en la negrura insondable de las naves. En los rincones, sombras negras de mujer, sentadas en el suelo, inclinaban la cabeza participando con toda su alma de las angustias y suplicios legendarios del Crucificado.

Al entrar y salir, hombres y mujeres se arrodillaban ante un Nazareno con faldas moradas, iluminado por una lámpara; después se abalanzaban sobre él y besaban sus pies, con un beso que resonaba en el silencio. Ponían los labios unos donde los habían puesto los otros.

Delante de los confesionarios se amontonaban viejas con mantellinas sobre la frente, y plañian y lanzaban en el aire mudo, frío, opaca de la iglesia, hondos y dolorosos suspiros.

XLIII

Fué, quizá, al ver la persistencia de Fernando en ir a la iglesia, la familia del administrador creyó que era el momento de catequizarle.

Un esolapio joven, profesor, que tenía fama de talentudo, comenzó a ir con más frecuencia a casa del administrador y a acompañar después en sus paseos a Fernando. Éste, que estaba asistiendo al silencioso proceso de su alma, que arrojaba lentamente todas las locuras misteriosas que la habían enturbiado, no solía tener muchas ganas de hablar, ni de discutir; pero el escolapio forzaba las conversaciones para llevarlas al punto que él quería, e inmediatamente, plantear una discusión metafísica. A Ossorio, a quien la discusión perturbaba la corriente interior de su pensamiento, no le agradaba discutir; y, unas veces, enmudecía; otras, murmuraba vagas objeciones en tono displicente.

Hubo ocasión en que llegaron no a discutir, sino a incomodarse. Fué una tarde que salieron juntos; hacía un calor terrible, el aire vibraba en los oídos, no se agitaba ni una ráfaga de viento en la atmósfera encalmada, bajo el cielo asfixiante.

Fernando iba, malhumorado, pensando en la idea que tendrían de él aquellos administradores para ponerle un ayo, y en la que tendría el curita de sí mismo y de sus condiciones de persuasión. Callaba para no ocuparse más que del cambio que

of them. In the spacious, dark atmosphere, you could see the altar illuminated by several candles shining in the darkness; the organ, after sobbing for the agony of Christ, had then remained completely silent. A silence, filled with horrors, resounded in the unfathomable darkness of the naves. In the corners, black shadows of women, seated on the floor, were bending their heads forward, sharing the legendary anguish and torment of the One Crucified with all their soul.

As they came in and went out, men and women would kneel down before a figure of the Nazarene, that was clothed in purple skirts, illuminated by a lamp; then they would throw themselves upon him and kiss his feet with a sound that resounded in the silence. Some were placing their lips where the others had placed them before.

Old women with mantillas over their foreheads were piling up in front of the confessionals, and they kept wailing and hurling their deep, doleful sighs into the mute, cold, gloomy air of the church.

XLIII

It was perhaps when they saw the persistent manner with which Fernando was attending church that the administrator's family concluded that the proper time had come to win him back into the faith.

A young Piarist, a teacher with a reputation for being quite intelligent, started coming to the administrator's house more frequently and accompanying Fernando on his walks afterward. The latter, who was witnessing the silent process of change within his spirit, who was gradually eliminating all of the mysterious foolishness that had been troubling him, was generally not very anxious to converse, nor to argue; but the Piarist would orient the direction of the conversations, in order to lead them to the point he was aiming at, and he would immediately introduce a metaphysical discussion. Because such a discussion disturbed the inner current of his thoughts, Ossorio didn't feel very much like arguing; sometimes he would keep silent, while at other times he'd mutter some vague objections in an ill-mannered tone of voice.

There was one occasion during which they reached the point where they didn't really have a discussion, but succeeded rather in upsetting one another. It took place one afternoon when they had gone out together; it was terribly hot; the air kept vibrating in your ears; not even a breath of wind was stirring in the calm atmosphere under the stifling sky.

Fernando was walking along, ill-humored, thinking of what a strange idea the administrator and his family must have of him that they would bring in a private tutor for him, and what a lofty opinion this ridiculous priest must have of himself and of his abilities at persuasion. He kept silent so that he could concern himself only with that change his spirit was undergoing with each passing moment; the

por momentos iba sufriendo su espíritu; el escolapio le miraba entre las cejas, como sí quisiera arrancarle el pensamiento.

Con lentitud y sin gran maña, después de mil rodeos y vueltas, el cura llevó la conversación, más bien monólogo, pues Fernando apenas si contestaba con monosílabos, a un asunto entre social y religioso: la autoridad que debía de tener la Iglesia dentro del poder civil.

– Si tuviera más en España de la que tiene, yo emigraría – murmuró Ossorio.

– ¿Por qué?

– Porque me repugna la clerecía.

El escolapio no se dió por ofendido; dió varias vueltas y pases al Poder civil y al religioso, y ya, como seguro en sus posiciones, dijo:

– Todo eso parte de la idea de Dios. ¿Usted creerá en Dios?

– No sé – murmuró con indiferencia Fernando.

– ¡Ah! ¿No sabe usted?

– A veces he creído sentirlo.

– ¡Sentirlo! Misticismo puro.

– ¡Psch! ¿Y qué?

A Fernando le molestaba la petulancia de aquel clérigo imbécil que creía encerrada en su cerebro toda la sabiduría divina. El escolapio miraba de reojo a Ossorio, como un domador a un animal indomesticable.

Iba anocheciendo; la caída de la tarde era de una tristeza infinita. A un lado y a otro del camino se veían viñedos extensos de tierra roja, con los troncos de las viñas que semejaban cuervos en hilera. Veíanse, aquí manchas sangrientas de rojo obscuro, allá el lecho pedregoso de un río seco, olivares polvorientos, con olivos centenarios, achaparrados como enanos disformes, colinas calvas, rapadas; alguno que otro grupo de arbolillos desnudos. En el cielo, de un color gris de plomo, se recortaban los cerros pedregosos y negruzcos.

Pasaron por delante de una tapia larguísima de color de barro. Se veía la ciudad roñoso, gris, en la falda del castillo, y la carretera que serpenteaba llena de pedruscos. Allá cerca, el campo yermo se coloreaba por el sol poniente con una amarillez tétrica.

Fernando miraba y apenas oía. Sin embargo, oyó decir al escolapio que trataba de demostrarle que Dios sostenía la materia con su voluntad.

– Yo no le entiendo a usted – le replicó Fernando – . ¿De manera que según usted, todo no está en Dios?

– ¿Qué quiere usted decir con eso?

Piarist kept looking right into his eyes as if he intended to tear out his very thoughts from him.

Slowly and with no particular dexterity, after endless circumventions and discursions, the priest brought the conversation, which was really a monologue, since Fernando was barely answering in monosyllables, to a question which was partly social and partly religious: the authority the Church should have in the realm of civil power.

"If it had any more than it now has in Spain, I would emigrate," Osssorio muttered.

"Why?"

"Because I find the clergy repugnant."

The Piarist didn't seem to take offense, made several circumventions and feints concerning the idea of civil and religious Power, and then, as if he were certain of his position, he said:

"All that stems from the idea of God. You probably believe in God, don't you?"

"I don't know," Fernando murmured indifferently.

"Aha! Then you don't know?"

"There have been times when I thought I felt his presence."

"Felt it! That's pure mysticism."

"Pshaw! And what's wrong with that?"

Fernando was disturbed by the arrogance of that imbecile of a cleric who thought he had all divine wisdom locked up in his brain. The Piarist looked askance at Osssorio, as an animal tamer would look at an untamable beast.

It was getting dark and the ending of the afternoon was pervaded by an infinite sadness. On both sides of the road, you could see extended vineyards growing in the red earth, and the vine stems looked like crows lined up in a row. In one place, you could see blood-colored patches of dark red, in another place, the rock-filled bed of a dried-up river, dust-covered olive groves, with stunted, century-old olive trees, like deformed dwarfs, bare, smooth hills; here and there, a group of small, naked trees. The rock-strewn, blackish hills were outlined against the leaden gray sky.

They passed in front of a very long clay-colored earthen wall. You could see the city, filthy and gray, on the slope of El Castillo, and the winding, stone-covered road. There, not far off, the setting sun was bathing the barren countryside in red, giving it a gloomy, yellowish tint.

Fernando kept looking, hardly listening. Nevertheless, he heard the Piarist say that he was trying to point out to him that God held all matter together with his will.

"I don't understand you," Fernando replied. "According to you, then, everything isn't a part of God."

"What do you mean by that?"

– Muy sencillo. Si Dios no es razón de todo, y si todo no ha venido de Dios, hay otro principio en el mundo.

– ¿Otro principio?

– Sí; porque oyéndole hablar a usted, parece que hay dos: Dios uno y la materia otro.

– No... Dios creó la materia de la nada. Eso lo saben hasta los chicos.

– Es igual, son dos principios: Dios y una nada de donde se puede sacar algo.

– Dios sostiene la materia con su voluntad. El día que no la sostuviera, quedaría aniquilada.

– ¿Usted creé que una cosa se puede aniquilar?

– Sí.

– Físicamente es imposible; químicamente, también.

– ¿Y eso qué importa?

– Nada; que no queda más que un aniquilamiento teológico, y a ese yo me sometería sin miedo.

Se iban acercando a Yécora; se veía el immenso lugarón con sus casas agrupadas y sus tejados pardos y sus chimeneas humeantes.

– Es orgullo lo que le hace pensar de ese modo – dijo el escolapio.

– En mí, que no afirmo nada, porque creo que no puedo llegar a conocer nada, es orgullo – replicó Ossorio con voz irritada– , y en usted, que afirma todo, que ha ordenado el mundo, que según parece, su Dios lo dejó en desorden, es humildad.

El escolapio no contestó; después, volviendo a la carga, dijo:

– ¿De modo que usted cree que la materia existe también en Dios?

– ¿Creer? Creer me parecería demasiado. Hay una creencia, que es afirmación: hay otra que es suposición. Supongo, creo, pero no afirmo, que Dios es la razón de todo, la causa de todo.

– Entonces es usted panteísta.

– No me importa el mote. Yo, como le decía antes, supongo o creo que hay en todas las cosas, en esa hierba, en ese pájaro, en ese monte, en el cielo, algo invariable, inmutable, que no se puede cambiar, que no se puede aniquilar... No... En lo íntimo creo que todo es fijo e inmutable. Y esto que es fijo, llámesele sustancia, espíritu, materia, cualquier cosa, equis, que a nuestros ojos, por lo menos a los míos, es infinito; yo supongo, a veces, cuando estoy de buen humor, que se reconoce a sí mismo y que tiene conciencia de que es...

– Se explica usted bien – dijo el escolapio sarcásticamente – . Tiene usted ideas muy peregrinas.

– No me choca que le parezcan peregrinas y absurdas, ni me preocupa esa opinión. Yo lo veo así. Si hay un Alma Suprema de las cosas, ésa debe ser la razón de todo.

"It's quite simple. If God is not the reason for everything, and if all things haven't originated from God, then there is another principle in the world."

"Another principle?"

"Yes, because, hearing you speak, it would seem that there are two: God being one and matter the other."

"No...,God created matter out of nothing. Even little children know that."

"It's the same thing; there are two principles: God and a nothingness from which you can obtain something."

"God sustains all matter with his will. The day he no longer sustains it, it would all be utterly destroyed."

"Do you really think that something can be utterly destroyed?"

"Yes."

"Physically, it's impossible; not even chemically."

"But what difference does that make?"

"None at all; but the only annihilation left is a theological one, and I would submit to that without any fear."

They were drawing closer to Yécora; you could see the immense, ugly town with its houses bunched together and its brown roofs and smoking chimneys.

"It is pride that makes you think that way," said the Piarist.

"With me, who affirm nothing, because I believe that I can't really get to know anything, it's pride," Osssorio replied with irritation, "and with you, who affirm everything and have set the world in order, which it seems your God has left in disorder, it is humility."

The Piarist didn't answer; then, renewing the attack, he said:

"So you believe that matter also exists as a part of God?"

"Believe? To believe would seem too much to me. There's a kind of belief that is an affirmation; there's another that is a supposition. I suppose, I believe, but I don't affirm that God is the reason for everything, the cause of everything."

"Then you are a pantheist?"

"The name you attach to it is of no importance. As I was telling you before, I suppose or I believe that there is in all things, in that grass, in that bird, in that mountain, in the sky, something invariable, immutable, that can't be changed, that can't be utterly destroyed... No... Deep down, I really believe everything is fixed and immutable. And that something which is fixed, you may call it substance, spirit, matter, anything at all, X, which in our eyes, at least in mine, is infinite; sometimes, when I am in a good humor, I suppose that this something is conscious of itself and is aware of its existence..."

"You express yourself very well," said the Piarist sarcastically. "But you have very peculiar ideas."

"It doesn't shock me that you find them peculiar and absurd, nor does that opinion disturb me in any way. I see it this way. If there is a Supreme Spirit of all things, then that must be the reason for everything."

— ¿Hasta del mal?
— Hasta del mal, sí. El mal es la sombra. La sombra es la necesidad de la luz.
— Nada, nada: dice unas cosas verdaderamente enormes... Y oiga usted, con esas teorías suyas, ¿qué fin le asigna usted al hombre?
— ¿Fin...? Yo creo que nada tiene fin; ni lo que se llama materia, ni lo que se llama espíritu. He pensado a mi modo en esto, y con relación a la naturaleza, fin y principio me parecen palabras vacías. El principio de una transformación es al mismo tiempo fin de una, estado intermedio de otra y el fin es, a su vez, principio y estado intermedio.
— ¿Y la muerte?
— La Muerte no existe, es el manantial de la vida, es como el mal, una sombra, una noche preñada de una aurora.
— Bueno, concretemos — dijo el escolapio con sonrisa satisfecha —. De modo que ese Dios que usted supone, ¿no tiene influencia sobre los hombres?
— ¿Influencia? Toda... o ninguna. Como le parezca a usted mejor.
— Bien. ¿No premia o castiga?
— No sé. Supongo que no. Además, ¿para qué iba a castigar ni a premiar a la gente de un pobre planeta como el nuestro, regido por leyes inmutables? Ni las fechorías de los hombres son tan terribles, ni sus bondades tan inmensas para que merezcan un castigo o un premio, y mucho menos un castigo o un premio eternos.
— ¡Vaya si lo merecen! Cuando el hombre abusa de la libertad que Dios le ha dado y con el don de Dios se opone a los designios de su Creador, ¿no merece una pena eterna?
— ¡Bah! ¡Abusar de la libertad que Dios le ha dado! Una libertad dada por Dios, creada por Dios, que tiene su corazón también en Dios, que Dios al otorgarla sabe su calidad y conoce con su omniscencia el uso que ha de hacer el hombre con ella, ¿qué libertad es ésa?
— No; Dios no conoce el uso que el hombre ha de hacer de su libertad; para eso le pone en el mundo, a prueba.
— ¿Pero él no sabe y prevé el porvenir del hombre?
— Sí.
— Entonces él sabe ya de antemano lo que el hombre va a hacer de su voluntad, ¿a qué le prueba?
— No, no lo sabe.
— En ese caso no es omnisciente.
— Sí. Figúrese usted un hombre subido a una torre que ve que dos hombres van a pelearse. Los ve y, sin embargo, no puede evitarlo.
— Porque es hombre. Si fuera Dios, sería omnipotente y su voluntad sería bastante para evitar el encuentro.
— ¿Entonces usted niega el libre albedrío?

"Even for evil?"

"Even for evil, yes. Evil is the shadow. The shadow is essential for the existence of light."

"No, not at all; the things you are saying are truly horrible... And let me tell you this, with these theories of yours, what end do you assign to man?"

"End...? I think that nothing has an end; neither that which we call matter, nor that which is called spirit. In my own way, I've thought about this, and as far as Nature is concerned, end and beginning seem empty words to me. The beginning of a transformation is at the same time the end of another one, the intermediate state of yet another, and so the end is, in its turn, the beginning and the intermediate state."

"And how about Death?"

"Death doesn't exist; it is the source of life, it is like evil, a shadow, a night that is impregnated with the dawn."

"All right, let's be specific," said the Piarist with a self-satisfied smile. "So this God that you assume, has no real influence over men?"

"Influence? All..., or none at all, whichever seems better to you."

"Very well, then. He doesn't reward or punish?"

"I don't know. I suppose not. Besides, why should he punish or reward the people of a pitiful planet like ours, which is ruled by immutable laws? The misdeeds of men are neither so terrible, nor their good deeds so immense that they should deserve a punishment or a reward, much less an eternal punishment or reward."

"Of course they deserve it! When man abuses the freedom that God has given him and opposes the designs of his Creator with the very gifts of God, doesn't he deserve an eternal punishment?"

"Nonsense! To abuse the freedom that God has given him! A freedom granted by God, created by God, which even has its very heart in God, which God, in granting it, knows its quality full well, and in his omniscience, knows the use man will put it to, what kind of freedom is that?"

"No; God doesn't know what use man will make of his freedom. That's why he puts him in the world, to test him."

"Then you mean He doesn't know or foresee the future of man?"

"Yes, He does."

"Then He already knows beforehand what man is going to do with his will; so why is He testing him?"

"No, He doesn't know that."

"In that case, He isn't omniscient."

"Yes, He is. Imagine a man who has climbed up high onto a tower, and who sees that two men are going to have a fight. He sees them, and nevertheless he can't prevent it."

"Because he is a man. If he were God, he would be omnipotent and his will would be sufficient to prevent the encounter."

"Then you're denying free will?"

– ¿Y qué?
– Con usted no se puede discutir; niega usted la evidencia.
– No discutamos.
El cura miró a Fernando de reojo, y repuso:
– Se va usted de la cuestión; no tratábamos del libre albedrío.
– No, yo por mi parte no trataba de nada.
– Usted cree – añadió el escolapio – que las acciones del hombre no merecen una pena o un premio, eternos e irrevocables; ¿no es eso?
– Eso es.
– Sin embargo, lo irrevocable debe de castigarse o premiarse de un modo irrevocable, ¿no es verdad?
– Sí, me parece que sí.
– Pues bien; hay acciones en el hombre que son definitivas, irrevocables. Un criminal que pegase fuego al Museo de Pinturas de Madrid, ¿no cometía una acción irrevocable? ¿Podrían volverse a rehacer los cuadros quemados? ¿Diga usted?
– No.
– Pues esa acción sería irrevocable.
– Físicamente sí – respondió Ossorio.
– De todas maneras.
– No. Físicamente, objetivamente, todo es irrevocable. La piedra que ha caído, ha caído irrevocablemente, no podrá nunca haber dejado de caer; el hombre que ha cometido una mala acción, por pequeña que sea, no podrá nunca haber dejado de cometerla. En el mundo físico todo es irrevocable; en el mundo moral, al contrario, todo es revocable.
– No se puede discutir con usted.
Habían llegado al pueblo. Fernando se despidió del cura, se fué a casa, y de noche, aburrido después de cenar, entró en el Casino y se sentó en el rincón de una sala grande y destartalada, en la que se reunían algunos compañeros de colegio. Le habían visto los amigos discutiendo con el escolapio y le preguntaron si trataba de catequizarle.
– Eso parece – respondió Ossorio.
– Pues ten cuidado – dijo uno –; te advierto que es un mozo listo.
– Sí, ¿eh?
– Vaya.
– No tiene más – añadió otro – que es un calavera. Ahora anda con la viuda esa recatándose...
– No, se recataba con la mujer de Andrés, el zapatero. Yo, que vivo en frente de Andrés, he visto a la zapatera sentada en las rodillas del escolapio.
Fernando se alegró de la noticia; dada su falta de resolución, aquello era un arma en contra de las pretensiones irritantes del escolapio.

"What about it?"

"It's impossible to discuss anything with you. You deny all the evidence."

"Then let's not discuss it."

The priest looked askance at Fernando and replied:

"You're getting away from the issue; we weren't dealing with free will."

"No, as far as I'm concerned, I wasn't dealing with anything at all."

"You are of the opinion," the Piarist added, "that a man's actions don't merit a punishment or a reward that would be eternal and irrevocable, is that it?"

"That's it."

"Nevertheless, what is irrevocable must be punished or rewarded in an irrevocable way, do you grant that?"

"Yes, it would seem so."

"Well, all right then; there are actions in men that are definitive and irrevocable. A criminal who sets fire to the Museo de Pinturas in Madrid, wouldn't he be committing an irrevocable act? Could the burned paintings be restored again? Tell me what you think?"

"No."

"Then the action would be irrevocable."

"Physically, yes," Ossorio answered.

"From any way you look at it."

"No. Physically, objectively, everything is irrevocable. The stone that has fallen has fallen irrevocably, and most probably couldn't have helped but fall; the man who has committed an evil act, no matter how small it may be, could not have helped but commit it. Everything in the physical world is irrevocable; in the moral world, quite the contrary, everything is revocable."

"It's impossible to discuss anything with you."

They had reached the town. Fernando took leave of the priest and went off to the house, and that night, since he was quite bored, he went out after dinner to the *Casino*, and sat down in a corner of a large, dilapidated room where several of his friends from his school days had gotten together. His friends had seen him arguing with the Piarist and they asked him if the fellow was trying to win him back to the faith.

"It seems that way," Ossorio replied.

"Well, be careful," one of them said; "I must warn you that he's a very shrewd fellow."

"Really?"

"That's for certain."

"The fact of the matter is," another friend added, "he's a real womanizer. Right now he's carrying on with that widow..."

"No, he was carrying on with Andrés, the shoemaker's wife. Since I live across the street from Andrés, I've seen the shoemaker's wife sitting on the Piarist's knees."[89]

Fernando was delighted with this news; considering his lack of resolution, that was a weapon against the irritating pretensions of the Piarist.

XLIV

A los dos o tres días la discusión se entabló de nuevo; pero ya no fué a solas, sino en presencia del administrador, de su esposa, de la hija y del yerno.

Fué la batalla filosófica y hasta literaria; primero se cambiaron argumentos expresados en forma suave; luego pasaron a razones, si no más duras, expuestas con mayor crudeza. Fernando temía exasperarse discutiendo; pero lo que decía el escolapio era una continua provocación; llegó a hacerle alusiones sobre los desórdenes de su vida, y entonces Fernando ya no se pudo reprimir y se desató en improperios y en bestialidades en contra del cura y de su administrador.

El escolapio, que comprendió que desde aquel momento tenía la partida ganada, reconoció que era un pecador que lo sabía...

Fernando no quiso oírle y bruscamente abandonó el cuarto, bajó las escaleras y salió a la calle.

El inmenso poblachón estaba silencioso, mudo. Hacía luna llena; los faroles de la calle, por este motivo, se hallaban sin encender. El pueblo, iluminado fuertemente por la claridad blanca de la luna, aparecía extraño, fantástico, con la mitad de las calles a la sombra y la otra mitad blanco-azulada. En la zona de sombra, encima de algunos portales, veíanse escintilar y balancearse vagamente farolillos encendidos que iluminaban los santos de las hornacinas. Ossorio, indignado con ideas rencorosas, subió hacia la plaza; en el suelo se proyectaba, a la luz de la luna, oblicuamente, la sombra de la torre. Fernando comenzó a subir al Castillo por la calzada.

A un lado se veían las puertas azules de las cuevas empotradas en el monte. Fué subiendo hasta lo alto; había algunos sitios en donde se levantaban extraños peñascales laberínticos de fantásticas formas, unos de aspecto humano, tétricos, sombríos, con agujeros negros que parecían ojos, al ser sombreados por las zarzas; otros, afilados como cuchillos agudos, como botareles de iglesia gótica, de aristas salientes que marcaban y perfilaban en el suelo y a la luz de la luna su sombra dentellada.

Al llegar Ossorio a una peña grande y saliente, avanzó por ella y se sentó en el borde. Desde allá se veía el lugarón, iluminado por la luna, envuelto en una niebla plateada, con los tejados blanquecinos y grises, húmedos por el rocío, que se extendían y se alargaban como si no tuvieran fin, simétricos, como si todo el pueblo fuera un gran tablero de ajedrez. Cerca se destacaban con una crudeza fotográfica las piedras y los peñascos del monte.

Al sentarse Fernando en aquella roca, vió muy abajo su silueta que se reflejaba

XLIV

Two or three days later, the discussion was resumed again, but this time they weren't alone, but rather in the presence of the administrator, his wife, his daughter and his son-in-law.

The battle was philosophical, even literary; first they exchanged a number of positions which were expressed in a mild tone; then they moved on to arguments, which if they weren't more harsh, were expressed with greater rudeness. Fernando was afraid he would become exasperated by the discussion; but what the Piarist was saying to him was a continuous provocation; he reached the point where he even made some allusions to the excesses in Ossorio's private life, and then Fernando could no longer repress himself and he unleashed a number of abusive remarks and ugly comments concerning the priest and his administrator.

The Piarist, who understood that from that moment on, the battle was won, affirmed that Fernando was a sinner and that he was aware of it...

Fernando could listen to him no longer and he ran from the room abruptly, went down the stairs and out into the street.

The immense, ugly town was silent, still. The moon was full; for this very reason the street lamps hadn't been lit. The town, intensely illuminated by the white brightness of the moon, seemed strange, fantastic, with half the streets in shadow and the other half a whitish-blue in color. In the shadowy part, you could see the small burning lamps vaguely scintillating and swinging over some of the front doors, illuminating the figures of the saints in the niches over the doorways. Ossorio, filled with indignation and rancorous ideas, walked up toward the square; the shadow of the tower was projected obliquely on the ground by the light of the moon. Fernando started to walk up along the road to El Castillo.

On one side, you could see the blue doors of the caves embedded in the mountain. He kept going up to the summit: there were a number of places where strange labyrinthine, rocky projections arose in fantastic forms, some with human appearance, gloomy, somber, with black cavities that looked like eyes when they were shaded over by the brambles; others, pointed like sharp knives, like the buttresses of a Gothic church, with projecting arrises, that marked off and outlined their serrated shadows on the ground by the light of the moon.

When Ossorio came to a large, protruding rock, he moved up along it and sat down at the edge. From there, you could see the ugly town, illuminated by the moonlight, wrapped in a silvery haze, its whitish and gray roofs moist with dew, that stretched out and lengthened as if they had no end, symmetrical, as if the whole town were a great big chessboard. Nearby, the stones and crags of the mountain stood out with a photographic coarseness.

When Fernando sat down on that rock, he saw his silhouette far down below, reflected over the gigantic shadow of the crag, falling on the top of a roof. Here

sobre la sombra gigantesca de la peña y que caía encima de un tejado. Alguna que otra luz salida de las casas del pueblo brillaba y parpadeaba confidencialmente.

Un perro comenzó a ladrarle.

Sin saber por qué, aquello reavivó sus iras. Él hubiese deseado que la peña donde se sentaba, que todo el monte, fuera proa de barco gigantesco o reja de inmenso arado, que hubiese ido avanzando sobre aquel pueblo odioso, sin dejar en él piedra sobre piedra. Él hubiese querido tener en su mano la máquina infernal, el producto terrible engendrador de la muerte, para arrojarlo sobre el pueblo y aniquilarlo y reducirlo a cenizas y terminar para siempre con su vida miserable y raquítica.

Pensó después en lo que iba a hacer. Si volvía al pueblo, podía caer en el engranaje aquel de la vida hipócrita de Yécora. Era necesario huir de allí, pero sin hablar a nadie, sin consultar a nadie. Volvió a su casa muy tarde; estaban todos acostados; arregló en su cuarto una maletilla, y luego, despacio, sin hacer ruido, salió de casa y se fué al Casino. Se hallaba desierto: en un rincón, en una mesa, estaba solo Cabeza de Vaca, el gracioso de la compañía de Yáñez de la Barbuda.

Fernando se sentó en otra mesa, e inmediatamente Cabeza de Vaca se acercó a saludarle.

– ¿Va usted de viaje? – le preguntó al ver la maletilla que tenía Ossorio.

– Sí.

– ¿Adónde va usted?

– No sé; a cualquier parte, con tal de salir de Yécora.

– ¿Pero usted no es de aquí?

– Yo, no. Y usted, señor Cabeza de Vaca, ¿qué hace a estas horas en el Casino?

– ¡Yo! Morirme de hambre y de *aburrición*. Ya sabrá usted que la compañía se disolvió.

– No sabía nada.

– Antes de todo, ¿usted quiere mandar que me traigan un café? Hace mucho tiempo que no como nada caliente.

– Sí, hombre.

– Con leche y pan, si puede ser, ¿eh?

– Bueno.

– Pues, sí; se disolvió la Compañía, porque don Dionis arramblaba con los cuartos y nosotros *in albis*. Luego, a Yáñez de la Barbuda le mandó buscar su madre y nos quedamos aquí parados. Gómez Manrique, aquel hombre negruzco de lentes, se marchó; no sé a quién le sacaría el dinero; el director de orquesta y las tres coristas,

and there, lights from the houses in town were shining and winking in a somewhat confidential manner.

A dog began to bark at him.

This seemed to revive his anger, although he didn't seem to know why. He would have wanted the rock on which he was seated, the whole mountain in fact, to be the prow of a gigantic ship, or the plowshare of an immense plow, that would have kept advancing on that hateful town, without leaving one stone on top of another inside it. He would have wanted to have the infernal machine in his own hand, the terrifying object that generated death, so that he could hurl it down upon the town and utterly destroy it, and reduce it to ashes and put an end to its miserable, sickly existence once and for all.

Then he started to think about what he was going to do. If he went back to town, he might fall into that gear mechanism that was the hypocritical existence of Yécora. It was necessary for him to flee from there, but without speaking to anyone, without consulting anyone. He went back to the house very late; everyone had gone to bed; in his room, he prepared a small suitcase, and then, slowly, without making any noise, he left the house and went off to the *Casino*. It happened to be deserted; in a corner, all alone at a table, was Cabeza de Vaca, the actor who played comic roles in Yáñez de la Barbuda's theatrical company.

Fernando sat down at another table and Cabeza de Vaca immediately came over to greet him.

"Are you going on a trip?" he asked him when he saw the small suitcase that Ossorio had with him.

"Yes."

"Where are you going?"

"I don't know; anywhere, as long as I get out of Yécora."

"You mean you're not from around here?"

"I'm not. And you, Señor Cabeza de Vaca, what are you doing in the *Casino* at this hour?"

"Me? I'm just dying of hunger and *boredom*. You probably know already that our company was dissolved."

"I didn't know anything."

"Before anything else; would you mind having them bring me a cup of coffee? I haven't had anything warm for some time."

"Of course, my dear fellow."

"With milk and some bread, if that's all right, huh?"

"All right."

"As I was saying; the company dissolved because Don Dionis made off with the cash and left us *in albis* (high and dry). Then Yáñez de la Barbuda's mother sent for him and we were left stranded here. Gómez Manrique, that dark-looking fellow with the eyeglasses, went off; I really don't know from whom he could have gotten the money; the orchestra director and the three girls in the chorus were contracted

se fueron contratados a un café cantante de Alcoy y nos quedamos la característica y sus dos hijas y el maquinista, que está arreglado con la Lolita.

– ¿Sí, eh? Si lo hubiera sabido mi primo el alcalde...
– ¡Ah! ¿Pero el alcalde es primo de usted?
– Sí.
– Por muchos años.
– ¡Psch! Es un animal.

Cabeza de Vaca hizo un guiño expresivo.

– Yo creo – dijo agarrando la taza de café con las dos manos y bebiendo con ansia– señor don...; no sé como es su nombre de usted.

– Fernando.

– Pues bien, don Fernando, creo que me engañé con respecto a usted; en el escenario el día que le ví le traté como un doctrino... perdone usted.

– No vale la pena. Y diga usted, ¿qué han hecho ustedes en este tiempo, la característica, sus hijas y usted?

– Ellas muy bien; *cabriteando* las pobrecillas. Lolita, sobre todo, ha sido la salvación de la familia. Usted sabe; todos estos señores de la ciudad enviando cartas y alcahuetas que van y alcahuetas que vienen, y visitas de señores serios y de curas que salían de noche embozados hasta la nariz en la capa. Las mujeres tienen esas ventajas – añadió Cabeza de Vaca cínicamente:

– Al principio, a mí Mencía me prestó algún dinero; pero desde que se enteró el maquinista, el amigo de la Lolita, que es un bruto, animal, que se emborracha a todas horas, ya nada. He tenido que vivir como los camaleones; aquí un café, allá una copa...

– ¿Y qué va usted a hacer?
– Pues no sé.
– ¿Y ellas se fueron?
– Hoy quizás salgan de la estación inmediata.
– Pues yo también me marcho.
– ¿Pero cuándo?
– Ahora mismo.
– ¿De veras se va usted? ¿Pero ahora, de noche?
– Sí.
– ¿No le da a usted miedo?
– Miedo; ¿de qué?
– ¡Qué sé yo! Si tuviera dinero para llegar a Valencia me iría con usted.
– ¿Cuesta mucho el billete?
– No; unas pesetas.

to perform in a cabaret bar in Alcoy, and so we were left here, the actress who plays the older ladies and her two daughters and the stagehand, who's involved with La Lolita."

"Really, eh? If my cousin the Mayor only knew..."

"Oh! Then the Mayor's your cousin?"

"Yes."

"My compliments."

"Pshaw! He's a stupid brute."

Cabeza de Vaca winked expressively.

"I think," he said, grabbing his coffee cup with two hands and drinking it eagerly, "Señor Don...; I don't really know your name."

"Fernando."

"All right, then, Don Fernando, I think I was mistaken with respect to you; that day when I saw you on the stage, I treated you as if you were a shrinking violet..., you'll forgive me."

"Don't let it bother you. But tell me, what have you all been doing all this time, the woman who plays older ladies, her daughters and you?"

"The girls have been doing very well for themselves; the poor things have found themselves soliciting clients. Lolita, more than anyone, has been the real salvation of the family. You know; all these gentlemen in the city sending letters and procuresses coming, and procuresses going all the time, and visits from proper gentlemen and priests,[90] departing at night all covered up to their noses with their capes. Women have those advantages," added Cabeza de Vaca quite cynically.

"At first, Mencía lent me a little money; but ever since that stagehand, Lolita's boyfriend found out, and he's a brute, a beast, who gets drunk at all hours, and so now, nothing at all. I have to live like the chameleons; a cup of coffee here, a glass of wine there..."

"And what do you intend to do?"

"Well, I don't know."

"What about the women, did they leave?"

"They may perhaps be leaving today from the next station."

"Well, I'm departing too."

"But when?"

"Right now."

"You're really going? And now, at night?"

"Yes."

"Aren't you afraid?"

"Afraid? Of what?"

"How should I know! If I had enough money to get to Valencia, I'd go with you."

"Does a ticket cost very much?"

"No; just a few *pesetas*."

– Yo se las daré.
– Vamos entonces, don Fernando... otro café no creo que estaría mal, ¿eh?
– Bueno, pero de prisa.
Tomaron el café; salieron del Casino y después del pueblo. Comenzaba a lloviznar; hacía frío; no hallaron a nadie; la noche estaba negra, el camino obscuro. A las tres horas estaban Fernando y Cabeza de Vaca en la estación del pueblo inmediato; lo primero que se encontraron allí fué a la característica y a sus dos hijas, que andaban embozadas en las toquillas, por el andén; el maquinista dormía en un banco de la sala de espera.

Fernando se dirigió a la cantina, y por la influencia de un mozo de la estación, antiguo conocido suyo, consiguió que le abrieran la taberna. Entraron allá la característica y sus hijas, Cabeza de Vaca y Ossorio. No había más que unas rosquillas con sabor de aceite y aguardiente, pero ni las tres cómicas ni el gracioso hicieron ascos y se atracaron de rosquillas y de amílico.

Cuando llegó el tren y entraron todos en el vagón de tercera, las mejillas estaban rojas y las miradas brillantes; el maquinista, indignado porque no le avisaron, se tendió en un banco a dormir.

Mientras el tren iba en marcha, la vieja característica, que se encontraba alegre, empezó a cantar trozos de *Jugar con fuego* y de *Marina;* siguió Cabeza de Vaca con canciones del género chico, y después Mencía se arrancó con unas soleares y tientos que quitaban el sentido.

– ¡Si tuviéramos una guitarra! – se lamentó Cabeza de Vaca.

¡Ahí va una! – dijo un hombre del mismo vagón, pero de otro compartimiento, que iba envuelto en una gran manta listada.

Entonces ya la cosa se generalizó: Cabeza de Vaca tocó la guitarra, la vieja y Lolita llevaban las palmas y Mencía cantaba canciones gitanas, sentimentales, que hacían saltar lágrimas.

Cuando querrá la Virge
del Mayó Doló
q'esos peliyo rubio
te lo peine yo.

Y la vieja palmoteaba, gritando desaforada un estribillo:

Ezo quiero, ezo quiero,
Eza pipa arraztrando po el zuelo.

"Then I'll give you the money."

"Let's be on our way then, Don Fernando... I think another cup of coffee wouldn't be bad, though, eh?"

"All right, but hurry it up."

They drank their coffee; they left the *Casino* and then they left town. It was starting to drizzle; it was cold; they didn't come across anyone; the night was pitch black; the road was dark. After three hours, Fernando and Cabeza de Vaca were at the station in the next town; the first ones they ran into there were the actress who played older women and her two daughters, who were walking along the station platform, all muffled up in their shawls; the stagehand was asleep on a bench in the waiting room.

Fernando walked over to the station restaurant, and through the intervention of one of the railway porters at the station, an old acquaintance of his, he succeeded in having them open the tavern. The actress who played older women, her two daughters, Cabeza de Vaca and Ossorio all went inside. All they had were some ring-shaped cakes tasting of oil, and some *aguardiente*, but neither the three actresses nor the actor who played comic parts turned their noses up at this and they all stuffed themselves with the round cakes and the cheap liquor.

When the train arrived and they all got onto the third-class coach, their cheeks flushed and their eyes shining; the stagehand, who was indignant, because they hadn't informed him, stretched out on a bench to sleep.

As the train was moving along, the old actress who played older women, who happened to be in a gay mood, began to sing some songs from *Jugar con fuego* (Playing With Fire) and from *Marina*;[91] Cabeza de Vaca followed with songs from popular musical comedies, and then Mencía broke into some *soleares* and *tientos*[92] that literally took your breath away.

"If only we had a guitar!" Cabeza de Vaca lamented.

"Here comes one!" said a man who was in another compartment of the same coach, who was all wrapped up in a striped traveling blanket.

Then everybody joined in: Cabeza de Vaca played the guitar; the old lady and Lolita accompanied him by clapping their palms while Mencía sang sad, sentimental gypsy songs that brought tears to your eyes.

When it is the wish of the Virgin
of the Seven Sorrows
that those dear blond hairs of yours
let me be the one to comb them

And the old lady kept on clapping her palms as she deliriously shouted a refrain:

That's what I want, that's what I want,
that pipe dragging on the ground

Y Mencía, más sentimental, con las lágrimas en los ojos entornados, arrullaba y seguía achicando la frente, levantando las cejas, poniendo una cara de una voluptuosidad enferma:

En el hospitaliyo
a manita erecha
ayí tenía mi compañerito
su camita jecha.

Y la vieja palmoteaba gritando desaforada su estribillo. Toda la gente de los otros compartimientos, levantada, gritaba y tomaba parte en el espectáculo.

Después que aburrieron de cantar, Cabeza de Vaca empezó a puntear un tango; Lolita se levantó, le pidió su sombrero ancho a un tipo de chalán o de ganadero, que iba en el vagón, se lo puso en la cabeza, inclinado, se recogió hacia un lado las faldas, y cuando el tren paró en una estación, comenzó a bailar el tango. Era el baile jacarandoso, lleno de posturas lúbricas, acompañada de castañeteo de los dedos, en algunos pasajes con conatos de danza de vientre; producía un entusiasmo entre los espectadores delirante. Jaleaban todos con gritos y palmadas. Al ir a concluir el baile, echó a andar el tren; Lolita perdió o hizo como que perdía el equilibrio, y fué a sentarse de golpe sobre las rodillas de Fernando. Este la cogió de la cintura y la sujetó sin que ella ofreciera gran resistencia.

– ¡Ande usted con ella! – vociferaban de todos los compartimientos.

Ella se volvió a mirar a Fernando, y en voz baja le dijo:

– ¡Guasón!

XLV

– Es extraño – pensaba Ossorio – cómo se desenmascara el hombre en algunas ocasiones; el sacarlo de su lugar, de su centro, pone claramente en evidencia sus inclinaciones, su modo de ser. Un vagón de un tren es una escuela de egoísmo.

El sitio en que Ossorio filosofaba, era la sala de una estación manchega, donde se cambiaba de tren para dirigirse a Valencia.

Los viajeros de primera y segunda, unos habían pasado al café; la mayoría de los de tercera quedaban en los bancos de la sala, durmiendo. Los cómicos habían entrado en el café con la seguridad de que Fernando pagaría, y Lolita, sentada junto a él, con pretexto de que tenía frío, se le iba echando encima, hasta que inclinó la cabeza sobre su hombro y se durmió. Fernando no se sentía romántico; cogió entre sus manos la cabeza de la muchacha y la apoyó en el hombro de la característica, a

And Mencía, even more sentimental, with tears in her partly closed eyes, kept cooing and contracting her forehead, raising her eyebrows and making a face filled with sickly voluptuousness:

> *In the hospital,*
> *on the right-hand side,*
> *that's where my sweetheart had*
> *his bed set up*

And the old lady kept clapping her palms, frantically shouting the refrain. All the people in the other compartments were standing, shouting and taking part in the performance.

After they all got bored with the singing, Cabeza de Vaca started to strum a tango;[93] Lolita stood up, asked a man who was riding in the coach and looked like a horse or cattle dealer, for his wide-brimmed hat; she put it on her head, at an angle, pulled her skirts to one side, and when the train stopped at a station, she began to dance the tango. The dance was lively, full of lubricious postures, accompanied by the clicking of her fingers and, in some portions, by attempts at belly dancing; it was producing a delirious enthusiasm among the spectators. They were all cheering her on with their shouting and clapping of their palms. Just as the dance was about to end, the train started to move; Lolita lost her balance or possibly made believe she had lost it, and she suddenly ended up sitting on Fernando's knees. He seized her by the waist and held her fast, and she didn't offer very much resistance.

"Go to it!" came the shout from all the compartments.

She turned around to look at Fernando and said to him in a low voice:

"You devil, you!"

XLV

"It's strange," thought Ossorio, "how a man unmasks himself on certain occasions; taking him out of his natural place, out of his usual milieu, he clearly puts his inclinations, his way of life, into evidence. A train coach is a school of egotism."

The place where Ossorio was philosophizing was the waiting room of a train station in La Mancha, where you changed trains to go on to Valencia.

Of the first and second-class passengers, some had gone off into the café; the majority of those in third-class remained on the benches in the waiting room, asleep. The actors had gone into the café, feeling certain that Fernando would pay, and Lolita, seated next to him, kept pressing up against him under the pretext that she was cold, until she leaned her head on his shoulder and fell asleep. Fernando didn't feel very romantic, so he took the girl's head between his hands and leaned it on the shoulder of the actress who played older women, and he told her he was going to

quien le dijo que iba a dar una vuelta, que podían dormirse: él les avisaría cuando llegara el tren. Pagó el gasto y salió al andén.

Entró en la sala de espera, convertida en dormitorio. Un mechero de gas en una lira de hierro, temblaba, iluminando con su luz roja y vacilante las paredes sucias, llenas de carteles de ferias y anuncios; los hombres dormidos, embozados en las mantas. Algunos iban y venían y taconeaban con furia de frío; otros, más tranquilos, hablaban recostados en las paredes; no faltaba la labriega de rostro atezado, vestida de negro, que con la cara indiferente y dura, y la mirada vacía, se preparaba a esperar sentada en el banco media noche, con la mano apoyada en la cesta, sín moverse ni pestañear siquiera.

En un rincón, un hombre vestido de negro, cepillado, limpio, con el tipo de empleado decente que se muere de hambre; su mujer y una niña de siete a ocho años, que asomaba su cara aterida y pálida por encima del embozo de un mantón raído, miraban atentamente los movimientos de unos y otros, encogidos los tres como si tuvieran miedo de ocupar más sitio que el preciso.

Fernando salió al andén.

En uno de los bancos vió tendido a un hombre embozado en la capa, que roncaba como un piporro. Había colgado su maleta, por las correas, de un farol y apoyaba la cabeza en ella. Encima del banco en donde se había puesto, estaba la campana para señalar las salidas de los trenes. Además de la maleta, el hombre llevaba como equipaje dos jaulas, altas como las de las perdices, pero mucho más grandes, y dentro, en cada una, un gallo.

Silbó un tren. Un mozo hizo sonar varias veces la campana. El hombre de los gallos entonces se incorporó, bostezó, se arregló la bufanda, cogió sus dos jaulas y entró en un vagón de tercera.

Fernando preguntó adónde iba aquel tren que llegaba; le dijeron que a Alicante; pensó que lo más fácil para escaparse de los cómicos, sería meterse allí; cogió su maleta, y cuando el tren comenzaba su marcha, se subió al estribo.

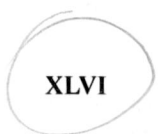

XLVI

¿Fué manuscrito o colección de cartas? No sé; después de todo, ¿qué importa? En el cuaderno de donde yo copio esto, la narración continúa, sólo que el narrador parece ser en las páginas siguientes el mismo personaje.

....

....

take a walk and that they could sleep for a while; he would let them know when the train arrived. He paid the bill and walked out onto the platform.

He went into the waiting room, which had been converted into a sleeping room. A gas burner in an iron frame in the shape of a lyre was trembling as it illuminated with its red and vacillating light the filthy walls, covered with posters for fairs and announcements; the men were sleeping, covered up in their travel blankets. Several men were pacing back and forth, furiously striking their heels on the ground because of the cold; others, calmer, were conversing as they leaned against the walls; there was the inevitable peasant woman, with her darkly tanned face, dressed in black, her face indifferent and hard, her expression blank, who was preparing herself to wait half the night, seated on a bench, her hand resting on her basket, without moving or scarcely even blinking.

In a corner, a man dressed in black, neatly brushed and clean, with the appearance of a very decent clerk who is dying of hunger; his wife and a little girl of seven or eight, who was poking her pale face, stiff with cold, over the fold of a threadbare shawl, were attentively watching the movements of the people all around them, all three of them hunched together as if they were afraid to occupy any more space than was absolutely necessary.

Fernando stepped back out onto the platform.

On one of the benches, he saw a man stretched out, all wrapped up in his cape, who was snoring like a bassoon. He had hung his suitcase from a lantern by its straps and was leaning his head against it. The bell that signaled the train departures was above the bench on which he had stretched out. In addition to his suitcase, the man was bringing two cages as baggage, about as high as those used for partridges, only much larger, and inside each one was a rooster.

A train whistled. A porter rang the bell several times. Then the man with the roosters sat up, yawned, arranged his muffler, grabbed his two cages and then climbed aboard a third-class coach.

Fernando inquired where the train that had just arrived was going, and they told him it was going to Alicante; he concluded that the easiest way to escape from those actors would be to get aboard; so he picked up his suitcase, and when the train started to move, he climbed up onto the steps.

XLVI

Was it a manuscript or a collection of letters? I don't know; after all, what difference does it make? In the notebook from which I am copying all this, the narrative continues, but on the following pages, the narrator seems to be the character himself.[94]

....

....

Ya no podía vivir allí. Tomé el tren y he bajado en la primera estación que me ha parecido: en la estación de un pueblo encantador. Como aquí no hay más posada que una, que está cerca de la estación, y deseo no oír ruido de trenes y de máquinas, he preguntado en dos o tres sitios dónde podrían hospedarme, y me han indicado una casa de labor de fuera del pueblo, en el camino real, y aquí estoy.

Mi cuarto es grande, de paredes blanqueadas; en el techo tiene vigas de color azul con labores toscas de talla; el balcón, con el barandado de madera carcomida, es de gran saliente y da al camino real.

Estoy alegre, satisfechísimo de encontrarme aquí. Desde mi balcón ya no veo la desnudez de Marisparza. Enfrente, brillan al sol campos de verdura; las amapolas rojas salpican con manchas sangrientas los extensos bancales de trigo que se extienden, se dilatan como lagos verdes con su oleaje de ondulaciones. Por la tierra, inundada de luz, veo pasar la rápida sombra de las golondrinas y la más lenta de las palomas que cruzan el aire. Un perro blanco y amarillo se revuelca en un campo de habas, mientras un burro viejo, atado a una argolla, le mira con un tácito reproche, con las orejas levantadas.

En el corral, que veo desde mi balcón, los polluelos pican en montones de estiércol; gruñen los estúpidos cerdos y andan de acá para allá con ojillos suspicaces y actitudes de misántropo; cacarean las gallinas, y un gallo farsantón y petulentes, con sus ojos redondos como botones de metal, y su cresta y su barba de carnosidad roja, se pasea con ademanes tenoriescos.

Aquí no se ven pedregales como en Marisparza; todo es jugoso, claro y definido, pero alegre. A lo lejos yo veo montes cubiertos de pinares negruzcos; más cerca, entre los viñedos, un cerrillo poblado por pinos de copa redonda. Arriba, muy alto, en el espacio azul, sin mancha, resplandesciente, se divisan los gavilanes, que trazan lentas curvas en el cielo.

Es la vida, la poderosa vida que reina por todas partes; las mariposas, pintadas de espléndidos colores, se agitan temblando sobre los sembrados verdes; las altas hierbas vivaces brotan lánguidas, holgazanas, en los ribazos; pían, gritan los gorriones en los árboles, revoltean en algarabía chillona golondrinas y vencejos; corren como flechas las aéreas libélulas de alas de tul verde y dorado; los mosquitos zumban en nube; pasan como balas los grandes insectos de caparazones negros brillantes; rezonguean las abejas y los moscones, curioseando por los huecos de tapias y paredes, y el gran sol, padre de la vida, el gran sol, bondadoso, sonríe en los campos verdes y claros de alcacel, incendia las rocas del monte con su luz vivísima, y va rebrillando en el agua turbia y veloz de las acequias que se desliza con rápido tumulto y ríe con gorjeos misteriosos por las praderas florecidas y llenas de rojas amapolas.

I could no longer live there. I took the train and got off at the first station that struck my fancy: at the station of a delightful town. Since there is no more than one inn here and it is near the station, and since I don't wish to hear the noise of the trains and the engines, I inquired in two or three places as to where I would be able to find lodging, and they suggested a farmstead outside town on the main road, and so here I am.

My room is spacious with whitewashed walls; there are blue-colored beams with roughly carved designs on the ceiling; the balcony, with a balustrade of rotting wood, projects far out and faces the main road.

I am happy, very satisfied to find myself here. From my balcony window, I no longer see the naked landscape of Marisparza. Opposite me, the verdant fields glisten in the sunlight; the red poppies sprinkle the vast oblong wheat fields with blood-colored patches that stretch out and widen like green lakes in a surge of undulations. I see the swift shadow of the swallows on the ground that is inundated with light, and the slower movement of the doves as they cross through the air. A white and yellow dog is rolling around in a field of beans, while an old donkey, tied to an iron ring, is looking at him with silent reproach, with his ears raised.

From my balcony, I can see the little chicks in the poultry yard, pecking around the piles of manure; the stupid hogs are grunting and go this way and that, with their suspicious, nasty, little eyes and their misanthropic expressions; the hens are cackling, and a rooster, looking very pretentious, very arrogant, is strutting around with the gesticulations of a Don Juan, his eyes as round as metal buttons, his comb and his wattle fleshy red in color.

Here you don't see the stony terrain as in Marisparza; everything is succulent, bright and clearly defined, yet still cheerful. In the distance, I see the mountains covered with blackish pine groves; somewhat closer, among the vineyards, a small hill, populated with pine trees with rounded tops. Up above, high up in the blue void, which is immaculate and resplendent, you can make out the sparrow hawks as they trace slow curves in the sky.

It is life, powerful life, reigning everywhere; butterflies, painted in splendid colors, flutter about, trembling over the green, cultivated fields; the high, vigorous grasses are bursting forth, languid and indolent on the sloping ground; the sparrows are chirping and shrieking in the trees; swallows and swifts flutter around everywhere in a shrill uproar; ethereal dragonflies, with wings of green and golden tulle, race by like arrows; mosquitoes buzz about in a cloud and large insects with black, shiny shells pass by like bullets; bees and bluebottles buzz past, prying about in the hollows of the earthen and stone walls, and the great sun, the father of life, the great and bountiful sun, is smiling on the green, bright fields of barley, lighting up the rocks on the mountain with its very intense light, and it keeps shining on the turbid, swift water of the irrigation ditches, that glides by with swift tumult and is laughing, with a mysterious warbling, through the blooming meadows filled with red poppies.

¡Oh, qué primavera! ¡Qué hermosa primavera! Nunca he sentido como ahora el despertar profundo de todas mis energías, el latido fuerte y poderoso de la sangre en las arterías. Como si en mi alma hubiese un río interior detenido por una presa, y, al romperse el obstáculo, corriera el agua alegremente, así mi espíritu, que ha roto el dique que le aprisionaba, dique de tristeza y de atonía, corre y se desliza cantando con júbilo su canción de gloria, su canción de vida; nota humilde, pero armónica en el gran coro de la Naturaleza Madre.

Por las mañanas me levanto temprano, y la cabeza al aire, los pies en el rocío, marcho al monte, en donde el viento llega aromatizado con el olor balsámico de los pinos.

Nunca, nunca, ha sido para mis ojos el cielo tan azul, tan puro, tan sonriente; nunca he sentido en mi alma este desbordamiento de energía y de vida. Como la savia hincha las hojas de las piteras, llora en los troncos de las vides y las parras podadas, llena de florecillas azules los vallados del monte y parece emborracharse de sangre en las rojas corolas de los purpurinos geranios, así esa corriente de vida en mi alma le hace reír y llorar y embriagarse en una atmósfera de esperanzas, de sueños y locuras.

Por las tardes, recorro la almazara y el lagar, obscuros, silenciosos, y cuando por alguna rendija de las ventanas entra un rayo de sol como un dardo de fuego o una vara de metal fundido hasta el blanco dorado, en donde nadan las partículas de polvo, siento una inexplicable alegría.

Estos rincones de la casa de labor, estas cosas primitivas y toscas, la zafra donde se tritura la aceituna, el molón de piedra grande y cónico, las tinajas de barro que parecen gigantes hundidos en el suelo, todo me sugiere pensamientos de algo que no he visto jamás y me produce un recuerdo de sensaciones quizá llegadas a mí por herencia.

Suelo comer y cenar en el zaguán, en una mesa pequeña, cerca de los hombres que vuelven del trabajo del campo. Éstos lo hacen por orden: los mayorales de mula y muleros, sentados; los chicos que llaman burreros, de pie. Rezamos todos al empezar y al concluir de comer.

No pinto, no escribo, no hago nada, afortunadamente. De noche oigo el canto tranquilo, filosófico de un cuco y el grito burlón y extraño de un pavo real que siempre está en el tejado.

¡Cuánta vida y cuánta vida en germen se ocultará en estas noches! – se me ocurre pensar. Los pájaros reposarán en las ramas, las abejas en sus colmenas; las hormigas, las arañas, los insectos todos, en sus agujeros. Y mientras éstos reposan, el sapo, despierto, lanzará su nota aflautada y dulce en el espacio; el cuco, su voz apacible y tranquila; el ruiseñor, su canto regio; y en tanto la tierra, para los ojos de los hombres, obscura y sin vida, se agitará, estremeciéndose en continua

Oh, what a spring! What a beautiful spring! Never have I felt, as I do now, the profound awakening of all my energies, the vigorous and powerful beat of the blood in my arteries. Just as if there had been an internal river within my soul, held back by a dam, and when that obstacle had been broken, the water had flowed through joyfully, in a like way, my spirit, which has broken the dike which has been imprisoning it, a dike of sadness and atony, now runs free and glides along joyfully singing its song of glory, its song of life; a humble note, in harmony with the great chorus of Mother Nature.

I generally get up early in the morning and walk with my head in the air and my feet in the dew, toward the mountain where the wind comes in perfumed with the balmy fragrance of the pines.

Never, never has the sky been so blue, so pure, so smiling to my eyes; never have I felt this overflowing of energy and life in my soul. As the sap swells the leaves of the pita plants, weeps in the thick stems of the vines and the pruned grapevines, as it fills the earthen walls in the mountain with small, blue flowers, and seems to become intoxicated with blood in the red corollas of the purple geraniums, in a like manner, that current of life in my soul makes it laugh and weep and feel enraptured in an atmosphere of hopes, dreams and wild fancies.

In the afternoon, I generally make the rounds of the oil mill and the wine press, so dark and silent, and when a beam of sunlight enters through a crack in the windows, like a dart of fire or like a metal rod smelted till it is golden white, in which the particles of dust keep swimming around, I feel an inexplicable sense of joy.

These corners of the farmstead, these primitive and rough things, the oil jar in which they crush the olives, the large cone-shaped millstone, the big earthen vats that look like giants buried in the ground, everything suggests thoughts to me of something that I've never seen and yet produces within me a memory of sensations which have perhaps come down to me through heredity.

I generally eat and have my supper in the outer vestibule, at a small table near the men coming back from their work in the fields. These men do this in a certain order: the overseers for the mules and the mule drivers are seated; the young men called donkey drivers are standing. We all pray when we begin to eat and when we have finished eating.

I don't paint, I don't write, I do absolutely nothing, which is fortunate. At night, I hear the tranquil, philosophical song of a cuckoo and the mocking, strange cry of a peacock, which is always on the roof.

"How much life and how much germinating life must be hidden away in these nights!" the thought occurs to me. The birds are probably resting on the branches, the bees are in their hives; the ants, the spiders, all the insects, in their holes. And while these are resting, the toad, wide-awake, will send its high-pitched, sweet note into space; the cuckoo, its peaceful, tranquil voice; the nightingale, its regal song, and in the meantime, the earth, dark and lifeless to the eyes of men, will begin to stir, trembling in continual germination, and myriads of living things will burst

germinación, y en las aguas pantanosas de loas balsas y en las aguas veloces de las acequias brotarán y se multiplicarán miriadas de seres.

Y al mismo tiempo de esta germinación eterna, ¡qué terrible mortandad! ¡Qué bárbara lucha por la vida! ¿Pero para qué pensar en ella? Si la muerte es depósito, fuente manantial de vida, ¿a qué lamentar la existencia de la muerte? No, no hay que lamentar nada. Vivir y vivir... ésa es la cuestión.

XLVII

Por más que hago, no he desechado todavía el prurito de analizarme, y aunque me encuentro tranquilo y satisfecho, analizo mi bienestar.

¿Es una idea sana que ha entrado en mi cerebro la que me ha proporcionado el equilibrio – me pregunto – , o es que he hallado la paz inconscientemente en mis paseos por la montaña, en el aire puro y limpio?

Lo cierto es que hace dos semanas que estoy aquí y empiezo a cansarme de ser dichoso. Como me hallo ágil de cuerpo y de espíritu, no siento el antiguo cúmulo de indecisiones que ahogaban mi voluntad; y una cosa imbécil que me indigna contra mí mismo, experimento a veces nostalgia por las ideas tristes de antes, por las tribulaciones de mi espíritu. ¿No es ya demasiada estupidez?...

Esta mañana he hablado en el café de la estación con un vendedor de dátiles que comercia en algunos pueblos de la costa, y enredándose la charla ha resultado que conoce a mi tío Vicente, el cual es pariente mío porque estuvo casado con una prima de Laura. Se encuentra, según me ha dicho, de médico en un pueblo de la provincia de Castellón.

Le he escrito. Se me ha ocurrido ir a verle. Creo que lo agradecerá. Este médico se casó muy a disgusto de nuestra familia con mi tía, la prima de mi padre; ella murió sin hijos al año, y el médico, probablemente aburrido de espiritualidad y de romanticismo, se volvió a casar con una labradora, lo cual para Luisa Fernanda y Laura fué y sigue siendo un verdadero crimen, la prueba palmaria de la grosería y de la torpeza de sentimientos de ese medicastro cerril.

XLVIII

He tomado el tren al amanecer. A eso de las diez de la mañana estaba llamando en casa de mi tío.

forth and multiply in the swampy waters of the ponds and in the swift waters of the irrigation ditches.

And at the same time as this eternal germination, what a terrible mortality is going on! What a horrible struggle for life! But why think of that? If death is the depository, the fountain, the source of life, to what purpose is it to lament the existence of death? No, we need not lament anything. To live and to live..., that is the question.

XLVII

No matter what I do, I still haven't been able to rid myself of the urge to analyze myself, and although I find myself tranquil and satisfied, I keep analyzing my sense of well-being.[95]

"Is it a sound idea that has entered my brain and has been provided to me for my sense of equilibrium?" I ask myself, "is it that I have unconsciously found peace of mind in my walks through the mountain in the pure, clean air?"

What is certain is that I've been here for two weeks and I'm beginning to get tired of being happy. Since I now find myself agile in body and in spirit, I don't feel the former burden of indecision that was stifling my will; and there is something absolutely stupid that makes me quite angry at myself, and it's that I sometimes feel very nostalgic for the sad ideas of the past, for the tribulations of my spirit. Now isn't that just too stupid for words...?

This morning I had a conversation in the café at the station with a date salesman who does business in several coastal towns, and in the course of our chat, it turned out that he knows my uncle Vicente, who is a relative of mine by the fact that he was once married to a cousin of Laura. According to what he said to me, my uncle now has a post as a doctor in a town in the province of Castellón.

I've written to him. It has occurred to me that I might go see him. I do think it will make him very happy. This doctor married my aunt, my father's cousin, much to the chagrin of our family; she died within the year without leaving any children; the doctor, probably bored with all that spirituality and that romanticism, married again, this time, a farm girl, which, for Luisa Fernanda and Laura, was and still continues to be a real crime, the living proof of the vulgarity and crude feelings on the part of that boorish quack.

XLVIII

I took the train at daybreak. At about ten in the morning, I was calling at my uncle's house.

El pueblo es grande. Cuando llegué, las calles estaban inundadas de sol, reverberaban vívida claridad las casas blancas, amarillas, azules, continuadas por tapias y paredones que limitan huertas y corrales. A lo lejos veía el mar y una carretera blanca, polvorienta, entre árboles altos, que termina en el puerto.

Se sentía en todo el pueblo un enorme silencio, interrumpido solamente por el cacareo de algún gallo. El tartanero, a quien dije adonde me dirigía, paró la tartana en una callejuela que tiene a ambos lados casas blancas, rebosantes de luz. Llamó y entré en el zaguán.

Mi tío salió a recibirme, me conoció, me dio la mano, pagó al tartanero e hizo que una muchacha subiese la maleta al piso de arriba. Mi tío tenía que hacer una visita y me ha dejado solo en la sala. He salido al balcón; el pueblo está silencioso; las casas, con sus persianas verdes, sus ventanas y puertas cerradas, parecen abstraídas en perezosas meditaciones. De vez en cuando pasan algunas palomas, haciendo zumbar el aire ligeramente con sus alas.

Ha venido la criada, y, llamándome *señoret,* me ha dicho que las señoras habían venido de la iglesia, que la comida estaba en la mesa. He bajado las escaleras y he entrado en el comedor con la sonrisa de un hombre que quiere hacerse amable. Me ha presentado mi tío a su mujer; la he hecho un saludo ceremonioso; he dado un apretón de manos a Dolores, la hija mayor; un beso a Blanca, una chiquilla muy graciosa; he acariciado a un niño de dos o tres años; hemos empezado la comida, y por más esfuerzos que he hecho para animar la conversación, la frialdad ha reinado en la mesa.

Después de comer, Blanca, que es una chiquilla muy traviesa y comunicativa, me ha enseñado la casa, que no tiene nada de particular, pero que es muy cómoda. En el piso bajo están el comedor, el despacho del padre, la cocina, la despensa y un patio que conduce a un corral; en el piso de arriba hay la sala grande, con dos balcones a la calle, y las alcobas.

Ha debido de ser cuestión de bastante tiempo el arreglarme el cuarto; yo, para dejar libertad, me he ido al Casino. Al volver me han enseñado mi cuarto. Es un gabinete grande, hermoso, enjalbegado de cal, con el suelo de azulejos azules y blancos, relucientes; tiene un sofá, varias sillas azules, un espejo, un lavabo y una cama de madera de limoncillo, ésta última muy coquetona, muy baja, con cortinas azules de seda.

El balcón del gabinete da a un terradito, en cuesta, hecho sobre un tejadillo del piso bajo de la casa. En un rincón nace una parra que sube por la pared; ya con las hojas crecidas, del tamaño del ala de un murciélago, y en la pared también hay unos cuantos alambres cruzados, de los que cuelgan filamentos de enredaderas secas. En el suelo, en graderías verdes, hay algunas macetas.

Estoy ahora aquí, sentado. ¡Qué sitio más agradable! Enfrente, por encima de las tejas, veo la torre de un convento, torcida, con su veleta adornada con un grifo largo y escuálido que tiene un aspecto cómicamente triste. Me ha parecido conveniente

The town is large. When I arrived, the streets were inundated with sunlight, and the white, yellow and blue houses, with earthen walls and heavier stone walls continuing alongside them, enclosing the kitchen gardens and poultry yards, were reflecting the vivid brightness. In the distance, you could see the sea and a white, dusty road that runs between tall trees and ends up at the port.

You were aware of an enormous silence throughout the entire town that was interrupted only by the occasional crowing of a rooster. I told the driver where I wanted to go and he stopped the *tartana* on a narrow side street with white houses on both sides, overflowing with light. He rang and I went into the outer vestibule.

My uncle came out to receive me, recognized me, gave me his hand, paid the driver of the tartana and had a girl take my suitcase upstairs. My uncle had a call to make and he left me alone in the drawing room. I stepped out onto the balcony; the town is silent; the houses, with their green shutters, windows and doors all shut; they seem to be absorbed in their indolent meditations. From time to time, some doves pass by, making the air buzz gently with their wings.

The maid came in, calling me *señoret*, told me that the ladies had just come from church, and that the meal was on the table. I went down the stairs and stepped into the dining room, with the smile of a man who wants to make himself very affable. My uncle introduced me to his wife; I greeted her very ceremoniously, I shook hands with Dolores, the older daughter; a kiss for Blanca, a very charming little girl; I fondled a little boy two or three years of age; we started the meal, and in spite of all my efforts to animate the conversation, a coldness reigned at the table.

After the meal, Blanca, who is a very mischievous and communicative child, showed me the house, which has nothing particularly unusual about it, but is quite comfortable. On the lower floor are the dining room, the father's study, the kitchen, the pantry and a patio that leads into a poultry yard; on the upper floor are the main drawing room with two balconies facing the street, and the bedrooms.

It must have been a question of considerable time for them to arrange my room; in order to leave them free, I went off to the *casino*. When I returned, they showed me my room. It is a large, attractive boudoir, with whitewashed walls and a floor of shiny blue and white-colored tiles; it has a sofa, several blue chairs, a mirror, a wash basin and a bed of *limoncillo* wood, this last piece being quite coquettish, very low, with blue silk curtains.

The balcony of the boudoir opens onto a small, sloping terrace, built on top of the tile roof over the lower floor of the house. A grapevine starts up in one corner and rises along the wall; its leaves are already fully grown, about the size of a bat's wing, and there are also a number of wires crossing one another on the wall, from which some dried up bindweed plants are hanging. There are several flowerpots on the ground, resting on green steps.

Here I am now, seated. What a pleasant place this is! Before me, over the tops of the tile roofs, I can see the bent tower of a convent, its weathervane decorated with a long, squalid griffin with a comically sad appearance. It seemed appropriate

hacerle una salutación, y le he dirigido la palabra: ¡Yo te saludo, pobre grifo jovial y bondadose – le he dicho – ; yo sé que a pesar de tu actitud fiera y rampante no eres ni mucho menos un monstruo; sé que tu lengua bífida no tiene nada de venenosa como la de los hombres, y que no te sirve más que para marcar sucesivamente, y no con mucha exactitud, la dirección de los vientos! ¡Pobre grifo jovial y bondadoso, yo te saludo y reclamo tu protección! Al oirme invocarle así, el grifo ha cambiado de postura gracias a un golpe de viento, y le he visto con la cabeza apoyada en la mano, dudando...

XLIX

En esta casa me tratan con gran consideración, pero con un despego absoluto. A mi tío le escuece aún el poco aprecio que hicieron de él los parientes de su difunta esposa, y de rechazo, no me puede ver a mí tampoco. Su mujer cree que soy un aristócrata; se conoce que le ha oído hablar a su marido de mis tías, como si fueran princesas, y que figura que, aunque todo me parece mal, no lo digo porque soy maestro en el disimulo.

Temo haber venido a perturbar las costumbres de la casa. La más asequible es Blanca, la chica, que suele venir a mi cuarto y charlamos los dos.

Por ella he sabido que ese cuarto tan alegre, con su cama de limoncillo y sus cortinas azules, es el de mi prima Dolores, así la llamo, aunque no seamos parientes. He buscado una ocasión de decirle a ésta que han hecho mal en privarla de su gabinete.

Dolores suele regar las macetas del terradito al anochecer, acompañada de Blanca. Andan las dos de aquí para allá, y por lo que hablan y lo que discuten, se diría que están dirigiendo la más trascendental de las cuestiones. ¡Lo que les intriga cada planta!

Un tiesto está colocado en medio de una cazuela con agua para impedir que entren en él las hormigas; el otro tiene una capa de arena o de mantillo; en él de más allá echan las colillas que tira el padre.

Hoy he esperado el momento de encontrar a Dolores sola. Ha venido con la regadera en la mano derecha y el niño en el brazo izquierdo. Yo me he hecho el distraído. La verdad, no me había fijado en mi prima hasta ahora.

Es agradable como puede serlo una muchacha de pueblo; es morenuzca, con un color tostado, casi de canela, un color bonito. Ahora, como las mujeres poseen la suprema sabiduría y la suprema estupidez al mismo tiempo, mi prima manifiesta la última condición, llenándose la cara de polvos de arroz a todas horas. Tiene los dientes muy blancos; una sonrisa tranquila y seria, los ojos grandes, muy negros, tenebrosos, con largas pestañas; las caderas redondas y la cintura muy flexible.

for me to offer some greeting to it and so I addressed it with these words: "I greet you, poor, jovial, kind griffin," I said to it, "I know that in spite of your fierce and rampant appearance, you are not in the least way a monster; I know that your bifid tongue is in no way poisonous like that of men, and that it serves only to indicate, successively and without any great precision, the direction of the winds! Poor, jovial, kind griffon, I greet you and I claim your protection!" When it heard me invoke it in this way, the griffin changed its position, thanks to a gust of wind, and I saw it with its head leaning on its hand, doubting...

XLIX

They treat me with great consideration in this house, but with absolute indifference. My uncle is still smarting because of the low esteem in which his deceased wife's relatives had held him, and to get back at them, he can't stand me either. His wife thinks that I am an aristocrat; you can plainly see that she has heard her husband speak of my aunts as if they were princesses, and she imagines that, even though everything here seems to be in poor taste to me, the only reason I don't say so is that I am a master of dissimulation.

I'm very much afraid that my coming here has upset the customs of the house. The most accessible one of all is Blanca, the little girl, who often comes to my room, where the two of us chat.

Through her, I've discovered that this cheerful room with its bed of limoncillo wood, and its blue curtains belongs to my cousin Dolores; that's what I call her, even though we aren't related. I have sought an opportunity to tell her that it was wrong of them to deprive her of her boudoir.

Accompanied by Blanca, Dolores generally waters the flowers on the roof terrace at dusk. The two of them walk back and forth, and by all their talk and discussion, you would think that they were dealing with the most transcendental of questions. How each plant seems to intrigue them!

One flowerpot has been placed in the middle of an earthenware crock with water inside to prevent the ants from getting in; another has a layer of sand or humus in it, and the one even further over gets all the cigar butts their father throws away.

Today I waited for the moment when I could meet Dolores alone. She came out with the watering pot in her right hand and the little boy on her left arm. I acted as if I were distracted by something else. To tell the truth, I really hadn't taken much notice of my cousin until now.

She is pleasant-looking, insofar as a small-town girl can be; she is very dark-complexioned, with a tanned color, almost like that of cinnamon, a pretty color. Nowadays, since women possess supreme wisdom and supreme stupidity at the same time, my cousin manifests this latter condition by covering her face with rice powder at every opportunity. She has very white teeth; a calm and serious smile, large, very black, tenebrous eyes, with long lashes; rounded hips and a very supple waist.

He esperado a que Blanca saliese del terrado por un momento para hablar a Dolores.
– Han hecho ustedes mal en darme este cuarto tan bonito. Si hubiera sabido que era el de usted, no lo hubiera aceptado.
No he concluído la frase y he visto a la muchacha que se ponía roja como una amapola. Me he quedado también azorado al ver la turbación suya y no he sabido qué decir; afortunadamente ha entrado Blanca y se han puesto a hablar las dos.
Hago mil suposiciones para explicarme su azoramiento. ¿Por qué se ha turbado de tal manera? ¿Ha creído que tenía intenciones de mortificarla? Me decido a volver a hablarla.
Después de cenar, en un momento en que su padre ha salido del comedor y su madre ha quedado dormida, la he dicho:
– Esta tarde me pareció que le había molestado a usted lo que dije; no sé lo que pude decir, pero creo que interpretó usted mal mis palabras.
– ¿Qué quiere usted? Soy muy torpe.
– Si alguna inconveniencia se me escapó, perdóneme usted; fué inadvertidamente.
– Está usted perdonado.
– ¿Eso quiere decir que estuve inconveniente, y que además le molesté a usted?
No ha contestado nada.
Me he levantado de la mesa incomodado por una estupidez tal. Indudablemente España es el país más imbécil del orbe; en otras partes se comprende quién es el que trata de ofender y quién no; en España nos sentimos todos tan mezquinos, que creemos siempre en los demás intenciones de ofensa. Estoy indignado. He decidido encontrar un pretexto y largarme de aquí.

L

Hoy me he levantado con la intención de marcharme. Como el tren sale del pueblo a la noche, me he puesto por la tarde a meter en mi maleta alguna ropa. En esta operación me ha visto mi prima Dolores al pasar a regar sus tiestos.
– ¿Pero qué? ¿Está usted haciendo la maleta?
– Sí; tengo que marcharme; una noticia imprevista...
Como no tengo costumbre de mentir, ni tenía para qué, no he dicho más.
– Vamos, que ya se ha aburrido usted de estar con nosotros – ha dicho ella sonriendo.
– No – he contestado secamente – , ustedes son los que se han aburrido de mí.
– ¡Nosotros!

I waited for Blanca to leave the roof terrace for a moment so that I could speak to Dolores.

"You all didn't do the right thing when you gave me this very pretty room. If I'd only known that it was yours, I wouldn't have accepted it."

I'd hardly finished the sentence when I saw the girl turning red as a poppy. I too was left in a state of embarrassment when I saw how upset she was, and I didn't know what to say; fortunately for us, Blanca came out and the two of them started to talk.

I keep making a thousand suppositions to explain her embarrassment. Why did she get so terribly upset? Did she think it was my intention to mortify her? I've made up my mind to speak to her again.

After dinner, in a moment when her father had gone out of the dining room and her mother had fallen asleep, I said to her:

"This afternoon, it seemed to me that what I said to you had upset you; I don't know what I could have said, but I think you interpreted my words badly."

"What do you want from me? I'm very slow-witted."

"If some impropriety escaped my lips, would you please forgive me, because it wasn't intentional."

"You're forgiven."

"Does that mean that I was impolite to you and that I also upset you?"

She didn't answer me at all.

I stood up from the table, annoyed by such stupidity. Spain is without doubt the most imbecilic country in the world;[96] in other places, one can understand who is the one trying to be offensive and who isn't; in Spain, we all feel so mean and petty that we always imagine that others intend to offend us. I am indignant. I've decided to find some pretext so that I can clear out of here.

L

Today I got up with every intention of going away. Since the train leaves town at night, I started to put some of my clothing in my suitcase in the afternoon. My cousin Dolores saw me while I was engaged in doing this as she passed by on her way to water her flowerpots.

"But, what's this? You're packing your suitcase?"

"Yes, I have to go away; an unforeseen piece of news..."

As I'm not accustomed to lying, nor did I have any reason for doing so, I said no more.

"Let's admit it; you've already become bored with being here with us," she said with a smile.

"No, I answered curtly, "you're the ones who have gotten tired of me."

"We?"

– Sí.

Hablando y discutiendo, no ha podido menos Dolores de comprender la verdad, que yo me marchaba por ellos, porque veía que molestaba. Ella ha protestado calurosamente.

– No, no – le he dicho – , comprenderá usted que no es cosa de estar en una casa en donde uno molesta, en donde se cree que uno se burla de la hospitalidad que recibe.

– Espere usted siquiera una semana.

Tras de la explicación hemos llegado a una buena inteligencia con Dolores y a la amistad cariñosa con Blanca.

He exigido que me muden de cuarto, y ahora duermo en una alcoba obscura del fondo de la casa. Me he empeñado en conquistar a la familia. La mamá está casi conquistada, pero el padre es terrible; no hay medio de desarrugar su ceño.

Por la tarde, la mamá y las dos muchachas cosen en el gabinete; ésta debía de ser la costumbre de la casa; yo entro y salgo en el cuarto y hablamos por los codos. Se ha roto el hielo, al menos en lo que se refiere al elemento femenino de la casa. Yo les hablo de París, de Suiza y de Alemania, y les tengo muy entretenidas.

Delante de su padre me guardaría muy bien de hacerlo, porque aprovecharía la ocasión para decir alguna cosa desagradable, como, por ejemplo, que los que tienen dinero para viajar son los que no sirven para nada, y ni aprenden ni sacan jugo de lo que ven.

Mi tío es especialista en vulgaridades democráticas. Mi tío es republicano. Yo no sé si hay alguna cosa más estúpida que ser republicano; creo que no la hay, a no ser el ser socialista y demócrata.

Ni mi tía, ni mis primas son republicanas. Ésas son autoritarias y reaccionarias, como todas las mujeres; pero su autoritarismo no les hace ser tan despóticas como su democracia y su libertad a mi republicano tío.

Al anochecer, las dos muchachas dejan el trabajo y andan de aquí para allá. Todas son sorpresas.

– Mira, Blanca, qué pronto ha brotado esta flor.

– Ay, *dona*, ya han salido las enredaderas que planté.

El otro día le dije a Dolores:

– Pues si tuviera usted un gran jardín, ¿qué haría usted?

– ¡Psch! Tenemos un huerto; pero no crea usted que me gusta más que este terrado.

Un conocido, que creo que es el fotógrafo a quien encuentro en el Casino y que trata de inculcarme el sentimiento de superioridad suyo y mío, por ser madrileños ambos, supone que me gusta mi prima, y no creo que esté en lo cierto.

"Yes."

By talking and discussing all this, Dolores couldn't help but understand the truth, that I was going away because of them, because I saw that I was getting in the way. She protested vehemently.

"No, no," I said to her, "you must understand that it isn't right to stay in a house where you only cause trouble, where they think you are making fun of the hospitality you receive."

"Wait at least a week."

After this exchange of feelings, Dolores and I have come to a better understanding and Blanca and I have an endearing friendship.

I insisted that they change my room, and now I sleep in a dark bedroom at the back of the house. I have persisted in my efforts to win over the family. Mama is almost won over, but the father is just terrible; there seems to be no way to stop him from frowning.

During the afternoon, mama and the two girls sew in the parlor; this must have been a custom in the house. I go in and out of the room and we keep chattering with one another. The ice has been broken, at least insofar as the feminine element in the house is concerned. I talk to them of Paris, of Switzerland and of Germany, and I keep them very well entertained.

I would be very careful not to do this in front of the father, because he would take advantage of the opportunity to say something unpleasant, as for example, that those who have the money to travel are those who serve no good purpose and don't learn anything or get any substance from what they see.

My uncle is a specialist in democratic commonplace ideas. My uncle is a republican. I don't know if there's anything more stupid than being a republican; I don't think there is, unless it's being a socialist and a democrat.

Neither my aunt nor my cousins are republicans. They are authoritarians and reactionaries, as are all women, but their authoritarianism doesn't make them as despotic as my republican uncle's idea of democracy and liberty makes him.

At dusk, the two girls leave their work and rush around in one direction or another. Everything is full of surprises.

"Look, Blanca, how quickly this flower has budded."

"Oh, *doña*, the climbing bindweed plants I put in the ground have already come out."

The other day, I said to Dolores:

"Tell me, what would you do if you had a big garden?"

"Pshaw! We have a whole orchard; but don't think I like it any more than I do this roof terrace."

An acquaintance of mine, who I think is a photographer, and whom I meet in the *casino*, and is trying to inculcate in me a feeling of his superiority and mine, because we are both from Madrid, is of the opinion that I like my cousin, but I don't really think he's right.

Dolores y yo no nos entendemos; siempre estamos regañando. Yo le digo que estos pueblos valencianos no me gustan: blanco y azul, yeso y añil, no se ve más, todo limpio, todo inundado de sol, pero sin gracia, sin arte; pueblos que no tienen grandes casas solariegas, con iglesias claras, blanqueadas, sin rincones sombríos.

— A Fernando no le gusta nuestro pueblo — ha dicho ella a su madre en tono zumbón —. ¡Como él es artista y nosotros somos unos palurdos! ¡Como no hablamos con gracia el castellano y no decimos *poyo* ni *cabayo* como él!... Pues *veas* tú si eso es bonito.

Hemos seguido discutiendo que si valencianos, que si castellanos, y yo para incomodarla, le he dicho:

— Pues yo, la verdad, no me casaría con una valenciana.

— Ni yo con un madrileno — me ha contestado Dolores rápidamente.

LI

He comenzado a hacer el retrato de Dolores, y ha transcurrido el día de la marcha y me he quedado.

¡Me encuentro tan bien aquí!...

El retrato lo estoy haciendo en el terrado al ponerse el sol. Dolores se cansa en seguida de estar quieta. El primer día vino con la cara más empolvada que nunca.

Yo le dije que tan blanca me parecía un payaso, y después estuve hablando mal de las mujeres que se pintan o se llenan la cara de polvos de arroz. Ella quiso demostrar que una cosa es distinta de otra; yo afirmé rotundamente que era igual.

Desde el segundo día de sesión viene sin polvos de arroz, pero se preocupa mucho por lo negra que está.

El retrato no me sale por más que trabajo, y podría ser una cosa bonita. La figura esbelta de Doloires, vestida de negro, se destaca admirablemente sobre la tapia verde, picoteada de puntos blancos, llena de manchas obscuras de las goteras.

He recurrido a un expediente, dentro del arte, vergonzoso; le he pedido a mi amigo el fotógrafo la máquina y he hecho dos retratos: uno de Dolores y otro de su madre, y un grupo de toda la familia. Después los he iluminado con una mezcla de barniz y de pintura al óleo. Un verdadero crimen de leso arte. Han parecido mis retratos verdaderas maravillas.

Lo que he hecho con gusto ha sido un apunte que me ha resultado bastante bien: el suelo, de ladrillos rojos; las gradas, verdes; las manchas rojas de los geranios en

Dolores and I don't understand one another; we are always quarreling. I tell her I don't like these Valencian towns: white and blue, plaster and indigo, that's all you see, everything clean, everything inundated with sunlight, but without any charm, without any art; towns that have no big, ancestral houses, only bright, whitewashed churches, without any gloomy corners.

"Fernando doesn't like our town," she said to her mother in a teasing tone. "Since he is an artist and we are only country bumpkins! Since we don't speak Castilian with charm, and we don't say *poyo* for chicken and *cabayo* for horse as he does...! And isn't that just too pretty."

We continued discussing whether Valencians or Castilians were the better, and just to annoy her, I said:

"Well, to tell the truth, I wouldn't marry a Valencian girl."

"Nor I a Madrilenian man," Dolores quickly replied.

LI

I've begun to do a portrait of Dolores and the day set for my departure has gone by and I've remained here.

I find myself very much at ease here...!

I am doing the portrait on the roof terrace after the sun has gone down. Dolores gets tired of remaining still very quickly. The first day she came with her face more covered with powder than ever.

I told her that as white as she looked, she resembled a clown, and then I started speaking ill of women who put on a lot of makeup or cover their faces with rice powder. She tried to show me that the one case is different from the other; I categorically affirmed that it was the same.

Ever since the second day of her posing, she arrives without any rice powder, but she is quite perturbed by how very dark she is. The portrait isn't coming along well no matter how much I work, and it could easily turn out to be pretty. The slender, graceful figure of Dolores, dressed in black, stands out admirably against the green earthen wall, which is dotted with white marks, covered with dark stains left by the water dripping from the spouts.

I've resorted to an expedient that is shameful among artists; I've asked my photographer friend for his camera and I've taken two pictures: one of Dolores and the other of her mother with a group of her whole family. Afterwards, I illuminated them using a mixture of varnish and oil paint. A real crime of perverted art. My portraits turned out to be real marvels.

What I have succeeded in doing with pleasure is a sketch that turned out rather well: the ground, of red bricks; the steps, green; the red patches of the blooming geraniums on the earthen wall, and above this, the blue sky with golden striae, and

flor sobre la tapia, y encima de ésta el cielo azul con estrías doradas, y la espadaña medio caída y ruinosa. Hay en este apunte algo de tranquilidad, de descanso.

No me podía figurar el reposo, la dulzura de estos crepúsculos. Se oye el murmullo de la gente del pueblo que a esa hora empieza a vivir, las golondrinas chillan dando vueltas alrededor de la torre, y las campanas de la iglesia suenan encima de nosotros.

Después de la sesión, cuando Dolores deja de pasear y se dedica a la costura, discutimos acerca de muchas cosas, de arte inclusive.

No comprende que se puedan pintar figuras feas, de cosas tristes; no le gusta nada torturado, ni obscuro.

Ella, si supiera pintar, dice que pintaría mujeres hermosas y rubias; a Dolores la rubicundez le parece una superioridad inmensa; pintaría también escenas de caza con ciervos y caballos, bosques, jardines, lagos con su correspondiente barca; cosas claras y sonrientes.

No se la convence de que puede haber belleza, sentimiento, en otras cosas. Es una muchacha que tiene una fijeza de ideas que a mí me asombra, y, sobre todo, un sentimiento de justicia y de equidad extraño en una mujer, que yo ataco con paradojas.

El madrileñismo mío, más fingido que otra cosa, porque yo nunca tuve entusiasmo por Madrid, le indigna.

– Después de todo – le digo yo – , crea usted que es lógico que la gente del pueblo, la gente ordinaria, trabaje para nosotros los elegidos, porque así se forma una casta superior directora, que puede dedicarse al arte, a la literatura.

– Vamos, que vivan los zánganos y que trabajen las abejas.

– Usted no debe decir eso.

– ¿Por qué? ¿Cree usted que soy zángana? Pues soy abeja.

LII

El fotógrafo, que trata de convencerme de la superioridad de todo hombre que haya nacido entre las Vistillas y el Hipódromo, tiene razón. Dolores me va gustando cada vez más. A medida que pasan días, encuentro en mi prima mayores encantos.

Tiene unos ojos que antes no me había fijado en ellos; unos ojos, que parece que van a romper a hablar a cada momento, sombreados por las pestañas que se le acercan a las cejas, y le dan una expresión de pájaro nocturno. Luego, bajo la apariencia de muchacha traviesa, hay en ella una ingenuidad y una candidez asombrosa, sin asomo de fingimiento.

El otro día estaban de visita unas amigas de Dolores. Al ver una lámina de un periódico ilustrado, en donde venía el retrato de Liane de Pougy, se comenzó a

the bell gable, partly collapsed and in ruins. There is some element of tranquility and repose in this sketch.

I couldn't imagine the repose, the sweetness of these twilights. You can hear the murmur of the people in town just beginning to come to life at that hour; the swallows scream as they make circles all around the tower, and the church bells sound above us.

After the sitting, when Dolores stops walking around and settles down to her sewing, we discuss many things, including art.

She doesn't understand that you can paint ugly figures, about sad things; she doesn't like anything tortured or somber.

If she knew how to paint, she says, she would paint lovely, blond women; for Dolores, rubicundity seems to be a tremendous superiority; she would also paint hunting scenes with stags and horses, forests, gardens, lakes with an ever-present boat; bright and smiling things.

You can't convince her that there can be beauty and feeling in other things. She is a girl with fixed ideas that astound me, and above all, with a sense of justice and equity that is unusual in a woman, and which I attack with paradoxes.

My Madrilenianism, more a pretense than anything else, because I never really was very enthusiastic about Madrid, makes her indignant.

"After all," I say to her, "you must believe it's logical for the masses of people, the ordinary people, to work for us, the elite, because in that way you can form a superior, directive caste, which can dedicate itself to art and to literature."

"Come now, let the drones live and let the bees work."

"You shouldn't say that."

"Why not? Do you think that I'm a drone? Well, I'm a bee."

LII

The photographer, who is trying to convince me of the superiority of any man born between Las Vistillas and El Hipódromo, is right. I am beginning to like Dolores more and more. As the days keep passing by, I keep finding greater charms in my cousin.

She has a pair of eyes which I really hadn't noticed before; eyes that seem as if they might break into speech at any moment, shaded by eyelashes that lie close to her eyebrows and give her the expression of a nocturnal bird. Besides, beneath her outward appearance of a mischievous girl, there is an ingenuousness and a candor that are astonishing, without the slightest hint of pretense.

The other day, some friends of Dolores were visiting her. When they saw a page in an illustrated newspaper, showing a picture of Liane de Pougy,[97] they began to talk about these famous hetaerae. They asked me if I knew any of them, and I told

hablar de estas héteras célebres. Me preguntaron a mí si conocía algunas, y les dije que sí, que había visto bailar a la Otero, a la Cleo de Merode y algunas otras.

– ¡Valientes tunantas serán! – dijo una de las amigas de Dolores – . Si yo fuera hombre, no las había de mirar ni la cara.

– Pues yo creo que si fuera hombre me gustarían mucho – saltó Dolores.

Todas protestaron. Después que se fueron las visitas, Dolores me dijo que hace colección de estampas de cajas de fósforos, y de eso conoce los retratos de la Otero y de las otras bailarinas y actrices. En un armario tiene unas cajitas con fotografías, cartas de sus amigas del colegio de Orihuela, en donde se educó, y otra porción de quisicosas guardadas.

Mientras me enseñaba estos tesoros, que yo iba examinando atentamente, le dije como quien no da importancia a la cosa:

– Es raro que nosotros nos hablemos de usted siendo primos.

– ¡Bah! Es un parentesco el nuestro tan lejano...

Blanca me ha ayudado, y ha hecho que, en broma, Dolores y yo nos hablemos de tú.

LIII

La noticia fué para mí terrible. Me dijeron que Dolores tenía novio. En el Casino me aseguraron que recibía cartas de Pascual Nebot, el hijo de uno de los propietarios importantes del pueblo. La noche pasada fuí al Casino por conocerle.

Es un hombre alto, fornido, rubio, de cara juanetuda y barba larga, dorada. No sé si notó algo en mí; probablemente me conocería; me pareció que me miraba con una atención desdeñosa. Es tipo de hombre guapo, pero tiene esa ironía antipática y amarga de los levantinos, que ofende y no divierte, una ironía sin gracia, que niega siempre, sin bondad alguna.

Este Nebot tiene fama de republicano y de anticlerical, y goza de un gran prestigio entre la gente del pueblo. Es también federal o medio regionalista, y hace alarde de hablar siempre en valenciano. Se le tiene por un tenorio de mucha fortuna.

A pesar de su fachenda, me parece que no ha de conquistar a mi prima. Yo estoy decidido a abandonar mi indolencia y a tener una voluntad de hierro. Me voy a encontrar gracioso echándomelas de hombre fuerte.

Anteayer acompañé a Dolores a las Flores de María. Como la madre no puede ir, fué ella acompañada de la señora Mercedes, una vieja criada de la familia, más negra y más curtida que un salvaje.

them I did, that I had seen la Otero[98] and la Cleo de Mérode[99] and several others dance.

"A fine lot of hussies they must be!" one of Dolores' friends said. "If I were a man, I wouldn't even look them in the face."

"Well, I think that if I were a man, I'd like them very much," Dolores burst out.

They all protested. After her visitors left, Dolores told me that she is collecting prints from match boxes, and that in this way she knows the pictures of La Otero and the other dancers and actresses. She keeps several small boxes of photographs in a closet, along with letters from her friends from the school in Orihuela where she received her education, as well as a whole lot of oddities she had stored away.

While she was showing me these treasures, which I kept examining carefully, I said to her in the manner of one who doesn't consider it important:

"It's strange that we should speak to one another with the polite *usted*, even though we are cousins."

"Bah! Our family relationship is really quite distant."

Blanca has helped me and has succeeded in getting Dolores and me to use the familiar *tú* in speaking to one another, if only in jest.

LIII

It was a terrible piece of news for me. They told me that Dolores had a suitor. They assured me in the casino that she was receiving letters from Pascual Nebot, the son of one of the important property owners in town. Last night I went to the casino to find out what he was like.

He is a tall, robust, blond man with a face with prominent cheekbones and a long, golden beard. I don't know if he noticed anything special in me, but he probably knew who I was; it seemed that he kept looking at me with disdainful intensity. He is a handsome sort of man, but he has that disagreeable and bitter irony so common among Levantine people, which offends but doesn't amuse, an irony without charm, which always negates, with no trace of kindness whatsoever.[100]

This Nebot has a reputation as a republican and an anti-clerical, and he enjoys great prestige among the townspeople. He is also a federalist or somewhat of a regionalist and he always makes a great display of speaking in Valencian dialect. He is widely considered to be quite a successful Don Juan.

In spite of his conceit, it seems to me that he isn't going to win my cousin's heart. I've now decided to abandon my indolence and assume a will of iron. I'm going to find it refreshing to play the role of a man of strength.

The day before yesterday, I accompanied Dolores to las Flores de María.[101] Since her mother can't go, she was accompanied by Señora Mercedes, an old family maidservant, darker and more tanned than a savage.

Dolores estaba preciosa; indubablemente no pudo resistir la tentación de darse algunos polvos de arroz en la cara; me pareció muy blanca, verdad que su cabeza estaba rodeada de negro: el pelo, la mantilla, el vestido; luego, para que se destacara más la gracia de su talle y de su rostro, llevaba a la señora Mercedes al lado, que parecía el monstruo familiar; una dueña fiel y espantable que iba acompañando a su ama.

Se lo dije así a Dolores y se echó a reir; la fuí acompañando, verdaderamente orgulloso de ir con ella; echamos por el camino más largo, por entre callejuelas. Me pareció que causábamos sensación en el pueblo.

Al llegar a la puerta de la iglesia, un arco gótico, en cuyo fondo negro brillaban mil luces de cirios, nos detuvimos.

— ¿Vas a entrar? — me preguntó ella.
— Sí. Entraré: te esperaré a la salida.

En la iglesia el aire estaba tibio, saturado de un olor voluptuoso de incienso y de cera. El altar brillaba con las luces, lleno de flores blancas y flores rojas, entre los adornos brillantes de oro...

Hoy he acompañado a la madre y a las dos hijas a misa mayor. Con el traje negro y la mantilla, Dolores estaba guapísima. Pasamos, al ir a la iglesia, por un grupo en donde se encontraba Pascual Nebot entre sus amigos. Pascual me miró con rabia; Dolores no quiso apartar sus ojos de los míos.

Terminó la misa, y al volver de la iglesia a casa estaba lloviendo. En el terrado suenan las gruesas gotas de agua al chocar en las hojas de las hortensias y dejan en el suelo manchas grandes y redondas, que al evaporarse el agua en los ladrillos caldeados, desaparecen en seguida. Cantan los gallos hoy más que otros días. Sobre el fondo negro de la torrecilla del convento se ve correr en líneas tenues y brillantes el agua que cae. El cielo está gris, con una reverberación luminosa, tan grande, que no se le puede mirar sin que ofenda los ojos.

Dolores, después de mudarse de traje, ha entrado en el terradito y traído las plantas que están en la sala para que les dé el agua. Ha venido una visita y con ella está la madre de Dolores, charlando en el comedor.

— Oye, Dolores — le he dicho yo.
— ¿Qué?
— Te tengo que hablar.
— Habla todo lo que quieras.
— Oye.
— ¿Qué?
— Te estás mojando.
— No es nada.
— ¿Sabes que estás muy guapa hoy?
— ¿Sí?...

Dolores was simply lovely; she was undoubtedly unable to resist the temptation to put some rice powder on her face; it seemed very white to me, though of course her head was encircled in black: her hair, the mantilla and the dress; in addition, in order that the graceful quality of her figure and her face might stand out even better, she kept Señora Mercedes at her side, who looked like the family monster; she was a faithful and frightening duenna, walking along in the company of her mistress.

I told this to Dolores and she burst into laughter; I kept accompanying her, truly proud to be with her, and we took the longest route possible, along narrow side streets. It seemed to me that we were causing a sensation in town.

When we reached the door of the church, a Gothic arch, in which a thousand candle flames were shining in its black depths, we stopped.

"Are you going inside?" she asked me.

"Yes. I'll go in; I'll wait for you when you come out."

The air in the church was warm, saturated with a voluptuous aroma of incense and candle wax. The altar was shining with all its lights, covered with white flowers and red flowers, amid all of the brilliant golden ornaments...

Today I accompanied the mother and her two daughters to High Mass. Dolores looked extremely attractive in her black dress and mantilla. As we were on our way to the church, we passed a group in which Pascual Nebot happened to be there among his friends. Pascual looked at me angrily; Dolores refused to take her eyes from mine.

The Mass ended, and as we returned to the house from church, it was raining. On the roof terrace, the heavy drops of water resound as they strike the leaves of the hydrangea and they leave large, round stains on the ground, which disappear immediately as the water evaporates on the heated bricks. The roosters are crowing today more than on any other day. You can see the water as it falls, running in tenuous, shiny lines, against the dark background of the little tower of the convent. The sky is gray and has a luminous reverberation that is so great that you can't look at it without it offending your eyes.

After changing her dress, Dolores came out onto the roof terrace and brought the plants from the drawing room with her so that the water might fall on them. A visitor has arrived and Dolores' mother is with her, chatting in the dining room.

"Listen, Dolores," I said to her.

"What?"

"I have to talk to you."

"Speak to your heart's content."

"Listen."

"What?"

"You're getting wet."

"It's no problem."

"You know you're very attractive today?"

"Really...?"

Y me ha mirado con sus ojos negros tan brillantes, que me han dado ganas de estrujarla entre mis brazos.
– Oye.
– ¿Qué?
– ¿Es verdad que Pascual Nebot te pretende?
– ¿Y a ti qué te importa?
– ¡Que no me importa! Tú contéstame. ¿Es verdad o no?
– ¿Pero a ti qué te importa, hombre?
– No, tú no me contestas – le he dicho yo tontamente.
– Claro que no te contesto. ¿Por qué te voy a contestar?
– ¿Es que tú no sabes que yo también...?
– ¿Qué?
– Nada...que yo también te quiero.
– ¿Crees quo no lo sabía? – ha exclamado ella, mirándome a los ojos y poniéndose de súbito ruborizada.
– Entonces, dime – y me he acercado a ella – . Deja ese rosal en paz. ¿Por quién te decides, por él o por mí?
– Por ninguno.
– No es verdad. Te decides por mí. Dolores, mírame, que vea yo tus ojos. ¿No ves en los míos que yo te quiero? ¿Di? ¿Quieres que seamos novios?

Ella ha murmurado also con voz débil, muy baja. Yo he sentido que mis labios se encontraban con sus mejillas, que estaban ardiendo. Inmediatamente se ha desasido de mis brazos; pero yo he tomado sus manos entre las mías.
– ¿Qué viene mamá! – ha dicho.
– No, no viene.
– Bueno, pues suéltame.
– No quiero. Tengo hambre de ti.
– Mira. Estás rompiendo esta mata de claveles. ¡Oh, qué lástima!

He vuelto la cabeza para atrás, y mientras tanto ella se ha escapado riendo.

Como no quiero que Pascual Nebot se me adelante, he decidido hablar a la madre de Dolores.

La buena señora es joven, guapa y gruesa como una bola. Parece que está hecha de mantequilla. Cuando la he hablado de mi propósito de casarme con Dolores, ha quedado asombrada. Sin consultar a su marido, ella no se decide; por su parte, le parece bien, aunque teme que yo sea un hombre informal. Cree que soy un tenorio que abandono a las mujeres después de seducirlas; yo me he defendido de tal suposición cómicamente, demostrando que ni lo soy ni lo he sido, aunque en

And she looked at me with her ever black eyes shining so that they made me want to squeeze her in my arms.

"Listen."

"What?"

"Is it true that Pascual Nebot is courting you?"

"What difference does that make to you?"

"You think it should make no difference to me! Answer me. Is it true or isn't it?"

"Heavens, what difference does it really make to you?"

"No, I see you won't answer me," I said to her foolishly.

"Of course I won't answer you. Why should I answer you?"

"Don't you know that I too. . .?"

"What?"

"Nothing...,just that I love you too."

"Do you think I didn't know it?" she exclaimed, looking me in the eyes and suddenly turning quite red.

"Then, tell me," and I drew closer to her. "Leave that rose bush in peace. Whom do you favor, him or me?"

"Neither one of you."

"That's not true. You favor me. Dolores, look at me, let me see your eyes. Can't you see in mine that I love you? Won't you tell me? Do you want us to be sweethearts?"

She murmured something in a weak, very low voice. I felt my lips brushing her burning cheeks. She immediately pulled free of my arms, but I took her hands between mine.

"Mama is coming!" she said.

"No, she's not coming."

"All right, but let me go."

"I don't want to. I'm hungry for you."

"Look. You're ruining this carnation bush. Oh, what a pity!"

I turned my head to look back, and as I did, she succeeded in escaping with a laugh.

Since I don't want Pascual Nebot to have any advantage over me, I've decided to talk to Dolores' mother.

The good woman is young, attractive and as plump and round as a ball. She looks as if she were made of butter. When I spoke to her of my intention to marry Dolores, she was astonished. She can't make up her mind without consulting her husband; as far as she is concerned, it seems all right, although she is afraid that I may be an informal sort of fellow. She thinks I'm a Don Juan, who abandons women after seducing them; I defended myself rather comically against such an insinuation, pointing out that I'm not at all like that, nor have I ever been, although on other occasions, it wasn't out of any lack of desire to do so. Dolores came in just

otras ocasiones, no por falta de ganas. En este momento en que peroraba ha entrado Dolores; ha habido explicación entre los tres.

Ahora estoy pendiente del fallo de mi tío que dirá probablemente alguna gansada.

Según me ha dicho Dolores, al comunicarle mi petición ha refunfuñado de mal humor.

LIV

Pascual Nebot ha averiguado, no sé cómo, la vida que yo hice en Madrid, que tuve algunos líos, y, además, ha dicho, y esto probablemente es invención suya, que he estado para profesar en un convento; por el pueblo me llama el *frare.*

Me parece que Nebot y yo vamos a concluir mal; yo no le provocaré, pero el día que observe en él la señal más insignificante de burla, me echo sobe él como un lobo.

Alguna amiga ha tenido la piadosa idea de contarle a Dolores las invenciones de Nebot, y he encontrado a mi novia adusta y de mal humor. Yo me preguntaba: ¿qué le pasará?

Teníamos que ir a un huerto de la abuela de Dolores. Salimos a las tres o tres y media de casa. Por delante íbamos: Dolores, Blanca, una amiga de las dos hermanas y yo, acompañándolas; detrás, mi futura suegra, la madre de la amiguita y mi tío.

Dolores, esquivando mi conversación y alejándose intencionalmente de mi lado. Llegamos a la casa de la abuela por un camino que cruza por entre naranjales llenos de azahar, que todavía tienen naranjas rojizas. Dolores echa a correr, y las otras dos hacen lo mismo.

— Nada, me persigue la mala suerte — murmuro, y me pongo a contemplar la casa filosóficamente. Ésta es de piso bajo solo, pintada de azul, y se halla casi al borde de la carretera. En el centro tiene una puerta que conduce al zaguán, y a los lados, ventanas enrejadas.

El zaguán, que ocupa todo lo ancho de la casa, termina por la parte de atrás en una hermosa galería, cubierta por un parral por arriba y limitada a lo largo por una valla, en la que se tejen y entretejen las enredaderas, las hiedras y las pasionarias, formando un muro verde de flores y de campanulas.

De la galería se baja por una escalera al huerto, y el camino que de aquí parte concluye en un cenador, un tinglado de maderas y de palitroques, sobre los cuales se sostienen gruesos trozos de un rosal silvestre lleno de hojas, que derrama un turbión de sencillísimas flores blancas y amarillentas.

A la entrada del cenador, sobre pedestales de ladrillo, hay dos estatuas, de Flora

at this moment of my peroration. There has now been an understanding between the three of us.

I am now hanging on the opinion of my uncle, and he will probably come up with something simple-minded.

According to what Dolores told me, when my request was communicated to him, he just grumbled in an ill-humored manner.

LIV

Pascual Nebot has ascertained, I don't know how, the kind of life I led in Madrid, that I was involved in a number of liaisons there, and in addition, and this is probably something he invented, he said that I was about to profess and enter a monastery; all over town he calls me *el frare* (*the monk*).

It seems to me that Nebot and I are going to end up having it out; I'm not going to provoke him, but the first time I observe the slightest hint of ridicule toward me on his part, I'll throw myself on him like a wolf.

One of her girlfriends had the very pious idea of telling Dolores all about Nebot's fabrications, and I found my intended sullen and ill humored. I asked myself, "What can be the matter with her?"

We had to go to an orchard that belonged to Dolores' grandmother. We left the house at three or three-thirty. Dolores, Blanca and the two sisters' friend were in front, and I, accompanying them; behind us came my future mother-in-law, the little friend's mother and my uncle.

Dolores kept avoiding any conversation with me and intentionally moved away from my side. We reach the grandmother's house after walking along a road that crosses through orange groves, with trees full of orange blossoms and reddish oranges still hanging from them. Dolores starts to run and the other two girls do the same.

"What's the use, my bad luck pursues me," I murmur as I begin to contemplate the house philosophically. It consists of only a lower floor, it is painted blue and is situated almost along the road. It has a door in the middle that leads into the outer vestibule, and has windows covered with grillwork at the sides.

The vestibule, which occupies the entire breadth of the house, ends up in the back part in a lovely gallery, which is covered by a bower of grapevines up above and bounded lengthwise by a fence through which the bindweed, the ivy and passionflowers weave and interweave, forming a green wall full of flowers and campanulas.

From the gallery, you go down along a staircase to the orchard, and the road that starts from here ends up in an arbor; a shed made of boards and small, rough sticks, over which thick cuttings from a wild rosebush are supported, covered with leaves, that pours out a shower of very simple white and yellowish flowers.

At the entrance to the bower, there are two statues resting on brick pedestals,

y Pomona; en el centro, debajo de la cortina verde del rosal silvestre, una mesa rústica y bancos de madera. Nos sentamos. Todos hablaban, menos Dolores, que parecía ensimismada estudiando las figuras de los azulejos de la pared.

– ¿Qué representan? – le pregunté yo, para decir algo.

– Es Santo Tomás de Villanueva – contestó Blanca – ; está vestido de obispo con un báculo en la mano, y un negro y una negra rezan a su lado.

– El pintor comprendió la grandeza del santo – le dije a Dolores – . El negro y la negra no le llegan ni a la rodilla.

Dolores mi miró severamente; habló con su hermana y con la amiga, y las tres, cruzando el jardín, subieron a la galería y desaparecieron. Dí un pretexto para salir del cenador, entré en la casa, anduve buscando a Dolores y no la encontré. Volvía a reunirme con mi tío, cuando oí risas arriba; levanté la cabeza: Blanca y la amiga estban en la azotea.

Subí por una escalerilla de caracol. Dolores, con la actitud que toma cuando se enfada, se apoyaba en un jarrón tosco de barro que tiene el barandado de la azotea, mirando atentamente, con los ojos más tenebrosos que nunca, las avispas que revolteaban cerca de sus avisperos.

A los lados del huerto, se veían marjales divididos en cuadros por anchas y profundas acequias, en cuyo fondo verdeaba el agua.

Por la carretera, cubierta de polvo, iban pasando, camino del puerto, carros cargados de naranja; alguna canción triste y monótona llegaba hasta nosotros.

Me senté al lado de Dolores.

En un momento que vi muy ocupadas a Blanca y a la amiga en llamar a uno que pasaba por la carretera y en esconderse después, pregunté a Dolores la causa de la frialdad y del desdén que me demostraba.

Hizo un gesto de impaciencia al oírme, y volvió la cabeza; al principio no quiso decir nada; después me reprochó mi falsedad acremente.

– Eres un falso, eres un mentiroso.

– Pero, ¿por qué?

– Tienes una querida en Madrid; lo sé.

– No es verdad.

– Si te han visto con ella.

– Pero ¿cómo me van a ver, si hace más de medio año que estoy fuera de Madrid?

– No, no me engañas; todas las mentiras que inventes serán inútiles.

Le juré que no era verdad, y apretado, sin saber qué explicación dar, le dije que había sido un perdido, un vicioso, pero ya no lo era. Desde que la había conocido estaba cambiado.

one of Flora and the other of Pomona;[102] in the middle, beneath the green curtain of the wild rosebush, a rustic table and wooden benches. We sat down. All of us were speaking, except Dolores, who seemed absorbed in thought, studying the figures on the colored tiles on the wall.

"What do they represent?" I asked her, just to say something.

"It's Santo Tomás de Villanueva,[103] answered Blanca. "He's all dressed up as a bishop with a crosier in his hand, and a black man and woman are praying beside him."

"The painter understood the greatness of the saint," I said to Dolores. "The black man and woman don't even come up to his knee."

Dolores looked at me sternly; she spoke to her sister and her friend and the three of them crossed the garden, went up to the gallery and disappeared. I made some excuse to leave the bower, went back into the house, walked around looking for Dolores, but was unable to find her. Just as I was coming back to join my uncle, I heard laughter above me. I raised my head; Blanca and her friend were on the flat roof.

I made my way up by a winding stairway. Dolores, in the pose she takes when she is angry, was leaning on a rough, earthenware urn that rests on the balustrade of the flat roof terrace, and she was looking attentively, her eyes more tenebrous than ever, at the wasps hovering around their nests.

Along the sides of the orchard, you could see the marshes, divided into squares by wide, deep irrigation ditches, at the bottom of which the water looked very green.

Carts loaded with oranges kept passing along the dust-covered road on their way to the port; a sad, monotonous song rose up to where we were.

I sat down beside Dolores.

I chose a moment when I saw Blanca and her friend busy calling to someone passing by along the road and then hiding themselves, and I asked Dolores for the explanation for her coldness and the disdain she was showing for me.

She showed a sign of impatience when she heard me, and she turned her head away; at first she refused to say anything; then she reproached me bitterly for my falseness:

"You're deceitful, you're a liar."

"But why?"

"You have a mistress in Madrid; I know all about it."

"That's not true."

"But you've been seen with her."

"But how could they have seen me if I've been away from Madrid for over half a year?"

"No; don't try to deceive me; all the lies you may invent will be useless."

I swore to her that it wasn't true, and since I felt hard-pressed and didn't know what explanation to give, I told her that I had been a rake, given to vice, but that I was no longer like that. Since I had known her, I was a changed man.

— ¿Y por qué no me has dicho eso? – preguntó Dolores.
— Pero ¿para qué te lo iba a decir?
— Porque es verdad.

Discutimos este punto largo rato; yo dí toda clase de explicaciones, inventé también algo para disculparme. Dolores es tan ingenua que no comprende la menor hipocresía.

Ya perdonado, le pareció muy raro que yo quisiera retirarme a un monte como un ermitaño, y cuando le explicaba mis dudas, mis vacilaciones, mis proyectos místicos, se reía a carcajadas.

A mí mismo la cosa no me parecía seria; pero cuando le hablé de mis noches tan tristes, de mi alma torturada por angustias y terrores extraños, de mi vida con el corazón vacío y el cerebro lleno de locuras...

— ¡*Pobret*! – me dijo, con una mezcla de ironía y de maternidad; y yo no sé por qué entonces me sentí niño y tuve que bajar la cabeza para que no me viese llorar. Entonces ella, agarrándome de la barba, hizo que levantara la cara, sentí el gusto salado de las lágrimas en la boca, y, mirándome a los ojos, murmuró:

— Pero qué tonto eres.

Yo besé su mano varias veces con verdadera humildad, hasta que ví que Blanca y la amiga nos miraban en el colmo del asombro.

Dolores estaba azorada y comenzó a hablar y a hablar, tratando de disimular su turbación. Yo la escuchaba como en un sueño.

Anochecía; un anochecer de primavera espléndido. Se veían por todas partes huertos verdes de naranjos, y en medio se destacaban las casa blancas y las barracas, también blancas, de techo negruzco.

Cerca, un bosquecillo frondoso de altos álamos se perfilaba delicadamente en el cielo azul obscuro, recortándose en curvas redondeadas. La llanura se extendía hacia un lado, muda, inmensa, hasta perderse de vista, con algunos pueblecillos lejanos con sus erguidas torres envueltas en la niebla; hacia otra parte limitaba el llano una sierra azulada, cadena de montañas altas, negruzcas, con pedruscos de formas fantásticas en las cumbres.

Enfrente se extendía el Mediterráneo, cuya masa azul cortaba el cielo pálido en una línea recta. Bordeando la costa se veía la mancha alargada, obscura y estrecha de un pinar, que parecía algún inmenso reptil dormido sobre el agua.

A espaldas veíase la ciudad. Bajo las nubes fundidas se ocultaba el sol envuelto en rojas incandescencias, como un gran brasero que incendiara el cielo heroico en una hoguera radiante, en la gloria de una apoteosis de luz y de colores. Absortos, contemplábamos el campo, la tarde que pasaba, los rojos resplandores del horizonte. Brillaba el agua con sangriento tono en las acequias de los marjales; el terral venía blando, suave, cargado de olor de azahar; por el camino, entre nubes de polvo, seguían pasando los carros cargados de naranja...

"Then why didn't you tell me that?" Dolores asked.
"Why should I have told you about it?"
"Because it's true."
We discussed this point for a long time; I gave her all kinds of explanations and I even invented something to excuse myself. Dolores is so ingenuous that she doesn't understand the slightest hypocrisy.

Once I was forgiven, it seemed very strange to her that I should want to withdraw to a mountain like a hermit, but when I explained my doubts, my hesitancy, my mystical projects, she burst into laughter.

Even to me, the question didn't seem very serious; but when I spoke to her of my very sad nights, my soul tortured by anguish and strange terrors, of a life with my heart empty and my brain filled with wild fancies...

"*Pobret!*" she said to me, in a mixture that was both ironic and maternal; I don't know why I felt like a child then, and I had to lower my head so she wouldn't see me cry. Then, seizing me by the beard, she made me raise my face, and I felt the salty taste of tears upon my mouth, and she looked in my eyes and murmured:

"But you're so silly."

I kissed her hand several times with true humility, until I saw that Blanca and her friend were looking at us with utmost astonishment.

Dolores was embarrassed and began to talk on and on, trying to conceal her distress. I kept listening to her as if in a dream.

Night was falling; a splendid spring twilight. On all sides, you could see green orange groves, and in their midst, you could make out the white houses and the thatched cabins, also white, with their blackish roofs.

Nearby, a small, leafy wood with tall poplar trees was delicately profiled against the dark, blue sky, tracing its outline in rounded curves. The flat terrain stretched out on one side, silent and immense, till it was lost from sight, with a number of small villages in the distance, with erect towers, wrapped in the mist; in another direction, a bluish mountain range, a chain of high mountains, blackish in color, with crags of fantastic shapes at the summits, bounded the plain.

The Mediterranean stretched out before us, the blue mass of which cut into the pale sky in a straight line. You could see the elongated, dark, narrow patch of a pine forest skirting the shore, and it had the appearance of some immense reptile asleep on top of the water.

In back of us you could see the city. The sun was hidden under the fused clouds, wrapped in red incandescence, like a great brazier, setting the heroic sky afire in a shining blaze, in the glory of an apotheosis of light and colors. We were all absorbed, contemplating the countryside, the early evening that was coming to an end, the red splendors of the horizon. The water was shining with a blood-red tone in the irrigation channels in the marshes; the land breeze was coming in, gentle and mild, filled with the aroma of orange blossoms; the carts, loaded with oranges, kept passing along the road amid clouds of dust...

Fué obscureciendo; sonaron a lo lejos las campanas del *Angelus*; últimos suspiros de la tarde. Hacia poniente quedó en el cielo una gran irradiación luminosa de un color verde, purísimo, de nácar...

El cielo se llenaba lentamente de estrellas; envolvía la tierra en su cúpula azul, obscura, como en manto regio cuajado de diamantes, y a medida que obscurecía, el mar iba tiñéndose de negro,

Sobre las hierbas, sobre las hojas de los árboles, se depositaba el húmedo rocío de la noche; temblaba el agua con brillo plateado en las charcas y en las acequias; el viento, oreado por el aroma del azahar, hacía estremecer con sus ráfagas frescas el follaje de los álamos y producía al agitar las masas tupidas y verdes de los bancales, visos extraños y luminosos.

La frescura penetrante de los huertos subía a la azotea, mil murmullos vagos, indefinidos, suspiros de los árboles, resonar lejano de las olas, susurro de las ráfagas de viento en las florestas, repercutían en el campo ya obscuro, y en el recogimiento de la noche armoniosa, alumbrada por la luz eterna de las estrellas, bajo la augusta y solemne serenidad del cielo y el reposo profundo de los huertos, comenzó a cantar un ruiseñor tímidamente.

Obscureció aún más; en el cielo brotaron nuevas estrellas, en la tierra brillaron gusanos de luz en las enramadas y la noche se pobló de misterios.

LV

Pascual Nebot no ceja en su empeño; le ha escrito a Dolores; en la carta debe hablar de mí desdeñosamente; el el Casino oí que decían unos amigos de Nebot, al pasar junto a ellos:

— Y si no fuera pariente de la chica, me parece que se ganaba unos palos.

Además de esto, mi tío favorece a Pascual; es correligionario, de influencia en la ciudad...; pero yo no estoy dispuesto a dejarme arrebatar la dicha. He hablado a Dolores y estoy tranquilo. Cuando la he expresado mi temor de que pudieran torcer su voluntad, ha dicho sonriendo:

— No tengas cuidado.

He sabido que efectivamente en la carta que Pascual escribió a Dolores hablaba de mí en tono de lástima.

He buscado a Nebot esta tarde en el Casino. Estaba en el billar jugando a carambolas.

Le he advertido que no quiero armar un escándalo; pero que no estoy dispuesto a permitir que nadie se entremeta en mis asuntos. Me ha mirado de arriba abajo, y al decirle que le enviaría dos amigos, ha vuelto la espalda para jugar una carambola tranquilamente. Los de su cuerda han reído la gracia.

It was growing dark; in the distance, the bells of the Angelus were tolling; the final sighs of the late afternoon. Toward the west, a great luminous radiation, of a color that was green, very pure, like mother-of-pearl, remained in the sky.

The sky was slowly filling up with stars; it was covering the earth in its dark blue cupola, as if in a royal cloak thick with diamonds, and as it kept getting darker, the sea kept taking on a black tint.

The moist night dew was settling on the grasses and on the leaves of the trees; the water was trembling with a silvery splendor in the pools and the irrigation channels; the wind, refreshed by the aroma of orange blossoms, was making the foliage of the poplars tremble with its cooling gusts, and as it kept agitating the dense, green masses of the terraced fields, it produced a strange and luminous shimmering.

The penetrating freshness of the orchards rose up to the flat roof terrace; a thousand vague, indefinite murmurs, the sighing of the trees, the far off resounding of the waves, the whisper of the gusts of wind in the thickets, reverberated in the now darkened countryside; in the quietude of the harmonious night, illuminated by the eternal light of the stars, under the august and solemn serenity of the sky and the profound repose of the orchards, a nightingale began to sing timorously.

It grew even darker; new stars burst forth in the sky; on the ground, glowworms were shining in the bowers and the night was filled with mysteries.

LV

Pascual Nebot is not slackening his efforts; he has written to Dolores; in his letter, he must speak of me disdainfully; in the Casino I heard some of Nebot's friends say as I passed near them:

"If he weren't a relative of the girl, it seems to me he would have gotten a good thrashing."

In addition to this, my uncle favors Pascual; he is a coreligionist and is influential in the city..., but I'm not inclined to let my good fortune be snatched away from me. I've spoken to Dolores and I am calm. When I expressed my fear to her that her will might be perverted, she said with a smile:

"Just don't you worry about it."

Actually, I've found out that in the letter Pascual wrote to Dolores, he did speak with a feeling of pity for me.

I sought out Nebot this afternoon in the *Casino*. He was in the billiard room playing carom billiards.

I warned him that I didn't want to make a fuss, but that I'm not inclined to let anyone meddle in my affairs. He looked me up and down, and when I told him I would send two friends of mine to call on him, he turned his back and calmly made a carom shot. All of his cronies laughed at this clever response.

– ¿Usted quiere, sin duda, que nos peguemos como dos gañanes?

El ha contestado en valenciano no sé qué; pero algo que debía ser muy despreciativo; yo, en el colmo de la exasperación, me he arrojado sobre él y le he hecho tambalear; él se ha defendido con el taco, dándome un golpe en la cara. Entonces, enfurecido, loco, he cogido yo otro taco por la punta, lo he levantado en el aire y ¡paf! le he dado en mitad de la cabeza.

El hombre ha vacilado, ha cerrado los ojos y ha caído redondo al suelo. Un trozo de taco me ha quedado en la mano. La cosa ha sido rápida como de sueño.

Unos militares han impedido que me golpearan los amigos de Pascual; me he alojado en la posada, y he escrito a mi tío lo que ha pasado.

Estoy impaciente por las noticias que me traen.

Unos dicen que la herida de Pascual es muy grave, que ha tardado no sé cuánto tiempo en recobrar el sentido; otros aseguran que el médico ha dicho que curará en ocho o nueve días.

Veremos.

LVI

Mi rival está ya curado del garrotazo que le pegué. Por nuestra riña se ha dividido la gente joven del pueblo en dos bandos: nebotistas y ossoristas; los forasteros y los militares están conmigo y me defienden a capa y a espada.

Como estoy dispuesto a tener energía, he ido a casa de mi tío a pedirle la mano de Dolores. Inmediatamente, al verme, ha empezado a recriminarme por mi disputa con Pascual; yo le he enviado a paseo de mala manera. Me ha dicho que Nebot está enfurecido y que me desafiará en cuanto se encuentre bueno.

– Que lo haga; le meteré media vara de hierro en el cuerpo– le he dicho.

Mi tío se ha escandalizado; ha creído que soy un espadachín y ha hablado de los holgazanes que aprenden la esgrima para insultar y escarnecer impunemente a las personas honradas. Yo le he dicho que era tan honrado como Pascual Nebot y como él, y menos orgulloso y menos déspota que él, que llamándose republicano y liberal y otra porción de motes bonitos, tiranizaba a su familia y trataba de violentar la voluntad de Dolores.

– Muy republicanos y muy liberales en la calle todos ustedes – concluí diciendo –; pero en casa tan déspotas como los demás, tan intransigentes como los demás, con la misma sangre de fraile que los demás.

Y ¡habrá estupidez humana! El hombre a quien quizá no hubiera conmovido con

"You undoubtedly want us to fight it out like two roughnecks?"

He replied in Valencian dialect with something, but I don't know what, but it was something that was probably very disparaging; at the very height of my exasperation, I threw myself on him and made him stagger back; he defended himself with his billiard cue, striking me a blow in the face. Then, infuriated, insane with rage, I picked up another cue by the tip, lifted it in the air, and wham! I hit him in the middle of his head.

The man wavered, closed his eyes and fell right down to the ground. A piece of the cue still remained in my hand. The whole thing was very quick, as if in a dream.

Some soldiers prevented Pascual's friends from giving me a beating; I took lodging at the inn and wrote my uncle about all that had happened.

I am impatient to hear the news they will bring me.

Some say that Pascual's wound is very serious and that he took I don't know how long to recover his senses; others assure me that the doctor said he will be cured in eight or nine days.

We shall see.

LVI

My rival has now recovered from the blow that I dealt him with the stick. On account of our fight, the young people in town have split into two factions: the Nebotistas and the Ossoristas; those not native to the town and the army people are on my side and defend me through thick and thin.

Now that I'm inclined to be more energetic, I've gone to my uncle's house to ask him for Dolores' hand. Immediately, as soon as he saw me, he began to recriminate me over my fight with Pascual; I really told him off, none too politely. He told me that Nebot is simply furious and will challenge me as soon as he feels better.

"Just let him try it; I'll run a foot of steel through his body," I said.

My uncle was scandalized; he must have thought I'm a skilled swordsman, and he kept speaking of those ne'er-do-wells who learn the art of fencing in order to insult and mock honorable people with impunity.

I told him that I was as honorable as Pascual Nebot and as he himself was, and far less haughty and less despotic than he, who calls himself a republican and a liberal and a whole lot of other pretty names, and keeps tyrannizing his family and trying to thwart Dolores's will.

"All of you are very much republicans and very liberal in the street," I ended up saying, "but in your houses you are as despotic as the others, as intransigent as all the rest, with the same friars' blood as the rest."

And can you imagine greater human stupidity! This man, whom I couldn't have

un río de lágrimas, se ha picado al oirme; ha llamado a su mujer y a su hija y les ha expuesto mis pretensiones. Delante de mí le ha dicho a Dolores los riesgos que corría casándose conmigo.

– Fernando – con retintín nervioso – no es de nuestra clase; es un aristócrata; está acostumbrado a una vida de lujos, de vicios, de comodidades. Para él, convéncete, eres una muchacha tosca, sin maneras elegantes, sin mundo... ¡Piensa lo que haces, Dolores!

– No, papá; ya lo he pensado – ha dicho ella...

....

LVII

Se casaron y fueron a pasar un mes al Collado; una casa de labor de la familia.

Fernando sentía amplio y fuerte, como la corriente de un río caudaloso y sereno, el deseo de amor, de su espíritu y de su cuerpo.

Algunas veces, la misma placidez y tranquilidad de su alma le inducía a analizarse, y al ocurrírsele que el origen de aquella corriente de su vida y amor se perdía en la inconsciencia, pensaba que él era como un surtidor de la Naturaleza que se reflejaba en sí mismo y Dolores el gran río adonde afluía él. Sí; ella era el gran río de la Naturaleza, poderosa, fuerte; Fernando comprendía entonces, como no había comprendido nunca, la grandeza inmensa de la mujer, y al besar a Dolores, creía que era el mismo Dios el que se lo mandaba; el Dios incierto y doloroso, que hace nacer las semillas y remueve eternamente la materia con estremecimientos de vida.

Llegaba a sentir respeto por Dolores como ante un misterio sagrado; en su alma y en su cuerpo, en su seno y en sus brazos redondos, creía Fernando que había más ciencia de la vida que en todos los libros, y en el corazón cándido y sano de su mujer sentía latir los sentimientos grandes y vagos: Dios, la fe, el sacrificio, todo.

Y llevaban los dos una vida sencillísima. Por las mañanas iban a pasear al monte; ella, ligera, trepaba como un chico por entre los peñascales; él la seguía, y al abrazarla, notaba en sus ropas y en su cuerpo el olor de las hierbas del campo. No era una felicidad la suya sofocante; no era una pasión llena de inquietudes y de zozobras. Se entendían, quizá, porque no trataron nunca de entenderse.

Fernando sentía un desbordamiento de ternura por todo; por el sol bondadoso que acariciaba con su dulce calor el campo, por los ároles, por la tierra, siempre generosa y siempre fecunda.

A veces iban a algún pueblo cercano a pie y volvían de noche por la carretera

moved with a river of tears, was stung when he heard my words; he called in his wife and his daughter and explained my pretensions to them. In front of me, he told Dolores about the risks she would run if she were to marry me.

"Fernando," with a nervous, sarcastic tone to his voice, "is not one of our class; he is an aristocrat; he is accustomed to a life of luxury, vices and comforts. For him, you can be sure of this, you are a rustic young girl, without elegant manners, without worldly experience... Think of what you are doing, Dolores!"

"No, papa; I've already thought it over," she said...

....

LVII

They were married and went off to spend a month in El Collado, a farm property that belonged to the family.

Fernando felt that love's desire, in both his body and spirit, was full and strong, like the current of a mighty, serene river.

Sometimes, this very placidity and tranquility of soul would induce him to analyze himself, and when he realized that the origin of the current of his life and love was being lost in the unconscious, he thought that he was like a fountain of Nature that was reflected in itself, and that Dolores was the great river into which he flowed. Yes; she was the mighty river of Nature, powerful and strong; Fernando understood then, as he had never understood before, the infinite greatness of a woman, and when he kissed Dolores, he thought that it was God himself who was ordering him to do it; an uncertain, suffering God who makes the seeds sprout and eternally stirs all matter with the shuddering of life.

He was coming to feel respect for Dolores, as if in the face of a sacred mystery; Fernando thought that there was a greater awareness of life in her soul and in her body, in her breast and in her rounded arms, than in all his books, and he felt great and vague feelings beat in the candid, wholesome heart of his wife: God, faith, sacrifice, everything.

And the two of them led a very simple existence. In the morning, they would take a walk to the mountain; she, very nimble, would scamper up the rocky terrain like a young boy; he would follow her, and when he embraced her, he would note the fragrance of the grasses of the countryside in her clothes and in her body. Theirs was not a happiness that stifles; it wasn't a passion filled with uneasiness and anxiety. They understood one another, perhaps because they never made an effort to understand one another.

Fernando felt an overflowing of tenderness for everything, for the bountiful sun that caressed the countryside with its gentle warmth, for the trees, for the earth, always generous and always fertile.

Sometimes they would go on foot to some nearby town and they would return at

iluminada por la luz de las estrellas. Dolores se cogía al brazo de Fernando y cerraba los ojos.

– Tú me llevas – solía decir.
– Pero me guías tú – replicaba él.
– ¿Cómo te voy a guiar yo si tengo los ojos cerrados?
– Ahí verás...

Algunas noches se reunían los mozos y mozas del Collado y había reunión y baile. Se efectuaban estas fiestas en el zaguán blanqueado, que tenía dos bancos a ambos lados de la puerta en los que se sentaban chicos y chicas. En la pared, en un clavo, colgaban el candil, que apenas iluminaba la estancia.

Templaba un mozo la guitarra, el otro la bandurria, y, tras algunos escarceos insubstanciales, en los que no se oía más que el ruido de la púa en las cuerdas de la bandurria, comenzaban una polca. Después de la polca se arrancaban con una jota, que repetían veinte o treinta veces.

Aquel baile brutal, salvaje, que antes disgustaba profundamente a Ossorio, le producía entonces una sensación de vida, de energía, de pujanza. Cuando, a fuerza de pisadas y saltos, se levantaba una nube de polvo, le gustaba ver la silueta gallarda de los bailarines: los brazos en el aire, castañeteando los dedos, los cuerpos inclinados, los ojos mirando al suelo; las caderas de las mujeres, moviéndose y marcándose a través de la tela, incitadoras y robustas. De pronto, la canción salía rompiendo el aire como una bala; la bandurria y la guitarra hacían un compás de espera para que se oyese la voz en todo su poder; los bailarines, trazando un círculo, cambiaban de pareja, y, al iniciarse el rasgueado en la guitarra, comenzaban con más furia el castañeteo de dedos, los saltos, las carreras, los regates, las vueltas y los desplantes, y mozos y mozas, agitándose rabiosamente, frenéticamente, con las mejillas encendidas y los ojos brillantes, en el aire turbio apenas iluminado por el candil de aceite, hacían temblar el pavimento con las pisadas, mientras la voz chillona, sin dejarse vencer por el ruido y la algarabía, se levantaba con más pujanza en el aire.

Era aquel baile una brutalidad que sacaba a flote en el alma los sanos instintos naturales y bárbaros, una emanación de energía que bastaba para olvidar toda clase de locuras místicas y desfallecientes.

LVIII

Dejaron el Collado. Fernando trató de enseñar a su mujer Madrid y París; Dolores no quiso. Habían de hacer como todos los recién casados del pueblo: ir a Barcelona.

night along a road illuminated by the light of the stars. Dolores would take hold of Fernando's arm and close her eyes.

"You are leading me," she would say.

"But it is you who are guiding me," he would reply.

"How am I to guide you if I have my eyes closed?"

"You'll see..."

On several nights, the young men and girls of El Collado would come together and there would be festivity and dancing. These fiestas would generally take place in the whitewashed outer vestibule where there were two benches on either side of the door, on which the young men and women would be seated. There was an oil lamp hanging from a nail on the wall and it barely illuminated the area.

A young fellow was strumming on his guitar, another his bandore, and after a few insubstantial broken runs, during which you could only hear the sound of the plectrum on the strings of the bandore, they broke into a polka. After the polka, they burst into a jota, which they repeated twenty or thirty times.

That brutal, savage dance, which had profoundly displeased Ossorio before, now produced a feeling of life, of energy and vigor for him. When a cloud of dust would rise up, on account of the heavy steps and leaps, he was pleased to see the graceful silhouettes of the dancers: their arms in the air, their fingers clicking, their bodies bent forward, their eyes looking at the ground; the women's hips moving, inciting and robust, outlined though the cloth. Suddenly the song leaped out, shattering the air like a bullet; the bandore and the guitar marked a rest in the music, so that the voice could be heard in all its power; the dancers, moving round in a circle, changed partners, and as the strumming of the guitar commenced again, the clicking of the fingers started up with even more frenzy, as well as the leaps, the *carreras* (two quick steps forward tilting to one side), the *regates* (dodging), the turns and the *desplantes* (oblique stances), and all the young men and women, shaking wildly and frenziedly, their cheeks burning and their eyes shining in the turbid air, barely illuminated by the oil lamp, made the paved ground tremble with their heavy steps, while the shrill voice, not allowing itself to be overcome by the noise and uproar, rose up into the air with even more vigor.

That dance was a brutal sight, which brought to the surface all the wholesome, natural and barbaric instincts, an outpouring of energy that was enough to make one forget all manner of mystical and unsound madness.

LVIII

They left El Collado. Fernando offered to show his wife Madrid and Paris; Dolores refused to go. They were supposed to do what all recently married couples from her town did: go to Barcelona.

En el fondo temía las veleidades de Fernando.
– Bueno, iremos a Barcelona – dijo Ossorio.
Fueron en un tren correo, completamente solos en el vagón. Salieron a despedirles todos los de la familia.
Comenzó a andar el tren; hacía una noche templada. El cielo estaba cubierto de negros nubarrones; llovía.
Al pasar por una estación dijo Dolores:
– Mira, ahí en un convento de ese pueblo decía Pascual Nebot que tú querías meter fraile.
– Antes, no me hubiera costado mucho trabajo.
– ¿Por qué?
– Porque no te conocía a ti.
Hubo un momento de silencio.
– Mira, mira el mar – dijo Dolores con entusiasmo, asomándose a la ventanilla.
Algunas veces el tren se acercaba tanto a la playa, que se veían a pocos pasos las olas, que avanzaban en masas negras y plomizas, se hinchaban con una línea brillante de espuma, se incorporaban como para mirar algo y desaparecían después en el abismo sin color y sin forma. Era una impresión de vértigo lo que producía el mar, visto a los pies, como una inmensidad negra, confundida con el cielo gris por el intermedio de una ancha faja de bruma y de sombra.

A veces, en aquel manto obscuro brotaba y cabrilleaba un punto blanco y pálido de espuma, como si algún argentado tritón saliese del fondo del mar a contemplar la noche. De la tierra húmeda venía un aire acre con el gusto de marisco.

Salió la luna del seno de una nube, y rieló en las aguas. Como en un plano topográfico se dibujó la línea de la costa, con sus promontorios y sus entradas de mar y sus lenguas de tierra largas y estrechas que parecían negros peces monstruosos dormidos sobre las olas.

A veces la luna vertía por debajo de una nube una luz que dejaba al mar plateado, y entonces se veían sus olas redondas, sombreadas de negro, agitadas en continuo movimiento, en eterna violencia de ir y venir, en un perpetuo cambio de forma. Otras veces, al salir y mostrarse claramente la luna, brillaba en el mar una gran masa blanca, como un disco de metal derretido, movible, que se alargara en líneas de espuma, en cintas de plata, grecas y meandros luminosos que nacían junto a la orilla y ribeteaban la insondable masa de agua salobre.

De pronto penetró el tren en un túnel. A la salida se vió la noche negra; se habia ocultado la luna. El tren pareció apresurar su marcha.
– Mira, mira – dijo Dolores mostrando un faro, y sobre él, una como polvareda luminosa. El faro dió la vuelta; iluminó el tren de lleno con una luz blanca, que se fué enrojeciendo y se hizo roja al último.

Producía verdadero terror aquella gran pupila roja brillando sobre un soporte

Deep down, she feared Fernando's inconstancy.

"All right, we'll go to Barcelona," said Ossorio.

They went on the mail train, completely alone in the coach. All the members of the family came to see them off.

The train started to move; it was a mild night. The sky was filled with black, heavy storm clouds; it was raining.

As they passed a station, Dolores said:

"Look. Pascual Nebot said you were going to become a monk there, in a monastery in that town."

"It wouldn't have been very much trouble for me before."

"Why?"

"Because I didn't know you."

There was a moment of silence.

"Just look, look at the sea," Dolores said enthusiastically, peering out of the train window.

Several times the train would come so close to the shore that you could see the waves a few feet away, as they came forward in black, lead-colored masses, swelling up in a lustrous line of foam, rising into the air as if to look at something, and then disappearing in the colorless, formless abyss. The sea gave you an impression of vertigo, when you saw it down at your feet, like a black immensity, blending into the gray sky with a wide band of fog and shadow in between.

At times, a white, pale fleck of foam would emerge and form whitecaps within that gloomy mantle, as if some silvery Triton were coming out of the depths of the sea to contemplate the night. An acrid smell with a flavor of shellfish was rising up from the damp earth.

The moon came out from the heart of a cloud and glistened on the waters. The line of the coast was drawn as if on a topographical map, with its promontories and its inlets, with its long, narrow shoals that looked like monstrous black fish asleep on the waves.

Sometimes the moon would shed a ray of light from underneath a cloud, leaving the sea colored with silver, and then you could see its rounded waves shaded with black, stirred up in a continuous movement, in an eternal violence of coming and going, in a perpetual change of form. At other times, when the moon would come out and display itself clearly, a great white mass would shine on the sea, like a disc of melted metal, quite mobile, and it would spread out in lines of foam and strips of silver, in Grecian frets and luminous meanders, coming to life close to the shore and forming a border for the fathomless mass of briny water.

Suddenly the train moved into a tunnel. When it emerged, the night was totally black and the moon had concealed itself. The train seemed to speed up its movement.

"Look, look," said Dolores, pointing at a beacon light which had something like a luminous cloud of dust above it. The beacon light made a turn; it fully illuminated the train with a white light that kept getting redder and finally turned completely red.

That great red pupil, shining over a black base and lighting up the sea and the

negro e iluminando con su cono de luz sangrienta el mar y los negruzcos nubarrones del cielo.

LIX

Llegaron a Tarregona y se hospedaron en un hotel que estaba próximo a una iglesia. Los primeros días pasearon a orillas del mar; el Mediterráneo azul venía a romper las olas llenas de espuma a sus pies.

Luego se dedicaron a visitar la ciudad. Fernando cumplía sus deberes de *cicerone* con satisfacción infantil; ella le escuchaba aquel día sonriendo melancólicamente. En algunas callejuelas por donde pasaban, las mujeres, sentadas en los portales, les miraban con curiosidad, y ellos sonreían como si todo el mundo participase de su dicha.

Entraron en la Catedral, y como Dolores se cansaba pronto de verla, salieron al claustro.

– Aquí tienes una puerta románica que será del siglo XI o XII.
– ¿Sí? – dijo ella sonriendo.
– Mira el claustro qué hermoso es. ¡Qué capiteles más bonitos!

Los contemplaron largo tiempo. Aquí se veían los ratones que han atado en unas andas al gato y lo llevan a enterrar; por debajo de las andas va un ratoncillo que es el enterrador con una azada; en el mismo capitel el gato ha roto sus ligaduras y está matando los ratones. En otra parte se veía un demonio comiéndose las colas de unos monstruos; una zorra persiguiendo a un conejo, un lobo a un zorro, y en las ménsulas aparecían demonios barbudos y ridículos.

Fernando y Dolores se sentaron cansados.

Hacía un hermoso día de primavera; llovía, salía el sol.

En el jardín, lleno de arrayanes, piaban los pájaros volando en bandadas desde la copa de un ciprés alto, escueto y negruzco, al brocal de un pozo; de dos limoneros desgajados, con el tronco recubierto de cal, colgaban unos cuantos limones grandes y amarillos.

Había un reposo y un silencio en aquel claustro, lleno de misterio. De vez en cuando, al correr de las nubes, aparecía un trozo de cielo azul, dulce, suave, como la caricia de la mujer amada.

Comenzaron a cruzar por el claustro algunos canónigos vestidos de rojo; sonaron las campanas en el aire. Se comenzó a oír la música del órgano, que llegaba blandamente, seguida del rumor de los rezos y de los cánticos, cesaba la música. Cesaba el rumor de los rezos, cánticos, cesaba la música del órgano, y parecía que los pájaros piaban más fuerte y que los gallos cantaban a lo lejos con voz más chillona. Y al momento estos murmullos tornaban a ocultarse entre las voces de la

blackish storm clouds in the sky with its cone of blood-red light produced a truly terrifying feeling.

LIX

They arrived in Tarragona and took lodging in a hotel that was next to a church. The first few days, they strolled along the shores of the sea; the blue Mediterranean came up to break its foam-filled waves at their feet.

Later on they spent their time visiting the city. Fernando carried out his duties as a cicerone with childlike satisfaction; she listened to him that day with a melancholy smile. On some of the narrow side streets they passed, women seated in the outer doorways would stare at them curiously and they would both smile as if the whole world were sharing their good fortune.

They went inside the Cathedral,[104] and as Dolores quickly tired of seeing it, they went out into the cloister.

"Here you have a Romanesque door that is probably from the xith or xiith century."

"Really?" she said with a smile.

"Look, see how beautiful the cloister is. What charming capitals!"

They contemplated them for a long time. In one place, you could see the mice that have tied the cat onto a litter and are taking it off to bury it; underneath the litter is a little mouse that is the gravedigger, with a spade; on the same capital, the cat has broken its bonds and is killing the mice. In another place, you could see a demon devouring the tails of some monsters; a fox pursuing a hare, a wolf pursuing a fox, and long-bearded, ridiculous demons appeared on the brackets.

Fernando and Dolores sat down wearily.

It was a lovely spring day; first it would rain and then the sun would come out.

The birds were chirping in the garden full of myrtles, as they flew down in flocks from the top of a tall, solitary, blackish cypress tree to the curbstone of a well; several large, yellow lemons were hanging from two lemon trees, from which some of the branches had broken off, the trunks of which were covered over with lime.

There was a restful silence in that cloister which was filled with mystery. From time to time, as the clouds ran by, a patch of blue sky would appear, sweet and soft, like the caress of the woman you love.

Several canons, dressed in red, started to cross through the cloister; the bells rang in the air. You began to hear organ music, which came to you softly and was followed by the sound of prayers and canticles. The sound of the prayers ceased, the murmur of the canticles ceased, the organ music ceased, and it seemed as if the birds were chirping more loudly and the roosters crowing with a shriller voice in the distance. And in only a moment, those murmurs were hidden once again among the voices of

sombría plegaria que los sacerdotes en el coro entonaban al Dios vengador.

Era una réplica que el huerto dirigía a la iglesia y una contestación terrible de la iglesia al huerto.

En el coro, los lamentos del órgano, los salmos de los sacerdotes lanzaban un formidable anatema de execración y de odio contra la vida; en el huerto, la vida celebraba su plácido triunfo, su eterno triunfo.

El agua caía a intervalos, tibia, sobre las hojas lustrosas y brillantes; por el suelo las lagartijas corrían por las abandonadas sendas del jardín, cubiertas de parásitas hierbecillas silvestres.

Fernando sentía deseos de entrar en la iglesia y de rezar; Dolores estaba muy triste.

– ¿Qué te pasa? – le preguntó su marido.

– ¡Oh, nada! ¡Soy tan feliz! – y dos lagrimones grandes corrieron por sus mejillas.

Fernando la miró con inquietud. Salieron de la iglesia. En la plaza, el secreto fué comunicado. Dolores tenía la seguridad. Una vida nueva brotaba en su seno. Fernando palideció por la emoción.

Volvieron al Collado. A los seis o siete meses, Dolores dió a luz una niña que murió a las pocas horas. Fernando se sintió entristecido. Al contemplar aquella pobre niña engendrada por él, se acusaba a sí mismo de haberle dado una vida tan miserable y tan corta.

LX

Dos años después, en una alcoba blanca, cerca de la cuna de un niño recién nacido, Fernando Ossorio pensaba. En una cama de madera grande que se veía en el fondo del cuarto, Dolores descansaba con los ojos entreabiertos, el cabello en desorden, que caía a los lados de su cara pálida, de rasgos más pronunciados y salientes, mientras erraba una lánguida sonrisa en sus labios.

La abuela del niño, con los anteojos puestos, cosía en silencio, cerca de la ventana, ante una canastilla llena de gorritas y de ropas diminutas.

Por los cristales se veían los campos recién labrados, los árboles desnudos de hojas, el cielo azul pálido.

El día era de final de otoño; los vendimiadores hacía tiempo que habían terminado sus faenas; la casa de labor parecía desierta; el viento soplaba con fuerza; bandadas de cuervos cruzaban graznando por el aire.

Fernando miraba a su mujer, a su hijo; de vez en cuando tendía la mirada por aquellas heredades suyas recién sembradas unas, otras en donde ardían montones de rastrojos y de hojas secas y pensaba.

Recordaba su vida, la indignación que le ocasionó la carta irónica de Laura en la cual le felicitaba por su cambio de existencia; sus deseos y veleidades por volver a

somber supplication that the priests were intoning in a chorus to God the Avenger.

It was a reply that the garden was directing to the church and a terrifying response from the church to the garden.

In the choir, the lamentations of the organ and the psalms of the priests were hurling out a formidable anathema of execration and hatred against life; in the garden, life was celebrating its placid triumph, its eternal triumph.

At intervals, the tepid water would fall on the lustrous, shining leaves; on the ground, the small lizards ran around the abandoned garden paths, which were covered with wild, parasitic weeds and plants.

Fernando was anxious to go back into the church to pray; Dolores was very sad.

"What is the matter with you?" her husband asked her.

"Oh, nothing. I'm so happy!" And two big tears ran down her cheeks.

Fernando looked at her uneasily. They left the church. In the square, the secret was communicated to him. Dolores was certain. A new life was blossoming in her womb. Fernando turned pale with emotion.

They returned to El Collado. In six or seven months, Dolores gave birth to a little girl who died a few hours later. Fernando felt terribly sad. As he contemplated that little girl he had engendered, he accused himself of having given her so wretched and so short a life.

LX

Two years later, in a white bedroom, beside the cradle of a newly born child, Fernando Ossorio was thinking. In a large, wooden bed that could be seen at the back of the room, Dolores was resting, her eyes half open, her hair unkempt, falling on either side of her pale face; her features more pronounced and salient, while a languid smile wandered over her lips.

The child's grandmother, wearing her eyeglasses, was sewing silently near the window, in front of a small basket filled with tiny bonnets and baby clothes.

Through the windows, you could see the recently cultivated fields, the trees stripped of leaves, the pale blue sky.

It was a day toward the end of autumn; the grape harvesters had long since finished their labors; the farmstead seemed deserted, a strong wind was blowing; flocks of crows were crossing through the air cawing.

Fernando was looking at his wife and at his son; from time to time, he would turn his gaze toward his tracts of farmland, some of which had recently been sown, and others where piles of stubble and dry leaves were burning, and he was thinking.

He recalled his life, his indignation, occasioned by Laura's ironical letter in which she congratulated him on the change in his way of life; his desires and uncertainties over whether to return to the capital, how he had slowly acquired a taste for living in the

la corte, lentamente la costumbre adquirida de vivir en el campo, el amor a la tierra, la aparición enérgica del deseo de poseer y poco a poco la reintegración vigorosa de todos los instintos, naturales, salvajes.

Y como coronando su fortaleza, el niño aquel sonrosado, fuerte, que dormía en la cuna con los ojos cerrados y los puños también cerrados, como un pequeño luchador que se aprestaba para la pelea.

Estaba robustamente constituido; así había dicho su abuelo el médico, y así debía ser, pensaba Fernando. El estaba purificado por el trabajo y la vida del campo. Entonces más que nunca sentía una ternura que se desbordaba en su pecho por Dolores, a quien debía su salud y la prolongación de su vida en la de su hijo.

Y pensaba que había de tener cuidado con él, apartándole de ideas perturbadoras, tétricas, de arte y de religión.

El ya no podía arrojar de su alma por completo aquella tendencia mística por lo desconocido y lo sobrenatural, ni aquel culto y atracción por la belleza de la forma; pero esperaba sentirse fuerte y abandonarlas en su hijo.

El le dejaría vivir en el seno de la Naturaleza; él le dejaría saborear el jugo del placer y de la fuerza en la ubre repleta de la vida, la vida que para su hijo no tendría misterios dolorosos, sino serenidades inefables.

El le alejaría del pedante pedagogo aniquilador de los buenos instintos, le apartaría de ser un átomo de la masa triste, de la masa de eunucos de nuestros miserables días.

El dejaría a su hijo libre con sus instintos: si era león, no le arrancaría las uñas; si era águila, no le cortaría las alas. Que fueran sus pasiones impetuosas como el huracán que levanta montañas de arena en el desierto, libres como los leones y las panteras en las selvas vírgenes, y si la naturaleza había creado en su hijo un monstruo, si aquella masa aún informe era una fiera humana, que lo fuese abiertamente, francamente, y por encima de la ley entrase a saco en la vida, con el gesto gallardo del antiguo jefe de una devastadora horda.

No; no le torturaría a su hijo con estudios inútiles, con ideas tristes; no le enseñaría símbolo misterioso de religión alguna.

....

....

Y mientras Fernando pensaba, la madre de Dolores cosía en la faja que habían de poner al niño una hoja doblada del Evangelio.

FIN

country, his love for the land, the vigorous awakening of the desire to possess something, and how little by little, all his natural and savage instincts had been forcefully restored.

And as if to crown his fortitude, here was that rosy-colored, sound child asleep in his cradle, with his eyes closed and his fists clenched, like a little fighter preparing for the fray.

He had a robust constitution; that is what his grandfather, the doctor, had said, and that is how it ought to be, thought Fernando. He himself was purified by his work and his life in the country. At that moment more than ever, he felt a tender feeling for Dolores that kept overflowing in his heart, for it was to her that he owed his well-being and the prolongation of his life in that of his son.

And he thought that he ought to be very careful with him and keep him away from all those disturbing, gloomy ideas of art and religion.

He himself could no longer cast aside that mystical tendency toward the unknown and the supernatural from his soul completely, nor that worship and attraction for beauty and form; but he hoped that he could find enough strength to keep them away from his son.

He would allow him to live in the bosom of Nature; he would let him savor the sap of pleasure and strength in the brimming udders of life, a life that wouldn't hold painful mysteries for his son, but rather ineffable serenities.

He would keep him away from the pedantic pedagogue who is the annihilator of all fine instincts; he would prevent him from being nothing more than a single atom within the sad mass, that mass of eunuchs of our own wretched days.

He would allow his son to be free with his instincts: if he were a lion, he wouldn't pull out his claws; if he turned out to be an eagle, he wouldn't clip his wings. Let his passions be impetuous, like the hurricane that raises mountains of sand in the desert, free like lions and panthers in the virgin jungles; and if Nature had created a monster in his son, if that as yet unformed mass turned out to be a human beast, then let him be so openly, frankly, let him go through life plundering, above the law, with the gallant gesture of an ancient chieftain of some devastating horde.

No, he wouldn't torture his son with useless studies, with sad ideas; he would not teach him the mysterious symbol of any religion whatsoever.

....

....

And while Fernando was thinking in this way, Dolores' mother was sewing a folded page of the Gospel into the swathing band that was to be put on the child.[105]

END

NOTES

Introduction

1. Pío Baroja, *Nuevo tablado de Arlequín*. In *Obras completas*, Vol. V. Madrid: Biblioteca Nueva, 1948: 95. Translation is mine.
2. Miguel de Unamuno (1864–1936) was the author of *The Tragic Sense of Life in Men and Peoples* (1913). Walter Borenstein is the author of an unpublished dissertation on the subject of the contradictory philosophy of Baroja. See *Pío Baroja: His Contradictory Philosophy*. Urbana, ILL: University of Illinois, 1954.
3. Miguel de Unamuno, *The Life of Don Quixote and Sancho*. Anthony Kerrigan, trans. Bollingen Series LXXX, Vol. 3. Princeton, NJ: Princeton University Press, 1967: 11–12.
4. César Barja, *Libros y autores contemporáneos*. Madrid: Librería de Victoriano Suárez, 1935: 306. Translation is mine.
5. Pío Baroja, *Familia, infancia y juventud*. Vol. II of *Desde la última vuelta del camino: Memorias*. 2nd ed. Madrid: Biblioteca Nueva, 1951: 69.
6. Baroja, *Familia*: 70–71.
7. Roberta Johnson, "Pío Baroja." In *Twentieth Century Literary Criticism*, Sharon K. Hall, ed. Detroit, MI: Gale Research Co., 1982: 589–90.
8. Baroja, *Infancia*: 99.
9. Anthony Kerrigan, "The World of Pío Baroja." In Pío Baroja, *The Restlessness of Shanti Andía and Other Writings*, Anthony Kerrigan, trans. Ann Arbor, MI: University of Michigan Press, 1959: 10.
10. Pío Baroja. *Juventud, egolatría*. Madrid: Rafael Caro Raggio, 1920: 70–72. The quotation is the title of the chapter. Translation is mine.
11. *Krausismo* was a philosophical movement begun by Karl C. F. Krause (1781–1832), a German disciple of Kant. The movement was very popular in Spain, where it was led by Julián Sanz del Río (1814–69), who attracted a group of intellectuals to his side. They favored self-education and sought a balance between reason, science and religion. They fostered tolerance and played a major role in education, with the founding of the Institución Libre de Enseñanza. Their impact on the Generation of 1898 was enormous.
12. John Dos Passos, *Rosinante to the Road Again*. New York: George H. Doran Co., Publishers, 1922: 86–87.
13. Dos Passos: 88. For additional material, see Walter Borenstein, "The Failure of Nerve: The Impact of Pío Baroja's Spain on John Dos Passos." In *Nine Essays in Modern Literature*, Donald E. Stanford, ed. Baton Rouge, LA: Louisiana State University Press, 1965: 63–87.

14. Juan Uribe Echeverría. "Baroja y su tertulia." *Indice de Artes y Letras* {Madrid} 6 (May, 1950): 3–4.
15. Johnson: 610.
16. Johnson: 610.
17. Kerrigan: 6.
18. Pío Baroja, *Juventud, egolatría*. Madrid: Rafael Caro Raggio, 1920: 287. Translation is mine.
19. Kerrigan: 6.
20. Kerrigan: 8.
21. Pío Baroja, *La dama errante*. Paris: Thomas Nelson and Sons, Ltd., 1914: xiii-xiv. Translation is mine.
22. Baroja, *Dama*: xiv.
23. Pío Baroja, "Soledad." *Indice de Artes Y Letras* {Madrid} 9, Nos. 70–71 (Dec.-Jan. 1953–54): 1. Translation is mine.
24. Baroja, "Soledad": 1.
25. Pío Baroja, *El escritor según él y según los críticos*. Vol I of *Desde la última vuelta del camino*. 2nd ed. Madrid: Biblioteca Nueva, 1950.
26. Federico de Onís, "Pío Baroja and the Contemporary Spanish Novel." In *New York Times Book Review* (May 4, 1919): 257.
27. Pío Baroja, *Páginas escogidas*. Madrid: Casa Editorial Calleja, 1918: 11. Translation is mine.
28. C. J. Brown, *A Literary History of Spain: The Twentieth Century*. London: Ernest Benn, Ltd. 1972: 31–32.
29. Brown: 32.
30. Salvador de Madariaga, "Pío Baroja." In *The Genius of Spain and Other Essays on Spanish Contemporary Literature*. Oxford: Oxford University Press, 1923: 115–17.
31. William A. Drake, *"Pío Baroja.* In *Contemporary European Writers. New York: The Jon Day Co., 1928*: 115.
32. Ramón Sender, "Posthumous Baroja." *New Mexico Quarterly*, xxx, No. 1 (Spring 1960): 7–9.
33. Kerrigan: xxix.
34. Kerrigan: xxix.
35. Ernest Boyd, "La busca." Rev. of *La busca*. *The Nation*, 115 (December 27, 1922): 720.
36. Madariaga: 114–15.
37. John Dos Passos, "Building Lots." Rev. of *Weeds The Nation*, 118 (January 9, 1924): 37.
38. Dwight Bolinger, "Heroes and Hamlets: The Protagonists of Baroja's Novels." *Hispania*, 24 (February 1941): 93–94.
39. V.S. Pritchett, *New Statesman and Nation* (September 26, 1959): 396.

40. Sherman E. Eoff, *The Modern Spanish Novel*. New York: New York University Press, 1961: 165.
41. Ernesto Giménez Caballero, "Miradas conmovidas a ilustres solitarios." *La Gaceta Literaria*, 5 (August 15, 1931): 6. Translation is mine.
42. Beatrice P. Patt, *Pío Baroja*. New York: Twayne Publishers, 1971: 88.
43. Johnson: 594–95.
44. Johnson: 595.
45. Uribe Echeverría: 3–4. Translation is mine.
46. Barja: 353. Translation is mine.
47. Pedro Lain Entralgo, *Mis páginas preferidas*. Madrid: Antología Hispánica, 1958: 28–29. Translation is mine.
48. Stanley Kunitz and Howard Haycroft, *Twentieth Century Authors*. New York: Wilson, 1942: 76.
49. Pío Caro Baroja, *La soledad de Pío Baroja*. Mexico, D.F.: Pío Caro Baroja Ed., 1953: 18–23.
50. Camilo José Cela, *Recuerdo de don Pío Baroja*. Mexico, D.F.: Ediciones de Andrea, 1958: 54.
51. Carmen Iglesias, *El pensamiento de Pío Baroja: Ideas centrales*. Mexico: Antigua Librería Robredo, 18 (footnote 39).
52. Pío Baroja, *Camino de perfección (Pasión mística)* New York: Las Américas Publishing Co., 1952: front.
53. Donald Shaw, *La generación del 98*. Tr. by Carmen Hierro. Madrid: Catedra, 1985: 133.
54. Ricardo Landeira, *The Modern Spanish Novel, 1898–1936*. Boston: Twayne Publishers, 1985: 45.
55. Luis S. Granjel, *Retrato de Pío Baroja*. Barcelona: Editorial Barna, 1953: 287–96. Sebastián Juan Arbó, *Pío Baroja y su tiempo*. Barcelona: Editorial Planeta, 1963.
56. Fernando Entrerios, "La censura bajo Franco." *Ibérica por la libertad*, 10, No. 6 (June 15, 1962): 6.
57. E. Inman Fox, "Introduction and Notes," *La voluntad*, by José Martínez Ruiz (Azorín). Madrid: Clásicos Castalia, 1982: 54.
58. Stanislaw Baranczak, "Introducing 'Zapis'." *Index on Censorship*, 7, No. 4 (July-August 1977): 10.
59. Pío Baroja, *Aquí Paris*. Madrid: Colección Literaria "El Grifón," 1955: 73–74.
60. Johnson: 613.

Road to Perfection

1. Juan Pantoja de la Cruz (1553–1608) was a leading Spanish portrait painter of the Renaissance. He came from Valladolid and studied in Madrid with Sánchez Coello. He served at the court of Felipe II and was known for his devotion to minute detail.
2. Alonso Sánchez Coello (1531–88) was the most important portrait painter of the Spanish Renaissance. He studied in Portugal and came to Madrid in 1555 to serve as the favorite court painter of Felipe II.
3. An entire sentence has been omitted in the edition of the novel found in the *Obras completas* of Baroja published in 1948 by the Biblioteca Nueva in Madrid. For a more complete explanation of the many expurgations in this edition, see the Introduction. The line begins with "First" and ends with "there." The expurgation can be attributed to the religious doubts expressed by Fernando Ossorio.
4. Santiago Rusiñol (1861–1931) was a Spanish impressionist painter from Catalonia. He was noted for his paintings of gardens and was also the author of several plays including *El místico*. He was a close friend of Baroja and accompanied him on several trips. The author speaks of him in his memoirs.
5. Ignacio Zuloaga (1870–1945) was a Spanish painter closely tied to the members of the Generation of 1898. In his work, he presents a stark, desolate and tragic vision of Castile. He is best known for his "Víspera de la corrida" and a portrait of the famous bullfighter Juan Belmonte.
6. Darío Regoyos (1857–1913) was a Spanish impressionist painter from Asturias. He was a follower of the style of Camille Pissaro, Alfred Sisley and Claude Monet. Baroja admired his work and compared his style as a painter to his own style as a novelist.
7. The Queen is María Cristina (1858–1929), the daughter of Ferdinand Charles of Austria and the Archduchess of Habsburg. She married Alfonso XII in 1879. When he died suddenly in 1885, she became the Queen-Regent for her infant son, who was born after his father's death, and who was to become Alfonso XIII. She remained Regent until 1902 when her son took the throne.
8. Caserta was the name given to María Cristina's son-in-law, Carlos María de Bourbon, the son of Alfonso, the Count of Caserta of Italy. He married María de las Mercedes, the Princess of Asturias, daughter of Alfonso XII, on February 14, 1901, shortly after acquiring Spanish citizenship. The marriage was highly unpopular in Spain, and the public identified even more with the princess after her untimely death in 1904. This gives us a possible date for the events of the novel.
9. La bella Martínez was a dancer of the period. The Romea Theater was one of many that offered programs of dance and music in Madrid at the turn of the century.

Notes

10. The expression using "los mansos" is a popular idiom of the time and has its origin in the terminology of bullfighting. The "mansos" were the tame animals brought in to pacify the fierce bull and induce it to leave the arena quietly, as was the custom in Portugal. The metaphor comes to imply using the aid of others to get rid of someone who is in the way.
11. The entire paragraph has been omitted in the edition of the *Obras completas*. The obvious factor is the reference to the immorality of the clergy.
12. This entire paragraph has been omitted from the edition of the *Obras completas* because of its implication of lesbianism.
13. Except for the first sentence, the whole paragraph has been cut from the edition of the *Obras completas*. It deals with an incestuous sexual relationship and was probably eliminated for being too explicit. It is surprising that allegedly pornographic material should be objectionable since there had not been extensive censorship of such material during the late nineteenth and twentieth centuries up to the time of the regime of Francisco Franco. All the previous editions of the novel had included this paragraph. Its exclusion was probably due to the power of the Church in questions of morality, as well as a tendency toward prudishness that had come to dominate publishing in Spanish society.
14. The *cante jondo* or *hondo* is typical of the *cante flamenco* of Andalusian gypsy music and poetry. The renowned poet Federico García Lorca (1898–1936) wrote a collection of poems called *Poema del cante jondo*.
15. The short paragraph is omitted in the edition of the *Obras completas*, evidently due to its irreverent tone, considered offensive by the censors.
16. Manuel Fernández y González (1830–88) was a major Spanish Romantic novelist who wrote over 200 historical novels. His best-known work was *Los siete Infantes de Lara*. Baroja speaks of meeting him in his memoirs (*Familia, infancia y juventud*, Second part, Chapter VII.)
17. La Guindalera is a section of Madrid in the northeastern part of the city. The author speaks of memorable crimes and executions he witnessed as a boy in 1888 in his memoirs (*Familia, infancia y juventud*, Fourth part, Chapter VI). The public execution of a woman, Higenia Balaguer, left a profound impression upon him as a child.
18. Ossorio starts out on his "road to perfection" by walking north along the Paseo de la Castellana. At the northern end is the Hipódromo, which was built in the latter part of the century to replace the earlier site where horses would race.
19. Cuatro Caminos is a suburb of the city of Madrid and lies northwest of the Hipódromo.
20. Fuencarral is small town some 9 kilometers north of Madrid on the road to Colmenar in the province of Madrid. The Palace of El Pardo, built in 1543, is located here. It was renovated by Francisco Sabatini in 1772 and served as

the summer residence of the kings for some time. Francisco Franco occupied it until his death.
21. Francisco Sabatini (1722–95) was a Spanish general and an architect. He directed the construction of many public buildings and was the inventor of a closed cart used to pick up garbage. These carts were known as "chocolateras de Sabatini."
22. Colmenar Viejo is a town in the province of Madrid, some 20 kilometers north of El Pardo.
23. Manzanares el Real is a small town located in front of the granite mountain backdrop of La Pedriza that rises 2227 meters. The castle to which Baroja refers is very close to town and is called El Castillo de los Mendoza. It was built in the 15th century in the Gothic/Mudéjar style and has been restored in recent years.
24. The author is referring to the Carlist wars that began over the succession to the throne in 1833 and did not end till 1874. The wars derive their name from the name of the pretender, Carlos, the brother of King Fernando VII. This is a stereotyped view of many Carlist leaders, often depicted as guerrilla bandits.
25. The line from "Before" to "brutishness" has been eliminated from the edition of the *Obras completas*. It can be seen as a disparaging remark about the Catholic Church.
26. Rascafría is a town 20 kilometers directly north of Manzanares el Real.
27. Rascafría is the town where the monastery of Santa María del Paular is located in the valley of El Paular. It was constructed for King Juan I in the year 1390 in order to fulfill the wishes of his father Enrique II of Trastamara. It was the earliest Carthusian monastery in Spain.
28. The character Max Schultze is based on a very close friend of Baroja named Paul Schmitz, a native of Basel, Switzerland. The author refers to him in his memoirs (*Final del siglo xix y principios del xx*, Part IV: Primeros Libros, Chapter I). We are told that he had studied in Germany and in Switzerland and had lived for a time in northern Russia. He had come to Madrid to recover from a lung disease and spent three years in Spain. He traveled with Baroja to Toledo, El Paular and the fountains of Urbión. Years later, the two traveled through Switzerland, Germany and Denmark. Baroja says that Schmitz opened his eyes to many aspects of life, literature, philosophy and art. Schmitz would read to him about Nietzsche at El Paular. Many years later, in 1931, Schmitz wrote an article under the pseudonym of *Dominik Müller*, in which he spoke of his relationship with the Spanish author and of his presence as a character in one of his novels. Azorín also speaks of Schmitz in Chapter XLII of his work *Madrid* (1941) and refers to Baroja's relationship with Schmitz and himself. He refers to him as Paul Smith in another work.
29. These two paragraphs have been removed from the edition of the *Obras completas*. They were clearly seen as sacrilegious.

30. The Guadarrama mountain range runs north to south for several hundred miles is only eight kilometers north of Rascafría. Its highest point is the Pico de Peñalara, 2430 meters high. Three of its passes are those of Guadarrama, Navacerrada and Somosierra.
31. "*Deutschland, Deutschland über alles,*" written by Hoffmann Von Fallersleben in 1841, became the national anthem of Germany in 1922. In 1952, the last stanza became West Germany's anthem.
32. The forests of El Espinar are a few kilometers north of the Guadarrama range near the Navacerrada pass. La Granja de San Ildefonso is some eight kilometers north of the forest and eleven kilometers from Segovia. It was built for King Felipe V, the first Bourbon king of Spain, in order to remind him of his beloved Versailles. The site had originally been occupied by a hermitage built for Enrique IV of Castile. Ferdinand and Isabel gave it to the monastery of El Parral and a farm (granja) was set up there. Felipe had the statues, fountains and gardens created in the French taste.
33. Cercedilla is a town located some 16 kilometers south of Segovia.
34. Joachim Patinir(1485–1524) was a leading Flemish landscape painter during the Renaissance in the north.
35. The Sierra de Gredos is a mountain range in Spain that runs between the provinces of Avila and Toledo and is separated from the Sierra de Guadarrama by the Avila Plateau.
36. The Cathedral of Segovia is a Late Gothic structure erected on the highest point of the old town, built between 1525 and 1593 to replace the older building destroyed when the *Comuneros* rebelled against Carlos V in 1520. It contains precious 16th and 17th century Brussels tapestries.
37. The Romanesque church of San Esteban was built in the 13th century and possesses one of the highest church towers in Spain, restored in the 18th century.
38. The Alcázar of Segovia is built on a steep crag between the valleys of the two rivers that join here in the western part of the city. It may date back to Roman times and served as a fortress in the 11th century and was rebuilt in the reign of Alfonso X in the 13th century. It later became a favorite hunting retreat for Castilian kings and was favored by Felipe II who was married here. It was destroyed by fire in 1862 and later restored.
39. Zamarramala is a small village north west of Segovia near the Church of the Vera Cruz. La Lastrilla is another village east of Zamarramala.
40. The monastery of el Parral, a Hieronymite house, was founded by Enrique IV in 1447. The church is in Isabelline style and contains a massive 16th century retablo and two alabaster tombs. It is not far from the Alcázar on the other side of the river and a poplar grove can be found to the east along the banks of the river.
41. The entire paragraph has been eliminated from the edition of the *Obras*

completas, probably because it seemed anti-Spanish and was an unsympathetic portrait of local types.
42. The remainder of this chapter takes Ossorio on a tour of the city of Segovia. After leaving El Parral, he crosses the Eresma River, passes by a Gothic church that may be the church of San Andrés and reaches the Plaza Mayor. He sees a Romanesque church that opens onto the square that could be the church of San Miguel. He spends some time her and makes his way to the outskirts and descends to the Arroyo de los Clamores that runs along the southern edge of the city. He then walks west along the Camino de la Cuesta de los Hoyos, passes by a ruined convent and goes on to the point where the arroyo meets the river near the Alcázar. He reaches a pine grove where he stretches out to admire the Cathedral and the Roman aqueduct, one of the best preserved aqueducts in the world. It joins two hills, has 118 arches and has two levels for a short distance. Water is still brought from the Sierra de Fuenfría, some 18 kilometers away. He also admires the old wall that surrounds much of the old town. They date back to the Iberian period and were improved and strengthened by the Romans. After Ossorio crosses a bridge over the Eresma, he takes a narrow road that passes close to the Convento de San Juan de la Cruz, a house of Discalced Carmelites, founded in 1576 by St. John of the Cross. On the opposite side of the road is the round church of the Vera Cruz, built in 1208–17, once a church of the Knights Templar.
43. Ossorio's trip with Señor Polentinos will take him south from Segovia to the Sierra de Guadarrama. They will travel southeast and stop at La Granja and then continue directly south till they begin to climb into the wooded hills of the sierra. At the pass, the Puerto de Navacerrada (5575 meters), they go by the Venta, now called the Venta de los mosquitos or Peña Agudilla, often known as La Cantina. There are many ski resorts today all throughout the area. The route was followed by the nobility in past centuries, on their way north from Madrid.
44. Torrelodones is a town south of Navacerrada and is some 24 kilometers from Madrid.
45. Las Rozas de Madrid is a town several kilometers north west of Madrid.
46. Aravaca is a suburb of the city of Madrid, just north of the city.
47. Illescas is a town about 34 kilometers south of Madrid. Polentinos intends to bypass the capital after reaching Aravaca and continue south to Illescas. Emperor Carlos V met the captured Francis I of France here in 1525 after the Battle of Pavía.
48. Sepúlveda is a town some 56 kilometers north east of Segovia.
49. The church of the Hospital de la Caridad contains five paintings by El Greco.
50. The parish church of La Asunción in Illescas dates from the 12th century and has a handsome Mudéjar tower from the 14th century.

51. Chapters XX to XLV take place in Toledo, a city with an ancient religious history. It was the capital of an Iberian tribe, was captured by the Romans in 192 B.C., and was a center during Visigothic rule from 534 to 712. The Visigothic king converted to Catholicism in Toledo in 589. During the period of Moorish domination, the city was a focal point for both the Muslims and the Jews. Toledo held the largest Jewish community in Spain. As can be seen in later chapters, Toledo played a dominant role in the life and work of El Greco. His *View of Toledo* is one of the most famous paintings in the world.

Once again, Ossorio takes us on a tour of this famous city. On his journey here, he travels the 34 kilometers from Illescas to Toledo in a wagon and arrives in the imperial city from the north through the Puente de Alcantara. The bridge was built by Romans, redone by Goths and Arabs and destroyed in 1257. King Alfonso X had it reconstructed. Ossorio chose to stay at an inn near the Plaza de Zocodover, the most popular gathering place in town. He tells us it was opposite a convent at the entrance to the plaza. The convent may be the Convento de Santa Fé. There had long been an inn there called the Posada de la Sangre or the Posada del Sevillano. In one of Cervantes's *Exemplary Novels, La ilustre fregona*, much of the action occurs at this inn and the author spent some time here as well. It was destroyed during the Civil War, rebuilt, and may now house government offices.

The world-renowned Cathedral of Toledo stands in the heart of the city and is the Catedral Primada of Spain. It in the Gothic style and was built between 1227 and 1493 on the site of the Moorish Great Mosque. In spite of its reputation and its many artistic works of sculpture and painting, Ossorio only enters the cathedral for a brief time in Chapter XXX.

52. San Juan de los Reyes is another Gothic-style church in the eastern part of the city and was built for Ferdinand and Isabella in 1477. It is best known for the magnificence of its cloister.

53. The Mudéjar-style Sinagoga del Tránsito is located in the old Jewish section of Toledo, the Judería. It was built in 1366 by Samuel ha-Levi, the treasurer to Pedro I.

54. Churrigueresque architecture refers to a style introduced into Spain in the late 17th century by José Churriguera (1650–1725) and his followers. He was a native of Salamanca, known as a sculptor and architect. The style is characterized by excessive ornamentation associated with the baroque period.

55. When Ossorio leaves the inn where he was staying, he leads us on a tour of the northwestern part of the city, where he hopes to find lodging at the boarding house recommended to him earlier. He takes us through the streets, plazas, churches and convents not far from the cathedral. He sees the churrigueresque-style church with its two towers near the Plaza de las Capuchinas and soon finds himself on the Calle de las Tendillas, with two

convents and their churches nearby, very likely that of Santa Leocadia and of Santo Domingo el Antiguo. The former was built over the house once occupied by the saint, and the latter reconstructed in the 16th century by Juan Herrera and containing paintings by El Greco.

Later, after taking up lodging at the boarding house, he hears of the Colegio de Doncellas Nobles, where the older daughter of the house is studying. This school was founded by Archbishop Siliceo, later a cardinal, in 1551, to offer opportunities for girls who could not afford it. It later became the Colegio de Nuestra Señora de los Remedios. Reference is then made to an occasional holiday stroll on the Camino de la Fábrica de Armas, where the steel blades were fashioned that made the city famous. The Provincial Council Building, the old prison and the Paseo de Merchán are all in the northernmost part of Toledo.

56. The entire paragraph beginning with "The priests" has been omitted from the edition of the *Obras completas* because of the allusion to the immorality of the priesthood, and the chicanery of the political leaders and businessmen.

57. The church of Santo Tomé was originally a mosque and was rebuilt by the Count of Orgaz in Gothic style in the 14th century with a beautiful Mudéjar tower. It was reconstructed in the 18th century. In an annex can be seen the painting by El Greco of "The Burial of the Count of Orgaz," reflecting the legend that the dead nobleman was carried to heaven by St. Stephen and St. Augustine in the year 1312. In the painting, the saints are wearing magnificent church vestments and some of the models for the figures are known to be contemporaries of the painter.

58. Cardinal Siliceo was Juan Martínez Guijarro (1486–1557). He had been a professor of philosophy at the University of Salamanca and later the archbishop of Toledo. In the novel, the author associates him with the school where Teresa is studying.

59. Santa Teresa de Jesús (1515–82) ranks among the leading Mystics of her time in Spain. Always associated with her native city of Avila, she joined the Carmelites of the Convent of the Incarnation in Avila in 1553. She is the author of a number of books, the most well known being *Camino de perfección*, *El Castillo interior* and *Libro de la vida*.

60. The Hospital de Afuera, also known as the Hospital de Tavera and the Hospital de San Juan Bautista de Afuera, is a complex of buildings erected between 1541 and 1599. It has a marble façade, done by Berruguete and a museum containing works by El Greco, Titian and Tintoretto. The painting referred to may be "The Baptism of Jesus."

61. Cardinal Tavera (1472–1545) had been the Archbishop of Toledo for many years and was a major force in the construction of the hospital. The painting of him by El Greco is near his sepulcher and was painted from a mortuary mask.

62. The twin-towered Puerta del Sol is of the 14th century and is in Mudéjar style. In the outer district of Santiago is the 13th century Mudéjar church of Santiago del Arribal.
63. The two paragraphs beginning with "On the following day," and ending with "commonplaces," have been omitted from the edition of the *Obras completas.* They speak disparagingly of Loyola and the Catholic faith.
64. Alfonso XII (1857–1885) was the son of Isabel II of Spain who was forced to resign and go into exile in 1868. He became king after the brief reign of Amadeo I from 1871–1873 and the First Republic (1873–74). The Second Carlist War had played a prominent role in weakening the young republic.
65. The National Institute stands northwest of the Cathedral, halfway to the Provincial Governor's Palace. It was once a famous university, and has a neo-classic façade.
66. The Duke of Aosta (1845–90) became Amadeo I of Spain after the expulsion of Queen Isabel II in 1868. General Juan Prim, the leader of the Progressive party, was his principal supporter and the new king came to Madrid in December 1870, the day the general was assassinated. The Unionists, who opposed him from the start, helped drive him from the throne and he was forced to abdicate in despair on February 12, 1873.
67. The first Spanish Republic was proclaimed on February 12, 1873 by the radical majority in the Cortes and the newly elected body was divided among different types of federalists. Emilio Castelar (1832–99) was elected as head of the government on September 8, 1873. He retired on January 2, 1874 and this was followed by a military coup led by General Francisco Serrano.
68. The Restoration began with the ascension to the Spanish throne by Alfonso XII in early 1875.
69. The governor remarks that everyone is an anarchist in Spain. Baroja had been interested in the anarchists in Spain and elsewhere in Europe for many years. In his trilogy of novels, *La lucha por la vida,* in his novel *La ciudad de la niebla,* as well as other works of fiction and many articles, he had dealt with anarchists and their impact on the society.
70. *Lagartijo* was the name given to Rafael Molina (1841–1900), a famous bullfighter of the time from Córdoba. *Frascuelo* was the name given to Salvador Sánchez Povedano (1842–98) a noted bullfighter from Granada.
71. The convent of Santo Domingo el Antiguo, also known as Santo Domingo de Silos (*Dominicus Siloecensis*) is located on a site founded by the Visigothic king Recaredo in the 6th century. It was built here by Santo Domingo in the 11th century and then reconstructed in the 16th century by Juan Herrera.
72. The main retable was the work of El Greco. There are five paintings of his in this convent.
73. Alonso Berruguete (1480–1561) was a famous painter and sculptor whose works can be found in Toledo, as well as in Granada, Salamanca and

Valladolid. In the cathedral in Toledo, he did biblical scenes for the upper tier of the choir, and his work can be seen in the Museo de Santa Cruz, the Hospital de Tavera and other places in the city.
74. The words beginning with "dreaming" to the end of the sentence are omitted from the edition of the *Obras completas*. They reflect a lack of religious faith in eternity.
75. *Loin du bal* is a piece of music for piano by Fernand Gillet (1882–1980), a French composer and music professor in France and the United States. The Teatro de Rojas in Toledo was built in 1878 and is still offering music, dance and theater. It is located on the Plaza Mayor.
76. The words beginning with "Morality" to the end of the sentence are omitted in the edition of the *Obras completas*. They deal with sexual ethics and an amoral philosophy.
77. Ossorio decided to return to Yécora, where he had gone to school as a boy. Chapters XXXII to XLIV will all take place in this town. Baroja's close friend and fellow member of the Generation of 1898, Azorín, speaks at length of this city, which is, in reality, Yecla, a town that is some 65 kilometers west of Alicante. Prehistoric ruins on the Cerro de los Santos can be found in this very old city.
78. La Estación de Castillejo is located in Toledo.
79. Albacete is an important Spanish city some 240 kilometers southeast of Madrid.
80. The words beginning with "contribute" to the end of the sentence are omitted from the edition of the *Obras completas*. They speak disparagingly of the teaching of the Piarist brothers and the church in general.
81. He uses a popular expression, "*capeo,*" very cynically. The term, said of the bullfighter waving the cape in front of the bull, is said here with the meaning of beguiling or deceiving the public.
82. The portion of the paragraph beginning with "The young priest," the five paragraphs that follow, and the part of the paragraph ending with "both of them," have been eliminated from the edition of the *Obras completas*. They deal with the worldly character and manners of the priests, their utter indifference to the parishioners whom they think they are deceiving and their immoral sexual behavior.
83. The school described here as being in Yécora is in actuality the school where Azorín, Baroja's close friend and fellow member of the Generation of 1898, attended classes as a boarding student. Azorín describes the school in Yecla in his autobiographical novel *Confessions of a Little Philosopher*. In Chapters VII to XXIII, Azorín tells of his trip to Yecla, the daily life at the school, his fellow students and the many priests who taught there. He quotes Baroja in the first lines of Chapter XIV. Although he does give us a view of the boredom he faced daily and the occasional cruelty of some teacher, he does

not approach the savage attack Baroja offers on the impact of life on the boys at such a school. I am also the translator into English of this novel as well as Azorín's *The Route of Don Quixote*.

84. The last four paragraphs of this chapter have been eliminated from the edition of the *Obras completas*. This is by far the longest section expurgated from all the earlier editions. It deals primarily with the impact of the system of religious training on the young boys attending school here. Baroja's anticlericalism is nowhere as devastating as it is here. The authorities in charge of censorship of books felt obliged to eliminate these paragraphs even though they did not see it possible to leave out the entire novel.

85. Paul Bourget (1852–1935) was an important French novelist and essayist. His works took a stern moralist point of view and his major novel, *Le Disciple*, dealt with the responsibility of a novelist for the actions of his readers. He was very popular with conservative Catholic intellectuals.

86. The author is probably speaking of Marcel Prévost (1862–1941), a noted French novelist and a minor dramatist. His works dealt mainly with women and he wrote of moral laxity in women's education. An important work was *Les Demi-Vierges*.

87. The sentence beginning with "There" to the word "feelings" has been omitted from the edition of the *Obras completas*. The words are seen as an indictment of Catholic moral teaching.

88. Saint Blaise, who lived in the early 4th century was a bishop of Sebaste in Armenia. He was associated with the care of the sick and his saint's day is February 3.

89. The two paragraphs beginning with "Really" and ending with "knees" have been omitted from the edition of the *Obras completas*. They deal with the sexual misconduct of a priest.

90. The three words "and of priests" have been omitted from the edition of the *Obras completas*. The entire list of the clients of the procuresses is left in and only the clergy are deleted.

91. These are two popular *zarzuelas* of the day. *Jugar con fuego* is a work of the composer F.A. Barbieri and *Marina* a work of the composer E. Arrieta. Both were originally performed at the Teatro del Circo in Madrid.

92. *Soleares* and *tientos* are terms used for playing the guitar. They are used for the melancholy Andalusian gypsy songs and dances.

93. The author is referring to the Andalusian tango. In his memoirs, Baroja informs us that the tango may have come from a variety of sources and that it became popular in the late 19th century. He refers to both Arabic and Argentine origins.

94. Ossorio becomes the narrator in Chapter XLVI and continues to be so through Chapter LVI. This fundamental change takes us away from the unknown observer narrator of the earlier chapters.

95. In Chapter XLVII, the author begins to use the perfect in place of the preterit tense. Doubtless through imitation of French, the perfect is often used, especially in Madrid, where one would expect the preterit. This use is especially important for Azorín, for whom time is an essential aspect of his style and his philosophical perspective. It is often an attempt to bring the past closer to the present.
96. The words from "Spain" to "world" have been omitted from the edition of the *Obras completas*. They do little more than denigrate Spain in the eyes of the reader.
97. Liane de Pougy (1870–1950) was a famed French courtesan. She was called Paris's Most Beautiful and Notorious Courtesan.
98. La Bella Otero was Carolina Otero (1868–1965) She gained her reputation during La Belle Epoque. A movie was made about her in 1954.
99. La Cleo de Mérode (Cleopatra Diane de Mérode 1873–1966) was a French beauty who earned her reputation in dance and ballet. After Leopold II of Belgium was impressed with her beauty, a certain aura came to exist around her and she was called Cleopold. She struggled over the years to maintain her good name.
100. Ossorio's feeling about Pascual Nebot is reduced to creating a stereotype of him. He refers to his character as being typically Levantine. For a view of Baroja's tendency to create stereotypes, see Walter Borenstein, "Baroja's Uncomplimentary Stereotype of the Latin American" in *Symposium*, Vol. XI, No.1 (Spring 1957), pp. 46–60. In addition, the author's reference to the man being a republican and an anti-clerical, a federalist and somewhat of a regionalist politically may reflect Baroja's negative feeling about Vicente Blasco Ibáñez who also held these attitudes.
101. Las Flores de María, known elsewhere as the Month of Mary are the many devotions during the month of May to the Virgin Mary. The custom of associating her name with the month of May is quite old and was fostered by many Jesuits over the centuries.
102. Flora was the Roman goddess of the spring and flowers and blossoms. The Romans offered prayers to her for the prospering of ripe fruits of field and tree. She was also a goddess of the flower of youth and its pleasures. Pomona was the Latin goddess of fruit trees. She was represented as a fair damsel with fruits in her bosom and a pruning–knife in her hand.
103. Santo Tomás de Villanueva (1488–1555) was a Spanish priest of the Augustinian order from the town of Villanueva de los Infantes. He became the archbishop of Valencia in 1544 and was known for his work among the poor.
104. Tarragona is a Spanish city and seaside resort 60 miles southwest of Barcelona. It contains more remains of the Roman period than almost any other place in Spain. Many consider it one of the most fascinating places

in Europe because it evokes a picture of the past as few other places do. The Cathedral stands on the highest point of a hill that was once the site of an ancient fortified settlement. It was built in the 12th and 13th centuries and represents a transition from the Romanesque to the Gothic. The author describes the Cloister in great detail.

105. The final chapter of the novel presents a situation found in many of Baroja's novels. The translator's dissertation, *Pío Baroja: His Contradictory Philosophy*, as well as a number of articles dealing with the *héroe fracasado* (the failed hero) of the Barojan novel take up this theme. The author's fascination with "the man of action" in so many of his novels and in his series of novels, *Memorias de un hombre de acción*, reveal this intense struggle between the man of action, prepared to confront the world and struggle to improve it and the man of thought who is doomed to failure because of his moral constraints. Ossorio wants to allow his son to grow into a man of action and he dreams of how he will prepare him to become so. And all the while, the child's grandmother is sewing onto his clothes the symbols of tradition and conformity that will restrain him. Ossorio's son will have to undergo the same struggle his father had faced.